A Passion Born . . .

"What now," she asked fearfully. "We have nothing, not even a bed. What's to happen?" She held tight to his strong arm, letting her thigh rest against his.

He laid her on the ground. He took her cloak and wrapped it around them both and in the warmth of its folds he rejoiced in her. There was no other woman in the world that he had loved like this. She put her fingers in his long yellow hair and they smiled at each other. It was all new. Out of an end had come a beginning . . .

Hall of Sparrows

HALL OF SPARROWS

BETH CARSLEY JONES

BERKLEY BOOKS, NEW YORK

This Berkley book contains the complete
text of the original hardcover edition.
It has been completely reset in a typeface
designed for easy reading and was printed
from new film.

HALL OF SPARROWS

A Berkley Book / published by arrangement with
the author

PRINTING HISTORY
Judy Piatkus (Publishers) Limited of London edition published 1985
Berkley edition / March 1989

ISBN: 0-425-11533-X

A BERKLEY BOOK® TM 757,375
Berkley Books are published by The Berkley Publishing Group,
200 Madison Avenue, New York, NY 10016.
The name ''BERKLEY'' and the ''B'' logo
are trademarks belonging to Berkley Publishing Corporation.

PRINTED IN THE UNITED STATES OF AMERICA

10 9 8 7 6 5 4 3 2 1

"To Robb"

"Your Majesty, when we compare the present life of man on earth with that time of which we have no knowledge, it seems to me like the swift flight of a single sparrow through the banqueting hall where you are sitting at dinner on a winter's day. . . . In the midst there is a comforting fire to warm the hall; outside the storms of winter rain or snow are raging. This sparrow flies swiftly in through one door of the hall, and out through another. While he is inside, he is safe from the winter storms; but after a few moments of comfort he vanishes from sight into the wintry world from which he came. Even so, man appears on earth for a little while; but of what went before this life or of what follows, we know nothing."

A History of the English Church and People by the Venerable Bede, AD 731.

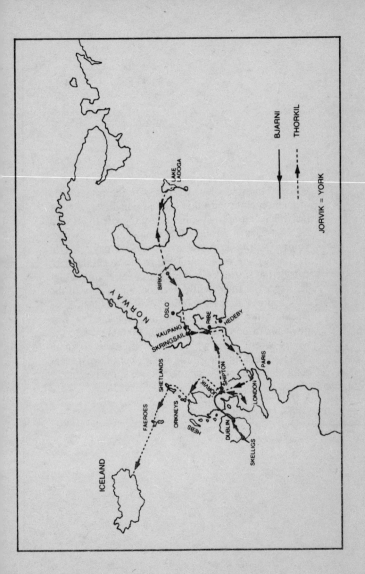

BJARNI
THORKIL

JORVIK = YORK

ICELAND

FAEROES

SHETLANDS

ORKNEYS

HEBS

DUBLIN

SKELLIGS

JORVIK

LONDON

PARIS

SHIPTON

RIBE

HEDEBY

KAUPANG

SKRINGSAIL

OSLO

NORWAY

BIRKA

LAKE
LADOGA

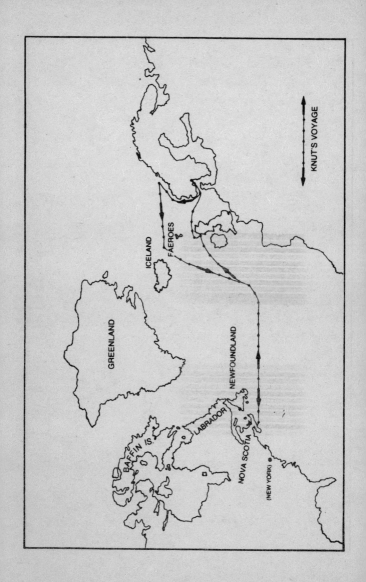

KNUT'S VOYAGE

GREENLAND

ICELAND

FAEROES

BAFFIN IS.

LABRADOR

NEWFOUNDLAND

NOVA SCOTIA

(NEW YORK)

Chapter
One

THE NIGHT WAS dark, without a moon. We came on foot for the last part, carrying our weapons. The wind was light on our faces, and warm. I thought with longing of the sea. Behind and to the side men made noise, but we four were silent, going as we always did: myself to the front; by my swordarm Skarphedin; at my shield my brother Bjarni. Olaf comes always behind, because these Danes are not our people. It is a fool who trusts strangers and soon he will be a dead fool.

Before a battle it is always the same. Fear makes men short of temper. If a man pushes too close or too hard he may die for it, because all are looking for courage. Somewhere in the darkness there came the sobbing that is a young man's fever grown too great and I wondered, because most have fought long years in this land. Someone's brother perhaps, newly joined. May Odin be his shieldman.

Those who had stormed this place the first time told of earth ramparts and a wooden fence above. There were stones too in parts, but much broken and easy to climb. I looked for more in this second coming, but saw nothing. Was it then a trap, to draw us on to a place of slaughter? The thought came but I sent it on its way. These people have grown soft in the years of plenty, they value their land too little. They will soon know what it is worth.

They were long in hearing us, though the rasp of our breath

1

was like thunder. The night air smelled sweet as honey. When the fence rose above us Skarphedin stopped and we three stopped also. With arms spread to the sky and the wild light coming into his face, he made his battle pledge.

I could sense that Bjarni trembled, and I know that Olaf did also.

"Shall we leave for the ship now, comrades?" I said to them but the laugh was overtaken by Skarphedin's howl. Even the memory of it now can chill me, as if Fenrir himself had broken his chains and stalked red-eyed amongst us. Mothers, hold your children close to the breast, for I am come to claim the blood-price; know then who comes here: Northman; Seastrider; Viking!

I ran the last oars-length to the palisade and made a step of my hands and Skarphedin put his foot there and leaped for the top. Then came Bjarni, then Olaf, for they were both needed to haul me skywards, complaining all the while that they could have stayed home and fished, for I was heavier even than a herring catch. The Danes were battering at the gate and torches raced through the night as men came running. I could not see where I was and stayed a moment, but then came a scream that rattled at the end.

"This way." Skarphedin was busy already. Thatch was blazing now and a man ran towards us, sword upraised. I stepped away and drove him through the belly. As I said, they are not used to battle. Skarphedin came from a doorway, his face wet with sweat.

"My blade is hungry."

"Come this way, my friend, and we shall find it a meal."

On then, through the twisting ways. The Danes were stayed by a knot of men and those we met were still travelling to the battle. They died before it ever began, so it seems. The screams of women rose up as we passed, and a child ran weeping before us. Skarphedin would have struck at it but I held him. "What, spoil the feast to come? Too small, too small." It brought an empty smile to his face and I knew he was not so far gone. Sometimes the battle made him senseless.

We were come then to a great hall, and first there for no fires burned and there were no sounds of battle.

"First pickings," cried Bjarni, and Olaf chuckled. Too often we headed the fighting and missed the treasure. Always

Bjarni wastes time looking for trifles, pretty things, while Olaf hunts for shoes, for his feet are short and wide and nothing suits him. It was left to me to shake the coin out of them, for Skarphedin took nothing of course. But it was a bare place. Cloth hung down the walls, but much faded and worn, so the pictures could not be seen. There was some old armour slung from the rafters, but that too was worthless, so I began to turn over the benches. I have found many a bauble there in my time, though the best is always buried and must be beaten out of them.

Skarphedin stood by the dead hearth, looking at nothing. That was always his skill, to go inside his spirit, to where the fire burns, and warm himself at the flame. Then, when the time came he could strike. There is no fear in such a man, and no pain either, for these are little things and he gives them up to burn. So he stood and waited, and we took care to move respectfully.

Then running feet, and the door burst wide. A man ran in and he was a Saxon to judge by his helm. It was of bronze and old fashioned, but clever in its working. He stood and gaped at us, amazed, and we stared back, wondering how to get the helm without breaking it. The boy, for he was little more, tugged at his sword.

Skarphedin grunted.

"Mine," I cried, for if Skarphedin struck, the helm would be in two and useless. The boy hefted his sword as best he might, looking from one to another. I stepped to the fore, but slowly, for he was looking at death and I would not send a man on that journey with too much haste. I saw the sweat on the hairs of his face and his tongue making play, but he did not turn aside. He would die well.

A gasp from the door and I looked to see only a woman there. I had wasted my time. I stepped right as if to strike at the boy, then left to wrong-foot him, and drove him through the open body. It was a killing stroke and he fell soundless to the floor, his sword tasting only the blood of the man who carried it. I bent to strip off the helm.

"This is a prize worth having." Bjarni had the woman by the arm. She had on her face the look of unbelief that comes when death hisses suddenly in your ear.

"Who are you?" I asked, in her own tongue. I spoke it moderate well and for that reason the others did not concern themselves with it, for it takes need to teach a man to speak a tongue not his own. Many's the time I've dickered for a whore for them, aye, and beds and food and ale. This woman did not answer me and I saw she was past speech. A servant, I thought, with her bare feet and unbound hair. Bjarni took off his helm and tried to cuddle her close, for he thinks himself matchless with women. She stood like stone and he began to fondle her breasts. They pressed against her clothing like the bosom of a ship, they filled each of his two hands. I felt my own blood begin to stir and thought that I would take a turn at her before too long.

Of a sudden she sprang to life. Her nails raked Bjarni's cheek, she twisted free and was at bay against the wall. Her face, strong and unlovely, was chalk white. I knew the things they believed of us and tried to calm her.

"Come now, come," I urged. "We won't hurt you, sweetheart. How about a little comfort for some sailors far from home? Your master here's in no case to object, I think."

She licked her lips. When she spoke her voice was deep, unlike a woman's, but softer still than a man's. "That is— that man is my husband. I am Emma, daughter of Beodar, who is a great and rich man in Mercia. If you touch me you will suffer for it. My father will pay dearly to have me returned to him."

I did not know what to say. Bjarni moved to get her again, but I stayed him. "No! She says she is noble and they'll pay ransom. Wait a moment."

"Noble? Her? Look at her clothes. No shoes, no jewels, nothing."

Olaf nodded in his slow way. "She looks worth a deal more in bed than out of it, Thorkil."

I considered. She was indeed dressed poorly, but it was night and a battle raged. And in her height, past my shoulder and I am a tall man, and her pride—even now she held herself straight—it might be as she said.

"What do you have to prove who you are?"

"There is no need of proof. I am who I say I am and you are barbarians." She tipped her chin and glared at me and I laughed.

"Hoity-toity," I mocked, and pretended to stroll down the hall looking at the hangings. These things are not easy to decide. If indeed there was a ransom all was well, but if I believed her and there was not the laughter would crack the rafters. Better the whole army had her than that. But the pickings had been poor of late—I was uncertain.

A shout from the men and I turned to see her coming for me, her husband's bloody sword clutched in her two strong hands. Out of the side of my eye I saw Skarphedin come to life, carrying axe and sword together. I knew she would have one blow only, for the weapon was heavy, and I prayed she would be quick. When it came it was close, and I felt the wind of its passing, but then I rushed her. I pinned her under me, knowing Skarphedin stood above. She fought and it pleased me to feel her legs pressed against mine. I was tempted to ride her then and there, I had a cock like a horse.

"Kill her! Kill her!" moaned Skarphedin and I thought that is one thing I'll not do, my friend. He had a loathing for women. They despised him because he was ugly.

She was kicking and trying to bite and I gave her a thump in the ribs to slow her up. Her tongue came out with the air and I seized my chance and ripped at her dress. I wanted to feel those tits. What I felt instead was a leather bag, nestling where I should have liked to lie, between two white pillows with tips like pink honey. I had struck harder than I intended and she lay sucking air like a fish, so I sat up to see what was in the bag. It was then that Skarphedin lunged, intending to take her head with the axe. Had I thought, I should have let him because a good friend is worth much, but before my dull head could come to it, I had seized his leg and thrown him.

I got to my feet, slow and dismayed. Olaf and Bjarni went to Skarphedin, like girls to their mother, but he snarled them away. He was in a white rage, and past himself.

"Skarphedin—old friend—" I held out my hand and he spat.

"I kill you," he hissed and picked up his sword from where it had fallen. His legs, so short and thick, were spread wide beneath him as if he were a table. It was his battle-stance and we laughed to see children copy him. To see it now and know I was his enemy filled my heart with fear and sorrow. I took off my helm. I threw down my weapons. I bowed my head for the blow.

When it did not come I looked up to see his face twisted and hateful. "Do not think you can turn fate aside so easily, Thorkil," he whispered. "The day will come." He turned

and went stiff-legged into the night. I was sickened. I knew
he would be as a fox in a chicken-run, killing until the mood
passed. I had the blood of children on my hands.

All thought of pleasure had gone from me. I could not look
at the woman, crouched like a cat on the floor, her arms
crossed on her breast.

"I have done a terrible thing," I said, and Olaf came to
me. He put his arm round my shoulder and gripped me with
his tough, shipwright's hand. His callouses were used to axe
and adze and plane, he had no touch of comfort. Yet he was
my friend from boyhood and I loved him.

We tied the woman's hands and led her with a rope. The
fighting was near finished and men were drunk and whoring.
It had not been a great battle. We looked for treasure and
found it, buried under hearths and lodged against the thatch.
Bjarni took a good saddle and some unforged iron, and
brooches too from the women. We found an unburned house
with ale in the pitcher and we turned the squealing peasants
out and took it. The woman we tied to a roof post and she
stared at us in hatred. Her eyes were clear as water. Then at
last sleep, with drink to dull regret of deeds we wished
undone.

I was weary when I woke. At sea a man may pass a day
and a night and another day without sleep and think he knows
how it is to be tired, but it is nothing to the heaviness that
comes after battle. I know not why it should be. Bjarni knelt
beside the woman, smiling and making signs, but her face
was like stone. Her husband's blood had dried in crusts on
her hands. I wondered what I should do with her.

"Leave her be," I said to Bjarni. "You'll not sweeten
her."

"You think not?" He stood up and I thought that if Bjarni
could not make her love us then the cause was lost. He was
tall and boyish slender, and his hair bright as corn. The girls
all fell for him and he was in love a dozen times a day,
though mostly with himself. Many's the hour he spent comb-
ing his hair and trimming his beard. He seldom slept alone.
Still, he looked to me for guidance in all things, I sometimes
thought too much. He did not think for himself.

I went to piss and Olaf rose grumbling and did likewise.
No-one spoke of Skarphedin. We had not been parted in years

and the strangeness was beyond discussion. Such things are like a raw wound that must be tended, but a man will let it fester rather than face the pain.

I took my knife and cut the woman free. She sat up and rubbed at her hands, for I had tied her tight and they were like dead fish. I knew for myself how it was when the feeling came back, but her face kept still. Her cheeks were flat, like a dog's, though her hair was lush as bracken.

"You say your name is Emma."

"You may believe it. Get away from me, Dane, you stink."

I picked at my teeth with my dagger. She was probably right for we had come upon the town in three days' march and no time to wash away the sweat. But the Saxons were a filthy race themselves. For the time, I let it pass.

"What was your husband called?"

"If you had not killed him you might have asked him yourself." She tried to pull her dress across her breasts and it unsettled my temper. I caught her by the hair.

"His name, bitch."

She spat, full in my face and at once I struck her. She fell to the floor and lay still.

Olaf rumbled his deep, slow laugh. "You'll not tame that one in a hurry. Sell her, Thorkil, you'll lose an eye otherwise. She has that look."

I grunted. It was only the thought of ransom that stayed me. When we left Norway to join the Danes I had hoped to earn my fortune once again, but for all the years of struggle we had little to show. Whatever we took, others had also taken and the price was low. It was coin that we needed. I wondered if we should go instead to Ireland and try our luck there, but, well, there were others there before us. I glanced at the woman, on her knees now and holding her head. I put a leg against her and pushed her down again.

"I asked your husband's name."

She lay in the stinking rushes and her fury was so hot you could warm your hands at it. Her face was swelling and I saw that her eye would soon close. My desire for her lessened. I squatted down beside her. "He died well for such a boy."

"He was older than I. He was always slight."

A beginning. I set myself to coax the words from her. "Some men never thicken. You have children?"

She shook her head, quick. I grinned to myself, for I had thought her too much woman for the lad. Strong pasture needs a man at the plough, it is no use tickling with a twig. I fell to thinking. "You come from Mercia, you say?"

"Yes."

"The king is Burgred, I think? I have the name right?"

"Yes—yes." She had drawn her knees up to her chin and her face was half hidden. I knew that she fought tears.

"And your father—he will pay for you, or so you say. Tell me, girl, why should he pay for a daughter with a face like sour ale? I warrant your husband took some finding as it was."

She raised her head and looked at me, the eye I had struck no more than a slit in swollen flesh. "My father loves me. He is a great man. As for my husband, we took the most wealthy. Next time I will find one that can fight."

I thought of the boy's headpiece, of bronze with figures overlaid; it was good, though too small for a Viking head. His sword was only fair, but these Saxons do not understand the craft. My own sword now, there was a blade. The iron was plaited together to make a weapon of great strength, even equal to an axe. Not for nothing was it called World Tree.

I stood and went to look for the bag I had taken from the woman, for I knew it would hold her treasure. I felt her watching with her sea-grey eyes, and I tipped the bag on to a cloth, where she could see it. Two silver coins, *sceatta* they call them. They come from the time of Offa, who was some ancient king or other; a gold ring, quite pretty; a few smaller, copper coins.

"Why so little?"

She shrugged. "Why more? The silver is much valued here. My father will pay in silver, of course. We did not keep our coffers here, we knew you would come. The ring was my mother's."

"And now it is mine." I saw her burn to claw me, and I laughed.

Bjarni came in with some bread and salt meat. We shared it amongst ourselves, noticing again that there were three where there should be four.

"Do we feed her?" asked Bjarni, nodding at the woman.

"Give her something. I may yet have to sell her."

"Pity you marked her," said Olaf, tossing some bread

across. The woman left it where it fell. "You think she lies about the ransom, then?"

I chewed on the meat and thought. That is the worst of these campaigns, the food. Stale, sour and too little of it. I hadn't eaten well since I left my mother's hearth in Vestfold. "I think she is noble," I said at last. "She comes from Mercia and Halfdan moves against there soon. I would like to get there first and claim what there is to be had. Bjarni, I do not want you prattling to some whore about this, mind. Tell no-one that we have her. I will ask a few questions in the town, and if I find she has lied it will be the worse for her."

There was a silence. At last I said what all were thinking. "Have you heard where Skarphedin rests?"

Both shook their heads. "He could find a bed anywhere," said Bjarni. "The Danes would be honoured."

Just so. But my friend, whose name would live in saga when mine was long forgotten, had been forced to seek shelter with strangers. The beloved of the gods, humbled, and over a woman. I was grieved and ashamed. I rose and took a rope and tied her once again, wrists tight to ankles and then to one of the roof posts. I was glad the others were there. If it had been she and I alone she would have suffered more. As it was she choked her cries in her throat. The dark little house was crushing me.

"Come," I said to Bjarni and went out.

The Saxons called the place Eorwic, which was Jorvik to the Danes, for they lack an ear for the language. As a stronghold it was well placed between two rivers, but for that same reason it was unpleasant, with stretches of marsh and bog close by. The day was clement and spring flies sat on the stagnant pools. Such things breed summer sickness. I would not understand the great pieces of stone that were everywhere, here part of a wall, there making a path through the slime. It was only when we came upon the ruins that I understood. A great building had stood here once, as great or greater than anything I had seen, and I have travelled the world. Pillars lay tumbled to the floor, like a child's sticks. I went in amongst the stones, wondering how this had come to be. It was eerie there, with weeds growing tall through the cracks.

Of a sudden a great white owl swooped from a niche, high

on a crumbled wall. Bjarni shrieked. I turned to see him blushing. "I thought—it was like a spirit, Thorkil."

"Some spirit to make you squeal like a girl." I wandered further in, but it was dangerous with pieces falling. "This is the work of giants," I said.

"I think you're right. Let us go now, Thorkil, there's nothing for us here."

I remembered his fears as a child, of the dark, of the byre, even of me when I came in with frost on my hair. He was a child still. A man learns that he does well to fear the gods, but not in darkness or sudden noises. I turned back and went into the streets, that were alive and bustling with Danes.

I went looking for Halfdan. Everywhere men were drunk and quarrelling, over women, loot, even over who had struck which blow. Remember this, if ever you take a place; plunder it at once, when all is confusion. In a day, or perhaps two, there will be a new king and new laws and rules and punishments, and you will be tossed into gaol for taking what could have been yours at the start. Take what you want, and hold it, though the last part is the hardest. When a man drinks, as he will after battle, he forgets how hard won was the booty. I knew a man, from Trondelag, he was called Knut. He went voyaging one summer in a ten-bench ship, and he thought to be back before the ice. He was gone three years and said he had travelled to Rome, which is a great distance and he was ever untruthful. But his treasure was seen by many, and is spoken of still. Silver, in bars and in the eastern coins, they call them *dirhams*; a great bronze saddle; silk, which is the finest cloth you can dream of, cool and light and of a brilliance that is like jewels; and a golden dish with pictures of people dancing, very clear and plain. Well, Knut came back with these things and there was such a feast as Trondelag had never seen, and much ale and wine were drunk for he had brought wine with him for his mother to try. In the morning he had but a pain like a split skull and three pieces of silver.

Many in Jorvik that day would wake to find less. Here and there men hailed me and I replied civilly enough, though we had always kept ourselves apart. I fancied that I saw things in their greetings that perhaps were not there. How many knew Skarphedin had left us? Many or none? Does that man there look mocking beneath his smile? At such a time a man who has squinted all his life may of a sudden seem to begin. For our standing with Halfdan was high just then, we headed the fight and were well rewarded. I looked to have much from him, and not so long to wait either, with the kings paying tribute. But it was all for Skarphedin. Berserks are always honoured of course, but even among the great there are some that are greater than the rest. Skarphedin was one such. His purpose was always true. There were some that said spears turned back on themselves rather than strike him. Others believed that his sword, which was Claw of the Raven, became as ten at the height of the battle, and could be seen striking the enemy down with no hand to hold it. I, who owed him my life a dozen times, had never seen such things. But perhaps it was my eyes that were at fault.

I went to where I heard Halfdan held the prisoners. It was a relief to me to see Skarphedin absent, for I did not want to greet him before them all. Halfdan sat with his guard around him. He was a big-bellied man, much troubled by his teeth. They called him Wide Embrace, and he was well-named, he held much. His brother, Ivarr, that was a bloody man, but Halfdan was less fierce, except when his teeth troubled him.

"'Thorkil Sigurdsson! You are welcome! A good night's work, I think. I looked to see Skarphedin with you?''

I grunted. Indeed, speech was hard when Halfdan put his arm around your shoulders, for his breath was as foetid as an ale-filled swamp. He was a warrior though, and clever. I was not sorry to serve him, nor Guthorm either.

He released me and I found my tongue. "The battle was good. I did not think to see so many prisoners." I looked at the lines of men, some holding to courage but others more plainly fearful. They had reason to despair, for Halfdan had a fancy to repay rebellion with blinding, or worse. Some would be slaves. The fortunate would die.

A priest was there, cleanshaven, and watching all with a long face. I knew him for Wulfhere, who ruled them in their religion here once, and now would do so again. He was obedient to the Danelaw. He drank from a cup of green glass, which he had through our goodwill, though he kept his lips tight as if it might be poison. I do not understand these men, I make no secret of it. What should it matter if a man worships this god or that, except to the man himself? Why, it might be that a boy would learn to sail and to fish and be so struck by the wonder of it, being so new, that he would make offering

to Frey. He of course has a magic ship that he keeps folded in
his pouch until he must use it. The boy would long for such.
Then, in his manhood and adventuring across the oceans he
would know the power of Thor, in the storms and the clouds
and the giant strength of the wave. That would be his god,
and rightly so. But if he came to battle why, who but Odin
could protect him? What good then to have made his offering
to Frey, who has more care for a less bloody harvest? Yet
here, these Christians as they call themselves demand that a
man should put his trust in one only. I dread to think of the
wrath that would befall the world if we all did so. Ragnarok,
it could be no less. I misliked Wulfhere and his doleful look.

"And where is Skarphedin? I would thank him."

"He comes later." I lied, and sweat put a salt taste on my
lips. I had seen Halfdan have a man's balls for less. Looking
for one to bear the burden of what I knew was my own
shame, I silently cursed the woman, and at the same time
prayed that Halfdan did not know we had her.

"You have a good house?" he asked and I assured him
that we were well suited. I kept my praise soft though, in case
he took a liking to our beds. It was always nervous, talking
with Halfdan.

He began to speak of the campaign. As I expected, we
would wait until Guthorm's ships joined us and then move
north to crush the Saxons altogether. Then it was to Mercia.
At that time Alfred was paying Danegeld for Wessex, the
East Angles were ours and with Northumberland taken once
again we were very strong. Before long I thought, the fighting will be over, and with it the chance of wealth. The
woman had to bring a good price.

They brought in some men, much cowed, their hands
bound and their feet hobbled, so that they shuffled along.
Their fear was very great and the smell rose from them, like
sour sweat.

Halfdan said, "Will you have one of these, Thorkil? Take
whichever you fancy, there are some strong ones there."

I came slowly to look, for I did not wish to be as a dog,
begging for bones. It was a poor enough gift and I had looked
for more. I gestured to a boy, his beard still thin, who shook
and shivered like a man with fever. He looked as if I would
jump on him and eat him alive, plucking a leg here and an
arm there perhaps. They believe such tales of us. I asked his

name, and when he had found his voice he told me "Aldwulf."
I had no wish for anything more fierce, for it seemed to me I
had already enough trouble in that way of thinking. So I took
him and thanked Halfdan as one man to another.

We left and went out into the street. Bjarni was at my
elbow, asking what did I think, what had he said, but I closed
my ears to his prattle. I needed to gather my thoughts. In the
distance was a figure I recognized. It was Skarphedin coming
towards me, young men with him on every side.

"He is here, I said to Bjarni.

"What will you do?"

"Hold the slave. I will talk to him."

I stood in the way, and he stopped also. "Well met,
Skarphedin," I said. His face was marked with rents, as if
from fingers. I knew they were his own. In the frenzy sometimes he does not know himself.

"Thorkil." His voice was raw with screaming. The young
men round him stood in awe and I alone saw even then that
he was lost. It showed in his eyes. For Bjarni was not his
friend, nor Olaf either, only me. I tended him, and brought
him to the fight. I found him bed, and ale, and a woman who
would not flinch. Where others saw strength I knew weakness. I knelt in the mud before him and touched his hand.

When I rose he said, "You owe me the woman."

"She is noble, Skarphedin. We are to ransom her."

"She is mine. I am owed her."

I swallowed. These things became fixed in his head and it
was impossible to move them. "Take it as my debt to you," I
said.

"She is mine. For sacrifice." He was croaking like a frog.

I took his arm and squeezed it almost to pain. "Come and
rest, Skarphedin. All will be well." He came, but I knew he
would not forget. Still, one problem at a time, that is my way
of thinking.

We walked back to the house and I stepped beside the
shivering Aldwulf. "Tell me, boy," I said kindly, but I
might as well have bellowed for he pissed himself. "Do you
know of a man called Beodar? He comes from Mercia, I
think."

"Beodar? Beodar?" The lad was a gibbering fool.

I gave his backside a kick to sober him. "Yes, Beodar.
What do you know of him, boy, be quick about it."

He gaped and swallowed and his nose ran and covered his face with slime. A loathsome boy, it had to be admitted, with lice thick in his hair. He mumbled something about Beodar being a great man and a friend of the church.

"Does he have a daughter, boy?"

A great sniff, like the death-rattle of a cow, and he mumbled, "She is Emma, wife of Aelthyn."

"What does she look like?"

"Er—look like, sir?" The boy was indeed an idiot. Most like Halfdan had chosen the idiots to give away, it was not impossible.

"Does she have two heads, green hair, feet like a goat? What does she look like?"

"She—she is tall, sir. Taller than her husband. She—she is fierce, sir."

"Fierce? What do you mean, boy?" I roared at him and it addled his brain. All he could do was whimper and run snot. If Bjarni had spoken the language he could have tried more softly, but as it was I had to hold my temper and try again. At length I discovered that this Emma was tall, plain of face but with long, reddish hair. She did as she willed and her husband could not manage her, though she was thought to be virtuous. There was a tale that a man named Egbert had tried to steal a cuddle and she had blacked his eye. The Emma I held was the Emma he knew, that much was clear.

"Is her father rich, boy? Does he have coffers filled with silver?" I smiled at him but he thought I meant to bite.

When he had picked himself out of the mud I asked the question again. "Beodar is—rich, sir," he bleated. It was enough. I was pleased. Skarphedin should not have her.

When we reached the house, I was in mellow mood. Skarphedin was once again my friend, we had a fine cow to take to market and the pitcher was filled with good ale. Only the food was bad, and I resolved to keep the drink from Olaf until he had cooked. One step through the door and my good temper fled. The fire was out, Olaf was nursing a bloody arm and the woman crouched like a cat in a corner.

"What is this?"

"I untied her, Thorkil. She was crying with the pain. But she seized the dagger and cut me, and in the fight the ale went on the fire."

"At least you did not lose her."

"Give her to me," said Skarphedin in that way he had, as if nothing could be said against him.

"I have taken her and owe you the debt," I said as calmly as I could. "Go, Bjarni, and fetch some ale for Skarphedin. As for you, bitch—" I went to the woman "—we will truss you like a bird for the pot." I took up the rope and stepped towards her, but in a second she was on her feet and facing me. She was a tall woman. If I had bent just a little I could have touched my lips to her forehead.

"Don't you dare lay your hands on me," she hissed, alight with anger and fear at one and the same time. "I'm not a slave! My father is a great and rich man. If he learns how you've treated me he won't rest until you're dead. I swear it!" The words meant nothing. Her breath came and went in a shudder, and I looked to see the swell of her bosom within the torn dress. Slowly I reached my hand up and drew the cloth close to cover her. She flinched at the touch of my fingers.

"You will do as I say," I said softly, "or I will give you to Skarphedin."

"Skarphedin?"

"His face is marked."

She looked across to where he sat, as shaggy as an animal in his coat made of the skin of a sheep. His black eyes watched her without blinking.

"He is mad," she said and could not keep her voice still.

"You will go to him if you disobey me,"

She raised her eyes to mine. I wished I had not marked her. "Only do not tie me."

"I will tie you at night. If you try to escape it will be the end of you."

She thought for a moment. Her head moved in a nod.

Bjarni came in with the ale and offered it to Skarphedin. Olaf wrestled with the fire, for the error was his own, and in no time the place was like a smokehouse, and we all pieces of fish. The woman talked softly to the slave, Aldwulf, and he sobbed into his hands. Her words seemed to calm him a little.

We passed the night packed close in the little house. The boy was as rank as an old goat and Bjarni complained of fleas, for they always relished his flesh. As for myself I lay and dreamed of a woman. I rode her like a stallion, I held her like a flower, I plunged like a ship on the sea. I woke to the sound of Bjarni scratching, my seed spent while I slept. A lad's trick that one, and unknown to me since. I fell to thinking.

There are times when a man remembers his father and the things he taught. When we sailed through the ice in search of walrus and reindeer in the land of the Lapps, when I was weak of arm and unused to rowing, he would sit by the spears and tell me what a man should know. To keep his weapons clean, and always close at hand; tell no-one what it is best that none should know; sleep always light, so that a rat's scamper will not go unnoticed. Those nights in the ice were cold as death and sleep itself was hard to come by. I remember that we spread the sail across the deck and huddled beneath it, with Ottar snoring drunk and myself longing to be home with my mother. Ah, what a time that was. There are people there that live all their lives in the ice and snow, and they trade hides and reindeer horn. Some of them have tame reindeer with which they entice the great herds that roam wild in the forests and on the tundra. Every year my father traded with one of these men, but one year the man was gone and the trade bad, and we never went back again. There was a moon-faced girl there that I think I might have bedded; but I was young and she unlovely, though to an innocent boy what is a little whalegrease when he thinks to have his first woman?

I had come very far since then. My father was long dead and had taken his sword and shield to Asgard. The farm was gone to Harald Finehair who looked to rule all Norway, and my mother nothing but a lodger in my uncle's house, and he poor enough. Bjarni and I had nothing but that we could hold in our own two hands. By now I should have a home and a hearthfire, a good wife sharing my bed. Oh Bergthora, Bergthora, my heart cried. For a man must go adventuring and leave home and love behind him. When he is sea-weary, when spear and sword and even the very waves of the ocean smell of blood, there is no comfort. Word-fame is his true reward, but who knows what others may say of him? My bones ached for the home I had lost.

Chapter
Two

THE HORSE THAT will suit me has not been foaled. I have more sickness on the bouncing back of some pony than ever in a longship, and I have sailed through storms that have even had Olaf hanging over the side calling for his mother. So my temper was foul from the minute we left the town.

We led the slave, Aldwulf, by a string round his neck. He trotted along well enough, for none of us would have him up behind and the land around Jorvik is as flat as a cake on a griddle. When the dawn broke, pink and chill, the walls of the town were only a line in the mist. I wanted no-one to know where we were bound, or who it was came with us.

Birds waded in the reedbeds and flew up at our approach. I watched their legs trail as they went and thought of the whore I had taken. As slack as an old shoe, though the others liked her well enough. Skarphedin did not want her, and that concerned me, for it was good for him to let the heat out now and then. He rode a shaggy pony, as short and wide as he himself. His black hair blew in the morning breeze, for he carried his helm tied to the saddle.

There was a sudden splashing in the marsh. A young deer was plunging away through deep water, sending spray to catch rainbows from the morning sun. With one mind we went for it, myself and Skarphedin drawing sword, Olaf reaching for his bow and Bjarni casting a spear. The deer jinked at swimming, turned and tried to rush past us. We all urged our ponies but my feet met each other underneath and I hung to the neckhair and cursed. Skarphedin it was that sliced the beast. His sword took it in the throat and he stood in the water and held it as it died. He reached bloody hands up and offered the head to his god. The rest Olaf took across his saddle.

We rode on, laughing, for it was a good omen. The woman sat silent on her pony. "A good kill," I said to her. Skarphedin was licking the blood from his fingers. She said nothing.

The day became warm and my spirits began to rise. Even on a pony I am happiest when travelling, when the place behind seems something best abandoned and the one before holds the promise of all that you would wish. If this meal is bad, why, the one we shall come to will be better. If it is good, how plain it is that this is a rich country and worth knowing. When a man ceases to long for things unseen then he is old indeed.

After a time I found the pony cramped me unbearably and I swung off and walked. A man is like a cripple when he walks after riding, but it was better. I held to the woman's saddle as I went.

"When we come closer to your home you must tell me the way."

"Yes."

The bruise was fading. I have never seen a woman who showed so little of her thoughts, or who wailed less either. I think it was for that I did not doubt her. I wondered if she were a witch.

"What metal is the blade that will kill you?" I mused, and she looked at me with her still face, so I did not know if she understood me. Then her eyes moved to the miserable Aldwulf.

"We are not all easy meat."

It was a strange answer. And indeed she was walking in my dreams. I resolved to make offering to Thor as soon as may be.

We came to a river with a beach of shallow sand and we stopped to water the ponies.

"Let us wash" I said and began at once to take off my clothes. I gestured to Aldwulf. "Get in, slave. Scrub your clothes as well, they stink." He uncovered his white and feeble limbs, shivering and sobbing the while. Bjarni dragged him in and ducked him, which was near drowning since the

starveling could not swim. We hauled him blubbering to the
bank and Olaf took a knife and used the edge to shave his
scalp, a little bloodily but at least ending the days of the lice.

Skarphedin and the woman sat and watched the while, for
both required privacy before they would wash. For myself I
stood in the stream and scrubbed at my chest, taking care that
she should see what I was made of. She watched without
blushing and I felt myself quicken, so that in the end I was
forced to cool myself with a swim. I could not better the
bitch, and I fixed on revenge.

Bjarni led the ponies in to drink and they stood belly deep
in the slow water. There was a clump of willows nearby,
trailing their leaves like hair.

"Go you," I said to the woman. "You may bathe beyond
the trees. We will not watch."

She looked at me and we both thought of escape. I squeezed
the water from my beard and let her think a little. When she
had gone behind the trees I called Olaf and my brother and
told them what I planned.

"I thought you had grown past such tricks," said Olaf, but
he laughed.

I judged it would take her some time to get into the water.
We harnessed the ponies and chuckled like boys. Then we
mounted and began to ride quietly into the shallow river, to
come at her round the willows. I caught sight of her through
the green strands, hair dark with moisture against the white
skin of her back. She was washing with long, slow movements of her arms. I looked at the others and they were
watching open-mouthed.

"Come on," I yelled and we kicked the ponies and charged,
roaring and splashing as if attacking a fortress. I do not know
what I expected. That she should run screaming, I think. But
after the first shocked start she only stood there. The water
was to her waist and she crossed her arms to hide her breasts.
Olaf's pony tripped and tumbled him in, and it was left to
Bjarni and me to whoop and plunge around her, and Bjarni
thought it the greatest joke. To me, it did not seem so funny
and I dragged my horse to a stop in front of her. Bjarni too
pulled up and went to fish out Olaf and catch his pony.

So close to the girl I saw that she was trembling. She had
such courage I was ashamed to have tried it for a joke.

"We meant nothing," I said.

She lifted her eyes to mine. "Only to bring me low. You have no honour."

That stung me worse than a bee in my breeks, for it has never been said that Thorkil Sigurdsson is without honour. I have paid my debts and fought my own battles and the man who can call me coward does not live. I raised my hand to hit her and she opened her eyes wide and waited for the blow.

"Damn your Saxon cheek, we should have stuck you along with your husband," I muttered, and rammed my legs into the pony. I could not have stayed there longer, with the water growing still and clear. Her belly was flat and tight and the hair at its base was as curly as a lamb's, wet as it was. I looked back once and saw her dressing beneath the trees. I resolved to find her a new dress, to make her think better of me.

We went on along the side of the river. There was much woodland and tracks wound through the trees, but I mislike travelling in forest. One may be attacked without warning. Some time after noon we saw a village ahead, no more than a dozen houses. We stopped and studied it for a time. I noticed that the woman was grey in the face and swaying, and of a sudden I remembered she had not eaten in days. She would die before we ransomed her, I thought with anger.

"We will lodge here." I led the way forward. As we approached figures ran between the houses. "Quick, before they fire arrows," I ordered, and we cantered on, the boy Aldwulf screaming as he was dragged at Olaf's saddle, the girl in our midst. We rode into a scatter of villagers, and moved amongst them, our swords drawn. Squealing peasants all of them, without even the wit to run. They stared at Aldwulf with his bloody shaven head, and at Skarphedin with his twisted face. They also gaped at me, for these people are small and dark and I am large and light of hair.

"Danes! Danes!" they whispered, and milled like frightened cattle. I got from my pony and went to a house which was larger than most. I went like a crab for I was stiff, but it only added to their terror. They did not think we were human.

They build their houses small, for small men. I ducked inside, at the ready for attack. None came. Only a baby mewed from the cradle by the hearth and in a moment a woman ran screaming past me and snatched it up. She thought I would eat it, I suppose. Meat and game hung from the

rafters and only the thought of it made my stomach growl. A
little more hungry and I might turn to babies. I stuck my head
out again. "This will do. Bring a hostage or two and come
in."

The woman all but fell from her pony and I caught her arm
to hold her. But she shook me off and walked straight-backed
to that poor house.

We got the mother of the child to cook for us while her
husband and a boy were tied in a corner. She took a hare and
skinned it, then hung it on a stick over the fire, turning it all
the while. They do not put their meat in water to cook as we
do, and you need strong teeth to tackle it. But it was good to
a hungry man, and the bread too. I watched most carefully to
see that Emma ate. At the first it sickened her but I brought
her a fresh bread cake and broke it for her with my own
hands. I did not care that the others laughed, nor that she took
it pridefully. She had said I was without honour.

It was clear to me that such a little village was in all
likelihood under the protection of some lord or other. I wondered when he should have warning of our presence. They
farm their land most strangely here, with each man in the
village taking a part of each field. They plough in strips and
the pieces in between are wasted. It is so there is fairness in
the good and the bad land but it seems to me that a man must
spend his life trailing from field to field, and a long time
getting rich with his lord waiting with an outstretched hand,
whether for food or service or the warmth of a man's woman.
I have heard that happens here, for all their religion. It may
be a tale though, for half the peasant women are fat and the
other half toothless.

In a strange land it is seldom wise to lodge within walls.
Why, I remember a time in Frankia when we left our ship and
went away from the river, and because I was young and
foolish we stayed in a great house and drove the people from
it. We drank and we feasted, and although it is said "there is
no better load for a man than much common sense and no
worse than too much drink" we were very much disguised.
My good friend Egil died that night, taken through the throat
by a spear. Even the watch we set was drunk. So in this little
village, so few of us in a hostile land, I stayed wakeful.

Emma lay wrapped in her cloak. I had found a linen shift

for her, plain but worthy. When I gave it her she did not know whether to thank me or throw it in my face.

"What is this?" she said at last.

"For you. If it is not good I will find you another."

"Steal one, you mean. You are nothing but a robber."

I sat down at her side and thought. "It is right that a man should prosper by the strength of his arm."

"Even a fool can be strong."

"But then he will not prosper. I am not a fool, lady."

She turned her grey eyes on me and I wondered if I was indeed a fool, for all my denial. I could not settle what I thought about her and that was strange, for I am not usually disturbed by women. My Bergthora now, she was soft and gentle as a dove, which is what a woman should be. This Emma was half Viking.

"Your husband was called Aelthyn, was he not?" I hoped I had the name right.

A little shock crossed her face as she wondered how I knew, and also in the remembering. "You had no need to kill him," she said at last.

"If he was any man at all he would not be a slave. Tell me, why is there no fight in you people? I have not yet met a man who can use a sword properly. See, the shield should come across the body, like so, ready to take a thrust. Did the lad not have a spear, perhaps?"

I could see she did not wish to speak of it, she brushed me aside like a fly. "Before you came we did not need to fight. Let me sleep, Dane."

"I have told you, I am from Norway," I said, but she had turned her back to sleep.

Skarphedin's eyes were on me, and on the woman. "She is weary," I said feebly, and knew he had contempt for me.

"She will bring you lower than a dog." He never spoke without he said something meaningful. I shivered to hear him. But it was his anger that drove him, I thought, he cannot know what he says. Yet such as he are closer to things of the spirit than ordinary men, he could see the cloth that the gods were weaving. I resolved to treat her more harshly.

We set off in the dark hour before the sun rises. I saw that Emma had put on her new shift and I smiled before I remembered. Olaf was troubled by his bowels and we did not make such speed as we might, waiting as he squatted and cursed in the bushes. A man's guts are a difficult thing. One bad fish and he would not care if the world was coming to an end, if only the churning would stop. I have seen a man happy to be drowned, rather than go on heaving on an empty belly. You can say what you like to a man whose guts are troublesome, he will not care.

Thinking these thoughts I turned to Emma. "If all the world had the gripes there'd be no fighting. Would that please you Christians?"

"We can fight well enough. You have not tried us."

"Tried you? We have tried and won, my girl. All over this land kings are paying us tribute, and if it is that little stand you made, well, it was soon past. I think you will not try again."

She turned her eyes on me. "You'll go in the end. You will have to because we will always hate you, for your cruelty if for nothing else."

"You think we are worse than we are. You tell each other tales to frighten in the dark."

"Is he a tale?" She nodded at Skarphedin.

"He is different. Berserk. A man honoured by his people."

"We would not honour one such. He is mad and should have the spirit driven from him."

"A kind of madness, perhaps. He is dedicated to Odin, who is the god of battle. He goes through life without wealth or family, he gains only honour for his people and his god."

She twisted in her saddle and pondered Skarphedin. He returned her look, his eyes blank, as always except when lit for battle. "He would kill me."

"Yes. He thinks you are bad luck. But so far I do not agree and you are safe."

The flies were biting and she scratched her cheek. "Why isn't he the leader?"

I could not answer. I was affronted. I turned my face to the track ahead, which was stony enough, and pretended not to have heard, nor Olaf's row either as he dragged at his breeks and rushed after us.

"He seems higher born than you."

She sat there, fine noble lady, and called me peasant. It was only a little false. My family has farmed and fished since anyone can remember and if we had slaves there were many others who asked us for service. So it is everywhere, except for the very greatest but even they answer to the gods. Why then should I be ashamed that these hands could drive a plough?

I said to her, "Go to Skarphedin if you wish, since he is of good family and I am but a ploughboy. There, I release you to him."

But she laughed at me and said only, "I thought you were a farmer." Olaf groaned and grumbled through the day and all the stopping slowed us. Then Emma slipped from her horse in a wood and walked away into the trees.

Skarphedin was after her in a moment and as he crowded her with the shoulder of his pony she cried out, "Call your dog to heel, Viking!"

I thanked my mother's milk that he did not understand her. Also I was pleased that she had called to me. I said, "Skarphedin, she goes on women's business. Let her be."

He urged his pony again, till she was hard against a tree. I stepped from my mount and came to him, catching his bridle and pulling the beast aside. Beside me was the woman's face, sharp and clear, and above the livid mask of Skarphedin, the scar like sap run from a diseased tree. In that moment I felt that one of us would die. A high whine rose in him, that was fury without escape. I moved to draw my sword, but instead my hand went to push the woman aside. She was not part of this, only the instrument of its making.

Then the cries of men in the attack, and the boy Aldwulf shrieking. By the time I looked they were almost upon us. Ten I think, perhaps more, though in battle men count in bushels instead of singly. Some were horsed, some on foot, and their leader wore mail. I went at him with my sword in two hands, roaring, for my head was bare and I knew if he struck I was a dead man. But he poked at me with a lance and my blade went into his knee and stuck. He screamed and I dragged it free, but before I could come again he was finished. Skarphedin, leaving aside his own dead to come to my aid. A man with a gashed face urged his horse away, but the beast was stupid and slow from the smell of blood. Olaf took him with an arrow.

All was quiet but for a moaning and that was soon ended. There was a silence in the trees as if even the wind had ceased, to mark the passing of the spirits of brave men. The grass was slimed with blood. The woman stood and watched us as Olaf went for the horses and Bjarni cleaned his dagger with the hem of a dead man's shirt. I could not look at the horror on her face. Skarphedin took two of the best swords and broke them. The pieces he cast into a pool for he asked nothing from battle but the victory itself.

I said to her "The word came from that village."

But she only stared again at the dead. I took her arm and led her to her horse, and there was blood on her skirt. For a moment I did not know where she had been struck and then I knew that it was women's blood, which comes like tears when she is not with child. The blood of women and of men, it is shed for the same thing, and that is the ending of hope. I lifted her up to the saddle.

"Will they come again?" asked Bjarni, as if I should know the thoughts of men who were strange to me.

"We will keep from the villages," I said. What more can a man do in a hostile land? We should not have travelled with so small a party, of course. The journey would be three more days at the least and it might be that we should take to the forests and hope that the trees would hide us better than them.

So it was that we camped beside a woodland pool that night, and lit a shielded fire. Noise came from far off, and no saying that it was not wolves. I had no fear of them in summer, in this rich land. I have sat at night wrapped in my cloak in forests deep in snow and watched them circle the fire, eyes like green glass in the darkness. Then a man has cause to be afraid, and think that his bones will go to grace a wolf-wife's den.

Neither did Emma have fear. She went amongst the trees and found plants which she brought to the fire.

"What is this?"

"For Olaf. It is dead-nettle, if I boil it on the fire it will settle his guts." She stripped the leaves from the stalk with strong fingers and put them into the pot.

"The witch will poison us. What is she doing?" Olaf was anxious. I told him what she had said and left the drinking of the brew to his own courage. At last the griping of his belly took command and he sluiced the draught down so hot it burned his throat. "I don't care if it does kill me," he gasped and the woman sensed what he said and laughed.

I saw Bjarni watching her again and I was sharp with him
for some hours after.

Our path led across a range of hills. On the next day we
moved out of the trees and the land became somewhat bleak.
A wind blew cold across rough heather and there were only
the curlews and here and there a flock of sheep, tended by old
men or frightened boys. We killed a ewe and ate sheepmeat
until our beards were shiny with grease, and we took the skin
and wrapped it in a parcel on a saddle, though Emma turned
her nose up.

"It will rot," she complained, and so it would, but worth
something for all that.

The slave, Aldwulf, was mighty sore of foot. It was Emma
that suggested he come up behind her but I would not have
that cess-brained fool clutching at her. I put him up behind
Bjarni and he and Olaf dickered as to whether they would
rather have the slave or the rotting hide to nurse.

I was not easy in myself. I called to mind the pony, the
threat of ambush or the hard going, but I knew it was none of
these. It was Emma. I think she had planned to escape on the
journey, without giving thought to how it might be done. For
she was watched. If she went on foot we were mounted and if
she was caught I had threatened her with Skarphedin. At
night one was always awake to raise the alarm, and we went
through wild country, where none could give her shelter. Still
she thought of it and watched what we did, and I watched
her, with equal secrecy.

It could only be that her father would not yield a ransom.
When I asked about this Beodar I had not understood that he
held sway so far from Jorvik. Was it likely that anyone would
know of him, except from the lips of Emma and her husband?
That fool Aldwulf would say what I wanted to hear. And
things were bad enough already between Skarphedin and
myself. If we made this journey and gained nothing he would
despise me. Even Olaf and Bjarni would look at me with
doubt in their eyes, and a man cannot lead where he is not
trusted.

One morning we sat and waited while Skarphedin bathed in
a little dip in the rocks, that held rainwater warmed by the
sun. He went alone and we sat apart.

"Is he so ugly?" asked Emma.

I pretended not to hear. It is not for me to tell tales for women to laugh at. She had plaited her hair so the wind could not tangle it and a fold of her cloak was turned into a hood. I seem to remember that the larks were singing, but it was long ago.

"There will be no ransom," I said.

Her face, which had been still, became set. "What have you heard?"

"Nothing. Except your thoughts."

She was silent awhile. When she spoke, she was strained. "You are mistaken."

"It is possible. I think not."

She swallowed. "I am worried that my father may be ill. I have heard nothing from him for some time, that is all that concerns me."

"Such a loving daughter. I wonder that your husband's family would not pay to have you back."

She drew a long, deep sigh and raised her face to the sun and the warm wind. There was the scent of mayflower and I know I remember that truly.

"You are very wise for a farmer," she said with a laugh. "And this is a lovely place to die. My father was rich once, and powerful. Then my brother died of a wasting sickness, and my mother of fever, and it made him strange. There was a monk, Brother Sebastian, he talked to my father. He said it was a punishment that God was striking Beodar for his lack of care for the church. He had been strong, you see. They raid from the mountains there, you have to be watchful. But soon my father was wearing monk's clothes. He fasted and did penance endlessly. Men began to drift away and no-one stopped them. He freed the slaves, though they had nowhere to go. The land was left fallow, he did not even concern himself with storing seed and we had always done that. People depended on us. Then the raids started, they never dared before. Wild men from the mountains. Villages burned. Cattle were driven off. I appealed to my father, but he did not care. He said I should marry and leave him to his prayers, but there was no-one for me, they had all gone away when they saw how things were. Then Aelthyn came. His father is a greedy man and he thought he could take me and have what was left. He is called Godric and he hates me. I married Aelthyn and all he got was the helmet, and you have that, a

few bags of silver and three horses. They died of a cowpox, I
did not know horses could catch that, did you?''

"They will die of anything. I mislike horses. This Godric
then, is he rich?''

She made a face. "Rich with other men's money.''

"How far to his steading?''

She looked at me with wide eyes. "He will not pay for me.
I was not obedient to him. That is why we went to Eorwic, to
Aelthyn's mother's kin. There was nowhere else to go.''

I sniffed, for we are a people that hold to the ties of family.
I had never before heard of such a casting-out, except for a
killing or some such. "I think I should mislike Godric as
much as that horse there. Where does he keep his money,
girl?''

There was color in her cheeks, the first I had seen. Her
grey eyes sparkled.

"Would you rob him? I should not mind dying if I knew
you had done that.''

"Less talk of dying, girl. Only tell me where to look.''

And this I remember most clearly. The witch smiled at me.

I did not tell the others that our plans had changed. There
was no need, they would fight where I told them. I have
never understood how it should be that good men like Olaf
should be pleased to have their lives ruled for them. It has
never been my way. Thinking back, I see that was why I was
with the Danes, for their lords were not mine and I was paid
for what I gave, no man forced me. There was a difference in
Skarphedin's following. He saved himself for the inner fire,
he had no time for the things of the body. As for me, when I
lay in the night and wondered how I should provide for all
that depended on me and the thoughts chased like fish that
would not be caught, it seemed that I was the fool. The men
sleep, saying to themselves, "Thorkil will know," and it is
only Thorkil that lies wakeful.

The downslopes of the hills were steep and covered in
shale. The ponies picked their way with care and I alone was
not happy to ride. I preferred to trust in my own strong legs.
Olaf sang as we went, contented now that his bowels were to
rights, and he taught the chorus to Emma:

"My mother once told me she'd buy me a longship,

A handsome-oared vessel, to sail with the Vikings.
To stand at the stern-post and steer a fine warship,
Then head back for harbour and hew down some foemen.''

Her voice was low and full, and to watch her sing roused
me. She stretched her long throat and at the base was a
hollow like a cup. I longed to sip from it, to lie in a meadow
and tickle her to smiles with a feather of grass, and this when
before I had been content with a quick stabbing at some slut
and the men standing round to watch. I was getting soft as a
girl. So I kept from her and let Olaf teach her songs. Skarphedin
and I made a pair of it, sitting apart and glowering.

When we came to the lowlands we travelled with stealth. It
was an empty land, with few villages, for the earth was still
poor. As we went on it grew richer and the people more
numerous, and I began to think they would see us and be
warned. So we rolled our swords in the sheepskin, covered
our heads with cloth and tried to look like country people
travelling. Emma laughed at us with white teeth.

When we passed farms I took note of how they defended
themselves. The villages were quite open, so I took it that
when attack came they drove their animals into the stockades
round the greater steadings. In the day men were out in the
fields without weapons, when we teach children to keep a
sword by them even when ploughing. Such a foolish people.
We were few, but if we surprised this Godric all should be
well.

We came to a country that was known to Emma. She sang
no more and her face became sombre. When we stopped to
rest the horses she came to me.

"It is a short ride to Barwic. What will you do?"

I gnawed on a piece of hard bread. "Take some good food
if nothing else."

"But you won't kill them all? Some of them were kind to
me."

"I cannot say what we will do. We are but four."

She looked at Skarphedin with a clouded face. "I am
betraying my own people. I can't set him on them."

"I am the one who sends him to battle, not you. Be easy, it
will soon be over."

I touched her arm but she pulled away from me. "I won't
take you there."

"Then we will strike where you have no enemies at all. We have come too far to go home empty-handed. Come, get on your horse. Your lies have brought us here, we will see if you can also speak the truth."

But she would not mount. She sank to the ground and when I pulled her arm she struck at me. I caught her up and she hung heavy as a dead fish, so I hit her and she bit me. The others stood amazed as we fought, for I could not bring myself to be truly harsh with her. At the finish I held her on the ground and dared not let go for fear she would claw me.

"We are here again," said Skarphedin in his thin voice. "I will kill her."

"No! By Thor's hammer I say no! Any man that touches her will have me to reckon with."

"It looks to me as if you've met your match with her," said Bjarni, as Emma turned her head and grazed my hand with her teeth. He and Olaf thought it a great joke.

"Will you stop this, Emma," I pleaded. "They are laughing at me."

She flung herself about and I felt the strings in her arms move as her fingers clutched uselessly. Then all at once the fight went out of her and she lay still. Her eyes were wet with tears. I bent my head and kissed her.

I have kissed many women in my time; a boy's first kiss when his nose, his hands, his tongue, everything gets in the way; the slobber of a man on a whore; a chaste promise on the mouth of a betrothed. But Emma—oh, Emma. Warm as a child's bed and soft as down, yet with the oiled sweetness of a woman's body for all that. I felt her tongue grow hard against mine, we met and grappled—and dissolved in pleasure. I groaned. She caught her breath on a sob.

"I'll hold her for you," said Bjarni, and I hit him and set his ears ringing. His shocked face lives with me still. Olaf took him by the shoulders and said something to him, but I could look at no-one. Emma rose from the ground, pulled her cloak around her and went to mount her pony. The slave was staring at her, so I kicked him. Without speaking we put our weapons close to hand, pulled on our helmets and prepared our thoughts for battle.

All was peaceful. A woman walked from a house, carrying a bowl, she went to a barn and when she returned the bowl was full. Flour, I thought. We were too far to see clearly. Emma and the slave were tied in the wood behind us.

"What if you are killed?" she asked. "What will happen to us?"

"Someone will find you." I did not wish to think of her. My head was turning with the fight to come, for I have found that it helps to spend time planning for what might happen. In the heat of the battle a man wil act without thinking, and rightly. But the plans he has made are like the deck of a ship, the firm footing for those actions.

We mounted our ponies and trotted briskly to the gate. No-one hailed us. A boy making hurdles stood watching, open-mouthed. As we crowded through the fence Skarphedin's battle-cry rose, swelled up and broke like a wave on the quiet houses before us.

We found silver, buried as she said, beside the hearth, and a gold bracelet in the corner of a chest. Pins and brooches from the cringeing crowd of women. Bread and meat and ale in a goatskin bag. We grabbed at it all, in haste to be gone. Five dead, and only one a woman who had thrown a stick at Skarphedin. Bjarni found us a horse to carry our finds, but it was lazy and we thrashed it through the gate with the flat of a sword. A bell began to toll behind us and we urged our mounts the faster. Into the trees then, and there was Emma, her face drawn, babbling questions. I was too strained to answer and snarled at her. She rode with her hands still tied, for I did not trust her. We rode long into the night.

Chapter
Three

"YOU HAVE WHAT you wanted. Now you must let me go."

Her hair glowed in the firelight as if it had captured the flame. I knew it for a false burning, gone in the day, and I turned my eyes away. "I promised nothing."

"But you must let me go! What more do you want from me, you have taken my home, you have killed my husband. And now you are rich. I have nothing more to give." She was pleading with me. This is all I have left, she said. Do not take it.

On the arrow of thought I went to the bags in the corner of the dark little hut, I knew what I looked for, a pin, taken from the dead woman. It was silver and held at its center a ball of blue glass. A noble thing.

"For you."

She took it and stared as if it were a toad. "This belonged to my husband's mother."

"A fat creature. She cursed like a sailor when we took this."

"You did not kill her?" Grey eyes, asking for the lie.

"I did not."

She sighed and a smile touched her. "Then I will take it. She worked me like a slave and then told Aelthyn to beat me. But he would not."

Outside the trees whispered. This was a woodman's house, deserted when we found it. Olaf and Bjarni slept by the fire, and Aldwulf with the horses, hobbled hand and foot. Skarp-hedin sat in the dark and watched me.

"Let us go out." I wrapped her cloak around her shoulders.

"It's nowhere near morning."

"I am not afraid of the dark." I led her to the door.

As I moved to close it behind us Skarphedin said, "You are a fool, Thorkil. You sow your seed in a spider's web."

The sky above the trees was light as the sea, but we stood in darkness.

"There is rain on the wind." I saw the flash of her teeth.

"We are safe yet awhile." I held her hand, strong and warm in mine, and led her to where the brambles hung over mossy grass. "Lie here."

Her fingers touched my face. "But I do not wish to lie with you."

I felt a joyful madness coming on me and I lifted her and laid her on the ground. I whispered in her ear, I love you, sweet, sweet Emma, let me drown in you. I will take care of you always, you are my love. For what does a man say at such a time? None of it is enough. I dragged at belts and buckles, laces and thongs, until I felt her breasts against me. I am covered in thick hair and she closed her fingers in it and tugged. So I kissed her to make her kind. And then when she was gentle I was not, I put my mouth to her arms, her breasts, her belly and she moaned as the wind was moaning in the trees above us. And then I loved her. I was like a god, powerful, huge, I rode her as a longship rides the storm. She cried to me, held to me, cursed me and begged, and I shouted aloud as I spent my seed in her.

She was a bird brought down by an arrow. Her white body lay helpless beneath me. "I will plant a forest of boys in you," I said.

I saw the shine as her eyes opened. "I thought you would let me go."

"Oh no. When my hand closes it seldom opens. Ask anyone.' And I took her again, and a third time, for I was indeed a god that night.

At last the rain came, just before dawn, and we went back into the hut. All seemed sleeping but there was fresh wood on the fire. Raindrops were jewels in her hair and I could have wept for joy. But she did not smile. I saw that there was blood on my hands and I wondered at it, until I knew that it was her blood. I was indeed bewitched, for it pleased me.

It was a good ride that morning. A strong woman at my side, a laden pony coming after and all around the comrades of my heart. The earth smelt green after the rain, it was a scent that brought remembering. I had been a good farmer in my youth, before I went after glory. It is a worthy life, to bring food and plenty from the soil, to match the spirit to the seasons. But it is no life for a lusty lad and many's the day I raged at my mother and begged her to let me go adventuring.

We had an old ox that was weary of the plough. In the mornings I would go to him and his rheumy old eye would meet my restless one and I knew we were of the same mind. Anything but this we both thought, but in the end I whipped him to it and we turned the field at a hectic pace, to find contentment in the struggle. One day he died and I shed tears, for he had been a friend to me.

We went quickly, for I was anxious to get to Jorvik. Halfdan would be looking for me. Perhaps it was the pace but no-one talked much. I came to notice it and made some little remark to Olaf, to have some speech from him. His reply was strained, and it was the same with Bjarni. As for Skarphedin I did not need to look to know what he thought. I glanced at the woman, sitting stiff and straight on her horse and of a sudden I knew that the only one of us that was pleased with that fine morning was myself. I struck up a song and called to them to join me, but no voice sounded. Then it was I turned.

"What is this? Scowling like a wife with a blackened pot? Yes, you, Olaf, and you, Bjarni, tell me."

Olaf wiped his nose with the flat of his hand, a habit he had since boyhood. "We are wondering what you are about, Thorkil."

"About? What should I be about?" I was blustering and I felt the heat come to my face. How could they know what I had said to her?

"Well—it puzzles me, Thorkil. First, there was an insult. It was not paid for. I take a slash in the arm, but that is no matter, you think only of the woman, that you will ransom her. Very well then, off we go. But there is no ransom. Instead we must fight, but why there and nowhere else we do not know. Only that she wills it. We gain handsomely, I'll give you that. Then, last night, you and she humping it till dawn and this morning grinning like a fool—I wonder who I'm following, Thorkil. It looks like a lovesick boy.''

I wanted to strike him. Anger was a flame within me, the stronger because I knew what he said was true. So I grabbed at his bridle, so hard that the pony shrieked. My knee was against Olaf's, my face felt his breath.

"Do you say I am unfit to lead you? Is that what you say?"

"Only that we don't know what you are about." He kept his stolid gaze on mine and met fire with earth, which always puts out the flame.

I laughed and let the pony go. "You are right. You do not know what I am about for until last night I did not know myself. And it is this. We are tired, all of us. There is nowhere that we can call home. It is time we stopped thinking that we will one day return to Norway and find our places there again, the only place for us would be under the thumb of King Harald himself, and that is no place for me. But a man should have his own hearthfire, he should raise children, and we have a good place for us all to settle at last. This summer's fighting will see the finish of it, I think, and I will ask Halfdan for land. We will have a house and a fine cow and good strong ale, for we have the money now. Does that sound good to you comrades? Olaf? Bjarni? Skarphedin?''

No-one spoke. Skarphedin stared into the distance as if he had not heard.

Then Bjarni said, "I knew you were tired of it."

"And who would not be tired? We have been years in the field, summer and winter, all the beds damp and all the bread stale. Perhaps I am getting old. In the end a man needs a home and a wife, that is all there is to it."

"You have forgotten my sister," said Olaf, but not as if offended.

"Forgotten? Never. She will not be looking for me now I think, not after all these years."

"Who then?" Olaf and Bjarni stared, as if they could not believe what was in their minds.

Skarphedin's laughter, rarely used, crackled like dried leaves. "He will take the witch. Look at her, she hates him but that's the hare he's chasing. Do you think she'll love you, Thorkil?

Do you think she'll bear your brats? Poisoned meat, Thorkil, poisoned meat."

Dark blood came to my face. I said, "She did not hate me last night. Her family is good. She will bear me fine sons."

They stared at her and she sat her pony as if they were not there. I was proud of her and I felt again the surging happiness of the morning.

We started on again and I let them weigh what I had said, like a piece of silver on the scales of a packman. Olaf was the first to spit.

"I have been too long from the sea, Thorkil."

I grunted. We had all been long from the sea. "She's a cold mistress."

"I was raised to build ships," said Olaf. "I'm no farmer. There may be work in Jorvik, I do not know it well enough. The wharf is broken down but it may suffice."

Bjarni whipped his horse closer to me and whispered fiercely, "She's breaking us up. It's as Skarphedin says, she's bewitched you. Do you think he'll be content to grub in a field?"

I studied my little brother. In these years with warriors he had come to see himself as greater than he was; still, he was right about Skarphedin.

"And you, Skarphedin," I said respectfully, "what will you do?"

The air hissed through his nostrils and his pony danced. As always we waited for him to speak. He said at last, "I warn but you are beyond hearing. Also I bear an insult at your hand, I do not forget it. Shall it then be said that Skarphedin deserted his friend? No. There is too much between us."

He fell silent and we were none the wiser. Bjarni was beside himself and kicked his horse next to the woman's pony, striking out at it with angry fists. The beast shied away, the stones of the path sliding beneath its feet, and Emma screamed at him.

"Come ride by me, Emma," I said and put myself between her and Bjarni. Her face was sharp with the effort of understanding.

"What is it? What do you say?" she asked.

"That I will take you to wife. They do not like it."

I watched as the color went out of her face. "But—you must let me go."

"Go? Where will you go?"

"To my father perhaps—I don't know—" she was bewildered and it touched a softness in my heart.

I placed my hand on hers as it held to the rein of her pony. "I will take care of you, sweeting."

She jerked her hand away and went again to ride beside Bjarni. It was a knife in me. But I laughed for the others to see.

"Poisoned meat," said Skarphedin. Soon the rain came again. We bent our heads into it until our beards were sodden. Boulders lay scattered on the hillside amongst the poor trees, that clung with their roots showing.

"We will look for a cave," I said and turned my horse upwards, for all his protesting. As I thought, there was a crack in the rock, a poor enough slit and dank, but at least we could shelter. The ponies stood heads drooping, and the slave Aldwulf crouched by them. The scabs on his head gleamed like stripes.

"Please. Bring him in," said Emma, but to revenge myself I did not. I felt her eyes watching me.

When the rain eased it was late, so we set about gathering dry fuel although there was little enough. Olaf got out his strike-a-light and tried to raise a spark, but nothing would catch. At the finish we cut a dry piece of Bjarni's shirt and started the blaze with that. The cave became lit with flame. Outside it was only a dull summer's evening, but against the fire it looked like night. There was a feeling in the air, of unease, of things about to happen. The hairs on my neck began to bristle and of a sudden the woman came quietly and sat by my knee. So I was not alone to feel it.

"Thorkil," said Skarphedin, and I shivered to hear him. Again he said, "Thorkil."

"Yes, Skarphedin?"

"I will take the slave."

I looked out past the fire to where the poor creature was lying, and though I had no care for him at all my heart was moved. "Why will you do this?" I asked.

"Because I am owed him. It is the price of it, Thorkil, my friend."

Olaf and Bjarni both stared at me, in terror lest I should oppose him. Yet it was my debt. There was nothing I could do.

He took his strong belt and went out beyond the fire. The slave cried out in fright, a little at first and then in terror as the knowledge came to him. Like a goat, falling to the wolf.

Emma caught at my arm, saying "Stop him! What is he doing?" but I held her close and hid her face against me. When she looked again the lad swung in the cold wind, for Skarphedin and his hanged god. And Claw of the Raven was stained with blood. We came to Jorvik in the afternoon, when the gates stood wide and the sentry hailed us from afar. Even then we could see that much was changed. The stockade was greater and the broken stones put up again. We did not mean to lose Jorvik a second time.

In the streets of the town all was bustle. There was building everywhere and it was hard to pass for the movement of wood and earth, and all the time the sound of axes. I saw Olaf brighten.

"Let us look at the wharf," I said and turned my pony to the river. Emma I led behind me, still shocked and silent as she had been for days. But I heard her gasp when she saw the longship, although it was small and broad in the beam.

Olaf hailed the men with the vessel. "Come far, have you?"

A hefty fellow with a straggled beard said, "Three days. from the East Angles."

"Good weather?"

He nodded. "Fair. The wind was against us some of the time."

Olaf swung down from his horse and squatted at the water's edge. "How does she sail against the wind? I fancy she's a little broad for it."

Bjarni caught the rein of Olaf's horse and we turned away. He would be there a good while, and we had things to see to. The town was crowded with men. It seemed to me that if we wanted a lodging there we would have to build it, unless we wanted to sleep in the halls with the Danes. We had never done so, although Bjarni sometimes hankered after the life. Fastened to my belt he had missed the drinking and whoring, the lads' games of strength that would have been his lot with others of his age. We all like it in our time and scorn it when that time is past.

The streets were thick with slop. I saw Halfdan coming through it on foot, and at once I stepped from my pony though the wetness was most unpleasant. Halfdan was not a man to like looking up. Bjarni came down beside me, but Skarphedin and the woman stayed.

"Thorkil Sigurdsson! Skarphedin!"

"Halfdan." I bent my head in all that I would allow of submission.

Halfdan went past me and reached his hands to Skarphedin in a firm clasp. "You are well? We have not seen you with us."

"We have been travelling." Skarphedin turned his face away and looked again at nothing. I found it possible to breathe once more. I had bought Skarphedin's silence with the life of that boy.

"Travelling, Thorkil?" Halfdan bared his brown teeth in a smile and I returned it easily.

"I am to take a wife," I said, trying for the bashful pride of the young bridegroom. It worried me that I did it so well.

"A wife! Well." Halfdan went to Emma and I prayed she would not kick him or some such. He smiled again and she stared at him in bewilderment. He looked at her face and then at me and said "Well. A wife!" as if he thought I might be silly with ale. "You travelled to fetch this?" he asked after a moment.

"To see her father only. He is dead," I said, finding a stiffness in my voice. It offended me to see him despise her.

"Dead. Oh." He looked again at Emma and put a hand on her knee, saying, "You've caught a man who'll keep you wakeful, my girl! A mighty ram is Thorkil." He was ever coarse-tongued was Halfdan, he would have spoken like that in front of his own mother, I do believe.

"She does not speak our tongue yet," I said with iron thoughts.

Emma urged her horse away from Halfdan and came beside me. "I do not like him touching me," she said clearly, and if she did not understand Halfdan he most certainly understood her. A moment's pause in which I thought we might be dead, and then he laughed and laughed and laughed.

"We'll have a feast for you, Thorkil, and your virgin bride. How will that one be between the sheets? 'I do not like him touching me', she'll squeal as you try and put it where it belongs." His laughter was taken up by the men

around him. They would laugh at a pig, the fools. I felt my
face become hot but I forced myself to smile.

At last they all passed on and we were left.

"By the hammer, that was close," said Bjarni. "Can't you
shut her up, Thorkil?"

"Hold your own tongue, brat!" I snapped, simply because
he was within striking distance. Bjarni glared but kept silence, knowing that I would land him a clout if he said more.
I turned to Emma to indeed tell her to shut up, but if her face
was calm her hands were shaking. I covered them with my
own and held them tight to still them. "Do not doubt me," I
said softly. "You are mine. You are safe with me." Her lips
parted in a small, tired sigh.

We paid a man to lodge in a house by the river, small and
dank but without fleas. There was no private place for Emma
and myself, but soon Halfdan would have his feast and we
would have a proper bedding. I lusted after it as if had been
the first.

It is strange to look back and remember Jorvik as it was
then. It was young and alive, men were at the beginning of a
thing. For it seemed to us that we were placing our mark
upon the country and settling where before we had been only
lodgers. Some men spoke of sending for wives and sweethearts from home and many a peasant girl found herself with
a Viking lover. It pleased me that the woman I had taken was
so far above them.

Part of our force moved to Torksey, further south, to
prepare for coming battles but we and many another stayed in
Jorvik, learning to live at one another's elbow. One forgets
when one has been at arms for so long. Of course Emma was
unused to the duties of the house, except for spinning and
needlework, and the brewing of herbs which is suited to
ladies, so even in our tiny lodging I had to find a woman to
cook. I bought her from a Dane and she was called Berthe.

On the first day Emma said to me, "That woman is a slut.
She will poison you all and it will be with filth."

I too had watched while she coughed into the cookpot and
spat on the floor, but used as I was to Olaf, who was never
very dainty, I had not taken offence. I waved a hand and said
loftily, "You see to it," though what she might do I could
not imagine. Within a day Emma had the woman clean and

respectful, and she ceased making eyes at us all besides. Life became a deal more comfortable.

The problem of a house was not overcome so easily. I wanted to build, but not to advertise wealth or station. At home on the farm we lived in a longhouse with a byre attached, but after our travels that seemed very humble. The greatest Saxons had wide halls with floors of wood or stone, and sometimes rooms above for sleeping. Ricsige, the king Halfdan had chosen to rule at his bidding, he lived in a house like that. Great chests and fine hangings were everywhere and it was said he slept in a bed hung all about with curtains. Still, if that's what a man's honour is worth, it's little enough, I suppose. And I did not mean to live in Jorvik for long, only until I could tackle Halfdan about land.

So we came to it. A house of wood with stone hearth and footings. At the entrance we would have a storeroom, and at the end two separate chambers for sleeping. The roof would be of thatch but we would have one door only, for we did not trust the Danes more than need be. It was a good plan and Olaf liked it, which was as well since it was to be his to build, we were just the laborers. As to the siting of it, we did not want to be hugger-mugger with the Danes so we took a place to the north of the town and left them in the rabbit hutches that contented them well enough.

Each day Olaf, Bjarni and myself went to the forest to cut wood. Because I dared not leave her behind I brought Emma too, and she sat with her spindle as we worked. There was a place in the house, beneath the wall, where I knew she was hiding things; a *styca* or two that I had let fall from my pocket, an old knife of Bjarni's that he thought he had lost. I could not understand what she was thinking of, but in that cramped house there was no private place to talk.

There was a strangeness between us, growing greater every day, and it was part shyness. We had lain together and found pleasure, but the memory was changing—it was no longer clear and of its own time, it took the color of other happenings. When I saw a man with a stupid woman and he not seeing how she was, I wondered if I had deceived myself with Emma, because I wanted her to be the woman of my dreams. She I knew could not look at any of us without her thoughts shadowed by Aldwulf's swinging legs.

Olaf complained a great deal, about unseasoned wood, we

two who could not strike a plank cleanly and most of all of
the waste of his talents when he could be building ships. One
morning as we made ready for the forest he said, "I shall go
fishing today."

Bjarni and I blinked at him. Skarphedin, who passed the
days in Halfdan's hall, was unconcerned.

I said, "And where shall you fish? The river's as filthy as a
cess-pool."

Olaf pulled on his breeks, as bright-eyed as a boy. "There's
a skiff going down river. We'll see how the catch is, we
might make open sea. Back tomorrow I should think."

I was angered. As their chief I alone had the right to say
what each would do. Yet I was going my own way. I said
"You should have told me." He grunted.

Bjarni said, "Is there room for me?" and soon he too was
making ready to go fishing. The thought came to me that had
it not been for Emma I would have gone too. But I dared not
leave her. So I tried to make it seem that I was letting them
have a holiday and I sent them on their way with smiles and a
slapping of backs.

Skarphedin was laughing, I swear it. He came closer to us
when the heat of battle was distant. "To think that I should
see you as a nursemaid," he chuckled, and went out with that
swinging stride of his, that made his short legs seem longer.
He would pass the hours teaching young men to fight, but he
would not touch a sword himself. It was not in him to
pretend.

Emma and I were alone but for fat Berthe, who squatted by
the hearth picking stones from the flour.

"Get outside, woman," I said, and she scuttled away
holding the flour in her skirt, her fat chins wobbling.

We were awkward with each other, more even than the
first day I saw her, when we knew nothing of one another.
Her cheeks were flushed as a maiden's. "I thought you would
go fishing," she said, and I jumped. I had not known she
understood.

"Who is teaching you what we say?"

She shrugged. "No-one. If you talk about something simple I can catch it. It isn't so very hard." She sat on the bench
and her neck drooped. When her face was hidden you could
think her beautiful. Under her eyes I went to the place by the

wall and took out her things, more now than before, and on top the silver pin I had given her.

"Why do you always want to run away?" I said and felt the shameful tears prick my eyes.

"But—I am your prisoner," said Emma in a gasping voice, almost as if she were laughing.

I struggled to explain it to her, taking her hands in mine and speaking as a lover. "You are only a captive of my heart, little one. I will tend you as a shepherd with his flock, and like a shepherd I cannot let you stray. What would you do without me, sweeting? Where would you go? It is for your sake I hold you, for your sake only."

"I would rather be free," she said and banged her fist on me so I would know how she felt.

"Free? When is a woman ever free? I do but take the place of your father and your dead husband. Come, be cheerful, I will buy you a dress for our wedding." I planted a kiss on her cheek, but when I saw her eyes I felt that there was a chasm between us. What could it be, I thought? Then I knew and at once made my decision.

"We will marry by the faith that is your own," I said with satisfaction. "There! Then it will all be shipshape."

"But—no!" She gaped at me and in an instant I knew what had been in her mind. To wed me by rites not her own, to be renounced whenever she thought fit. I was angered, I can tell you.

"Faithless bitch," I said, taking her by the shoulders and shaking.

"I shall always hate you—" her teeth were rattling but she spat "—heathen!"

"You liked our coupling well enough," I yelled.

She dragged herself free of me and stood apart, trying to catch her breath. Her hair tumbled all about her. "I have hot blood for a woman," she said.

The thought of it grew between us. We did not speak but only went to the bed.

It was a powerful joining. I gazed at her face with its closed eyes and saw her pleasure. Lines came and went in her forehead, her lips moved as if to kiss. Here was one harp I had the skill to play and the knowledge made me strong.

When she lay peaceful beneath me I said, "You will be a good wife to me. I have a great need of women."

She took little pinches of my skin, holding to pain and then letting go. "You do not know what you are doing. It is the wedding of horse and cow."

"What's wrong with that? Marriage is for house and children, there is no more to say."

"My church will not permit it." She tried to escape from under me, but I held her.

"We will speak to Wulfhere," I said, and met her glare with a smile.

I watched stone-faced as Emma knelt and kissed the hand of Wulfhere. He rested his palm on her bright head and then raised her up from the flags. She began to speak to him in a low, rushed voice, so that I could not hear, and together they paced the hall, Wulfhere's head bent to her. His tunic was of fine wool and I swear the cross that hung from his neck was of gold. A pretty custom that, it must be admitted. One of the hangings showed a picture of men in the fight and I strolled also, pretending to look. Snatches of their speech came to me.

". . . so I am sure, Father, you will agree with me. These people are barbarians. I have suffered at their hands."

Wulfhere nodded and said "We are sorely tried. Let us consider what our Lord wishes us to do in this case, my child . . ."

From time to time they looked at me as if I were a bargain on a stall in Birka market, perhaps even a piece of bad fish. I began to be angered and I took out my dagger to clean my nails. Let me see what would be the finish of it if he tried his foxy tricks with me. Many's the priest I have strung up in my time, I can tell you, and a shrieking, cowardly bunch they were too. Their monks though, that trail about in cloth that would be untender for a sail, some of them have courage. They go to their deaths chanting prayers and charms, calling down blessings on us for sending them on their way. Very strange.

". . . so it is a trial laid upon your shoulders, child. It is given to you to bring them to Christ."

I grinned to myself and put away my dagger. Halfdan had chosen his man well.

"And that is all you can say?" I smiled to see Emma's temper muffling itself.

"I will bless your union myself and I will ask that you be
granted courage to hold to your duty." He touched her forehead with his thin lips, and she knelt to him.

"We are all of one mind then," I said contentedly as we
passed back through the streets. Men had laid pathways of
wood and wicker which we stepped on gratefully. Emma
would not speak. I slipped my arm round her waist and said,
"I am marrying a hag, so it seems."

"The choice is yours. No-one's forcing you."

"I never knew a woman so anxious to be sold into Frisia.
They like a good strong cow there."

I saw her face quiver and I held my peace, to let her think I
might mean it.

Some feasts a man will remember to his dying day, and my
wedding feast lingers in the memory of more than myself.
There had been no great celebrations for some while, and
now we were coming to be settled and to put down roots like
windblown seeds, well, we had cause to be merry. Oxen were
slaughtered, and sheep, and men brought in deer from the
forest. There was a great brewing of ale and as luck would
have it a ship came in with Rhenish wine and spices. The
men sailing her could not believe their luck for they had set
out unhopefully, thinking the country might still be in uproar.
They would carry back a great tale, as well as what we had to
sell, which at that time was mostly hides and slaves. In later
years of course, we sold grain and made-up things such as
combs, but then we weren't so well set-up.

For Emma I bought a most rare thing, a brooch from
Gotland, and it cost more than I thought sensible I might say.
It was of silver gilded in some way, and like a box so that it
stood out from the shoulder. The design was of tangled
animals, which is a Norse habit, and I worried a little in case
she should not like it, for as I say, it was expensive. The
Saxons have a fancy for plainer things. Perhaps that it why
they like their religion, there is less of it to concern them!

The feast began at noon or thereabouts and Emma and I
walked to it in all our finery. I had on a tunic of blue wool,
new-made, which was a pity because it became spattered
during the feast and never looked the same. Emma looked—I
hardly know how to say it. Noble, perhaps, with her hair
coiled upon her head like rope. She wore a white shift and

over it a green tunic, because that is a lucky color. It is the
Viking style for women to bare their arms, but she would not,
saying that I was taking a Saxon and that was what she would
be. No man could think her lovely. All thought her a prize.

We were seated of course beside Halfdan and we drank a
few cups and ate honeycakes and so on until we saw that
there would soon be no room for men to move in the hall for
the press of those wanting to come in. So Halfdan cried for
benches to be set up outside and for the wedding to take place
at once before we all forgot what we were there for. Off then
to the church, which was plain and chill after the warm sun,
and the monks and the priest all solemn and we Vikings
roaring drunk for the most part. At last Wulfhere became
fractious and Halfdan called for silence, which came of a
sort, with much giggling and belching, and every now and
then someone dropping a dagger or a handful of coin.

The priest began to mumble at us and sometimes they
nudged me to make me say "Yes," as if I would have been
there if I intended otherwise. It might be that the Saxons force
men at the point of a sword, in which case I doubt if they
would refuse even if asked. Still, an oath is an oath I suppose, even when a man cannot understand it. The men were
getting restless and I called out to them to have a little
patience, which someone of course turned into a lewd remark
for it was a wedding after all. In the midst of the laughter the
door opened and Skarphedin came in.

I do not know how it should be that one man can enter a
place and all be aware of it, even though they cannot see him
for the press. I knew from the silence who it was, and
Emma's grey eyes flew to mine and I felt her fingers tighten.

"He has come then," I said to her, trying to make light of
it.

Men made a path for him. He was Skarphedin, shaggy
black in a sheepskin coat, saying nothing but by his very
silence bringing meaning to a thing. He stood to the side,
where the monks should be, but none dared ask him to move.
His hands rested on his sword and the tip of his sword upon
the church floor.

"He is cursing us," whispered Emma, staring into his dead
black eyes.

The fancy had come to me too. I dropped her hand and
went to Skarphedin. "Wish us well, my friend," I said.

He brought his gaze to me as if from a far-off place. "A man's destiny is his own. My sword is with you, Thorkil, I can give no more."

I stepped back to Emma and again took her hand. Wulfhere began his mutterings once more, and in that way I was married.

Oh, the feasting and the singing and the telling of tales! Halfdan passed his horn to me time and again and Emma drank from the palm cup that was his gift to her. I saw her blinking like an owl in daylight and I thought, "This is my wife." At last I was started on that path I had been chased from years before. At last I would make something that no-one would take from me.

When the drinking and the singing has lasted long enough, there comes time for the telling of tales. One Attar, who was a master at it, was dragged to standing and his friends called for quiet. What tale should it be? Wellund, he decided, the tale of Wellund the Smith. For myself I thought it unsuited to a wedding, but then it was the joining of enemies. Perhaps it was not so ill-timed. I tell it again for you here:

"There was once a smith, and his name was Wellund. He was a craftsman greater than any other, for in his hands the strong iron bent and twisted like reeds. Great were the things he wrought, mighty swords and pretty rings amongst them, and there was magic too in his making. Who can know if Claw of the Raven was the work of Wellund the smith?"

At this there was a great shouting, although I and many another know that sword was made by a man in Trondheim. Rather one should ask, from whence came World Tree? That is a true mystery, for I took it from a man in Sweden. To go on with the tale:

"A king in those days, Nidud, wanted Wellund to travel to his land and work at the king's own forge, but the smith was unwilling. So the king sent warriors to Wellund and they captured him, and at the king's command they cut the strings of his legs and crippled him. Then Wellund laboured, long and bitterly, at Nidud's forge and of the things he made the greatest was a web of iron revenge. The king's son came to him with a sword for mending. Wellund took the sword and mended it, and took it up and slew the king's own son. And of his skull he made a cup, the like of which is not seen in these days, for there was magic in it.

"Then came the king's second son, and he too brought work for Wellund the smith. With a smiling face the iron-worker gave him his brother's head from which to sip wine, and the lad drank his fill. When the cup was finished he too gave his head for the smith to craft.

"Still Wellund plotted, uncontent with the grief he had brought to an unwise king. Nidud's daughter, Bodvild, vis-ited the forge, and with her she brought a broken ring, made in ancient times and full of ancient magic. 'Mend this for me, Wellund' she said sweetly and held it out in a fair white hand. She was used to men's honour and had no fear of the crippled smith. Wellund took the ring and with it the power. He fell upon Bodvild and ravished her, while she screamed and beat at him with those same white arms. When he left her, sobbing, he took up the magic ring and turned into a bird, taking to himself feathers of bronze made on his mighty forge. Away he flew, high from the place of his dishonor. Such is the tale I tell you, of Nidud and his bitter harvest."

The tale was ended and it was not fit for a wedding. I saw that Emma drooped with weariness and I said to her, "Come," for she had no women friends to go with her. Men whooped and yelled as we pushed our way to the door but her flat cheeks did not color. Only her fingers trembled, held tight in mine. We went through the streets on a tide of friendship, and the fresh air made me know that I was very drunk. Emma too, I think, for she staggered against me. Honey wine is strong.

At last, the house. I pushed Emma before me and thrust out my lewd and curious friends, barring the door against them. The peace was like cool water.

"Well, Emma," I said, "you have me now."

"I think it is still the other way," she said and sank wearily on to the bench that Bjarni and I had struggled to cut straight. It wobbled all the same.

"Here. I have this for you. A bride-gift." I held out the brooch and she took it.

"It is very strange."

"Strange? It is very rare, girl, that is what it is. That brooch cost more than I would care to tell you, there won't be another woman wearing one this side of the sea. I hope to see you treat it carefully." I knew when I said it that it was not the right thing. I could hear in my head what Bjarni would have said in my place. "This is for you. It took much getting, but I do not grudge it. You are more precious than a brooch." But could I say it? No. So she gave me a look that measured my worth and put the brooch down so that it chinked noisily on Olaf's good table.

I swallowed my anger and began to take off my clothes. "Let us get to it then."

"Not yet. I am thirsty." She went to the pitcher for water but as she lifted the ladle to sip I caught her arm. The water went over her dress.

"You are hurting me."

"A good wife does not anger her husband. It is time for the bedding."

But she took up the ladle with her other hand and drank, more slowly than I would have thought possible. I would have struck her if I had not feared my friends would laugh at the marks, and besides, I did not like to beat her. So it was at her pleasure that she took off her clothes, and lay down for me on the bed. I knew I was insulted but there seemed nothing to do. So drunk as I was I joined with her, although being drunk it was over in an instant. I rested my head on the pillow of her breasts and groaned.

"I will have a pain in the head in the morning."

"You are hurting me now. Get off."

I rolled aside, saying, "Wait until you are bearing my strong boys. They won't be shifted so easily."

Fuddled as I was, it seemed that her eyes were cold as glass. "There are some things you will not have, Viking," she said, and turned her shoulder to sleep.

Chapter
Four

WHEN SHE WAS a girl she lived in Mercia, in her father's strong house. He was ealdorman to Burgred, who was king then, and they had riches and honour. It was a happy time, that seemed in remembering to be all warm fires and sunshine. Their sadnesses were little ones only.

Sometimes, when she was still quite small, she rode with her brother after boar, going deep into the forest where they live in thick tangles of brush. Only the hounds can go where the boar lie hid, in the dark pig-smelling thickets, and she would wait with the men on the narrow ride, her pony dancing under her. She was afraid, but that was nothing when she sat beside her brother, a boy like a slender whip and the joy of all their hearts. He too trembled at the thrill to come and his boy's cheek twitched. He could never quite master himself, she always thought, it was as if he burned through his skin, like an over-bred horse, with more fire than was good for him.

One day stuck fast in her memory, the first on her good grey mare that was then too big and too strong for her. The noise from the trees was fierce, they could hear the boar snorting and the hounds shrieking after it. Her heart beat so hard it hurt her ribs and the pony quivered under her. It was a big boar. It broke on to the track in front of them, they saw the gleam of white tusks and its little red eye and they were away, flying over the grass with the young men shouting and bawling and she hanging to her pony for dear life. They ran fast and dangerous, a horse fell with his foot down a rabbit hole, a lad was swiped from his seat by a branch. The boar made his stand soon after, against a rock wall with trees at the side, making the approach narrow. He took two hounds before they finished him, one of them a brindle. Emma wept for her hound, that lay dying with its belly slit. She hid her tears on her sleeve.

As ealdorman her father was obliged to keep men at arms, for there were often raids in the district. Men would come at night and fire thatch, driving the cattle off in the confusion. How they would talk about it, complaining all the while about the lawlessness that was come upon the land. They had such innocence. Word of the northmen reached them from time to time, of raids on monasteries and churches to take silver and gold, and to stain the old stones with blood. Remote as they were, they shook their heads and went on about their business, raising crops and children in the gentle rhythm of the seasons. When change came it was of a different order.

There was a monk, his name was Sebastian. He had lived all his life in a priory in the east, and when the raiders came from the sea he fled to take sanctuary with the Mercians. It seemed to Emma that terror had affected his mind somewhat, for there was a wildness in him, a white-faced, fearful strength. He passed some time with Burgred who, doubtless tiring of fervour, sent him to his ealdorman, to help teach his son Latin.

At first they all laughed at him behind his back, with his tales of torment and punishment, his warnings of suffering to come. But in a while Beodar began to change. He spent nights talking to the monk, much of his day was spent in prayer, and all at once Emma saw that her father was old. He felt death stalking him. He was afraid.

It was as if a cloud covered her sun, at one moment warmth and light, the next cold gloom. Her father was distant, both from her and from her mother, who was so much younger than he and so bright and full of fun. She came from the mountains, as dark and lovely as the hills themselves, and it was said her own mother was a witch. Emma's mother knew charms, that was sure enough, although herself a Christian woman. But from the first she hated the monk and in that Emma joined her. They began a silent war, on the one side

women with their herbs and blandishments, a curse doll hid in
a chest, on the other the pale, hard monk, who offered
eternity as the prize. Beodar was past women, the fires of lust
had long since burned to ashes, and his daughter, once a
pretty child, was grown strong-faced and shy. Sebastian took
the victory with ease, and life was joyless.

News began to trouble them. A great army of Danes had
landed and was conquering in the east. Wessex was beleaguered, for which they were all very sorry, but not so sorry as
to send aid. Mercia and Wessex were always testing strength
in those days and for too long Wessex had been the greater,
their king always Bretwalda. They were safe in the west. But
Sebastian told tales of heathen Vikings who plucked the
hearts and lungs from the bodies of their victims and ate them
while they still quivered with life! They could not believe
such barbarism. Then they heard that the army had left its
ships and moved away into the country, conquering as it
went, and no-one raised a murmur when Burgred sent silver
and begged to be left in peace.

Distant wars stretched long fingers into Mercia. The land
was in turmoil and the roads thick with travellers, those who
had lost all they had or who had nothing in the first place.
Slaves without masters, goldsmiths without gold, they all
looked for somewhere new. Those that wandered as far as
Beodar's steading were fed for a day or so, and if he was a
craftsman, a stonemason or some such, stayed. Skilled men
are always hard to come by. Lonely as she was, Emma's
mother would often talk with the strangers, gracing their fires
with her presence while Beodar grew callouses on his knees.
One man was sick when he came and she brought him a
posset, and the next day she was sicker. Neither one of them
lived above a week.

Those days were a cloud in Emma's mind and in it she saw
faces, the monk, her mother, her father's dry eyes. She and
her brother clung to each other, and he talked, fiercely, of
leaving to fight the Vikings. She knew she could not bear it if
he went, she knew she could not live with such loneliness.
She made a charm to keep him by her. He became thin, his
eyes were round holes in his face, so she burnt the one charm
and made another, to bring him to health. Perhaps she did it
wrong, there was no-one to ask. His skin hung yellow on his
bones and as each day passed he grew weaker. He faced

death as he had his life, with a boy's high courage, and
Emma clung to his clawed fingers and sobbed. There was
no-one to comfort her, nowhere to turn but a church that had
given her nothing. Such pain is only suffered once. No
trouble after was as bad.

Yet she still hoped, for she was young enough to believe in
it. Perhaps tomorrow her father would love her again, perhaps
it was all a dream, soon ended, its horror remembered in clear
day. And she was trained to endure and to show a brave face,
from her earliest years she had known it was expected. When
she laughed at a snarling hound her father called her his
precious and took her up on his saddle in a mad, hectic
gallop, so surely now, when there was so much more to fear,
her courage would have its reward. But her father was a grey
old man and she just a woman without looks or fortune.

She was lucky in her Viking, she well knew, for in that
time women were no more precious than oxen and were
treated as meat. To be paid for your virtue was remarkable,
most turned their children's faces to the wall and prayed to be
still alive when it was over. To gain a husband was a miracle.

But it is easy to marry and harder by far to live with a
husband, especially a foreigner and an enemy. Emma turned
in on herself. Her life was apart from them, in her head, in
her memories. Her first marriage had been so short, a scant
five months. She had been fond enough of Aelthyn, she
supposed, though she found his touch unpleasant. He wanted
her every night, even if they slept in a room with others, but
he fumbled at her and every moment's pleasure was likely to
be suddenly shot through with pain. She learned to let her
mind drift while he pumped, she found herself thinking of
men, once even of Godric, Aelthyn's father. What would a
man be like she thought to herself, while her boy husband
worked between her legs. How would it feel to lie with a man
who had loved many women? And now she had her Viking
and she knew.

Her life seemed very hard, for the house was like nowhere
she had ever lived before and she did not understand much of
what was said to her. Bjarni and Olaf were kind enough, but
the creature, Skarphedin—sometimes she crouched in her bed
rather than stay by him, feeling his black eyes watching her,
judging her. In the night when Thorkil wanted her, lifting her
breasts in his great hands, she knew he was listening, that

they all were. On her wedding night, when it was so like Aelthyn she thought, there then, they give up the fondling when they marry, but it was only the drink. She came to long for the nights, and in the day her mind lingered on the taste of the night before. If only the others need not know. Thorkil would boast a little, saying, "She was a wild one last night, friends, I can tell you. I had a job to settle her," and she would see Bjarni watching her, wondering what it was she did to please his brother so. Skarphedin too, his cold gaze seeing even into her dreams.

Yet both Bjarni and Olaf had women, she knew. Olaf had found himself a fishwife near the wharf, whose husband was away a lot. It meant that they were never short of herring and she asked Thorkil to build her a little stone oven by the fire to bake it. She learned to put herbs in when the guts came out, and to wrap the fish in leaves, and the men all praised her for it, far beyond its worth. She began to take a pride in her cooking, and to move Berthe from the hearth, because the men thought so much of what she did. Sometimes she made special things for them, Bjarni in particular. He made her think of her brother, he was so young, there was so much burning in him. He chased all the girls of course, lifting skirts everywhere, but he never seemed satisfied. Emma thought he should try Olaf's fishwife, she would teach him a thing or two.

Those Vikings seemed a busy people. Day in and day out men flocked to Halfdan's hall, with plans and messages, disputes and feuds. A great army was camped within walls and there was much fighting. Once Emma stepped out to buy meat and in the flyblown mess at the back of the shambles, in amongst the sheeps' heads and bones, was the body of a man. She stood gaping at it, unable to believe what she saw, then turned and ran. When she told Thorkil, gasping, her eyes wide, he only grunted and told her to stay within doors. He went out to see about it. Later he told her that it was the brother of a man he knew, killed in a fight over *hnefatafl*, a game of theirs played with a board. Thorkil's friend was demanding the bloodprice but in the end he took money as *wergild*. Thorkil doubted it would settle it, there was too much honor at stake.

In contrast the country round about was quiet, and it was not hard to see why. When the Danes first came they sent parties out and attacked towns and monasteries like wolves in a sheepfold, until only a whisper of their coming sent people running to the forest. Soon they could ride where they liked, and the talk turned to farming and settlement. It was what Thorkil hoped for, he made no secret of it, and he had set his heart on the hills above Shipton, no more than a day's ride from Jorvik and as far from the sea. Emma hoped for it too, for she had never lived in a town before and she did not like the noise and smell, and the sense that your business was as much another's as your own. Sometimes her life exhausted her, it was so coarse and strange, at least on a farm she would know herself again. Sheep don't change because their master does.

Then a day came when Thorkil told her that the army was to move against Mercia. She was sewing a patch on Bjarni's breeches and she stabbed herself.

"Sweet Jesu, I am bleeding! You are mistaken, Thorkil. Mercia has paid to be safe."

"Then they will have to find more. I knew this was coming. Hey-ho, how will you like to be a soldier's wife?"

She eyed him crossly, not believing they would fight, not in Mercia, though the thought of it was making him merry. "I will stay here and sew," she snapped.

"You can do that on the march. I am not as young as I was, I need a wife to tend me in the line." He lifted a linen square and picked at some honeycakes that were covered against the flies. She slapped at him, and he took two to spite her.

"Are you worried about your father?"

She shrugged. "I don't know. You'll never get that far."

He grunted and suddenly alarmed she asked sharply, "Will you?"

"How can I tell? But Halfdan is in the mood for a fight, I think. We all are."

The patch was finished. She shook the work and folded it, strong hands neat and purposeful. Her face looked at Thorkil, he did not know what she thought. "I will come. I would rather see what happens, you'll never tell me the truth."

"Sweeting! When have I lied to you?"

"Vikings are born liars."

He laughed, but it was true.

*   *   *

They crossed the hills in a straggling, dusty line. Thorkil and the others rode ahead and Emma was left with the carts and the baggage, the women and the squalling babies. What a mixture, she thought to herself, these Viking comforters. Whores in scarlet dresses, lousy hair blowing; Danish housewives, brought from across the sea, and here and there a slavegirl with skin the color of bronze. Emma was amongst the most respectable, with her bunch of keys and her chaste hood, but secretly she would rather have been a slattern, shouting insults at the men and taking their money. From time to time Thorkil came to see how she was, and the girls yelled "There's a mighty one" and worse. He played up to them at first and roared back, but then he saw his wife and was at once the virtuous husband. It made Emma laugh to watch him.

"This is bad company for you, Emma. I am sorry."

"Don't be. I like it, it's so strange. But I should like to ride with you for a little, the dust is choking me."

He thought for a moment and then said, "My wife should ride with warriors. Come."

She was surprised. Not even her father in the days of her favor would let her ride with him when he was with men. So she sat straight in the saddle and sent her tired horse in a tight canter down the line, like a warrior woman from days of old. She had once told Thorkil the tale they had of a queen who rode barebreasted into battle, but he had thought it a great joke and he and the others rolled about laughing. They offended Emma, who knew in her heart that she would have been a great queen. They would not have laughed at her, they would have quailed, and her followers would have died for her. Women were so helpless nowadays.

Thorkil's horse crashed into hers and he cursed it. She drew up neatly and pointedly beside Olaf.

"How goes it?"

He grunted and spat politely, on the far side of his horse. "We will stop soon. They've caught a few sheep."

She saw the poor beasts, lashed upside down and alive on either side of the packsaddles, which was a sure way to make the meat tough. She coughed the dust from her throat and looked more thoroughly about her, for it was all new and strange. Skarphedin rode a little apart, for no-one dared crowd him, but whenever she looked his way he was watching her, or so it seemed. Thorkil told her it was not so, that everyone felt it in his presence, but it seemed to her that she alone held his gaze. On this hot day he had cast off his sheepskin and wore only a leather jerkin, studded with metal. The skin of his arms was striped with scars and his knuckles were calloused from the rubbing of sword and shield. He watched her watching him. She turned away.

"Where is Bjarni?"

Thorkil rubbed his groin, where the horse pressed. "I sent him to Halfdan. He goes ahead to look out the way."

"Why him? What does he know that another does not?"

Thorkil smiled at her guilelessly. "Nothing."

Her eyes widened. It was a lie, she knew it. Thorkil had spent long hours at Halfdan's table, talking of this campaign; he alone knew Mercia and he had sent his brother as a guide. She looked at Olaf, chewing like a cow on dried meat, but he would not meet her eye. They would indeed reach her home country, because her husband was pointing the way. So much for his care for her.

She dragged her pony out of the line and sent him at a run back the way she had come. It was dangerous for the road was thronged with men and wagons.

A man pulled his horse across her way, she screamed and her pony struck him. It fell to the ground, winded and groaning. Emma lay bruised in the dust. The man rushed to her and lifted her up, and she saw that it was Attar, who had told a tale at her wedding. His hands were cool and light.

"Lady Emma. Are you hurt? I'm sorry, I didn't see you."

"The fault was mine. No, no, I am well, but I think I have done for the horse." The beast was lying with its neck stretched out, his body swollen as a bladder.

Attar went to look at him. "Not so bad, I think. He won't die. Here, take mine lady, he's a sweet one."

"And what will you do?"

"Walk at your side like a little, faithful dog." He smiled at her and her heart lifted. In this mass of uncouth men he was neat and trimmed and clever. She laughed and took his horse.

They went slowly, leading the winded horse behind them, and soon they were passed by wagons and milch cows and then all the draggletailed end of the line, with its children and baskets of hens. Her horse plodded and though her leg was by his hand, Attar did not once reach to touch her.

"What is your family?" she asked. "You're not like the others."

"Why do you say so?"

She shrugged. "You don't blow your nose on your fingers."

"Not in your presence perhaps. In theirs I do. I don't like to seem different."

"Then you are different."

"My father is reeve to the Danish king."

He spoke with pride and she nodded. She had thought as much. The column ground on and they moved further and further back. Now they were with the groups of spare horses that came last of all. Attar began to bargain with a man to change Emma's pony for something better, and she studied the beasts, shaggy all of them, not one as lovely as her old grey mare. She had died when given to Godric. They laughed at her when she cradled the mare's gentle head and watched the bright eyes dim, and they took the tail to stuff a cushion and took the hooves and boiled them.

"I would like that one." A dappled pony, small and thick, but as grey as her old mare.

"Then you shall have him." Attar haggled with the man and soon she was mounted on the grey. He was tough and wilful. She liked him.

"Emma!" It was Thorkil, with his pony blowing beneath him, and small wonder for he was too big for it.

"Thorkil Sigurdsson." Attar rode forward in greeting. "I regret I have injured your wife, or her pony rather. I got in her way and she fell. Thankfully there was nothing broken but the horse was bruised and I have made amends for my carelessness by finding her another."

Thorkil stared at him and Attar stared back, an enquiring smile on his face.

"I will thank you to know, Attar Gunnerson, that my wife's mount is my affair. Tell me what it cost."

"But the fault was mine, Thorkil! Take it as a bride-gift if nothing else."

"I'll not take it at all. Your mother was a whore and your father a licker of arses, so you can keep your breeks fastened and leave my wife to me. Come, Emma. I'll return the animal later."

She did not know what to do. It galled her to ride meekly after Thorkil, leaving Attar scarlet and insulted. But she could not stay, so instead she took her time, turning to Attar and saying, "I am sorry for my husband, it is most rude of him." Perhaps it took her longer than it might have, for she was still not easy with the language, but she saw no reason for what came after.

When he realised she was not behind him Thorkil turned his pony, charged back and swiped her from her horse. The pony squealed and so did Emma, but then Thorkil tangled his fingers in her hair and dragged her to her feet.

"Emma. I said come," he hissed, hauling her half across his saddle. Then he kicked his much-tried pony and carted her off.

That night—the memory of it always made her wince. Their only privacy was that they could scream at each other in English, which few understood. Thorkil cursed her for a whore and she called him a lying murderer, and worse. She had learned the words from him anyway. She was also rude about Bjarni, which really inflamed him, as insults about family will. He hit her when she called him a peasant.

But after the screaming came the time when they lay together under the blankets with aching heads and sore hearts and wondered what would happen in the morning. They had a tent held up on sticks and it was very dark inside it. They had no choice but to lie close.

"Now I have no pony," she said, her throat thick with tears.

"It is what you deserve."

"I told you, he didn't touch me."

"If that were not true you'd both be dead."

They lay silent for a time and then she said, "You had no need to bring them this way."

His hand rested on her thigh. "You were wrong in thinking that. Halfdan goes his own way, it has nothing to do with me."

"I wish I could believe you." That bold hand was burrowing up her shift.

"I would not wage war on my wife's family. Ah Emma, there is honey between your legs, I will suck it like a bee."

But she was not finished with him. As he bent his head she caught her fingers in his hair and said, "Attar wears his hair short. He trims his beard."

"Attar fucks boys."

"He doesn't!"

Thorkil grunted and put his head down to her. She combed his hair with her fingers and groaned at the warm pleasure of it, until a voice outside the tent said cheerfully, "Would you like some help, Sigurdsson? The heifer's in distress."

"Get stuffed," said Thorkil, and mounted her. She muffled her cries against his shoulder and he whispered to her, would she get this from Attar then? How did she like a real man inside her?

When they were finished and lay back, gasping, the voice said, "I'm glad that's over. Now we can all get some sleep.' Thorkil laughed and cuddled her against him.

"I'll die of shame in the morning," she whispered.

The next day she rode on a wagon and talked only to women. A Danish girl gave her some salve for her bruises, which were from Thorkil and the fall from the horse. All the men seemed to be staring at her. In the afternoon Thorkil rode up on a new, larger pony, and he led the little grey.

"What is this?" She was bewildered.

"For you."

"Did you buy it from Attar?"

"No, no. He had sold it to a man and is saying there is bad blood between him and me. But he hasn't the guts for a fight."

She said nothing, but stepped from the wagon to the pony. He bucked a little and she checked him. The Danish girl watched with round eyes.

"You look better on that than the other," said Emma to Thorkil.

"I like it no better. Come up with the men, wife."

So again she rode by her husband in the line.

After a time, when her thoughts were drifting, she realized that Skarphedin rode beside her and Thorkil was ahead.

"What do you want?" she asked quickly. She hated him to be close, there was a smell about him, with him even when he bathed. She thought it was death.

"What should I want of you, a woman who betrays her kind?"

"I have betrayed no-one."

"Who will believe that when our swords taste Mercian blood? I know you, lady. Your heart is black."

"Then yours is blacker. Please, remember I am married to your friend."

"And he dreams of strong children, poor ignorant fool. I know a witch when I see one and I know what is in her womb!"

"What? What do you mean? I'm not a witch!" She stared at him, and at his scar that was filled with dark blood. She thought she would be sick, he couldn't know. Could he? What were a few herbs now and then, no-one could know what they were.

She pulled her horse away and went back, to ride with the women. There was sour fluid inside her mouth, she could not swallow it. Everyone knew she could cure fever and gutrot, what harm was there in that? But she knew it was wrong, it was a witch's trick, told by her mother, from her mother before her, and she was certainly a witch. There was a certain plant, you picked it when the moon was on the wane. The leaves were crushed very small, and mixed with the devil's spit, that hangs on the flowers sometimes. If a woman took it deep into her body it turned a man's seed aside, and who could blame her for that? The Viking was an enemy, she wanted no son of hers to look like that, all blue-eyed, lying smiles. And for Aelthyn, she had only used it a month or two, because she wanted to spite his family, which was no more than they deserved, the grasping peasants. Why should she lie down for these men, serve them, pleasure them, and suffer the anguish of childbed, just as they willed it? This one thing was hers to with-hold and she would keep it for as long as it pleased her. If only Skarphedin did not know.

She dreaded that he would speak to Thorkil, who would kill her if he knew. His whole hope was of children, in the night he would rub her belly and whisper of the sons he would have, that he thought he might even then be making. As if he could have even that from her. If Skarphedin spoke she would deny it, though she knew no-one would believe her. There could be no victory if she died for it. Suddenly she rode her pony into the scrub bushes by the road, holding her while she crouched down, as if to relieve herself. She took the pouch from under her skirt and threw it on to the earth,

piling twigs and leaves to hide it. Now what would become of
her?

She stood on the hill and stared down at the jagged line of
men with their pikes and bows, their staves and pitchforks.
No match for a Viking shieldwall as even she could tell, but
Burgred was an honest man and could not perceive dishon-
esty. He was to pay for his trust. She wondered if there was
anyone she knew, but so far away she could see only blurs of
faces. Turning, she went back into the camp.

The day was dark. It was quiet in the encampment, as men
gathered their thoughts and prayed to their heathen gods.
Emma kept her prayers to herself, for what should she wish
for? Even now she might be with child and she could not
want it fatherless.

Thorkil spoke quietly with his men. "They look weak, but
even the weakest can strike a killing blow. Keep together, but
give Skarphedin room. Do not cross his path or you will
suffer for it. We will strike at the center while Halfdan comes
round behind."

He saw Emma watching him and she turned away. He
came and stood against her, his mailshirt rought against her
bare, Viking arms. "Stay in the camp, Emma."

"Do you think I will betray you?"

"I think that you think of it. It is only to be expected. I
have asked Gunnar's wife to stay with you, her name is
Marjolein."

She was stung. "A gaoler! I have caught myself a fine
husband indeed!"

"Not so stupid as you would like. Here, sweeting, kiss me.
I need your luck."

But she would not. Thorkil glowered and went to put on
his helmet, that dipped in a mask over his nose. Dressed like
that they were not men to her, but things of metal and leather
and cloth. They had looked the same when she first saw them
and she was glad she had saved her kisses.

The woman, Marjolein, came to sit with her. She was not a
Dane but came from Francia, and after the first sullen greeting Emma was glad of the company. Marjolein was pretty,
with fine yellow hair and a little face that was never still.
Everything about her was narrow and light, and Emma felt
stolid in comparison.

Marjolein made a face, all lips and big blue eyes. "Shall we sit here sewing, Emma, or shall we go to look?"

"Thorkil said—I thought I was not allowed to look."

"What harm is there in sitting on a hillside? We will talk to no-one, and you can't do anything without talk. Or will you run away? I couldn't stop you."

Emma's still face moved to smile. "There's nowhere to go."

"But your family? Surely there is someone?"

Emma told her dismal little tale as they walked. She had thought Marjolein's to be somewhat similar, but it was quite different. Gunnar had gone to Francia trading, for her people were strong and wary and he could not seize his prizes. He had seen Marjolein and she him, and from that moment they had loved. Emma could understand it, Gunnar was a fine, longlimbed man and Marjolein was pretty as a kitten. They made a pair of it. The only obstacle was that he was a heathen, so he obliged by being baptized. Emma was shocked.

"He's as heathen as the rest," she declared, but Marjolein shook her head.

"Oh no! It is the water makes the difference, Emma, he is Christian now."

Emma snorted. Vikings would do anything to get what they wanted.

At first the couple lived in Francia, but within six months Gunnar was on the move. Back to Denmark they went, but here again he could not settle, especially when their first child died. They had come to England in a party with some others, to join Halfdan and make a new life.

"But the travelling is bad for me," said Marjolein. "I miscarry."

"Do you so? You are right, you should rest. But tell me when next you quicken, I will give you something. It doesn't always work though."

"Gunnar said you knew herbs. He said—but I won't tell you!"

Emma was at once aflame with curiosity. "What did he say? Tell me, I won't mind."

"Won't you? I do so want to be friends, there are so few women of the right sort here. He said—he said you had charmed Thorkil!" She giggled at her own daring, pressing

one fluttery hand to her mouth as she watched what Emma
would say.

Despite herself Emma cooled towards her. "If there is a
charm for such a thing I do not know it." She gathered her
cloak around her and turned a shoulder to Marjolein.

Below on the plain men moved slowly, as it seemed from
so far away. The Mercian line straggled, with weak places
here and there, but they outnumbered the Vikings, who had
divided their force. Emma wished she had not come to look,
she wished she did not know what they planned. Thorkil
believed that the gods decided men's lives and that men had
no part of it. Perhaps it was so. She gathered her cloak still
closer and sat without moving.

It was peaceful on that windy hillside, with the shouts of
men rising faintly through the dull air. A hare lolloped
slowly by, looking at them from pop eyes. All at once, on the
battlefield, there rose a shower of flighting arrows, falling
silent like black rain, and as if at a signal men began to rush
forward, holding their shields high. When they clashed there
rose a furious howl. The Mercians were thickest in the center,
the pikes were like trees in the forest. She could not tell if
Thorkil was there, or Skarphedin, but the fighting was desperate. She saw a man take a spear in the belly. Another lost
his head to an axe.

"We're losing," shrieked Marjolein, wringing her pretty
hands.

But then there came a cry to chill the blood, a scream taken
up by Viking throats as they hurled themselves forward on to
the jagged pikes. It was Skarphedin, and with him Thorkil,
her husband. She had not even kissed him.

She began to pray, for what she did not know. The air was
thick with the spirits of men who lay like leaves on the
battlefield. Again Skarphedin's howl and again a surge, and
she was praying that Halfdan would come quick and end it.
She had taken a splinter from Bjarni's finger only that morning. Was that sweet boy now dying?

But men were falling back. A Mercian pikeman pushed his
way through the ranks of his fellows and raced for the hills,
tripping and stumbling in his haste.

"Hold! Hold the line! Stand fast!" Staunch men rallied to
the cry, they had more than honor at stake. But the Vikings
sensed the weakness, they pressed harder. All at once the line

broke, men ran and left their fellows, who unsupported, fell.
And then, when they were not needed, Halfdan's force swept
into view, trotting neat and unruffled on their ponies.

"You'd think the son of a whoreson cow could have come
a little faster!" Thorkil raged as Emma bound a gash on his
arm. He had another on his shoulder and a rip in his mail,
which distressed him more than the wound. The battle had
shocked his wife and she was more than gentle.

"He is a Dane. I say no more." Skarphedin slumped by
the fire. He had not even washed the black from his face and
was now so exhausted that he could barely lift a cup. Yet he
bore not a scratch, discounting a finger galled by the grip of
his sword.

"We are owed something for this day! They almost had
us."

"But the English cannot fight," said Emma, with only a
little spite.

Enmeshed in his own thoughts Thorkil did not hear her.
"Here is Olaf with a barb in his shoulder, and Bjarni with his
wits addled—I tell you I'll have that farm from Halfdan for
he's had Mercia from me!"

She hushed him with warm ale mixed with wine. Men had
died that day and some were his friends. Marjolein's husband, Gunnar, looked to lose an arm and his pretty wife sat
stunned and unbelieving.

Emma brought food to them, but Skarphedin could not eat.
His breath came hard as if in some desperate illness.

"The victory was yours, my friend," said Thorkil and
knelt beside him, wincing with the pain. He took the food and
fed Skarphedin from his own hand, like a woman with a
baby. Emma watched amazed.

Bjarni was groaning again, for he had taken a crack on the
head and did not know where he was. Emma soothed him
though he thought she was his mother. He had gone to the
fight shaking and now he was hurt. She stroked his hand and
herself cursed Halfdan. If he had come sooner Thorkil could
have taken care of his brother.

They were bringing prisoners into the camp, groups of ten
or twenty men, bloody and dispirited. Emma tried not to
look, dreading that she would see someone she knew. All the
same her eyes were drawn. Was that Aelthyn's brother? No,

too short. But that other behind, surely the son of my father's friend? Her mind turned fat men into thin ones, old into young. At last she rose and took up the water pitcher as if going to fill it. She would look and make sure, it was better to know than wonder.

They were men like any others, sad, frightened and weary. They looked at her with eyes too dull to see, and there was nothing she could say to them. Some would live, some die, and it rested on a Viking's whim. Men prayed and tried to find some comfort. She gave water to a dying boy.

"Emma! By Christ's blood, it is! Emma!"

She jumped and almost dropped her pitcher. The grimed faces all seemed the same, every one as strange as every other, when before she had known them all. Then she saw him, in the midst of the press. Godric.

"Well met," she said feebly, pushing at her hair. He had always said she was untidy, and here she was with blood on her skirt and her hair coming down.

"Why are you here? Where is Aelthyn?" He was as sharp as ever, with the hairs on his upper lip drooping as he trained them to do, like fruit trees in a monastery orchard. A bloody bandage circled his arm and he was muddied from head to toe. Gradually her shivers subsided. He could not touch her now.

"Aelthyn is dead. I can only give you water."

"I thought as much, I'd heard nothing. But why are you here? Are you a slave?"

Not a word of kindess from him. He was not changed, that voice had hectored her for long weeks, he had laughed when she cried and made Althyn tell how she was in the night. She poured him a cup of water.

"I am a Viking wife now," she said. "It was he who defeated you, he fought where the battle was thickest. Where were you, Godric?"

He was silent a moment. Then he sipped his water and said, "You were always a light woman. I tell you, boys, that one would lie with anything."

She hissed at him. "How you wish that were true! I see you still have the mark where I hit you. Tell me, how is your fat shrew of a wife, Godric?"

"She is dead. The Vikings killed her. They came raiding in the spring."

She put her hand to her mouth. She should have known he would never tell her the truth. She turned to walk away but they called to her. "Help us! Don't leave us here, bring a knife, anything! What will happen to us?"

But Godric said "Let her go, boys. She's cursed by the devil and her mother was a witch. Even a Viking won't get joy from her, I rue the day I laid eyes on the ugly cow, that I do. Even her father turned against her."

Her heart skittered, and hurt her, as if it had been stabbed. She had forgotten his cruelty, that he knew best how to wound.

"I hope they kill you," she said.

She went back to the campfire, turning her eyes from men in agony. From nearby a man screamed.

"Gunnar," said Thorkil. "They're taking his arm."

She found that her legs were shaking and she sat down, too quickly. Thorkil put a hand on her shoulder.

"I wish I had kissed you," she said.

"No matter. I came through without."

She wondered if he thought her kisses cursed. Gunnar screamed again and she could hear Marjolein sobbing herself into a fit. Emma knew she should go to her, but she could not.

"They have Godric," she said. "My husband's father."

Thorkil grunted. The sobs rose to a peak and then quietened. "Did you speak with him?" he asked.

She nodded. "He hates me still. He says you killed his wife."

"I did not."

"But one of you. She was dead when you left."

He drew her close to him. "No. He says it to hurt you only. You must see these things, Emma, you believe too much."

"It's true he hates me. Right from the first. He wanted to bed me, he was angry when I refused."

"I know such men. They do not forget a woman's rejection. No matter. I will talk to Halfdan in the morning."

"What will you do?"

"No matter. I am tired. We must sleep."

She lay in the warmth of his body and thought about Godric. She should have lain with him, let him roll her in the

barn like some slut of a peasant. Then he would have loved
her, sheltered her, made her his pet. They would be there
now, all of them, Aelthyn, Aelgifu, Godric and Emma. She
should have let him. From the first he touched her, on the
thigh, round her waist, a squeeze of her breast, but she
thought nothing. He was her husband's father, he would be
hers too, to take the place of the one that was no longer hers.
She liked him to be kind to her. But then he caught her by
herself and begged "Touch me here, Emma, please, Emma,
kiss me." Every day he was at her, and at last, in the barn,
she hit him with a spice box. And Aelgifu came in and saw
her husband with his breeks open and a broken head, and
Emma all indignant with her dress torn. Yet it was Emma that
took the brunt of it, which wasn't fair at all. Sin or not she
should have gone to his bed.

In the morning Thorkil went to Halfdan. She knew why he
went and she said nothing. So in the end she won.

Chapter Five

THEY PASSED THAT winter in Jorvik, piled uncomfortably in the little house. Thorkil spent much time talking with Halfdan, who had thoughts of a move to Ireland. His brother Ivarr had campaigned there and made himself rich, or so it was said. Emma could not believe there was that much gold and silver in all the world, and still more to come if the tales were true. She was afraid that Thorkil might go after it; there were Norwegians in Ireland now and she was coming to know her husband and his nose for gain.

Of them all, only Olaf was content. He worked on the wharf, building fishing boats and sometimes mending the longships that put in with their dragon prows and fierce, exhausted men. Sometimes when the short winter days lay heavy in her hands, Emma went to watch him. He worked slowly, or so it seemed, but the job grew even as she watched. She knew him for a great craftsman and wondered that he should be happy. His arm still pained him where the arrow pierced, and sometimes he would stop and circle his shoulder to ease it. When he was working he would not speak, but at these rests he would talk to her. It took his mind from the pain and the unfinished task.

"What was Thorkil like as a boy?" she asked one day, stirring her toe in the woodshavings.

"A boy like many another. No better, no worse." He sat down on an upturned fishbarrel. Further down men were landing a catch, piling fish into baskets ready to take to market. In the years to come, when she thought of Olaf it was always with that scent of fish and tar and leather in her nostrils.

"I don't understand why you all follow him. Why not Skarphedin?"

His eyebrows lifted to his coarse brown hair. "That would be a thing indeed. A leader must think of the rights and wrongs of a thing before does it. He must care for his men. Too much courage makes a man foolish, too little and he is despised. Thorkil has it about right."

"Well then, why not you?"

He laughed. "You think Thorkil would do as I said? No, it has always been the same. When we went after birds' eggs it was Thorkil who thought of it, I just dangled at the end of his rope. Which sounds a bad bargain but he never dropped me, and I had eggs to eat from it. It is the same now."

"Don't you want to marry? Have children?"

Olaf glanced at her curiously. Suddenly she thought that he would think she was in haste to be rid of him and she touched his hard hand, saying "Don't think I want it! I would miss you."

"I remember when you would have killed me." He grinned as he said it.

"Things were different then. You would have done the same."

"But I am not a woman."

She laughed and her teeth showed sharp white. "So it seems. Talking of such things—Olaf, Thorkil tells me that Attar is a man that likes boys."

His roar of laughter made people turn to look. He slapped a hand on his apron and wept tears of mirth. "Did he so? Attar? Well, I'll be. Did you believe him?"

She felt foolish. "I don't know. He is very neat in himself."

"Only the better to please the ladies. Attar is a bigger stud than Thorkil in his day, I doubt there's a wife's bed in this town that he hasn't visited. The pretty ones that is."

She got up to go, for the day was ending and if she left the house to Berthe there would be no comfort for anyone. The woman had not even the wit to poke the fire if Emma was not there to tell her.

Olaf was looking at her. "Do you like Attar?"

Her cheeks flamed and she could think of nothing to say.
At last she said, "He is like the men I used to know.
Sometimes I think I am with wild men and I know it seems
strange but—he makes me remember how it was. Nothing
more, Olaf."

She wondered if he knew that Attar went out of his way to
stop at her door when he knew the men were elsewhere. She
did not send him away.

"That is good." Olaf nodded, believing, and prepared to
start work again, weighing a length of timber in his hand.

"You can't make do with a fishwife for ever," she said.

He chuckled. "That is the beauty of it, I do not have to
think about for ever. Be off with you, Emma, or there'll be
more talk about us than you and Attar.'

When Thorkil came into the house she knew at once that he
had something to tell. He stroked his beard too often and his
fingers strayed to the little bronze hammer that he wore round
his neck, a Norse habit copied from the Christians. Emma
hated it, seeing in that small thing a sign of how it was in
everything, that they came, and stole, and belittled all the
lives of others. But Thorkil only thought it a handy charm and
in a while she took his view. It altered nothing.

"Tell me now or I shall not be able to eat," she said.

Everyone looked at her in bewilderment, but Thorkil burst
out laughing. "Witch! My thoughts are snails hiding from a
crow and you will crack, crack, crack with your hard beak
until you have them. Well, I have something. It is the farm."

Bjarni let out a yelp of excitement and Olaf landed a punch
on Thorkil's shoulder that would have felled a lesser man.
Only Skarphedin sat unmoved, but they were used to that.

"Did he say certainly? Can he go back on it?" Emma had
learned their distrust of Halfdan.

"It is agreed. Be easy, wife, it is the land above Shipton,
and all I owe for it is a duty of arms, and none too heavy at
that. We will travel to it tomorrow and decide what to do."

Bjarni let out another whoop and leaped from bench to
bench like a goat, nearly spilling the pot on the fire.

"Stop it!" Emma slapped at him in passing. "What of the
people there, Thorkil? Where will they go?"

His eyes were round and innocent and blue. "There is
no-one there."

"Are you sure?"

"But yes. When last I looked at the place it was empty."

If that were true it was because Thorkil had chased them away, she knew it as truly as if she had seen him. She was coming to know her husband and his ways. But to have a farm and escape from this hovel—her mind wove a picture of her father's steading, with wide halls and rich hangings. To begin with there would be less of course, but in time it would be so. In the midst of all the horror she would have plenty and peace.

When the meal was finished she was thoughtful. "Will you come with us, Olaf?" she asked, knowing that the others would not put the question.

"You'll need someone to take care of the house here," he said in his peaceable way.

Thorkil rested a hand on his shoulder. "You know my heart, friend. My hearth is lonely without you."

Olaf clasped his hand with his own and his eyes swam, for they saw no shame in a man's tears, especially over friendship.

"You can take care of Skarphedin," said Emma comfortingly.

They all looked at her. "Skarphedin comes with us," said Thorkil.

She flushed, a deep color that touched her hair. "But— why? You say yourself he's no farmer."

Skarphedin's laughter rattled the logs on the fire. "Did you think to be rid of me, witch? I am the wolf that follows your steps in the snow."

"The rat that gnaws at the corn barrel," she snapped. "Will he dirty his hands, Thorkil? Or is it too lowly for his noble blood, which is far less noble than my own?"

Skarphedin rose and came towards her, and despite herself she hid behind her husband. The berserk's face leered at her, large and twisted, like something from a dream when you wake up haunted. "Listen to the barren witch! You ask for fruit from a thornbush, Thorkil Sigurdsson."

Thorkil stood between them. "Be easy, old friend. She is a shrew but no more than that. I shall beat her a little."

"Will that make her swell? How many times must a man sow before he knows his field is sour?"

And Thorkil turned and looked at her.

She rode her little pony to Shipton, trotting along neatly

while Thorkil sweated behind. He had said barely a word to her since last night and her nerves were tighter than the girth of her pony. She was very afraid. Was it possible that a Viking would sell his wife for a slave, only because she was barren? She did not know.

Each month now she hid the blood from him, knowing how he would look, how he did look. All around women conceived, swelled and were brought to bed, and she alone was the object of their compassion. And Marjolein, she reminded herself, but she would not let her husband touch her. Whereas Thorkil, her prize bull, covered her almost nightly and in the day faced the sympathies of his friends. She was sickened at herself.

When they came to the village she looked about her with stiff-backed scorn. The houses clustered above the road, full of dull-faced people and one ham-fisted smith. She despised it. And then she thought, this is England for you now, it is what we have come to. If she valued a place like a magpie, a Viking, searching for jewels and gaudy rubbish, what could she hope to be given? She must be worthy if God was to listen to her. So she crossed herself and muttered a prayer.

Of late she had seen fit to pray often, sometimes before the casket said to hold the bone of Christ's finger. Thorkil said it was nothing but a pig bone, sold by a Dane who was making a profit at the game, but whether it was or not she prayed there. At the very least the priest might add his pleadings, and God would listen to him when He ignored others. But it was clear to her now that he thought little of the daughter of a witch who practised charms.

A one-eyed man on the path beside her held up the stump of a hand and begged. She threw him a coin and he called ''Bless you'' which so pleased her that she gave him some more. Thorkil shouldered him out of the way with his horse, and she glared at him, but he would not meet her eye.

The farm was on rising ground above the village. There were many trees, and their seedlings were sprouting in the small rich fields, a sure sign that the men have died or been driven away. The scent of charcoal drifted on the breeze and they glimpsed ragged figures in the woodlands at the side; the burners' children, that lived like wild foxes deep in the forest. As they passed they raised their hands to ward off evil and Emma was chilled.

"The people hate us," she said miserably. "We can't live here."

"It's always like that at the beginning," said Thorkil, who was cheering the nearer they came to the farm. "Next year they won't remember a time when we weren't amongst them."

"You mistake us. We're not so light."

He laughed. "Decide which you are, wife," he said easily and pushed his tired horse to a canter. She followed and they burst from the trees onto a sunlit upland where the air was cold and new. Thorkil stopped his sweating pony and looked about him. "It is good," he said finally, nodding to himself with the long gold hairs of his beard blowing in a haze about his face.

"Is there a house?" asked Emma, who could see nothing but burned-out walls and crumbling bothies.

"I will take you to it," said Thorkil, and in the distance a boy with a little flock of sheep hurried away. Emma's hopes began to rise, the wind was making her eyes water and she could smell grass and sun after weeks of a town's rank stench. Perhaps this would be a new beginning.

They mounted a little crest of a hill and in the dip was the house. She looked at Thorkil and then at the house and then at Thorkil again.

"There is a stream," he said. "The water is good."

Emma turned her back. She rode towards the mud-walled, sagging hovel, weeping as she went. She knew how it would be, she was a peasant now and would never be free. In winter the skin of her hands would be cracked to the flesh and she would be too weary even to rub grease into them. Such women were everywhere and their toil only ended in death. She would never bear a child. She left her pony picking at rank grass and went to sit by the stream. The sun did not strike into this place, it was cold and gloomy, a fit place for her tears.

"Emma." Thorkil squatted on the far bank and watched her across the dark water. "If you do not like the house I will build you another."

She rubbed her wet cheeks and whispered "I am barren. You'll sell me for a slave." Her heart thumped inside her and she felt sick.

After a little time he said, "I would not sell you."

"What then?"

He seated himself on the shale of the bank and began to cast pebbles into the stream. She watched them sink, one after the other, Christian pebbles, thrown for a witch from a heathen hand.

"We have not done everything," he said at last, and the pebbles went on falling, plop, plop, plop.

"I have prayed and asked the priest to pray for me. I have given to the poor and put a corn charm under my bed, I even put herbs in your drink, but nothing works."

"I always said yours is a feeble god. We will make offering to Frey, and also to Freyja, his sister. I have never known it fail."

In her head she saw Aldwulf, and his purple tongue. "What will you do?" she whispered hoarsely, and Thorkil saw her thoughts in her wide eyes and laughed. He tossed the pebbles away and dusted his hands. "Goats only." He stood up. "Come, wife, and tell me where you would wish me to build you a house.'

They stood in the glade and the trees rose mightily around them, stretching thick arms up into the sky. Sunlight fell in a pool at their feet, while around it was dark and dim. The two goats cropped unconcernedly, but Emma shivered.

Skarphedin had brought with him a small leather bag and he spread the things it held out on the grass. Grain; a stoppered flask of water and another of wine; an empty bowl; a stick with runes in a magic form; a little bronze statue of the god Frey, his manhood huge. She was very fearful. Thorkil had told her what would happen and she had accepted it, without thinking as it seemed to her then. Now that they stood in the grove with the pagan things spread before them, she knew herself to be dealing in devilish rites. What were herbs and dew and sunwarmed feathers when set against this, that went back to black night when men had no knowledge of God? If she did this thing she knew she would be far from the love of the Father. As if to witness the truth of it a cloud passed briefly across the sun.

She turned to Thorkil. "I cannot."

His eyes were blue and cold. "You must. I want a boy."

"You and Skarphedin must do it, I will watch. It will be enough."

"The gods would know you mocked them. If you will not do this thing, Emma, I will not answer for it."

She knew herself threatened and lifted her chin to him, daring him to do what he would. But then she thought—my God has failed me. I am not a woman if I cannot bear a child.

"It is time," said Skarphedin in his high, thin voice. Without a word to her husband Emma swept her skirts and strode to the place where the sun spangled the grass. She lifted her face to let it fall on her and closed her eyes for a long, long time. Her thoughts became light as the air she breathed. The golden sun shone through her eyelids, filling her head with its own bright heat.

"This is for you." Skarphedin held the bowl to her lips and she bent her head to drink. It was wine spiced in some way. As she looked up she gazed into his eyes and saw there what she knew was in herself; a purpose that had holiness in it, a raising of the spirit to the things that are not of this earth but yet give it its being. He reached his hands up and unfastened her cloak, so that she stood all in white linen. Once she would have flinched at his touch, but now he was as she, a servant only. He pressed grain into her hand and she closed her fist upon it; the other held the runes.

He brought the goats to stand before her and tied them together, male to female. He held the bowl over them and she dropped grain into the wine and passed the stick across the surface, and then again she drank. The sunshine filled her as Skarphedin shed the blood, life flooding out into the bowl and onto the good, strong earth. When at last the goats were still she let out her breath in a long sigh. She saw that Skarphedin's face, that was so ugly, seemed clean and pure, and she smiled at him as she took off her dress and pressed her hands in the blood, where it pooled on the grass. He began to make magic marks on her skin, anointing breasts and belly, brushing gore on her lips, and all the time singing to himself in a thread of sound. She felt that a god was touching her.

"Come, Emma." She turned in a daze to see her husband, and she did not know him. He was of the world and she was not, and he was only a man that could put into her that which she lacked. If need be she would have taken Skarphedin. But it was Thorkil that served her, planting his seed for a god. At the last, with the heat in her, she looked up and saw Skarphedin, and it was he that she called to, as her husband spent himself.

She sat in the doorway of her house, her fingers smoothly working the wool that fed the spindle. It was a task that suited her, needing as it did hands without cracks or rough places that would catch the wool, and also a calm mind. She was more than calm in those days, she was joyful, for the child grew in her belly and her husband labored to build her a house. The heat and stench of Jorvik sickened others but not she.

"Well then, Emma." It was Attar, as cool as other men were hot, wearing a thin linen shirt and a pair of tight trews. They showed what he wished her to see and she smiled to herself.

"I am surprised to see you. Everyone is off farming these days."

"You of all people should know I am no farmer." He brushed a strand of hair that had escaped her cap and let her feel the cool touch of his fingers.

"Have you heard the news?" she said, only for something to talk about.

"You mean Ivarr? Everyone is talking of it. He was a great king."

"I doubt that the men he killed so bloodily would think so,' she said tartly, for it seemed to her that judging a man depended more on where you stood than what he did.

Attar ducked the argument. "Halfdan is after his kingdom. As the brother he has the right."

Her hands jerked and the thread of wool broke. "He will not take all the men surely? Attar, I couldn't bear it, all the way to Ireland, and on the sea—"

"I doubt that many would go. Besides, Halfdan needs a force to hold the land here."

"Does he move against Wessex?"

"Sweet lady, how should I know?"

She looked darkly up at him, thinking that all their lives were ruled by battle and death. Attar put a better face on it than most, no more than that. The Danes had it all their way just then, or so it seemed. Burgred of Mercia was fled to Rome, and in his place was Ceolwulf that no-one even pretended knew what to do unless some Dane told him. In

Wessex the people lived in fear of further attack, and it did not seem that the young King Alfred could stand against Guthorm and his men. But Ivarr, who had held bloody sway amongst the Picts in the north, and also most mightily in Ireland, was now dead. It could mean change.

Attar watched her with his eyes half closed. "Tell me what will happen," she said softly, stroking him with her voice. The skin of her face was thick, like cream.

"What will you give me for a secret?"

She chewed on the tip of a finger. "What would you like?"

"The chance to serve you."

She giggled and said, "Olaf tells me that you serve all the wives in Jorvik."

"Olaf is a dumb shipman. There is only one wife I long for."

"And who might that be? Pretty Marjolein, who won't let her husband touch her? Or Hella, she's a fine cow. Or gentle little Gunhild, who blushes when you speak to her and always smells of violets, she'd be sweeter than I. You chase them all, Attar."

He leaned down very close and whispered, "The wife I want is tall and clever, with a mane of red hair and breasts like filled wineskins. I would serve her if she would but let me."

She put her mouth close to his ear and murmured, "Tell me your secret, Attar. If you love me you must tell."

"What will I get for it?" His hand rested on her shoulder.

"What it is worth." His fingers slipped into her dress but she caught his wrist and stopped him.

"Well then—Halfdan leaves for Ireland soon, and he takes with him young men only. Your husband is not with them, more's the pity."

"And Guthorm? What about him?"

"He moves against Wessex any day. He means to rule there."

"Does he now?" Again she chewed her finger, and with her thoughts elsewhere Attar's hand burrowed. He cupped her breast in a cool palm and she jumped. "Stop that! It was not enough of a secret after all. Go away, the woman across the way is watching us."

"Let her watch" he whispered, teasing her plump nipple. "You don't know what I could do for you, Emma."

She pushed him aside and got to her feet, letting her dress outline the swell of her belly. "I have a husband who does it more than well. He builds me a house and he gets me with child, which is what a man's for after all."

Attar was hot for her but she knew it was mostly to cheat Thorkil. There would never be kindness between them.

He caught her wrist and turned it to the soft white inside. It was a strong wrist, but the bones were cut fine. "Does he tell you you're beautiful? Does he liken your skin to the softest down and worship at your shrine?"

His voice oiled her thighs and she said slowly, "I like his loving well enough." It was true. She liked very well what Thorkil did, but she thought she might like Attar too. His touch was featherlight, he would drift into her softness, where Thorkil was a ram. Sometimes he all but crushed her.

But the woman was indeed watching, try as she might to absorb herself in sweeping, and Emma pushed Attar away, saying loudly, "Make up to someone else. I have been twice a wife and I know how far a silk tongue can stretch." She went inside and shut the door.

That night she wished very much for someone in her bed, she burned.

Thorkil built her a good house. He placed it high on the rise of a hill, so its back was sheltered from the gales but the sun warmed it in the morning. Stone was not lightly come by in those parts, and was used only for the standings for the walls and the hearth, but they found some flat, riverwashed slabs for the floor of the main hall. Thorkil built a chamber for he and Emma in a spur leading from the hall, and that spur and the hall itself made two sides of a courtyard. The third side was a great roofed barn, wooden pegged like a ship, and the fourth was Emma's sewing shed. It was this that pleased her most, though Thorkil said it was a habit much used by his own people. The building was small, of wood, with a little hearth in it and two great doors that took up the whole side. These could be flung open to let in light and air, so that if she was weaving she could see the work clearly and also what passed in the courtyard. She thought of it as her own place, though Thorkil did leather work there and

Skarphedin sat and did his strange and twining carvings, in those few days of tranquillity. The smithy was set apart, for it is always a place of smoke and stench. Bjarni and Skarphedin had their own lodgings in the upper part of the barn, and the slaves also, but above the animals as was fitting.

It was called Shiptonthorpe, which is Norse for the farm near Shipton. In time there were other farms, and each of them was Shiptonthorpe, so it came to be the farm by the grove, taking its name from the trees nearby. And as the years went by, the people said Grove Farm, Shiptonthorpe, and it was forgotten that the village had been Shipton once, it was forever Shiptonthorpe. It offended Emma to hear them call the place so, it was as if nothing was kept from the old time, it was all new. She felt that they were truly conquered when even the names were changed.

But in that time of waiting she was at peace with herself, wrapped in her womanhood as if in a cloak. There was nowhere that was settled but the farm, that was guarded by charms hid in the walls when they were built. All else was change and strife, as men fought for what was theirs or might come to be if they were strong enough.

Each day Thorkil and Bjarni laboured till their muscles cracked, at the plough or the scythe, or with a billhook clearing the saplings that were creeping everywhere. It was as if the forest fought where the people could not, waiting to snatch back whatever they took if they looked elsewhere for a moment. Emma knew of the woodspirits, all men had worshipped them once, in the days of their unknowing. Perhaps they felt the country's anguish. She knew herself to be prey to strange fancies, at night sometimes she thought of death, but not fearfully. She was well grown. She would survive.

Thorkil bought two slave girls, stout Saxons that would work on the farm and tend the milch cows. He had not the money for more and the hard, grinding toil fell to Bjarni and Thorkil himself. They grew brown in the sun and the scars on their arms and breasts began to fade. Emma took it for a sign, that they were become men of peace at last.

Only Skarphedin was still the warrior, passing the days till he should fight again. He carved a little and sometimes lent his strength to lift boulders that broke the plough, or took an axe to a tree that Thorkil was determined to be rid of however huge it seemed. For the rest he sat quiet enough and the others went carefully round him.

One day Emma said, "Have you tired of war, Skarphedin?" She was in the courtyard making soap and the task was tedious. They had killed a pig and the fat must be boiled before it went bad, but melting it stank and for that reason they always did it outside. Emma always saw to the soap herself for the girls were not clean and would let muck and pieces of grass fall into the pot, or would add the lye too quickly. She scented it with lemon balm and other herbs sometimes.

The fat was bubbling before Skarphedin replied. "Can a bird tire of flight?"

She wrinkled her nose at him and said tartly. "You are not a bird. Men should not kill each other."

He looked at her from very far away. "It is the one true glory."

The smell of the fat was choking her, for she had melted it twice and was sick of it, so she snapped, "If that is how you feel I am surprised you sit around here all day, getting under my feet!"

When it was said she wished it was not, but again he was silent. She stirred her noxious brew while he sat in his thick clothes and frightened her with his thoughts. He lived in a world of elves and demons and when she looked in his eyes she lived there also.

"I go to match with a weak young boy," he said suddenly, "Who is stronger than he seems."

"What do you mean?"

But he had said all he intended and rose on his short legs. She watched him go, knowing he would be away till evening at least, though where she did not know.

When the soap was done she took up a basket of bread and cheese and went to find Thorkil in the fields. He and Bjarni laboured with a stubborn pair of oxen that had never worked in an open field before but only between banks, so they were frisky and troublesome. The men stopped work gratefully and stretched out in the shade. Thorkil rested his hand on the swell of Emma's belly.

"Soon we will see my son. A good strong boy."

"He'll need to be. This land will take till he's grown before it's broken." Bjarni sank a weary head on to his knees. He was sickened by toil and unused to the loneliness. Emma teased him a little, seeing her brother in the slenderness of his neck. "Aren't there girls enough for you? Just think, when you go back to Jorvik you'll be quite forgotten."

He gave her a small, sad smile and she lay back on the grass, letting the sun soak into her. The larks were singing. Far off came the call of a snipe.

"We should have a hawk," she said. "I have often gone hawking after snipe."

"Oh, the grand lady," said Thorkil, waggling his head from side to side, but he was not angered. She touched his face with her fingertips, knowing she had lied a little, since her hawk was a merlin and too small for much. Her brother had gone after snipe, Bjarni had made her think of it. That and the warm, still day.

Her mind drifted. "I think Skarphedin plans something," she said sleepily.

"What is that?" Thorkil tickled her with a grass.

"He said, 'I go to match with a weak young boy.' I don't know what he means."

"Ah. It is Wessex."

She sat up, awkward and suddenly cross. "There is an agreement. Do you Vikings never keep your word?"

"It was Guthorm's word, nothing to do with me," said Thorkil peacefully.

"I'd like to go." It was Bjarni. They both looked at him, flushed and his hair flat to his head with sweat. They saw that he meant it.

"What is this?" rumbled Thorkil. "You are needed here, lad, on the farm."

"I'm no farmer, it's no life for me."

"Neither are you a warrior, I think. I do not like to say this to you, little brother, but where would you be now without Skarphedin and myself to help you? How many times have we cheated the fates for you? I do not doubt your courage, only your skill."

"If it wasn't for you I wouldn't be in the press, it's always fiercest where you are." Bjarni trembled a little, his eyes bright with tears that might yet fall.

Emma reaching her hand to him. "We need you this year," she soothed. "Wait till the spring."

"But Guthorm is moving now! I have to go. Or would you rather I went with Halfdan?"

"He is not the man his brother was," said Thorkil. "He does not know when to make peace."

"At least he's a man still and not an old woman tending her garden!"

At this Thorkil leaned across and clouted Bjarni round the ear. The boy yelped and rolled in the grass, like a puppy ducking from a slap. Emma clung to her husband as Bjarni screamed at him, "Curse you, Thorkil! D'you think I'm a child?"

"Still too small to give me your cheek," said Thorkil. "You will stay here and work like the boy you are, while men decide what should be done. I have nursed you like a mother with a new-born babe and you are no more fit to go off by yourself than a child learning to walk."

Bjarni struggled to his feet, his face scarlet with rage and frustration. "Who are you to talk—shagging your Saxon cow night and day—"

A growl rose in Thorkil's throat but Emma clutched at him, putting her swollen body between the brothers. "Go away, Bjarni," she pleaded. "You don't know what you say!"

Himself appalled, Bjarni turned and ran back to the house, stumbling over the lumpy ground.

Thorkil put Emma from him and flung himself down again. "That boy needs a whipping."

"It wouldn't do any good."

"You don't understand. I have always looked after him, I know him too well."

Emma eased herself heavily down beside him. "He's grown, Thorkil. He's too old to be told what to do."

"But you know how he is about girls! I have bought off a dozen outraged fathers, if it weren't for me he'd have been leg-shackled before he had a beard. And in battle, I keep one eye for myself and one for Bjarni, and Olaf does also, and he has two eyes of his own and needs them, all to take care of one boy's hide. Where would he be without us, eh?"

"As he says, he would not be there. He would find his own friends. He would fight with them." Her belly weighed heavy and she was hot and upset. She pulled off her cap and let her hair tumble. Thorkil tangled a hand in it absently.

"Die with them, more like. I am surprised at you, Emma, he is less able to take care of himself than you."

"But I am with child and I need a man's strong arm," she said meekly, resting her breast on the arm she spoke of.

Thorkil laughed and pulled her to him. "You need more than that girl! Come, let us take some pleasure from this sour afternoon."

Bjarni left the house that night and Emma wept because of it. She felt that she had lost her own brother once again. Another day and Skarphedin was gone also, and the farm was quiet with loneliness. It was the silence that oppressed her, clouding her days with thoughts of death and suffering. She dreamed that Bjarni lay bleeding, with maggots in the flesh and none to cleanse him, though she knew that being Bjarni there would always be a woman.

It was left to Thorkil to think of Skarphedin, for to stay and farm instead of standing by his friend in battle seemed to him a betrayal. Emma was in turmoil in case he left her, she knew how long she would keep the farm in that wild and bloody time.

But each time he travelled, to Jorvik or Wicstun, he came back. Once he brought fish and once a farm boy who was strong but very thick in the head. Thankfully the girls despised him and he slept with the cows because he had no more sense than an animal about pissing where he felt like it. Some of the people thereabouts were very strange, for even the church could not prevent too close matings in families. Peasants in these places were often the same, thought Emma, brutish and idiot. Sometimes she could not believe that they were all the same creatures.

Late that year she was brought to bed of a son. She never spoke of it, only that the child died, for that is often so, a babe brought forth with the life squashed from it and the woman lucky to survive herself. She was ill afterwards, and as she said to people, she remembered so little.

She labored for two days all told, at first as brave as might be, smiling at Thorkil between the pains. At the end they tied her hands to the bedposts to stop her tearing at herself. She screamed till there was no breath in her. They brought a woman up from the village and she was kind, though there was nothing she could do, for the child would not come out. And when at last it was forced into the air, that fine strong boy she had longed for—they took it away. They left her lying on that bed as drained as an empty cup and they took her little boy away. If she had once held him it would have been enough, if they had let her look at him—but her husband would not. He denied her even that. She lay on her dreadful, bloody bed, straining against ropes, and begged for her child, begged to be told what was wrong. They would not speak. In a while the woman came and gave her warm ale and she asked "Where is my baby?" No-one ever told her.

Chapter
Six

WHEN IS A man ever content? Even when he's dead and in Valhall, the greatest meadhall of them all, he longs for battle, so they say. When I had the battle I longed for peace. When I had the peace I found myself dreaming of battles I might fight.

It was no wonder that Skarphedin decided to go, for in my heart I knew it was no life for him. The flame that was his being sank to nothing when his days were spent quietly. As well use a sword to cut corn. But Bjarni should not have gone, he had no wisdom whatever his years, and I was surprised that Emma did not see it.

Do I sound like and old man? I suppose it must be. Youth has no fear and sees no danger, it is age shows a man what he owes to luck. That and the graves of friends. Lying beside my wife in the night I thought of the many, many things that could happen and resolved again and again to take up my sword and shield in the morning and go after them. But in the morning there was Emma and work to be done. And in the end a man must stop tearing things down and build.

That was the trouble with Halfdan, you know, he thought he could battle for ever. Even Ivarr knew better, and there was never a bloodier man than he. I think that was the kernel of it, the littler brother trying to sail faster than the greater, and wrecking his boat while doing it. For the men had had enough, they had seen too many places not to know that

mostly there is nothing to choose, except that in a new one
you may die whereas here you are most certainly alive and
likely to stay so. Halfdan sent men up and down Northumbria,
laying waste what could have been ours to hold, and in the
end no-one would follow him. So he took the young hot-
heads, like Bjarni, I admit it, and set sail for Ireland. Thank
the gods that my little brother was too late to catch the ship
for it was the end of Halfdan. I tell the tale as a man told it to
me, and I do not judge the truth of it.

Halfdan took to raiding in the land of the Picts, much as his
brother had done before him but with less success. In the time
since Ivarr's death his kingdom in Ireland had come under the
rule of Bardr, who was Norwegian and a fairish sort of man.
Somewhat boastful, I hear. Anyway, Bardr had a foster-son,
Eysteinn, who was married to the daughter of an Irish king,
and the ruling of Bardr and Eysteinn looked to be settling the
land. So Halfdan on a dark and windy night sent men out to
kill Eysteinn stealthily, with none to know who was responsi-
ble, which shows how foolish Halfdan could be. He had too
few men to try such a lie. The Irish king, who was Aed
Findliath, came to Halfdan's hall and sat drinking with him,
and when they were all past thinking Aed Findliath called to
his men and they burst into the stronghold, screaming to
avenge the widowing of their king's daughter.

Halfdan broke from the hall with a handful of men only,
but the fates were hard on his heels. He took to sea in three
small ships, one a good longship but the others only tubs, and
Bardr put to sea also. Even the wind failed Halfdan, as it will
when a man has used his time. I think he knew it was the
end, for the fight was not fierce. He took a sword in the
throat and died in a rush of blood.

There is a sadness that comes when a man hears of such a
death; a warrior who had fought and ruled with courage
ending his days like that. Is it better so than by his own hearth
with his sons forgetful of the deeds of his youth? For Halfdan
perhaps, though I think that in Valhall he will still sit below
Ivarr.

It was a good year on the farm. We planted corn and peas
and some flax, and one of the cows calved well though the
other looked to be barren. It is the air in that country. We
slaughtered her when the milk dried, for I was tired of leading

the beast up and down to Erik's bull and each time a gift of cheese, or salt meat, or some of Emma's soap. It paid to have an open hand though, for Erik came to help at our harvest when even Emma, swollen like a plum, had to stack sheaves.

"That cow looks ready to drop," joked Erik, which was somewhat coarse and offended Emma. She put her nose in the air and moved away and Erik looked as surprised as a dog kicked for fetching a bird. "I'm sorry, Thorkil—I did not mean—"

"No matter, friend. She has a lady's ways, that is all. And a better bull than you have, it seems!" I gave him a punch on the arm to show that there was no offense and he began to roar about his bull, as good as any and had fathered half the cattle in the country—that was probably the trouble, he'd exhausted the creature. I resolved to keep my bull calf and have done with Erik. The farm lad was coming to be useful, and in my heart I believed that next year would see Bjarni home again.

He had sent word that he was with Guthorm, which relieved my mind a little. Guthorm had rare sense, he never fought if he could dicker and he never dickered for long. Also he planned beyond the next battle, which is rarer than you might suppose. Still, he needed a good head for a good one stood against him, surprising though it was. I speak of that sickly boy Alfred.

Alfred was one of five sons, Athelstan, Aethelbald, Aethelbert, Aethelred, and then Alfred, the youngest. I find these Saxon names a little more than hard I can tell you, but since the father was Aethelwulf you can understand it. He had run out of "Aethels" by the time he came to Alfred, and we may thank the gods for that. Aethelwulf died and there was the usual mishmash of argument about who should rule, as is always the case when there are many sons, but before long the only one left alive was Alfred. Now personally I should have been wondering what this Alfred was up to on dark nights, but he was a studious lad, poor in health and much favoured by his father, and he was thought to be guiltless in the deaths. As a boy he was trailed round Frankia and then to Rome, while his father sought help against us Vikings. They would have done better staying home and looking to their army, and it seems Alfred was of the same mind for now he had come to be king he began to rally his people. Sometimes he made peace with Guthorm and paid him off, other times he fought, and the ups and downs of those battles went on for years. It was this that Bjarni joined, and Skarphedin, but since land was the prize and honor not thought of, I did not think they would stay with him long.

Thinking of the way that year ended I am glad that they were gone. There are some things that a man cannot say even to his closest friend and the presence of that friend only adds to his loneliness. Strange to think, but Skarphedin might have understood, and he alone of them all. He had never felt the comfort of another's thoughts, and that is not to say he did not long for it. Some men are set apart and it is their burden as well as their luck. I was like the seal lying maimed on the ice, half dying in the white of a cold land. No one can come to him. There is no comfort but perhaps the high, thin song of a fellow sounding from far away, where he too lies lonely. Skarphedin would have sung for me.

Emma was brought to bed in the evening, after a day of restless discomfort. Her belly weighed heavy upon her and her limbs were swollen. It was as if the life within had drained even the color of her hair, which hung dim and lank about a dull-eyed face. When the first pains came she laughed up at me.

"I am so glad it is starting. Will you mind if it is a girl?"

"It is a boy," I said happily, and kissed her. We were joyful and if there was fear we did not show it. I did not know what it was to lose the thing closest to your heart. I did not fear it.

But it was soon clear that the child would not come forth easily and his struggles stretched my sweet girl as if she were gripped by a monster. I put cloth between her teeth for she was bringing blood from her lips, and in the dark hours before morning one of the girls lashed her hands. I cried for her, I know that, and as soon as it was light I rode like a madman to fetch a wife from the village. It shames me to admit it but there was relief in being out of that house, filled as it was with anguish. Men say it is a woman's lot and men can bear no blame, but it was my lust that had brought her there. I had drunk the sweet wine and left Emma with the lees. Still, that is the way of it.

The wife was a good woman, and understood. "When the babe comes out she'll think it a small price," she soothed, but that was before she went inside. Then her face stiffened. She put leaves in Emma's mouth and told her to chew them, she heated cloths on the fire and laid them on her belly and sometimes she reached her hand in to see if she could feel the child. On the evening of that day Emma was weak, and weaker still by morning. The wife, now all sweat-soaked, came out into the air. "You must pray to your heathen gods," she said. "I shall pray to sweet Jesus and His lovely mother, who knows what it is to bear children. And you must send for the priest."

I wiped my face with a hand that shook, and my voice shook also. "I warn you wife, it will be the worse for you if she dies. She needs no priest."

"This is what comes of marriage with a heathen," she snapped, and went to rinse her face and hands in a bucket. Then back she went to the thick air, and Emma hoarse from screaming. That is that made me unjust to a good woman.

She brought the child out in the afternoon. No-one was there, only she and I, for the girls cowered in the barn stopping their ears. The woman used all her skill to drag the creature free, and it lay on the soaked cloths mewing.

"By the Blessed Saints," said the woman, and crossed herself.

"It isn't dead," I whispered, for it waved its limbs.

Emma was calling out in a voice too weak to understand. The woman looked at me, the sweat standing in beads on her lips. Then she bent and cut the cord that tied the offspring to its mother, and afterwards she took a thick wool blanket. Emma was calling again.

"I must see to her," said the woman, and held the bundle towards me. "This is a heathen thing. It is not for a Christian woman."

I saw that she had covered even the face. I took it, and it was not light.

I went out into the darkening afternoon.

The trees stretched claws into a grey sky. I felt that they tore at my heart. I stumbled as I went and sometimes the creature mewed, but my sobbing drowned the sound in my head. Once I fell but I clutched my burden close and it took no harm. That had been done long since, by sowing a seed for a god. I should have known that Frey could not be trusted,

nor Odin neither, and we had asked the help of his bondsman.
All around me the birds seemed black. They were the ravens,
come to claim their carrion meal. I cursed them, I stood on
the slope of that windy hill and I stretched my fist up and
cursed.

"Strike me now if you will! Tear the living heart from me
for you have done this thing and I curse you for it! Was it
you, Thor, angered because I neglected you? No. This is
Odin, the foul god. I curse you! I curse you!"

But even the birds only rose from the fields and then settled
again. So little is a man's anger.

I went back to the summer grove. Now there were no
leaves and I felt that I saw the truth, shrouded before in a
liar's pretty dress. Now I saw the twisted hands, the faces of
ghouls in the naked bark. I put my bundle on the rank grass
and opened it.

It was a boy. His head was huge; if it had not been for the
skill of the wife he would have killed his mother. The limbs
were twisted and mishapen. Yet even as I looked and saw
how terrible was the body, that in no way could it live, I saw
that the face was sweet and clear. They had trapped my son in
this foul carcase. I held him close to me and I wept, my tears
as bitter as the wind. The salt drops fell on that swollen head
with its little crown of hair. I had dreamed of the hair of my
son, red like his mother's and blowing in a warm wind as he
ran on sturdy legs. The child I held had two cramped twigs
that would never learn to run.

Towards morning a peace came on the grove. The trees
ceased their moaning, as if they had done with their triumph.
Even the birds were quiet. In the dimness the white skin of
the child was very still, yet I knew that he lived. I held my
son most tenderly. Then I drew my knife, and set him free.

Winter in Northumbria is a bleak time, when men huddle
within doors in dim houses. At home it is quite different,
there is a clean, white light that is of the snow. The cold cuts
to the bone, it does not scratch like a wife's long nagging.
Sometimes we would skate, winging across the ice like birds
in the air, and we would light fires to warm ourselves and
cook fish. I brought my skates to the farm but the ice never
froze thick enough. That winter was wet, it smelled of cow
dung and the rotting of leaves.

We could not speak to each other. Emma was more wounded than if she had been in battle and she lay in bed for many days. Once, soon after, she said "My baby . . ." and held to my arm as I lifted her. I shook her off and told the girl to give her something to make her sleep. It was wrong to be so silent, it was as if we allowed skin to form over an arrow's barb when there is no way that it will cease hurting, but I could not speak. The pain was beyond words and beyond Emma's understanding.

Come the bitter gales of March and she was mending. She would rise in the mornings and see to her work, and then lie down again in the afternoon. But there was no brightness in her. She was empty and silent. When we sat in the evenings, she was so still it was as if she were a rock, even her eyes were of stone, unblinking. Always before she had busied herself with sewing, or spinning, yet now she did not care what needed doing, she would only sit, quite still.

She was very cold towards me. For others she would make a little attempt, perhaps mending a rip in a farmboy's shirt, or mixing up a posset, but for me she would do nothing. Sometimes I thought she could not bear even to look at me and I thought, if I gaze in her eyes I will see then if it is grief she feels, or truly hatred. But when I did look all I saw was the cold, like ice on a distant ocean, with no feeling in it.

Once I asked her to make honeycakes, which I liked to eat. She could bake them better than anyone and I thought, if she makes them for me I will tell her so. A little thing, a bridge perhaps, that I could cross to warm her. That day she baked nothing, nor the next, nor the day after, and what was I to say? I had no right to anger, for the child was all my doing. The guilt was my own, and not for the child's death but for his life.

A man can face a thousand perils and have courage, but then to find that he cannot even reach out to his wife and say to her "This is a pain shared. I feel it also." It is to wonder what he has learned in all his wanderings, why he should have come so far if he is only the boy he was when he set out. I had many strange thoughts in those days, that I was a man cursed, set apart by the gods for this suffering. Whoever touched my life suffered for it, even my own brother had run from me. So it was that I moved through the days, alone in the midst of people, my thoughts locked in my head to seethe amongst themselves, and brewing something near to madness.

We slept in the same bed still, but the little space between us was wider than an ocean. If we touched we moved away again. Once in the night I woke to hear her crying, and I stretched my hand to her without thinking. I stopped it on its way. What could I say to comfort when our lives seemed as black as the night itself and the gods jealous and vengeful? I fancied that the world was ruled by tricksters who found it a great joke to prick old Thorkil with their pins.

"Give him what he wants and see how happy it makes him," they cried to each other, and drained their drinking horns to the music of my tears. We were so close, she and I, yet we were lost to each other, each in our own loneliness. One dull and windy morning I went to see Olaf at the wharf in Jorvik. The road seemed long that day and it was thick in mud. Everywhere I looked, in every hamlet and village, there were cripples and men without hands. That is the legacy of war.

It was late when I came to the town and Olaf was cleaning his tools, sitting on a barrel in the midst of woodshavings, and to the side the shell of a little faering. Half the planking was in place, held tight with wooden nails and stringing. He made a sound craft, did Olaf.

"A neat little thing," I said, jerking my thumb to the boat as I squatted amongst the shavings. Olaf grunted and went on clearing the dust from his plane. It was as if our last meeting had been but an hour before, but so it is with true friends.

"I shall get some good cooking at last," said Olaf.

"Emma did not come. She is not well."

"Oh. I heard it died."

I nodded and the tears welled in my throat. I wished I had not come. But Olaf dropped a hand to my shoulder and said, "We will beg a meal from Hilde. Her husband's at sea."

"Still the same one? She must be a charmer."

He chuckled. "She is like bread, strong and plain and good on an empty stomach."

We went to a little house nearby where the fishheads were piled for the pigs. "It does not smell like bread," I complained.

"Ah, you are getting old, Thorkil. Too much marriage makes a man too nice in his ways." He went in the little door and I ducked after him. It was warm and dim but I tripped on the downstep and fell amongst them.

"I think your friend's drunk," said the wife. I thought perhaps I was. The little body was as round as she was tall, with a front tooth missing and her eyes small and black. But she looked merry enough and made us most welcome.

We ate fish soup and bread, which we chewed at thoughtfully without daring to glance at one another. Hilde fussed around us, pouring ale and taking a flask of her husband's honey wine that was hid in the rafters. I thought of my own things at home. Emma would give those up as easily.

"Your friend can sleep here," said Hilde shyly. I saw that she was much in love with Olaf, who was no more than fond in return. But then he was always a calm sort and it was perhaps as much as he would ever feel for a woman. Some men are like that.

I got to my feet and struck my head against a roof timber. "I'll be getting back to the house," I said. "My thanks to you, Hilde. You come along later, Olaf."

"I'll walk with you. Give me but a moment."

I stood outside in the dark while Olaf quieted his ladylove with promises. It was long since I had been in a busy town at night and I found the noises strange and threatening. I found my hand straying to my knife in case the men who passed in the shadows should attack me. It was a feeling I remembered from my first trip to Birka and the great market there. I was a ploughboy once again.

The old house was as draggled as you would expect, with only Olaf as master. Gear and boat-shackles lay everywhere and a lumpish sort of lad uncurled himself from the hearth as we entered and stirred up the fire. Olaf went straight to a chest in the corner and unlocked it. I could see bags inside.

"Is that your treasure-store?"

"Yes. I am saving for a share in a longship." He opened a bag and dropped in two coins, then closed the chest up and locked it once again.

"Do you have a ship in mind?" I asked, and saw Olaf looking at me with that old smile.

"You're a farmer now," he said. "You cannot go adventuring."

"I can dream," I answered. "Which ship is it?"

"You will not know her. Skimmer, they call her. Twelve benches only."

"And she is for sale?"

He nodded. "Toki wants me to come in with him. She's a good vessel but needs some work. She knows her way around everywhere I want to go."

"And where is that?"

He grinned. "Somewhere different. I am tired of a safe bed."

I got up quickly and went to reach for the ale, which was half-buried under a pile of leather ropes. "This is cow-hide," I said.

"You try and get walrus here. I will go and fetch it myself, I think." He stretched out before the fire and scratched his beard, like a cat almost. It annoyed me greatly.

"When have you ever found you own way?" I snapped. "You'll be back in a week thinking you've found Paris."

"Maybe so. Toki's not much use, I admit. But you are up to your neck in dirt so I must make the best of it. If we go down you will hear my crying on the wind 'Thorkil! Thorkil!' and you'll cock an ear and say 'That's Olaf.' You'll be warm in bed, remember that."

I was silent for a time. "I am not so warm as I was," I said at last. My friend chewed at some meat, then spat a tough piece on to the floor. So easy is life for a man on his own.

"You do not care for her then, your English wife?"

I shrugged. "It is no part of it. The—the child changed things. And I do not think there will be another."

"Why so? It's not uncommon to lose one, and the first at that. She's young and strong, and you've tamed her well enough. I know it seems good to go off for a bit but the girl needs a brat at her breast. They can be strange when they lose one."

I thought of telling him that my seed was cursed. The words became iron in my throat. So instead I said, "She would not mind if I went. She'd be glad to see the back of me."

Olaf chewed a bit more. "For a day perhaps. I doubt it's that bad."

"How would you know, your wife is borrowed only. Oh, it is like sour milk, you cannot make it fresh again whatever you do."

"Then make it into cheese," said Olaf, and threw the rest of the meat on the fire. It hissed and spat as the fat went into the flames. All as we were we rolled ourselves in blankets and went to sleep.

*   *   *

In the morning we went to see Skimmer. She was moored upstream and looked a dowdy thing with her mast down and rubbish and dirty water where the deck was lifted.

"Bit of work would see to her," said Olaf, patting the sweep of her prow. She raked nicely but some fool had nailed a high stern to her and it spoiled the line.

"That will have to come off," I said. "The man who sailed her did not like to get wet it seems."

"And who can blame him," said Olaf. "Remember how it is when the salt rubs sores where your clothes touch?"

"Aye."

We kicked at the planking and unfastened the side rudder. The wood was rotted here and needed replacing, also I like a system where you can take the rudder up more quickly, even if it does mean you may lose it in a storm. It is by the shore that a rudder is needed, at sea oars and sail will suffice. There is no time to be struggling with a stubborn block when the men are armed and ready and you want to beach. Too long a wait and someone is like to decide that he does not feel like a battle today, and before long you have all chosen to go home instead and take up sewing.

"Is there a sail with her?" I asked.

"None that I would use, you can see through it. There is some rigging but much needs replacing. Toki is settling the price to take account of it."

I nodded. The trouble was that ships were hard to come by in Jorvik and even a hulk like this could cost you. At home in Vestfold where men spend their lives building ships no-one would look at such a wreck. But we had no choice, it was this or no other.

"I will talk to Emma," I said.

Olaf let out his breath through his nose, like a blowing horse. "I'm glad you didn't marry my sister after all. How's the girl going to manage with you gone?"

"I'll talk to Erik, he farms on the other side of the hill. He will work the land for half the crop."

"You have it all thought out, I see. And what about her? She's no beauty but when she walks by everything with balls turns to look."

"She is safe enough on the farm. No-one comes there."

He passed a hand across his brow and stared at me. "You're a bastard, Sigurdsson. What she needs is a husband and a

baby, not to be left in the middle of nowhere without even a
sword to protect her. What's she done to make you so bitter?
Won't she let you into her bed any more?''

I felt again the urge to weep. Talk of Emma did this to me,
I could not endure it. So I said only, ''She has been too ill for
that. But she is bitter about the child. We are better apart for
a while.''

''You mean to come back then?''

I had not thought further than the going. Who knew what
would happen? The spark of my life was weak just then,
perhaps a seastorm would blow it out. So I looked Olaf in the
face and said ''I will come back'' with a fair show of
honesty.

I rode back to the farm with a lightened heart and even the
beggars looked less gruesome. I had bought a present for
Emma, a comb made of deer antler. The best combs are ivory
but very expensive, so I chose an antler one from a little shop
in Hartergate. But when I rode up, mired to the knees and the
horse in worse case, Emma was in her sewing shed and did
not come out.

''I want you, wife,'' I called as I took my things from the
saddle.

''I am weaving. I can't come now,'' she said coldly.

I went to the door and leaned on it. She had lost so much
flesh that her face was quite changed. In the light of the fire
she could be beautiful.

''I have brought you a present,'' I said, and held out the
comb.

She looked at it and turned her head back to her work. ''It
is fine. I am busy now, I will look at it later.''

In the old days I would have thrown it straight in the fire.
But instead I squatted down and turned the comb in my
hands. It was a fine comb and had taken a man many hours to
make. ''Is there no mending it, Emma?'' I said softly.

Her hands paused in their work, went on and then fell in
her lap. ''I don't know,'' she whispered.

''We were wrong to ask Frey—it all went wrong. I'm
sorry.''

''Yes.'' Tears were falling on her hands, but her face did
not change. Then she said, ''I cannot feel warm towards you.
I am cold inside. I don't want to be.''

We were silent, I turning the comb, she so still and white. "I am going away," I said, and my voice shook like a child's.

"I thought you would. With Olaf." She did not look at me.

"We are buying a ship. We might make a bit of money with it."

"When do Vikings think of anything else?" she said tartly and jerked at a loose thread in her weaving. The cloth bunched and she hissed at it.

"Erik will work the land. You'll be all right."

"I don't like Erik."

"You cannot do it yourself."

"Since I have no child and no husband I shall have nothing else to do."

I scratched at my head and wondered at her. She was calm when I was not there, it was only my presence that maddened her. I could sense the mood come upon her the longer I was near, as if in a moment she would spring to claw me. I felt the pain as if she had done it.

"Then I will get another lad," I said.

She nodded and went back to her weaving, her fingers flying from side to side. The cloth was coarse and brown. Before the child she had done fine work in pretty colors, she had even made me a patterned belt, done most carefully on a handloom before the fire in the evenings. Time and again she had stretched it round me and laughed to find it too short.

Of a sudden my face crumpled into tears and I sobbed openly, not bothering to be quiet. But Emma went on with her weaving.

In the next month I traveled several times to Jorvik. The pony became sore and I more so, but at least I was busy. I found Emma a good lad, a Danish boy whose leg had been broken in battle and now was somewhat short. He limped but he was strong. Emma hissed "Is a cripple the best you can do?" when I brought him, but to his face she was kind. His name was Leif and for him she would make honeycakes.

The ship was coming on well. There was a little strife in that Toki seemed to think that he would captain it, but after a discussion he decided he would rather stay at home. I was not surprised. Shipboard life is not for a man with a broken jaw.

As for a crew, there was no shortage of men. Many wished to travel to fetch wives or sweethearts, and to oblige them we said we would put in somewhere along the way, though not too early as I did not want to lose the whole crew at the first port. I was having no women on my ship, if they wanted to leave they might do so but I would find single men to take their place. There are always men willing to take a chance on a thing, but whether you wish to take your chance with them, that is the question. A fine time to discover you have a thief on board when you are three days out and need him to row. I once had a man whose sea chest bulged with the things he had stolen from his fellows, but he was strong so we left it till we came safe to harbor. But he took what he could carry and went over the side and it took us two days to catch up with him in town. He had spent almost everything, but it cost him his life.

You have no idea of the stores a man must set by for a voyage, not only food and drink but bowls and cups, waterbags, a caldron and stand for cooking, medicines, blankets, spare gear for the ship, wooden blocks and ropes, resin and tar, the list is endless. Then of course there are the trade goods. We took combs, hides, grain, some wooden things, salt meat, iron things and some jewelery. For my part I did not think Saxon work as good as elsewhere, but it would be different and that is always valuable. I thought of taking slaves, which would have fetched the best price of all, but we had not the room. But I took some bags of silver hid beneath the decking to buy things that I thought would sell more dearly back in Jorvik. So perhaps I did mean to return, I don't know. It made Olaf happier, I know that.

He had much trouble with the sail, for there was a special resin that he liked and could not find. In the end he found something that he thought would do, but the sail stretched more than we would like. It caused some difficulty.

I said we would sail in three days. It seemed impossible that we would be ready, but that is always how it is. If you did not set a time to depart you would never go, but always find something else you might need, or a man you must see, or even an omen that demands you should delay. Scared men see omens, that must be admitted. Brave ones don't look. So I was by the ship sorting stores when I sensed that someone was near. I did not look up at once, though I knew who it was. Skarphedin.

"Well then, friend." I held out my hand and he took it. He was unchanged, being dark and squat, his hair thick with grease as such men often wear it. I recognized again the horror of his face. After a time without seeing it I would forget, and then when I looked I would think, "Yes, so it is. Dreadful." What can it do to a man to carry such a face with him all his life? For Skarphedin there was never a moment's forgetting, the grim looks of others reminded him.

"I knew you were going."

"How so? Did someone bring word?"

He did not reply, but only gazed down at Skimmer. I knew that if someone had told him he would not say, but let me think he had sensed it. But again, he could sense such things. Before a battle he knew which would die, and I have no reason to deceive you. It was in his eyes when he looked at a man. His gaze came back to me and I could not meet it.

"You have had trouble," he said.

"And who has not? Tell me, how is Bjarni? Is he with you?"

"I have no shieldman now. A man does not take a child into battle."

I felt ashamed that I had left him. I thought that he wanted me back at his side. I said, "I need to go to sea, Skarphedin, I cannot stay here."

He stretched his hand down again to help me out of the boat. "Come," he said in that way he had as someone who would never be denied. The strength of his grip matched mine, but when we stood together on the bank he was barely to my shoulder. I was like a giant beside him as we walked, to a place of his choosing, near a cooper's shop where the wood was stacked. We sat on the piles of timber and I was most uncomfortable.

"Did I not tell you she was a spider?" he said.

It was little enough, but it inflamed me. Of a sudden I wanted to kill him. Where before I could not look now I glared into his empty black eyes. "It was not her doing. It was you and your foul god that did it. Don't say you didn't know, I am sick of your lies!"

"I have never lied to you. You asked it of me and I gave, the rest was not mine."

"Are you saying it was mine then? That I could—that he could—you didn't see it! You cannot know!" And all at once my anger turned to tears. No grief has ever been so bitter.

"So you killed it," said Skarphedin, as if from a great distance. He was a bird, high above me.

"He was my son. I loved him and I could do no other."

"And his mother? What did you do with her?"

"Why—nothing. She barely lived. But you can rest easy, there is no kindness between us now. It is as you wanted."

Skarphedin grunted. "I tell you, Thorkil, I knew only that there would be pain. Perhaps this is the end of it, I do not know. You do as you will, I cannot stop you."

I stood up. "A man's destiny is his own, so they say. If he knew what it was he'd kill himself. I have some more work to do, but after I'd like to drink a cup or two and talk. About Bjarni."

"If you wish. I thought once that he would come to something, but now I think he will not. He is weak."

I grinned. "Young only. You forget, Skarphedin. We all forget."

"All but the gods," he said, and went away with his swinging stride.

In the evening we sat by the fire, myself, Skarphedin and Olaf, who worked shaping a block for one of the ropes. Spares are always needed, especially when the wood is not all you would wish. The best wood comes from the forests at home. There is wood in Northumbria, of course, but not the same skill with it. For myself I like a pine mast, it flexes better.

Skarphedin told how it was with Guthorm, and it was not as well as it might seem. He brought the army into Wessex from the land of the East Angles, and at first they went with caution. Then of a sudden they moved quickly, to conquer a place called Wareham. Alfred followed, fearful of a trap, and he and Guthorm made peace. But it was not a true deciding for Guthorm struck again and took Exeter. His plan was to unite with a force landing from a fleet on that coast, coming from Ireland. How clearly was it shown that our lives are ruled by wills other than our own, for there was a great storm and many ships were lost. When Guthorm learned of this he saw that he would have to make a peace, so he took money from Alfred and took his force to Mercia. That was where things rested. We did not doubt that Guthorm would win in the end, and be the richer for it in the meantime, but the task was not proving easy.

Olaf shook his head wonderingly. "This Alfred is a brave little wolf-cub. You'd think he'd have some sense and give in."

"He's seen Rome once. Perhaps he didn't like it. Now Skarphedin, what of Bjarni? He has not done so bad, by all accounts."

"He spends his days and nights drinking and whoring," said Skarphedin, for all the world like somebody's grandmother. "It is no way for a warrior. He takes up with the Danes, the young men that comb their hair and chew scented leaves. They do not think of battle."

"He fights, doesn't he?" I asked, alarmed. Never let it be said that a brother of mine shirked a battle.

"Oh, he fights," sneered Skarphedin. "If that is what you call tickling frightened men into running at the point of your sword. Bjarni takes more prisoners than any. It is said he sings to them." He was all outraged scorn and I hid a smile in my beard. Bjarni had stood beside me in battle and I did not doubt him, but he had no liking for it. Sometimes he hung back when he should have gone forward, he thought too much of his enemy, who he was, that kind of thing. It was dangerous and we had spoken to him on the matter. As for Skarphedin, he had never taken a prisoner in his life except for Emma. He spoke of it as some loathsome habit that Bjarni had begun, like buggery or some such.

"What else does he do?" rumbled Olaf on a belch.

Skarphedin sniffed. "He neglects his religion. He talks to their priests. I have heard that he goes with Guthorm when he speaks to King Alfred."

At this both Olaf and I sat up. We had not thought that Bjarni was so well considered. "What does he do there?" I asked, amazed.

"Fondles the women," snapped Skarphedin. "It is all he is good for."

We could get no more from him. It was clear to me that he had taken offense at Guthorm, who held Bjarni in higher regard than Skarphedin. There was a sense in me that the world was changing. Perhaps the time was coming when men like Bjarni would rule, and men like Skarphedin pass away. It was coming to be rare for a man to know more of the sword than the plough or the lathe or the forge. Skarphedin was revered in battle, but in peace men turned their eyes away.

* * *

On the next day we lined the men up to see how many were still sober, of the same mind and had not lost an arm or a leg since we asked them. They were a fair bunch, one or two somewhat older than I would have wished, but then I was no longer a boy myself. Indeed I felt older then than I do now, each day I wrenched myself from my bed as if I was going to my death. Still, I was their chief and as such had a part to play. I spoke bravely of the good ship Skimmer, I could have spoken no better of a vessel twice the size. I told them of the strange lands they would see, and the riches they would gain if they were stout of heart and trusted me.

I took a chicken and shed its blood on the deck of the ship, and of a sudden my gorge was in my throat and it was all I could do not to cast my guts up. Chickens have such thin necks, you see. But I mastered myself and poured wine into the thick water of the river. Perhaps no-one noticed the shaking of my hand and I gathered my wits soon after when I spoke of what they might bring on board. To begin with I knew none of them and all were equal in my eyes, so one chest apiece, that was the rule. As time went on and the good sailors became known and moved before the mast, they gained the right to space in the cargo. I have always found it to be a good ruling. You will be amazed how hard a man will fight to save a ship that carries his own wealth.

When they were scattered about their business Olaf said, "I thought you were going to puke."

"So did I. Did they notice, do you think?"

He shrugged. "Perhaps. It's a sign of a bad conscience, that's what I think. A man has a duty to his wife, child or no child."

I looked at good, solid Olaf who never saw more than the surface of a thing. To him if there was an insult and you made it good it was as if the offense had never been. He could not believe that it might rankle and he would not thank you for telling him.

"She does not want me to stay," I said.

"What has that to do with it? You could sweeten her if you wanted. Yet here you are not even bothering to go and say goodbye." He shook his head wonderingly and I was back again to when we were boys. Just so had he looked when I fought with a lad three years older and was slow to make it up.

"It is not so simple," I said, and could find no words to explain it to him.

He was upset because I would not talk to him and held himself aloof through all the shouting and bawling that comes before setting off. One man tried to bring a fur cape aboard that took up the space of two men and would be soaked within a day.

"My wife wants me to take it," he bleated, so we slung it at his pale and sobbing wife, wringing her hands on the quay, and we pushed off. It is best to get away quickly. I myself found it hard not to search the crowd for a face that was not there.

"Together—pull!" cried Olaf, as Skimmer swung out into the tide, but it was a ragged effort and I swore at them.

"Do you want them to think you a load of girls? Put some muscle into it!"

I took an oar myself to give them the stroke, and the weight of it came back like remembered pain. I felt the cracking of muscles in my arms as I pulled, and at once I shifted to move the strain to my back. One forgets the knack so easily. The men around were grunting and spitting and one caught the flesh of his finger and cursed. I dreaded to think of the picture we made, our proud boat with its bushel of spears at the stern, the shields ranged smartly along the sides, and crewed by a bunch of landlubbing whoremongers who could no more row than fly. Olaf moved amongst us, advising and correcting, and soon we were more respectable, though sadly we were out of sight of the town by then.

"I had forgotten how hard it is," said the man behind me. "If I'd remembered I'd still be at home."

I laughed and swung my oar one-handed, for it is important for them to think you strong. If a man sees his leader working without strain when he himself is near to breaking, he will think "If he can do it then surely so can I" and he must never know that his leader is wondering how long it will be before his heart bursts. The men who slave in the galleys die like that, with the blood coming up through their mouths like a fountain.

We traveled slowly for we had to correct the trim and arrange the men properly before we reached the sea. I knew that in just a few days we would be back in the way of it, but at the beginning men fell over one another and grew angry simply because they were unused to the cramping. There is no room at all in a ship, and if ever you find there is then leave it at once because it is sure to be on fire. What with men and stores and cargo, one man's sneeze is another's pain in the back. One grows used to it, that is all that can be said.

We stopped that night in a patch of reeds where we thought no-one could come upon us soundlessly. Men eased aching backs and put salve on their blisters. My own hands were hard still from the farm, it was a different sort of pain I had to face. It seemed that all around men were going to something, be it riches or family, adventure, or even just a different sky each morning. Whatever I might say to myself I was the one that was running away. It came to me that I could leave now, only telling the watch that I had to go ashore and not coming back. Half a day would see me at the farm.

I felt a sudden desire for a woman, something that had not troubled me in months. I remembered how it had been with Emma, losing myself in the soft billows of her breasts, plunging in her till she wept. No woman would be as sweet to my taste as Emma, I thought. And yet—it was as if I had been eating a meal, a good hot meal that pleased me, and a friend called before it was half gone. I went away for a little and when I came back the food was cold. I was not hungry enough, it was not hot, whatever the cause we could not come together happily, that food and me. There is never a good time to go back.

The dawn mist woke us, lying heavy across the river. Heron nested in the reeds where we rested and flapped like huge ghosts in the damp air. All noise was muffled as if by a blanket but above us the sun shone bright. As we set to our oars and I gave the order to pull the mist cleared and the water was speckled with gold. The fog in my head cleared also.

I became busy with the business of the ship. My mind was taken up with the men and their differences, for it was as well to learn them before our lives should rest on a thing unknown. There was a tang in the air that was of the sea. I felt my heart lift a little. The warmth of the sun reached my bones once again.

A longship passed us on its way upriver to Jorvik. There were gaps in the shieldwall and the men rowed like veterans.

"Well met!" I hailed, and the chief nodded to us warily, for the boat was loaded deep and they were in no mood to lose what they had brought so far. It came to me that if it had been night we could have had them, but it was too close to home and they were battlehard while we were home-fed boys on an outing. So I smiled and waved and smelt again the sharp excitement of life waiting to be molded in a man's hands like a pot.

As the day wore on we met fishing boats with a catch to sell, and we took good herring on board. The fishermen eyed us strangely.

"You'd do better to stay at home," said one. "There's no new prizes to be had."

"The world's a lot bigger than you think, my friend," I said. "And there's more to life than a few fish and a lusty wife."

I was thinking of Olaf's woman, and perhaps Olaf was also for he looked thoughtful.

"Would you be named Sigurdsson?" asked one of the fishers.

I looked more closely at him, but even under the salt I did not know him. "Who wishes to know?" I asked, for no man wants to admit to a debt or some such.

"You do not know me. I recognized the ship. There is a message from your brother."

"He would not send a message," I said. "Besides, he would send it to the farm."

The fisherman shrugged. "I was told to pass it on, it means nothing to me. Your brother told a man in Wessex who took ship for the East Angles. We put in there and he told me, that is all." He began to coil a rope and wind up the net in the way they have, that seems all tangled and yet comes out straight. We do it better in Vestfold.

"I am Sigurdsson so you can give me the message," I said, and my heart pumped a little hard.

The fisher hawked and spat. "Your brother is accused of stealing. They were waiting to bring him before Guthorm, for it looks like there's a plot against him. He's upset someone's wife or something. I was told to say he did not ask for help, but only sent the message."

I let out my breath in a gasp. "May the whoreson leper rot! He's been climbing up the wrong skirts again, that's the story! And now he wants me to rescue him."

"Will you go?" Olaf was picking at his teeth with a twig. He watched me with steady brown eyes. Just so had Emma watched me, saying, "Leave him, Thorkil, he's grown." Was I now to leave him to have his hands cut off?

"He has Skarphedin," said Olaf.

"Thank the gods for it. Chances are by the time I got there it would be over. Will the boy never grow up?"

The men were looking at me, anxious in case I should leave them. I turned back to the fisher. "How long has this been coming to me? Will it be over now?"

"I think it has taken two or three weeks to get here," he said thoughtfully, balancing on the deck as if born to it. Perhaps he was. I nodded my thanks and tossed him a coin. He at once took out his knife and nicked it to see if it was good, and since every man does that sometimes you can get a coin as frilled as a girl's skirt.

We pulled away and went on. I sat in the stern watching the dip and sway of the men's backs. More than one had joined us because of my name. Was I now to go nursemaiding once again? What if I left my ship and found all settled when I got there?

The river was wider now, soon we would reach the sea. I said to Olaf, "If it had come three days sooner I would have gone to him."

"It's time he stood on his own two feet," said Olaf.

"Aye, but will he still have them left to stand on?" We looked at each other and laughed. All at once my heart and my will came together, like two horses in a wagon. They would pull together and take me across the sea. In the end a man's fate is his own, woven to his own pattern, I could not shape Bjarni's and he had no hand in mine. Brothers we were, but men before that.

"We will set the sail," I said and felt my heart rising on a new, fair wind.

Chapter
Seven

THEY HAD KEPT dogs in this hole before him, great brown hounds, they kept them for going after boar. They roamed round the pit unchained and Bjarni would have given anything for even so little freedom. He wondered what had happened to the dogs, for no-one hunted these days, the country was too troubled. Perhaps they had sold them. Perhaps Thorkil would see them in some market and say, "Fierce enough, eh? I wonder where they're from."

Tears pricked at his eyelids and he slumped back on the greasy straw, forgetting the chain. It caught him a blow on the cheek and the sudden stab of hurt was too much for him, he began to sob and snuffle. They said he had stolen some silver and taken another man's wife. Well, he had. Except that the silver was stolen long before he took it and now they had it back, and as for the wife, he'd lay money he wasn't the first strange tup in that field, only the first to be caught. If she'd kept quiet they'd both be a lot better off now and that was a lesson to be learned; no more restless wives.

If they took off his hand he wouldn't have anyone, women were funny about things like that. He'd rather be dead, but more than that he'd rather be free! Bjarni heaved on the chain, straining till his joints cracked, but all that was achieved was a little lessening of his inner, burning rage and two weals on his wrists. Besides, the grating was ten feet up and next to it one of Guthorm's guards, that needed to chop a head a day to keep himself sweet. No escape. No hope but a hasty message that might not even reach its destination.

The tears welled again and Bjarni fought them, for they were shameful proof of his poor courage, and for once there was no way of hiding it. Olaf joked about his fear before a battle and Thorkil's hand trembled before the fight, but neither was truly afraid. They did not, could not know how Bjarni's stomach churned itself liquid, how his very fingers tingled, until it was all he could do not to turn and run away. It was the battle he feared, but more than that he feared his own terror. There was no place for a man without courage.

The bars of light on the grating were starting to dim, so that was another day almost gone. Soon they'd bring him some food and then he'd spend hours in chilly dozing, waiting for the dawn. You'd think Guthorm could remember him a little, ask after him perhaps, or send a blanket. Guthorm favored him. The uneasy thought came that he might favor Sven also, who was a Dane and fought in his guard. Again Bjarni thought, this can't be real; people like me, they know my brother, and besides, I've done nothing others haven't.

The grating was moving aside. As he expected, they were bringing the food.

"Come on up, Sigurdsson." A rope was dangling down to him. Bjarni blinked at it for a long moment and then with sudden, surging hope grabbed at it and scrambled up from the hole, tripping at the top over his chain. He shaded his eyes from the light, covered in straw and dog mess, knowing himself to stink.

"They keep their rats in a sound pen."

Bjarni jumped. He turned round slowly, trying to brush away some of the straw. "I'm sorry if you've been troubled on my account," he mumbled. "It's really all nothing—"

"Foolish boy's games," snapped Skarphedin. He stood short and wide and glowering. "For you I have humbled myself. Come. Guthorm would speak with you."

They walked away together, one tall and beautiful, the other as ugly as a dwarf, and yet it was Bjarni that felt small and foolish and weak. Skarphedin had his swordbelt looped across his shoulder, a habit he had taken to of late for it held the blade away from him as he walked. It tapped Bjarni's leg at every stride, like a little caning.

Guthorm held court in a great stone hall, with screens at

either end. He was a softer man than Halfdan, there were
women about him and he liked music. As they entered,
shielded from view by the screen, someone was playing a
pipe and the talk was hushed. Skarphedin cocked his head to
listen and Bjarni looked at him. As the notes played clear and
sweet Skarphedin's face smoothed, like linen when it is pressed.
If he had known how to smile he would have done so, but the
scar held his mouth in a grimace. When the tune ended he
turned to Bjarni and said, "I would forgive you much if you
knew music. Come." They rounded the screen and made
their unequal progress through the hall.

Guthorm's high seat was pillared with oak and it was
carried with him from place to place. He sprawled in it, a
little the worse for drink, wagging his grizzled head as someone spoke to him. He sat up when he saw Skarphedin approaching, and gestured his plump wife to leave. She slipped
behind the far screen, summoning her ladies with a lifted
finger and they went to her like a flock of bright birds.

Bjarni smiled at one and she wrinkled her nose at him. He
was so good-looking was Bjarni Sigurdsson, but not a man
you could ever take seriously.

Skarphedin stopped a distance from the high seat with men
ranging the benches on either side, anxious to see how much
honor was to be conferred on the berserk. Guthorm had
never liked him.

"Guthorm."

"Skarphedin." He did not rise to his feet.

"I am come to pay the *wergild* for this boy," said
Skarphedin, and he unlooped his sword and rested it before
him. "If you wish I will pay it in blood."

Guthorm raised an eyebrow. "Come, come, Skarphedin,
we are talking only of a little silver."

"He is the brother of my friend and we are talking of
honor. I have never known that to be counted in silver."

There was a silence. Then Guthorm said, "Bjarni Sigurdsson,
you are accused of taking another man's goods. I know not
what those might be—" there was a ripple of laughter along
the benches "—but it seems that something was lost. Would
it damage your honor to pay for it?"

Bjarni began to grin, caught Skarphedin's eye and grimaced instead. He licked his lips. "I am inexperienced in

these matters. I can only say that if there's been a mis-
understanding I will gladly settle it.''

"She thought that you loved her!" yelled a voice and was
drowned in laughter.

Skarphedin's face grew taut. He lifted his eyes as if to look
far beyond the present unruly scene. Bjarni glanced uncomfortably at him, longing to join in the laughter and knowing
that to do so would be to side with a mob against his brother's
friend.

Guthorm raised a hand for silence. "I will take a payment,'
he said at last. "I will pass it on in silver. I will take
Skarphedin's service for a year.''

There was a gasp. Skarphedin owed no duty to Guthorm.
"It is too much," said Skarphedin in his thin, passionless
voice.

"Then I will take the boy's hand.''

All urge to laugh left Bjarni with the color that drained
from his face. He was suddenly aware of his hands, each so
cleverly made, working so well at his bidding, even now
clenching obediently at his sides. Surely no-one could do
such a thing? Other men lost their hands, other people went
through life crippled, but never, ever him! His fingers tingled
with terrified life, it was his own sign of fear and now so very
meaningful.

Skarphedin stepped forward and drew his sword from its
sheath. He swung it in a slow circle at the length of his long,
strong arm. "This is Claw of the Raven," he said softly.
"You seek to bind him. Why do you want this from him,
Guthorm? Will it make the gods love you? We shall see. You
demand what could have been yours as a gift and you shall
have your prize. When the greater one is lost to you remember this day, for the gods will not forget it.''

The sword whirled in a circle of light, it passed a breath
from Guthorm's beard and sent men crashing backwards away
from the ice-sharp blade. Bjarni stood stockstill, his heart
thudding with slow relief. When Skarphedin left the hall with
his rolling stride Bjarni followed close behind, for all the
world like a dog.

Bjarni sat uncomfortably by the hearth with Skarphedin. He
wondered if everyone felt as unhappy alone in his company,
including Guthorm. It seemed likely. Skarphedin made peo-

ple feel threatened and unsure, he looked through doors that
others preferred to keep closed, it was only Thorkil who
never seemed uneasy with him.

As if catching the thought Skarphedin said, "I did this for
your brother, not you."

"I'm sorry. You needn't have—I thank you. I was foolish.
Will you take me for your shieldsman, Skarphedin? I owe it
to you."

Skarphedin eyed him gloomily. "You lack courage. Go
fight with the boys and leave the men to the killing."

"All boys grow up," said Bjarni.

"That is an untruth if ever I heard one. I cannot see you
standing close in the fight."

"I can try. If I fall then the matter's settled. But you need
someone. The things Thorkil did for you—I can do them. He
is your friend and I am only his brother, but I can do this for
you. I must."

Skarphedin thought. It was true he was finding life hard
without someone to smooth the way for him. Now he was
condemned to spend the year with Guthorm, who did not
honor him. Bjarni's help might be worth the irritations of his
presence. Skarphedin stood and began to unbuckle the belt
that held his sheepskin tight around his waist. "Go find me a
woman," he said.

The summer days slipped away like links on a golden chain.
Bjarni stayed bound in uneasy servitude, he and Skarphedin
held together by mutual need, separated by mutual distrust.
The army moved constantly but the battles were few. The
futility of it weighed heavy and brought even Skarphedin to
conversation. One autumn day as they urged their ponies over
the broken cobbles of a road he said, "Your brother was right
to put to sea."

Bjarni was taken aback. "When did he do that?"

"In the summer."

"But who is at the farm?"

"Only the spider. She will weave herself a fine web, all
alone in her own dark corner. But now she must catch another
fly."

"I never knew what made Thorkil so mad for her. She's
not like us."

"She is a witch. Every man that looks at her thinks only of

the bedding. Brother or not you would have tried it if you had dared.''

They rode on a little, with Bjarni pondering this unexpected news. He looked at Skarphedin. ''Did you ever want to lie with her?''

There was a silence. At length Skarphedin said, ''I am still a man, for all my ugliness.''

Bjarni supposed that it was true. From time to time he went and found a whore and brought her to Skarphedin. He put her into the dark house and sat outside until it was over, and though he paid them twice what they asked they would never come again. The girls sometimes refused to let him touch them at all and the word had spread so that Bjarni found it harder and harder to find someone. It gave him a sense of what it was like to be Skarphedin.

''Will Thorkil come back?'' he asked.

The dark man looked away to where a few huts burned. The cries of cattle and women rose in the air. ''Perhaps. She has clouded his mind, it will take time for the sea to clear it.''

''She's only a woman'' said Bjarni.

''She's a witch.''

The army encamped for some months, waiting for no-one knew what. When Christmas came the whole of Wessex celebrated, and King Alfred's army stood down and went home, as was the custom. Guthorm called Skarphedin to speak with him, in the great stone hall that was so chill men's breath formed clouds that froze on their beards. Guthorm sat enveloped in a fur, but he shed it when Skarphedin entered. The berserk watched warily as Guthorm stepped down to him.

''I am so glad you could come, Skarphedin.'' The chief stretched out a hand but Skarphedin did not take it and instead looked away to the empty window high in the stonework, where the snowflakes blew in on the gale.

''You may save your sweet words,'' he snapped. ''I fight for my honor, not yours.''

Guthorm withdrew his hand and coughed. He would have liked to go back to his fur but he dared not. Men were saying that he had offended Skarphedin and soured the luck, that they could not win Wessex if the berserk was out of temper and whispered to his god.

"Will you take ale?" Guthorm wheedled, but Skarphedin never moved his eyes from the window. He seemed at once so noble and so contemptuous that all around him became tawdry, venal and dishonored. Guthorm felt his temper slipping. "We are to march on the West Saxon king and take him in his hall," he snapped. "The men will go more easily if they know you are with them in heart as well as body. I called you here to ask for your word on it."

"Who is this Guthorm to ask for the word of a bondsman?" Skarphedin murmured, as if talking to himself. "Is he a king or something much less? For how should a man tell?"

The color began to rise in Guthorm's neck. Men were listening to the encounter, he could not afford to be bested. Yet Skarphedin held the luck and must be tamed. "Where is Sigurdsson?" he demanded and men ran to look. In the minutes of waiting Skarphedin stood motionless while Guthorm and the rest eyed him uncomfortably.

At last Bjarni came in, snow spattering his hair. "Skarphedin."

No reply. The berserk seemed to be entering a trance. Guthorm gestured to Bjarni and drew him aside.

"What's the matter with him?" he whispered.

"He is offended. He thinks you do not honor him."

"The men think he's going to curse me. I tell you this, Sigurdsson, we are to strike at Alfred in the next few hours. We must have his luck with us. What shall we do with him?"

Bjarni thought for a moment. He wished that Thorkil was here, he alone understood how to handle Skarphedin. How would Thorkil have done it? By making Guthorm surrender a thing first.

"You must release him from his bond," said Bjarni firmly. "Ask him to serve you as a gift. It's all you can do."

"Curse it, that is your bond!" snapped Guthorm.

Bjarni returned his gaze blandly. "It is what upsets him, sir."

Guthorm shot him a darkling glance and slouched back to Skarphedin, turned to stone in the center of the floor.

"Skarphedin," he said grimly. "I was wrong to seek to bind you. It was foolish and I am sorry for it. Today I release you. If you would serve us in this battle we would count it a great honor for us all."

Very slowly Skarphedin's head moved from its rigid, up-ward gazing and turned to look at Guthorm. "Is it a king after all?'' he said thinly. ''Does he see now that he cannot trick the gods?''

''I was wrong,'' said Guthorm, the words almost strangling in his throat.

All at once Skarphedin laughed, and it raised the hairs on the backs of men's necks. ''My luck is with you, Guthorm. Show me your shieldwall, I will take its center. Skarphedin will bring you the victory.''

All around rose voices, joining together in a great shout. ''The victory! We shall have the victory!'' and the echo warmed cold hearts. Men that had doubted went eagerly to put on armor, they kissed their wives as if going out for a morning's hunting. In the midst of it Bjarni felt a shiver.

''Come,'' said Skarphedin and clamped a thick hand on his shoulder, a gesture more familiar than any before. Bjarni's smile was less than weak. ''Now you will learn what it is to be a warrior,'' said the berserk happily. ''We will sink our teeth into these Saxons, we have waited long enough.''

They went together into the bitter wind, that at least hardened the ground and made it possible to travel.

''We took oaths on the holy ring,'' said Bjarni.

''What, to hold off from them? It is their foolishness that they believe them.''

''We have sent hostages too. They will suffer.''

''This Alfred is a soft man. Guthorm knows that.''

Bjarni nodded, suddenly depressed. He did not want to die in a bloody, frenzied battle against men who believed themselves to be at peace. He did not want to count this wild man as a friend. He held himself rigid under Skarphedin's comradely hand.

They rode through fields dusted with snow. Once rich, Wessex was a land in torment, with good crops burned and cattle only bleached bones in a ditch. It unnerved Bjarni to see the haunted faces of the people.

''You need not fight with me if you are afraid,'' said Skarphedin, his eyes fixed on a point lost in the blossomflakes of snow.

''I should be ashamed to desert you,'' muttered Bjarni. ''But this is a filthy fight.''

Skarphedin grunted. The rights and wrongs of battle had

never concerned him, it was the fight itself that mattered.
"This Alfred is a soft boy," he declared.

Bjarni let out his breath crossly. "He is not soft. He is a
good and clever king, he cares for his people. Men at his
court read books."

"Books?" Skarphedin was shocked.

"Yes, books. When I saw him before I thought—this is a
higher thing. He tries to learn and understand, with him it
isn't just grab, clutch, take, how much did it cost? It shames
me to let him see what we can do. When we cheat him it is
we who are dishonored."

Skarphedin shook his head somberly. "I worry about you,
Bjarni. There is a taint here. It is of their religion."

The ponies trudged on, stumbling here and there over the
ruts. The noise of their passing hung in the cold air, the chink
of harness and mail, the murmur of talk, the misty gasping of
animals and men. Bjarni hitched at his thick wool breeks,
patched at the sides with leather. He was heavy with fear, but
was it fear of the battle or only of being seen to be frightened? If only Thorkil were here, to lighten the moment with a
joke, to take the responsibility.

It was almost dark. They were to creep through the dusk on
foot and fall upon a feasting hall. When the time came to
dismount Bjarni's guts were churning.

"Do not fear, little one," sang Skarphedin in his nasal
drone. "Death is a cradle and pain your lullaby."

"They are not expecting us," hissed Bjarni, but Skarphedin
was moving into the distant state of excitement which was for
him the purpose of war. He hummed to himself and now and
then chuckled softly.

Men who thought themselves brave and wished to prove it
clustered around Skarphedin. Bjarni looked at their blackened
faces and felt like a rabbit in a pen of stoats, as yet unrecog-
nized but soon to be unmasked. Oh to have Thorkil before
him, and solid Olaf with his calm eyes. He fingered his sword
anxiously.

They did not quite catch the court unawares. One of those
white-faced peasants had run through the fields to bring desperate warning and when the Danes came upon the stockade
they found the gates barred, with warriors bristling the palisade. Bjarni sighed with sudden relief. He could not have
borne to fall upon peaceful merriment. It was very dark. He

remembered the night they had taken Jorvik, when he had felt a thrill as well as terror at the coming fight. Now there was nothing but the terror and it was hard to bear. This was no way to die, nor even to live. Above the fence rose the dark shape of the great wooden circle where the people sat when their king spoke to them. Bjarni had been amazed when he saw it, and humbled too. It was easy enough to burn such a thing down, but who amongst his people could build it? The king also, so small and grave and courteous, had seemed something finely made. In his presence Bjarni felt a barbarian.

Skarphedin took his place at the gate, ready to storm it. Men brought a tree trunk to batter at it with only a little rain of arrows to impede them, sure sign of few men within. Skarphedin was singing again, high, thin and eerie. As the gate splintered the sound thickened to a growing howl and the northmen flew to the fight on the wings of his battlepledge.

A face appeared before Bjarni, nameless in its helmet. He put his shield to it and sliced with his sword, striding on over the twitching limbs. He must keep beside Skarphedin, howling as he ploughed a bloody furrow through the enemy. The soil was greasy with blood. He saw Horda fall, not to a killing stroke, and screamed "Someone get Horda!" to those behind who were less pressed. A pike missed his groin by a hairsbreath, but his sword did not miss the pikeman. Skarphedin was ahead and unprotected. Bjarni lunged past a shield and took his place again. They had put their best men at the gate, the battle was become a bloody, thrashing struggle, with the breath of your enemy on your cheek as you thrust at him. Skarphedin was invincible, his sword leisured, almost peaceful as it struck and struck again. Bjarni was lulled by the rhythm of it, swinging at his side as he matched his will against that of the man before him.

Then they were through. There was space and good ground beneath your feet. Skarphedin went howling forward and Bjarni stumbled after him, his wits confused by the suddenness of it. A child stood in a doorway sobbing, and was snatched by his mother back into the dark house. Bjarni wished he had not seen that. They were firing the buildings, great halls with their shining wood and stone going to nothing in a roar of smoke and flame. When he had come there before he had seen books painted in green and gold, embroidery so rich it was like jewels. It was all burning.

Soon they were gathered in a knot before the greatest hall of all.

"Did they get the king?" men were asking. "Guthorm wants him alive."

"He would not be alive if I had seen him," gasped Skarphedin. He was near to falling and Bjarni took his arm.

"He escaped while they held us at the gate," he said. It was a relief to him. When Ivarr captured King Edmund it was said he had carved the blood eagle on him, taking his lungs from his back and spreading them wide like wings. Alfred was a greater king than ever Edmund had been.

The strength was draining out of him like so much water. "Come, Skarphedin," he said. The two men looped their arms around one another and staggered away.

They were weary still in the morning. The army was despondent; if they did not have Alfred they did not have Wessex. It was said that Guthorm was furious.

"He will blame us for it," said Bjarni.

"He would do better to blame his own foolishness. Odin does not forget."

There were grooves of fatigue on Skarphedin's face. It occurred to Bjarni that he did not know how old Skarphedin was, he seemed ageless, like wood. Perhaps the little stiffnesses of the passing years were not unknown to him. As he himself said, despite his looks he was as other men. Suddenly Bjarni was near to tears. He ducked his head into his chest and blinked at them, but in the end he hid his face in his hand.

"You fought well," said Skarphedin. "I did not think you had it in you."

Bjarni sniffed. "There's no pleasure in killing."

"You deceive yourself. There is a joy in killing, and you feel it as much as the rest of us. You do not want to feel it, that is all. You were with your mother too long, boy."

After a time Bjarni went out to see if he could discover what was happening. He hated the morning after a battle, with the pain and the terror. He hated to see pretty women cry. Surprisingly men hailed him with respect, one even saying to him, "How long before you hold Claw of the Raven, I wonder?" but carefully, in case Bjarni should take offense.

"That's not for me," he said quickly.

"There is no other that Skarphedin trusts."

Bjarni nodded but walked away. The smell of charred wood hung in the air with the smell of damp wool, for the hangings had been part burned before someone doused them. It was all ruined. All the loveliness that he remembered was gone. The great wooden seating place where Guthorm had met with Alfred was no more than charred timbers pointing accusingly to the sky. In his rage Guthorm was burning everything, his men were even smashing the stones in the graveyard. It had been such a gracious place, it seemed to Bjarni that here he had glimpsed life on a gentler plane. It was to do with their religion of course, they had no fierce gods. They were easy prey to a wilder faith.

He was glad that Alfred had slipped away, that small and sickly king who had such fineness in him that even Guthorm was affected, and made treaties he did not intend to keep. Guthorm's anger now was part embarrassment, that Alfred should know him false. For he was like a father, grieved but forgiving, ceaselessly urging his young children to strive for the better thing, pointing another way than destruction. They would be chasing Alfred again, that much was clear. The Saxons would not surrender until the king was gone and perhaps not even then, so there would be fighting aplenty, if that was what he wanted.

It seemed to Bjarni that he stood at a crossroads in a mist, without even a stick to help him find his way. Here he was now, close to Skarphedin and glory. One little step further and he too would be blacking his face and howling. It was a strange thing but when he had first gone into battle it had all seemed frenzied and without form, blows fell from all directions without reason. Now there was a pattern to it. He knew why Skarphedin was never marked, it was a sense that came to you, of the skill and the fear of the men around. He had learned it, as Bjarni was learning now. He rose in the battle to link his spirit to the men he would kill. There was no passion like it, and when it was raging all else seemed weak and pale. In a little time Bjarni too would be living for the fray.

Yet where did the other roads lead? One trudged back to the farm, where nothing was his and he had no place except to be always the younger brother. It was a comfort to him, thinking of it, but he would not go back yet awhile. He might see how Emma was doing, but no more than that. A man does his living and then goes home to tell of it.

He remembered that he was hungry, and that Skarphedin would be also. He rose from the charred bench on which he sat and went slowly back through the cold streets, his cloak muffled about him. A woman caught his arm, a Dane.

"I am Horda's wife" she said. "You saved him."

"Not me. I saw him fall only."

"He told me what you did." There were smudges like soot running into the creases of her eyes. Bjarni stared at her a little too long, his mind drifting to other times, other women. "You are a good man, Bjarni Sigurdsson. My thanks to you."

They parted and he went on, a little comforted.

They learned that Alfred had fled to Athelney, a place of swamp and tangled bushes. He hid there with his family and Guthorm was on his trail like a rootling boar. But the sullen, weary people would not give him up, torture and kill as the Danes might. Tales began to spread, telling of Alfred and a few brave men harrying the enemy when they least expected it. The tales grew in the telling, but the Saxons would not settle and Danish farmers could not sleep easy in their new-found beds. They complained again and again to Guthorm, who responded fiercely, leaving whole tracts of Wessex empty of people. Still the fight went on, it was like trying to squash bubbles in a boiling pot. After a day spent burning farms they had burned before, Bjarni and Skarphedin slumped together by the fire.

"It sticks in my throat," said Bjarni.

"Be patient. There is a battle coming, I feel it in my bones."

"I'm not waiting for it." He wiped a thick sweat. That day they had gathered the people into a little knot while they fired the buildings. One of the girls was pretty, but they did not touch her, they were hated enough as it was. Bjarni had smiled at her, to take the edge from what they were doing, and she had spat full in his face. For a moment he had known the urge to kill her. It frightened him.

Skarphedin scraped a piece of bread round his bowl and ate it thoughtfully. "Where will you go?"

"The farm. Best see how Emma is."

"You won't see much from a witch's bed."

"I'm not going for that." It occurred to him that he had not slept with a woman in months. He was almost shocked. He had become like Skarphedin, saving all his passion for the fight. The two men's eyes met.

"Whose brother are you now, I wonder?" said Skarphedin.

Bjarni put out his hand and clasped his shoulder.

They parted in the morning, Skarphedin walking away quickly with his rolling gait, Bjarni swinging a leg over his little, shaggy pony. It was raining and the roads were muddy slop. He had never felt so lonely. As he rode he passed Danes that he had drunk with once, and they saluted him cautiously. He was apart from them, they were not his friends. Who was his friend, except Skarphedin? In a little while the rain ceased and here and there in the decimated country someone worked at the plough. A man might think that all was ended but it was never so. Bjarni wondered if he might make a farmer yet.

He came to a river landing where a bargeman worked slowly loading timber.

"Will you take me to the coast?" he asked.

The man had but one eye, it swiveled unnervingly. "For a price."

"Make it the horse," said Bjarni and swung down.

"I don't need a horse," said the bargeman.

"If you need your life you'll take it."

He left the pony tied to a bush and went to sit in the barge. His beard itched, he wondered if it might have lice in it. Come the summer he would swim every day, he was tired of dirt and cold. While he sat there the sun came out. He was surprised and turned his face up to it. Had there been any sun in this winter with Skarphedin? If so he had not seen it. They had lived, the two of them, in an underworld. Only now was he climbing up into the light.

Chapter
Eight

THEY WERE BUILDING a new bridge over the river in Jovik. Bjarni stood and watched for a time as the wagons trundled to and fro, bearing their loads of wood and stone. A row broke out when two spars slipped into the water, narrowly missing a boat, and it only ended when someone got a ducking. Bjarni laughed and went on his way.

He had no money for a horse and was forced to hitch a lift on a wagon traveling round the farms selling dye and cloth and pots.

"Do you go to my sister's farm?" asked Bjarni. "The Grove Farm, Shiptonthorpe."

The carter shook his head. "They don't need nothing. They've got their own trade they have."

It was a bumpy ride and Bjarni was glad to step off at a farm some miles from his own. They had spent the night sleeping under the wagon and he was stiff and hungry, he would enjoy a walk with the promise of a good meal at the end of it. He picked up his pack with its few belongings, looped his sword over his shoulder and set off.

It was a blustery day and the still leafless trees swayed like girls dancing. He thought that he should have brought Emma a present, she had been very kind to him in the past. The thought of a good fire and spiced ale spurred him on, he would take her a bunch of the little yellow flowers that grew like stars in the grass. When they were gathered he stuck them in his pack, as his goodluck charm as well as his gift. Where the track was narrow spiders' webs tangled in his hair.

Soon he stood on the hill above the farm and looked down upon it. Three or four geese wandered about and smoke rose from the house, the sewing shed and the forge, speaking of work and people. A woman stepped from the house to the barn, but it was not Emma. She carried a heavy pail. Bjarni began to scramble down the hill, filled with a joyful sense that he was coming home. The geese began to cackle. "Emma! Emma!" he called. The gander was hissing at him and Bjarni was marooned at the entrance, with the geese wildly hissing and flapping their wings.

Emma came to the door of the house. She was dressed in green with a scarlet overtunic and a little green cap was set on her lush bronze hair. The strong face, skin as white as milk, broke into wreathing smiles. "Bjarni! It can't be! Have you dropped from the clouds, come in, come in."

"I would if these brutes would let me. I hardly recognize you, Emma."

She sent the geese away with a wave of her skirt and Bjarni went to take her in his arms. "You look so rich! Silver brooches no less and I'll swear these beads are amber. All this from corn and cows?"

"And sheep, and pigs and hens and cloth and cheese and butter and—everything. We work hard here." She squeezed his arm as he held her. "You've got a man's muscle, lad."

"I have indeed." He was suddenly aware that he was holding her and at once let go. She smelled of violets. "I am filthy, Emma, and half starved. Any chance of a bath and a meal for a poor soldier?"

She turned her back to go into the house, saying over her shoulder, "Not so poor if I know anything of it. Did you win much?"

"Nothing."

She swung round in the doorway. "But they are rich in Wessex."

"Aye. But I fought with Skarphedin."

Her face became still. After a moment she went into the house and Bjarni followed.

There were hams hanging from the rafters, brushing against bunches of herbs and dried flowers. The place smelled of food and warmth and spice. The yellow flowers that Bjarni had picked were here already, scattered in the rushes on the floor.

"I brought you the wrong flowers," he apologized, holding out his posy.

"They are welcome just the same. They are monk's hood." She twisted a stem with deft fingers and tied the blossoms in her girdle. Bjarni was touched.

"But where is the child?" he asked, suddenly jovial. "Let me see my nephew. It was a boy, wasn't it?"

Emma did not reply. She went instead to the pitcher, but her hands fumbled and she splashed ale on her dress.

"Was it a boy?" asked Bjarni again, feeling unsure.

She nodded. "It was a boy. It died." She thrust the cup at Bjarni and bustled to the door, calling for the girl to come quickly and stop loafing around where no-one could keep an eye on her, it was an age since she had gone for that milk. The girl rushed from the barn, her pail slopping in her anxiety.

Bjarni raised an eyebrow. Emma was a hard mistress, it seemed.

They fed him ham with peas and bread, all of it as fresh and good as he had imagined. Bjarni wiped a crust round the grain of his plate and said, "I am amazed, Emma. I did not think to find you so prosperous. Tell me, do you have trouble here? Things are not so settled that a woman alone can be sure to keep what she has."

"I can be sure," said Emma and bent to take his plate. Her breast brushed his hair and her long white fingers touched his hand. He felt the heat rising in him, he had forgotten this about Emma.

For a moment he was distracted and then he said, "But who does the work here? Surely Thorkil did not leave you quite alone."

She looked at him wide-eyed. "But for a crippled lad, yes. His name is Leif and he's a Dane. He's a good farmer and not a bad smith either. He'll be in later."

Bjarni did not understand it, either then or when all the household was gathered together, being the two maids, one with a swollen belly, an idiot farmboy and Leif, the Dane. He it was who had been serving the girl, but Emma seemed not to mind how things stood. Bjarni noted that they all spoke to her with respect and somehow it surprised him. The farm seemed too great a concern for a woman.

Again he asked, "Do you have trouble holding the place?"

Emma's eyes were wide, too wide. "I told you, no. We are not so lawless as we were."

Everyone began to chatter, to fill up a space in which he might have asked questions. "We are selling butter to Wicstun now, down the hill," said Emma gaily. "And our own red cloth, we dye it with whelks, do you do that where you come from?"

"I don't know."

"Do you not? How strange." She was nibbling at a hazel-nut, for all the world as nervous as a squirrel.

"Why don't you trade with Jorvik?"

"We do, we do. It's a long way."

"The carter says he brings you nothing."

Emma laughed at him. "You don't trust me, brother! Do you remember Marjolein, Gunnar's wife? She brings me things and takes stuff back, I pay for it. Her husband lost his arm, you know."

He suppressed a small shudder. "I remember."

He sensed that they were passing messages round the table only by looking at each other, but he could not catch it. She had a man in her bed, that was all it could be, the cow had a bull that served her for the sake of her nice green pasture. What a treachery!

"Do you hear from Thorkil?" he asked with a smile.

"We heard that he is in Norway, they said a name but I didn't understand it. Perhaps we'll hear in the summer, more people travel then."

"Yes." There was no hint from her face of what she felt, he had forgotten that about her. The woman was made to be false.

But the tallow dips made pools of yellow light, her hair was rich bronze and the wine felt sweet upon his tongue.

"Tell us all the news," she said, and her lips were soft and moist. She was clouding his mind.

"We didn't catch Alfred," he began.

Emma chuckled. "You see. We're not so stupid after all."

He gazed into her eyes and wondered.

* * *

When it was time to go to bed Emma said "I have made your place ready in the barn, Bjarni."

"I'll be all right here. I'm used to the benches."

"Oh, but it's too uncomfortable! Come, I'll light your way." She took the light from the wall bracket but Bjarni caught her wrist, saying cheerfully, "I'll not sleep in a soft bed, I've grown too tough. Ah, if you knew the places I've slept lately you'd know this is luxury."

He saw Emma bite her lip. He would not go and she knew it. With a pretense at laughter she said, "As you will. You'll be wakened early though, we don't lie in bed here."

"I'm glad to hear it."

She brushed her lips against his cheek and swept off to her chamber, shutting the heavy plank door with more than a little force. Bjarni tapped a finger against his lips and then made his bed close to the fire, simply throwing a thick wool blanket over a bench. Then he went out to piss. It was a starry night. The hillside below was touched with silver, the trees were black shadows and the stream a quiet gurgle in the silence. His water hissed as loudly. When he was done he left his breeks unfastened and stood for a moment, savoring the peaceful night. He noticed that the geese were shut up. When he went to his bed he slipped his dagger under the blanket with him.

After a little he heard a door open, Emma's door. In the dark he saw the white of her shift move stealthily across the room, but he made no move until she passed close to him. Then he shot out a hand and grabbed at her skirt. Emma choked on a shriek and flung her fist at him.

"Let me go, Bjarni! Can't I even leave my own house when I want to?"

Bjarni sat up. "I really don't know, sister. What would you want to leave it for, I wonder?"

"If my stomach is curdled it's my affair. I was trying not to wake you." She went across to the fire and agitatedly stirred the embers, lighting a dip or two from the little flame she found. There was less flesh on her than before, she had more bone than a milch cow that has seen a hard winter. Her hair hung in lush coils to her waist.

"Thorkil should never have left you."

She shrugged. "I was glad to see him go. As you see, we manage here. We do what we must."

"But a woman needs a man in her bed."

She laughed, tightly, and her fingers played with her hair. Bjarni tried to swallow what felt like a stone in his throat. He wondered if he was in love with her, he had never felt so giddy over a woman. Without thought he moved closer to her. What would she do if he touched her? If he cupped her breast in his hand it would weigh heavy as a bag of coin, but oh, so much softer. His fingers, moving with another's will, brushed her thigh.

"He is your brother," said Emma softly.

"I am trying to forget it." He lifted a strand of rich hair and let it fall through his fingers. She watched him, a slight wary smile on her lips, and then she turned away.

"What would you say if I said I was come back for good?" he asked.

"You'd like it no better than last time. I'll not have you in my bed."

"Who then?"

She spun round to stare at him, eyes like clear water. "Attar. You knew it from the first, you waited only to catch me out. How else do you think I've held this place? He is strong enough and rich enough, and I haven't a husband to stand by me."

"Beads and silver brooches," sneered Bjarni, who had only brought flowers.

"Strong men and good horses," snapped Emma. "He could be coming soon, he's late. And don't you dare to be rude to him for he was there when I needed a man which is more than can be said for you or your brother. He's very well respected."

"He licks the right arses you mean." Bjarni hawked and spat on the rushes.

"Don't do that! If you can't behave better than a pig you can go to the barn."

"You're very nice for a whore."

"And you are particular for a heathen. Go away!"

They glared at each other, sharply angry.

"I've nowhere to go," said Bjarni.

"That never stopped a Viking. Go and steal something."

"But what would I do next?"

Emma tipped her head to one side, wondering at him. He seemed almost shy. "You may do what you want," she said helplessly. "See here, Bjarni, you can roam the world only to look at it, it's women and cripples that have to stay at home. What else do you want? What else is there?"

He shrugged and his eyes slid away. She didn't understand, how could she? Like Thorkil she was brave and sure and strong. "I can't go back to Skarphedin," he said.

"If you are sick of killing then we are truly blessed," she sneered, but the bewilderment on his face checked her. He was so like her brother. She reached out a hand to touch him. "We all grow up in the end, lad. You find a place that isn't perhaps all that you would wish, but it's good enough. You're not your brother and neither are you Skarphedin, but there's many another way of doing things. Look at Olaf, when he's gone there'll be good strong ships to mark his passing and that's more than many can say."

There was the sound of a horse in the courtyard. They looked at each other.

"This is my place," said Emma. "It's good enough for me."

"That you should put him before Thorkil!"

"Thorkil isn't here," she hissed, and went to open the door. She stood in the wind with her shift blowing about her and Bjarni thought soon she will lie down for Attar to love her. He hated Attar. Emma stood aside from the door and he came into the house.

He was as neat as ever, his beard trimmed square, his nails white-rimmed. When he saw Bjarni his hand went at once to his sword.

"It's all right," said Emma quickly. "He won't fight."

"I'm glad to hear it," said Attar. "I should hate to hurt you, boy."

He strolled into the room, relaxed but cautious. Bjarni remembered that Attar always had made him feel like a peasant. He threw himself onto a bench and grinned insolently up at the older man. "I've no need for you to make promises, Emma. It's Attar who has to explain himself."

"I'll do nothing of the kind. Who do you think you are, boy? Let's see how cocky you are on the other side of that door, eh?"

"Just try," said Bjarni, and he smiled. The look of him curdled Emma's guts, the anxious boy had gone.

"Leave him," she said to Attar. "He's spoiling for a fight." There was a tautness about Bjarni like wet rope, she knew that in a moment he would kill Attar.

"I don't want him here," said Attar again. "There is no place for him."

"Yet you are in my brother's place. Fucking my brother's wife," said Bjarni and was ready for the lunge. He side-slipped Attar's blade and caught him unbalanced with the dagger. Blood spurted freely and Attar screamed.

"Damn you for a fool, Bjarni," shrieked Emma. "Get out of here. If you've killed him I'll never forgive you."

"It's a gnat bite only," said Bjarni, his nerves jangling with unreleased tension. Attar was breathing without depth, his hands pressed to his side and gore welling between his fingers like mud from a swamp. Bjarni wondered why he had done it. By Thor's hammer, he was more like Skarphedin than he knew.

Emma ran to call the girls, bright bloodstains spreading over her shift. All kindness was gone from her, when she looked at him her face was the face of that girl in the village, who spat at him when he smiled.

Bjarni was sickened at himself, he could not think why he had done this. He wanted to tell Emma, "I'm sorry, I didn't mean it!" if only to have her look kindly again. Why should he grudge her a little loving when Thorkil had abandoned her? How frightened she looked now. And he did not wish Attar dead, in fact he could feel a faint pity for the man lying gasping there, white and in pain. You did not escape Skarphedin just by leaving his side.

"Will he die?" he asked Emma as she rushed for more cloths.

"Go away," she hissed, tears thick in her throat. He saw that her hands were shaking.

Bjarni looked about him, at the warm, clean house with its peace and order that was now cast into confusion by his own unthinking hand. Unnoticed, he picked up his sword, his pack, his few meager belongings, and went out.

The hills were wide and high and lovely. Bjarni trudged them till the wind blew his thoughts away and at night he slept in the bracken. Sometimes he lodged with a Norse family farming the bleak lands and glad to talk to anyone, but mostly people shrank from the wild man with his hair grown long enough to tangle in his beard. One night he fell in with a shepherd guarding his flock in a hurdle pen, and they sat together and ate rabbit, unable to talk but friendly just the same. They were each as wild and strange as the other.

The day came when in the distance the blue of the sky merged into something more solid. He was come to the sea. Bjarni stood on his high hill and knew that the time of his escape was ended. He was sorry and at the same time glad, unfastening his fingers from his loneliness as if letting go of a rope, that bound him as well as held him safe. In dreams he could reach for moonlight and stars and find them in his hands.

He was curious about where he was, for he did not know this coast at all. Out to sea was the dark shape of distant land, visible from this high place. The fancy to visit it came to him. He began to walk the cliffs with a purpose, looking for a village, and when at last he saw a few huts, clustered on the sea's edge like ducklings at the edge of a pond, he at once decided to go down to them. He knelt by a stream of clear water and began to tidy himself, putting on a clean shirt from his pack that was now too tight across his chest. As for his hair, he wet it and combed it back from his face, startlingly fair against the brown of weathered skin.

When he came down to the village the people stared at him, goggle-eyed. He gave them a greeting, uncertain if they would understand him, but they nodded. Some small currachs were drawn up on the beach, by nets hung ready for mending. A young man was there, clutching a gutting knife in a hand too large for his arm, which is a sure sign of a fisherman. Bjarni nodded to him.

"What land is that over there?" From here it was a stain on the sea no bigger than a thumbprint.

"Ireland," said the fisher, feeling the handle of his knife with nervous fingers. Only by looking at him Bjarni could tell he had never fought a man in earnest, and felt the lack. But he had no wish to prove the young man's courage, when a far place called to him. Many riches had come from Ireland.

"I should like to go there," he said, and sat down on a

creel, which was wet. The gutting knife wavered, then disappeared into the lad's wool wrap. Their clothes were hardly sewn at all, they warmed themselves with lengths of cloth bunched round them, men and women both. The lad's legs were bare and brawny.

"There's nothing there that isn't here and better so," he said firmly.

"All the same I've a fancy to look at it."

Now the children, growing brave, were clustering round Bjarni staring at him. Suddenly he made a face at a dark-haired little girl and she ran screaming to her mother. Bjarni laughed at her as she peeped round her mother's skirts.

"Will you eat with us?" asked the lad abruptly. Bjarni nodded and accepted the offer for what it was, rough friendship from a people unused to strangers. Fish hung drying on racks propped against the small dark houses and they ate a stew made of fishes and drank a liquor so strong that it made Bjarni cough.

"This is good," he said weakly.

"A drink for a man," agreed the lad and poured some more, ignoring his mother's furious look. The fire was warm, if very smoky, and in a while Bjarni ceased to notice that everything smelled of fish. He knew he was drunk and wondered if perhaps he was drunker than he had ever been in his life, but if so it was good. He was among friends, this lad and he were close as brothers.

"I wish we had a woman," said Bjarni. "I haven't had a woman in ages."

"I haven't had one at all," said the lad.

Bjarni was at once moved in pity. He clutched his friend to comfort him and such was their comradeship that they began to sob together, wetting each other's beards with their tears. In the midst of it the lad began snoring, but Bjarni continued to weep, wiping his nose on the fisherlad's arm. Life was good sometimes.

In the morning they were like blind men. Bjarni's head throbbed like an open wound.

"We must go down the coast a little," said his friend, his eyes almost closed against the light. "My mother says there's a boat going to Ireland."

"Let's go tomorrow" said Bjarni, who had caught the stench of fishguts and wanted to puke.

"My mother says today."

Bjarni would have grinned if there had been less pain in it. The old woman was a dragon and no mistake, she had this big lad trussed and bound for market. She stood at her door and watched them as they staggered down the beach, to where the little boats were drawn up on the shingle.

"Goodbye mother," called the lad, but she glowered at him.

The boats were of skins stretched across a wood frame, small and light and difficult to row. The lad had the knack of it, and Bjarni slumped in the bottom groaning. After a while he leaned over the side to be sick and felt better. The sea breeze was fresh and clean, blowing his head clear and filling him with strong, sweet air. Already the village was distant. Behind and to the side of them mountains loomed, as solid as the little boat was frail. Little waves lapped against the sides. It was a good day.

"What will you do over there? Will you rob?"

"Not all Norsemen are robbers."

"Are they not? We hear how they fall upon the farms, killing and burning and ravishing the women."

Bjarni laughed. "So you'd like to be a Norseman, eh? Stick to the fishing, it's better in the long run." He craned his head to see round the lad's bulk and as he had thought, he could see a mast. There was a ship close in at a bay, with a village barely larger than the one they had left. As they drew nearer he could see that the vessel was small, only eight benches at a guess and as wide as a nag's mouth. Only by looking he could tell it would roll in any sort of sea.

The lad kept on rowing, sending their little boat forward against a fierce current and soon they were in the shallows. Bjarni leaped out and waded across to the ship. There was a man on deck, small and wide as his ship and working a new block with a chisel.

"That's a handy ship you have there."

"If you think that you're no seaman." Only from the accent Bjarni could tell he was from Norway. He stuck out a hand. "Bjarni Sigurdsson. From Vestfold."

"Gunnar Olaffson. Rogaland." He only nodded at the outstretched palm and Bjarni grinned.

"I'll be straight with you. I'm looking for a trip to Ireland

and I've little enough about me to think of taking ship in this tub, if my stomach will stand it. I'm a fair seaman. Always before the mast.''

Gunnar Olaffson stopped work. "Sigurdsson. Do you have a brother?''

"I tell you now I am not as good as Thorkil. The sea is his mother.''

Gunnar nodded. "You can take an oar, though I warn you we are but five counting you and she's a cow to row. We leave on the tide.''

Bjarni looked about him. "Where are the others?''

"See that bothy at the end there?'' Gunnar stood up in a shower of shavings, the better to point to it. Bjarni was a foot the taller.

"I see it.''

"There's a woman in there will open her legs for a penny.''

Bjarni looked across to where the fisherlad sat patiently by his currach. He thought of the lad's fierce mother, it was a crime for a boy to be hamstrung like that.

"Will you lend me a bit? You can take it out of my pay.''

"Who said anything about pay? But I need an extra man and we brought some good slaves this trip. You're worth something, I suppose. Here.'' Gunnar tossed two coins to Bjarni, who caught them with a supple wrist. The older man raised an eyebrow. "You good with a sword?''

"Yes. I was shieldman to Skarphedin. You may have heard of him.''

Gunnar blinked. "By the Raven. Here lad, have two more and think well of me.'

The girl was stone-faced, she took the money and went alone into the house to hide it. Then she came out and beckoned the lad in. Bjarni sat on a bank and waited, watching the seabirds swoop and call, and behind him through the rag that served as a door hearing the fisherlad grunting. He wondered if he would take a turn at her later, but somehow he didn't feel like it. A man had to be high in drink or passion to use a whore, and this was a country one with no gloss to her. One of the men from the ship said she'd lost her man in a Viking raid and had taken to this out of need.

Two small children were watching him round the end of

the house, thumbs in their mouths. Bjarni looked away. They might not be hers. Then he got up and went to wait by the ship, where he need not look at them.

When the lad came to find him he was flushed and wondering, like a man who has seen a vision. "You are a true friend," he said to Bjarni.

"Why don't you marry her? Then you could have it every night."

The boy laughed uncertainly, for there was no humor in Bjarni's words. "I've got to go now. My mother's waiting."

Bjarni nodded and they hugged each other, swearing to meet again when Bjarni knew that in a week this boy would be long forgotten. But it might be that the boy would not forget a Viking and would speak of his friend to his children.

"Stand up to your mother," he urged, and stood on the shore watching as the lad rowed away.

He picked up his pack and the loop of his sword and made for the ship where men moved grumbling about the deck, making ready to sail. Gunnar tossed him some smoked fish and Bjarni chewed at it while he settled himself. His oar was poorly balanced with the collar too far from the handle, and he adjusted it to suit himself. The others were looking at him from the corners of their eyes. Bjarni gazed out at the waves, whipped by the breeze into stiff crests.

"I apologize now to the man before me," he sang out. "I shall soon be puking down his neck."

"I thought you were a seaman," said a thickset man with a grizzled beard.

"So I am. But my stomach doesn't know it."

They all grinned. "Tell me where you have traveled," said Gunnar, and Bjarni leaned on his oar and told them. Once to the north, with Thorkil, so see the white bears running on the ice. Twice to Denmark, and then a little trip to Francia to make the crossing to England.

"What about the islands?" asked Gunnar. "That is the way for Norwegians. You followed the Danish path."

"But I am come to my senses now," said Bjarni easily. "By the way, have you heard anything of my brother? Last word was from Norway and nothing since."

Gunnar picked a fishbone from his teeth. "I heard he went a-viking to the Rus."

"Did he so? Ah well, he was a good brother once. He never could stand to stay at home, I knew it would lead him into foolishness." He tutted and they laughed.

"My cousin fought with him one time," said the man with the grizzled beard. "He was a good man to follow."

"You look to be of the same mold," said Gunnar. "Lambs from the same ewe."

Bjarni shook his head. "Thorkil leads men. I take care only of myself."

"And Skarphedin," muttered someone.

"As to that, it is a matter for the gods," said Bjarni, and by his face they knew that was not a thing to speak of.

It was a wild crossing with the boat dipping over the short seas like a bucking horse. The wind was gusty and backed the sail from time to time, so that they were forced to keep working the oars only to hold to their course.

Bjarni was not sick though others were, and Gunnar cursed them for puking dogs. Sometimes they shipped water and the boat wallowed while they baled. But after a while they could see the land as a clear dark line between waves and rushing clouds. It seemed that the clouds were gathered in a mass over it, heaped up like smoke from the hearth of a giant. Soon they could see trees and green fields, and behind them the darker stain of hills. Bjarni felt a thrill. It was long since he had come to a new land across the sea.

Once in the shelter of the shore they could take down their sail and row with some semblance of order. They had missed their landing point, which was a place called Dubhlinn, built by the Norsemen at the mouth of a river. They worked slowly up the coast, tired and wet, and before long decided to make a landing and wait till morning before going on. They pulled the boat up on a shingle beach, watched at a distance by wary, dark-eyed people in short tunics that left their legs bare.

"Be warned," said Gunnar to Bjarni. "They are strange people here, and they have dark ways. Keep your sword by you."

"Where do they come from?" asked Bjarni, who could see no dwellings thereabouts.

"They have sod huts in the forest, but they move around. I tell you they're wild, these shorefolk."

Now when Bjarni looked at the tangled figures watching he felt a threat. So he slept that night with his sword close by and woke at the slightest sound.

They went on next day, though it was raining.

"That is the trouble with this country," said Gunnar. "It always rains."

"That's what keeps it so lush, I suppose," said Bjarni. "You feel you could plant a stone here and it would grow."

"Perhaps it would if you found the right spell. They're full of spells and curses here, and you should see their holy men! They're like berserks but without the killing."

Bjarni lifted an eyebrow. He would not be drawn on that subject, he would not live on another's legend.

By noon they were within sight of the rivermouth that led to Dubhlinn. Theirs was a poor vessel in comparison with some, great longships with prows higher than two men, *knorrs* deep enough to hold a herd of cattle. Men hailed them as they rowed and looked hard at Bjarni. He knew that his name and reputation would be known to all before the day was out. There was a feeling both of strangeness and of coming home. He could have been in Kaupang or Jorvik, but the green country proclaimed it to be otherwise. When they tied up at the end of a row of boats each lashed to the other, and all to be crossed before reaching land, he picked up his things and took his leave of Gunnar.

"You can take an oar with me any time," said Gunnar. "We cross each week or so, when we've a load of slaves or what have you."

"I'll remember that. Tell me, where do the slaves come from? The people we saw looked very poor."

"You'll find out, lad. They fight all the time here, us and each other. Take care you don't end up in a slaveship on the way to China, it's not unheard of."

The night found Bjarni lodged in an alehouse, gathered around the fire with some five or six others, and smelling of peat smoke and damp wool. It was the smell he came to know in Ireland and whenever after someone dried a cloak before a fire he was back there in that first lodging, with an unsure feeling that spoke of little money and an empty tomorrow. He would have to earn something, but he had no wish to hump sacks or stoke the fire for a kiln, which was all that seemed likely. Besides, he wished to see a little more of the country than this Norse stronghold with its palisades and flagged walkways, stout matrons and blushing young girls. He could take arms, he supposed, with any of three chiefs, but he was wary of it. It was too soon, he remembered Attar too well. A man can become too thirsty for something he had once thought never to drink.

He asked the man next to him what was valued in this country, and after a little thought he said, "Slaves. Cattle. And flax, it grows like weeds here and you can sell it spun or woven."

In the morning it rained still, a fine shining mist that hung in the air and coated a beard with silver drops. Bjarni went down to the wharf and looked about him, then went upriver to where they beached the boats to work on them. One large boat was drawn up amongst smaller ones, a whale in the midst of minnows. Its bottom was thick with weed and barnacles, and one of the planks was stove in. One man worked on it.

"There's a deal of work here," said Bjarni.

"Aye."

"What will you pay for two weeks' work? I learned the trade under Olaf Trygvasson of Vestfold."

The man kept on scraping with a thick blade of iron. "This is no work for a shipwright."

"I'm not a shipwright, I worked under him only. This I can do."

The man handed over his scraper. "Give me a morning's work and then we will talk about payment. I'll give you what you are worth."

"I ask no more and no less," said Bjarni, and took off his cloak and jerkin, the better to tackle the task.

In the days that followed Bjarni worked stolidly on the boat, pretending to himself that Olaf stood at his shoulder chiding him. From time to time men came and talked to him, asking was he the one they called Siggurdsson, and why then did he not take service with this one or that one who was looking for a good man. All he said was "I am suited here," and after a while they went away. It occurred to Bjarni that he had learned more than one thing from Skarphedin, that there was power in saying little. But it was a graceless way to go on and he felt again that he had not found himself. He was many men and each one different, and if there was a point at which they met he had not reached it.

When the boat was as clean as a plate, with its bottom tarred and the broken plank mended, Bjarni took his wages and left. "There's a job for you here if you want it," said the boatman, and was thanked for the offer.

Bjarni had other plans. He found himself a cart and a sturdy black pony with scarred legs, and he drove through Dubhlinn's gates and into the countryside that very afternoon.

Chapter
Nine

"FOR THIS COW I will take two bales of flax, a bushel of cabbages and that coin." He was becoming weary of argument. They wanted the cow, they needed the cow for they had ten children and all of them pasty, but they could not bring themselves to pay for it. So he was set here for the night most like, which was not so bad since outside it was wet and growing chill. Much longer though and he would forego half the flax and the cabbages, and might as well give them the cow for all the profit it would make him.

The woman was tall with long red hair, she reminded him of Emma. She was making a stew with some of the cabbages and was besides heating water in a pot, simply by putting stones in the fire and then scooping them out and dropping them in the water. When ashes rose to the surface she skimmed them off with a deft flick of a piece of wood. He would have liked to talk to her, but it was impossible, the men did not like it. Bjarni wondered if he should settle for only half the cabbages.

One of the children ducked in through the curtained door and stood waiting to tell some news or other. His father was relating a long tale, most not understood, about the poor season and the plague that had cursed his crops. The boy jigged a little in his impatience. At last the father turned his head and asked what was the matter, at which the boy jabbered away at him excitedly, shifting about on his thin white legs. Bjarni began to feel uncomfortable. They always said you should not lodge in an Irish dwelling, if they themselves did not kill you their enemies would.

The smoke from the fire was thick and pungent, and when the door curtain swung aside it billowed around the tiny dwelling. Through streaming eyes Bjarni saw a tall, muscular figure with a black skirt kilted up to show his knees. Tonight of all nights a monk was come this way, putting a wily Norse trader out in the cold. They would have no time for him now, these Irish treated their monks like gods.

He moved grudgingly back from the fire to let the stranger in. "Well met," he said with sourness.

"In the name of Christ Jesus," said the monk in the thick, Irish tongue. He smiled at Bjarni out of a large, red peasant face and settled down beside him, seemingly unaware that he had jostled an elbow from the Viking's knee.

Bjarni dug the same elbow hard at the monk who said ingenuously, "Did I knock you? I'm sorry, let me give you some more room, it's a wee bit cramped here."

He tried to squeeze his raw bones into a smaller space and out of common courtesy Bjarni said, "I have enough room now, thank you."

The wife was putting grain into the soup. "That smells good," said the monk, his large nose twitching.

"The grain is for your benefit. I was to get cabbages."

"To the glory of God."

Bjarni snorted. There would be no deal done tonight, that was certain. He would leave this place in the morning and take the cow with him whether they wanted it or not, and let that teach them a lesson. With his bad temper decided upon he ignored the monk, and after a few hopeful questions the man turned instead to the family. They sparkled for him, laughing and talking as if to mark the silence there had been before. Bjarni knew then that he could not know these people, that they would always be closed to him, shutting up their lives when he came to their houses and turning always a blank and hostile face. He was suddenly sad.

The woman began ladling the soup, with the men to eat first while the children watched from the shadows, like so many mice. But Bjarni could not believe his eyes. Instead of wood or cracked pot, as was usual in these places, they were passing the monk a silver dish. It was much blackened by

smoke but the scroll and fish decoration was still clear and at
the edge was the ring where it should hang on a chieftain's
wall. What was such a thing doing here, in this hovel? He
took his own cracked bowl and absently sipped at it, burning
his lips. To think he'd been trading for cabbages.

The monk was drinking noisily and some of the soup
dribbled down his chin. Bjarni despised him, for this was a
peasant sure enough, dressed up as something better. He
began to be curious. "Come this way often, do you?" he
asked.

"Why no. I have never traveled before, this is the first
time. It is very—enlivening." There was a formal touch to
his speech, which was the monastery no doubt, polishing a
rough stone.

"Where are you going?"

There was a pause. "I am sent on a pilgrimage," said the
monk and buried his large face in the dish. A flush was
turning the tips of his ears pink below an ugly fringe of hair.

"Get in trouble, did you?" asked Bjarni, but the monk
looked away and would not answer. The night wore on.
Outside the rain hissed on the roof and Bjarni's cow mooed
piteously because far away in the forest the wolves were
howling.

In the morning Bjarni was up early and set about hitching
the pony to the cart. He was brisk and trim, and while he
worked he chewed on a crust of stale bread. The cow looked
as if it might be sickening for something, it stood dejected in
a corner of the bothy with its eyes half-closed. Bjarni said to
the farmer, "You can keep the cow, I'll take the flax for it."
He swung the bales up on to the cart and climbed up after
them, gathering the reins in haste to be off.

But the monk, all tousled from rising, stood in his way.
"I'll ride with you please." He was grinning like a fool and it
annoyed Bjarni because now he must rebuff him, and before
the farmer.

"There isn't room."

"I don't mind a squash. I'll sit up here, I'll be no trouble
to you." He stretched up a muscular leg and Bjarni had a
view of his crotch, where his balls nestled in a scrub of
orange hair. He looked man enough, though it was said these
monks did not have women. It seemed an awful thing and

Bjarni would have been kinder if he had not, for this one day, wanted to be alone. But the monk was steadfastly cheerful, as the Viking was grim. There was no shifting him. With a sigh Bjarni flapped the reins at the pony and they set off through the mud. The pony labored with the heavy cart.

"There's too much of a load," said Bjarni. "It seems you'll have to get off."

"I'll give you a push till you get on firmer ground," said the monk, without any apparent conception of how unwelcome he was. He leaped enthusiastically into the mire and splodged round to the back of the cart, reaching under the cover to gain a purchase. Bjarni had the sudden feeling that this was fate, that the monk and he had been placed here together for just this happening.

"No," he said hopelessly, knowing what the monk would find. As the monk's hand gripped his peasant face became crestfallen. He was holding the silver dish.

"Now you see what comes of poking your nose in where it's not wanted." Bjarni reached for his sword, close to hand as always.

"This is a bad thing that you are doing. You are taking another man's goods." The monk took no notice of the weapon.

"As to that, the man has my cow, and a cursed fine animal she is."

"The beast is near dry! You can wave your heathen sword as much as you like but it is stealing you are doing, and from folk so poor they cannot even feed their childer." He seemed near to tears and Bjarni could not understand it. The bowl was useless to them. It wasn't so very bad.

The monk swung round and paddled back through the mud to where the farmer stood bemused. Bjarni bellowed "Bring that back. It'll be the worse for you," but the monk took no notice and thrust the bowl into the farmer's filthy hands. Bjarni could have gnashed his teeth with rage, and again when the monk returned and composedly swung himself back onto the cart.

"If you think I'm giving you a ride after that you're more stupid than I thought," he said sourly. He realized he was still waving his sword and he put it away, feeling foolish.

"We had best get on," said the monk with an attempt at distance.

"Curse your idiot face," said Bjarni, and lashed the reins at the pony. The animal strained in its collar, the wheels of the cart left the mud with a long suck, and they heaved out onto the track.

They bounced along in silence for a while and then Bjarni said, "What's your name?"

"Brother Colman."

"And I am Bjarni Sigurdsson, here to make money, not trail about with a holy man. You're lucky I did not lose my temper."

"As to that, you'd have won no profit from sin, none at all. Ah, hell must be a terrible place these days, full of Vikings."

"Hel? You mean the underworld? We believe—people believe—it is a world of dwarves."

"It is not! I guess there might be some of them in it, but hell is a place where people get a roasting. Eternal torment for our sins on earth, it's not to be thought of. The devil's place."

Bjarni shook his head doubtfully. The morning had been chill and grey but now the sun was coming out, sparkling on puddles as if they too were made of silver.

"You should thank me, you know," said Colman cheerfully. "The word would have traveled. They'd have killed you for it and then you'd have known about hell. You didn't think of that, did you?"

Bjarni shifted uncomfortably. They were a treacherous lot these Irish, quite untrustworthy. He cast a sidelong glance at the monk, who seemed honest enough with his strong legs spread wide while he scratched at a flea.

"Where are you headed?" he asked.

"To the islands. I am to pass a year there." Now Colman was a little subdued, and Bjarni probed further.

"It's a monastery you're going to, is that it?"

Colman gulped, and then as if confessing said, "It's a place of penance. I am to be quite alone there, to test my obedience to Father Abbot."

Bjarni nodded. He had heard of these men, sent to barren places for months on end, passing their days in solitude, fasting and prayer. He understood it, because suffering was a common thread in worship and this monk would be renouncing the world very much as did Skarphedin. Yet for Colman it was clearly not his own wish. It was a punishment.

"Did you do something wrong?" he asked, and Colman sighed.

"It was wrong because it was not as I was instructed, and of course it is the discipline—but it was not wrong in itself! I still think it, and I know it to be true." His fleshy mouth set in an unaccustomed line. Bjarni decided to coax the tale out of him.

Colman was a tenth child, sent to the monastery young to be trained as an illustrator. He was nothing of a scholar but he had a skill in painting and spent his days working on the manuscripts that were the order's main task. It was not an easy life. Sometimes it was so cold that the brushes froze in the paint, and sometimes so hot they had to bind their heads in cloth to prevent sweat falling on the work. But when set against the lot of his brothers and sisters Colman was fortunate, for he was fed and clothed and on holidays allowed to play games. Mostly though he painted, and it was this that was the cause of his trouble.

Some years past one of the brothers, Bernard, had taken white martyrdom and traveled through foreign lands to Rome. Just when they had thought him gone for good back he came, bringing with him new and fanciful ideas. No longer was it good to draw a deer as a man saw it, running on slim legs in the forest, now it was given a neck so long that it tangled back on itself, and its horns traveled half down the page to wind around the text. Figures were not to look like men any more but if they appeared at all were stiff, as if frozen.

It was the new style and obediently the monks accepted it. All except Colman. Perhaps part of it was that Brother Bernard turned his nose up at the raw and hearty country boys that thronged the monastery, for he was come from a more elegant people. He had a permanent wrinkle in his nose, it seemed to Colman. And besides, Colman's pleasure in his work was the creation of something that brought to life the long ago tales of Christ and his saints, or Noah with the beasts in his Ark, or even David that slew Goliath with stone. To make something that had no people in it seemed to Colman foolish and without point.

"We do the work to make things plain, not to hide them," he explained. "I could not do as he wished, and so it was put to Father Abbot. And now I am sent away. To test my obedience."

"And this Bernard does as he pleases?" asked Bjarni.

"As God wills it," hissed Colman, for his teeth were gritted.

A little time later Colman said, "I can show you my work if you like." He fumbled in the pouch that hung at his side and brought out a roll of vellum, wrapped in cloth. Bjarni pulled the horse to a halt under a tree and spread the thing out to look at it. The colors made him blink, all green and gold and purple. It was the figure of a man, all wreathed about with patterns, but only half of it was done and to Bjarni it seemed quite lacking in style and sophistication. Child of a distant sun, his tastes were otherwise. He began to have some sympathy for Bernard.

"It is very colorful," he said doubtfully.

"They are the colors of heaven. You see, we are making again what was stolen and burned by your people and there are more than a few in hell for that, I dare say. But can you see the wings here? It is an angel, a messenger of God. I saw one once."

"Did you so? I once saw a spirit on the sea, it would be much the same I think." They grinned at each other, feeling an understanding.

They passed through country that was green and wooded, where the cows milked well and the people prospered. When they stopped at a farm Colman was made welcome, and in the warmth of it Bjarni traded flax for cured leather and bought a length of fine linen with some coin. He began to see what the monk could do for him, for this country was not what it seemed, that was clear enough. What treasures might he gain if the people trusted him? On his own they seemed closed and brutish, but with Colman at his side it was all quite different. Even the women talked shyly to him now, laughing at his accent and blushing at his compliments. In an excess of warmth for Colman Bjarni called to him to bring out his picture. The household gathered round to look.

"I like it to seem as if the hand could reach and touch you," said Colman, and indeed it might be so. But Bjarni was embarrassed by it, for it seemed to set out clearly what was best hidden away, almost as if a good woman had seen him naked in the street. Give him patterns anyday, and circles and close nets to hide the meaning. He left Colman to his audience and turned away.

*   *   *

In the night, as he and Colman lay in the warmth of the fire waiting for sleep he said, "It is fate that has sent you to me. I see it now."

"As to that, we are in the hands of the Father, you as much as me. I am surprised you do not see it."

"It is much the same thing," said Bjarni.

A little time later, when a softly falling turf had them both stirring, he said, "I have heard tell of a hall, a great Irish hall. The king is Maelsechnaill."

"I have heard of that," said Colman sleepily.

"They say he has men within his rath that can twist gold as fine as spun flax. And there are women with their hair hanging down that sing like birds."

"Do they say so?"

"I have heard it. Would not you like to see such a place, Colman? You could show the king your painting."

Colman settled down again. "I could not do that," he said unhappily. "I am to go to the islands, it is my duty of obedience."

"It seems to me that since I would take you to the islands most swiftly on my wagon, then the greater obedience would be to come with me to Maelsechnaill," said Bjarni guilelessly. "We would not stay above a night or two. Who knows, such a king might have a need of a monk such as you. This could be the way it was meant to be."

Colman pushed himself up on an elbow. It was very hard to decide what to do like this, he had made barely half a dozen decisions of his own since he joined the monastery, and one of those had caused him to be sent away. It was very difficult. It might be that he should never have taken up with this trader, though good had come of that already in the return of the bowl. Perhaps it was meant to be. "Maelsechnaill is a Christian king," he said almost to himself.

"Indeed he is, and as gorgeous as any angel so they say. How I should like to see such a place, the harps are like voices from the skies."

Colman could not decide what he should do, and besides he was very tired. Life outside the monastery was exhausting him and it was all the fault of Bernard, who had traveled half the world and earned nothing but praises while Colman, locked in obedience, was despised. "We must talk about it in the morning," he said.

*   *   *

The high plank gates of Maelsechnaill's stronghold were guarded by warriors who wore red kilts and whose necks were hung about with amber. Their hair was tangled and they looked fiercely out from the midst of it, holding their spears in readiness. Bjarni had prudently put away his sword and he nervously fingered his dagger hid beneath his shirt. All the day he had wondered if this was wise, for though the people hereabouts were heavy with silver the country smelled of war.

"What do you here?" questioned a soldier, looking from the blond Viking to the monk.

Bjarni coughed a little. "Brother Colman is making pilgrimage, we seek only your hospitality. I am a trader, I have pretty things for the girls to see—" He held out a pouch of beads but they did not reach to take it. Instead they whispered to each other and watched him warily.

Suddenly one said to Colman, "Is this one Norse? What does he want?"

Colman looked quickly at Bjarni who said smoothly, "Would you hold the door against two good Christians? We wish only to pass a night or two here, this country's dangerous for peaceful men."

"There's not so much peace in Maelsechnaill's hall," said one, in an accent so heavy that it could hardly be understood. Bjarni grunted and reached back into the wagon. He brought out a flask of liquor, traded from one of the earth bothies and with some taste in it, beneath the fire, of the place of its birth. "Like to try a little? You'll find this hotter than a whore's crotch. Only let us in, you can see we bear no arms."

The men sniffed, looked at each other and then swung the gate. They were like soldiers anywhere, for all their bare knees and red hair. The weary pony plodded slowly into the stronghold.

Within the rath the houses clustered together, surrounded by a broad path next to the fence that was filled with rubbish and dogs and children. There was a smell of peat fires and mud, and as the wagon creaked in a crowd of children gathered, bare toes wriggling in the mire.

Colman was disappointed. "Where is the silver? Where is the king? It is not even so grand as the monastery."

"We shall see him," reassured Bjarni, himself somewhat dismayed at the look of the people. These children seemed to him to be as hungry as any. He tossed the flask to the guards and steered the pony slowly between the dungheaps and woodpiles until he came to a wider space where he thought he might leave his wagon. A little girl stood watching, thumb in mouth and he tossed her a wooden figurine saying, "Take this home, sweeting, tell your mother to come and see my cloth." The child ran off and he began to set out his wares.

"What was that drink?" asked Colman. "Should I like to taste it?"

Bjarni laughed. "There's another flask here. I warn you, it's strong." He took a mouthful himself before handing it over to Colman and he shook his head, feeling the heat spreading through him. There were some very good things about this country, there was no doubt about that. He looked appreciatively at the women gathering cautiously round, white-skinned and slender. He would give a lot to lie with one of these.

They liked the cloth best, and the flax, for these people were fighting with a neighbor and often as not the fields were torched. Bjarni thought it a pity he had not still the cow, he could have asked more for food than anything. They were rich, but what use silver when there's no food to buy?

"I'll bring flour and cattle next time," he promised and a man who was buying a knife said, "And you will profit from our wars. You are a curse, you heathens."

Bjarni looked innocent. "Me? I'm a good Christian man."

It was growing dark and the people began to drift away to their homes. Bjarni looked for Colman, but he could not see him anywhere. Perhaps he had gone to eat in someone's home, he was always assured of a welcome. Bjarni felt a little aggrieved that he should be so easily forgotten. He put away his unsold goods, mostly dark cloth which they did not like, it seemed, and as he was finishing a warrior with a fighting sword came up to him. Bjarni felt for his dagger, still within his shirt. It was too easy to kill a friendless man in the dark.

"You are to dine in Maelsechnaill's hall. Come."

Bjarni did not know what to think. Was this a trap or an honor? "I have to find my friend," he said cautiously.

"Maelsechnaill waits for no-one." Nonetheless Bjarni took time to pull a comb through his hair and swill his mouth with water, for if he was truly to see the chief it would not be wise to appear ramshackle.

The soldier looked contemptuous. "You think to charm our women," he said.

The hall was set at the center of the rath, raised up on a small hill, and at first sight it did not seem imposing. Within the walls the blue peat smoke hung in wreaths below the rafters and Bjarni blinked at it, struggling to see the king. His guard pushed him forward and Bjarni turned to glare. "Do not push me, friend. No man has the right." He stepped forward of his own accord, towards the dais where Maelsechnaill sat entroned. When he was a dozen steps from him he stopped. The king said nothing, neither did he move and Bjarni saw that he was old and creased and grizzled. One great hand hung weary at his side and the other held a jeweled cup, though he appeared to doze, his eyes half-hooded. Bjarni shivered and his courage drained away. But if there was one thing he had learned from Skarphedin it was composure at such times, that a man has power in silent waiting. He hooked his thumbs in his belt, lifted his head and looked about.

It seemed to him a poor sort of hall, for it was short and low with the roof supported by pillars at the side, for the walls were not strong enough to take the weight alone. Along its length were tables newly spread with food and the men were starting their meal in the Irish fashion, with low talk. In a Viking stronghold the shouts and laughter would already crack the rafters, but here they began quietly and grew raucous later on. He looked back at Maelsechnaill, who slowly raised his cup and sipped from it.

There was a screen behind the king, hiding a portion of the hall from view. A movement at the edge caught Bjarni's eye and when he looked he caught his breath. A girl stood there watching him, her eyes, cat's eyes, green and staring. She was small and thin as a wand, with hair that flamed against pale skin and as he looked he saw her tongue licking her pink lips, like a cat after eating. The hair on his neck prickled beneath her gaze and then she was gone behind her screen. He felt breathless.

A man was speaking to Maelsechnaill, resting a hand on the chief's arm, so it was the son, no-one else would dare. He had not Maelsechnaill's wily look though he had his size, as tall as any Viking and muscled with it. The chief's own hand was brown-spotted with age and his arms had the slackness of strong muscle grown weak. Maelsechnaill's time was almost done.

At last the son came down the hall. "He would speak with you," he said.

Bjarni inclined his head in mock graciousness, taking his time in coming at an old man's bidding. Was he not Viking and ruler of the world? He puffed himself up in his own importance, yet still he felt himself humble. There was power yet awhile in this old man.

"Why do you come here?" A fierce, dry whisper. Round his neck the chief wore a thick silver chain, as wide as Bjarni's two fingers.

"Who has not heard of the great Maelsechnaill? Who would not wish to see the glories of his hall?" He had a sudden vision of the dogpit from which Skarphedin had rescued him. Would they have such a pit here? Or something worse. He felt aggrieved that the monk, who had agreed to come with him, should now be so cravenly in hiding.

"We are honored that a Viking should think us so glorious. They have never before troubled themselves with us except they came to steal and burn and dishonor our women. Perhaps there will be others in your wake. Perhaps you come to see how strong is an old man's fortress?"

"Trade only, lord, I swear it. Two Christian men traveling together."

Maelsechnaill coughed a little and took a shallow, rasping breath. "Yes. There was a monk, I am told. A strange pairing. But I would speak with him."

"He has—he is—lodging somewhere." It sounded feeble even to Bjarni's ears. Curse the monk for a whore's bastard. He searched for an ingratiating remark. "You have a fine son, lord."

"I have four fine sons and eight grandsons grown, tell that to the men who would conquer me."

"I come in peace, lord. To trade."

"And what do you trade? Irish slaves? Irish women?"

"Only cloth, lord. And cabbages. And good strong knives."

Maelsechnaill tapped his finger on his lip and on that finger glowed a jewel. Bjarni cursed himself for trusting to a monk, who was not even here when he was needed. Suddenly Maelsechnaill snapped, "Ivarr lit cooking fires on the bodies of his enemies."

Bjarni swallowed. "I have heard it said," he agreed cautiously. "But Ivarr is dead and those battles long over."

"Are they so? We learned a wildness from them, I know that. In my young day a warrior honored the body of his enemy, it was Ivarr taught us another way, he taught us treachery." He rolled his great head from side to side, an old man remembering a time when the world was fresh and green and there was nothing in it that he could not understand. Bjarni forced himself to keep his hands by his sides when his fingers tingled to hold a weapon. He had walked bare-headed into a hornet's nest and it was not likely that he would walk away unscathed. He fixed his eyes on the low beamed roof and saw that a pair of antlers hung above the dais, the biggest he had ever seen and wider than he was tall. What manner of beast could it be that had so huge a headdress? What manner of place was this?

"I need men."

Bjarni jumped, he had thought the chief lost in his thoughts. "I am but one lord. The monk—is a monk."

Maelsechnaill waved an impatient hand. "I need a strong band and I can pay in silver. In the country nearby there is a young chief, and he covets my lands and my wealth. He is in league with another such as he, but who can I, Maelsechnaill, turn to? Only the strong. Only the brave. I ask you to fetch me—a Viking band." He fell back, coughing, and drops of spittle formed on blue-grey lips. Yet he saw the surprise on the Viking's face, Bjarni watched him mark it. There were such men to be had, selling their swords to the Irish chiefs. How to tell him they were not at Bjarni's disposal?

The king was exhausted. The son brought men to lift him up and carry him from the hall. A voice at Bjarni's elbow said, "Will you eat now, then? It is the king's order." Bemused and not at all hungry, Bjarni allowed himself to be led to a table.

They fed him well on goose and soft Irish bread and afterwards two women came into the hall with harps. Neither was beautiful but their voices were more lovely than any face. As they sang Bjarni thought of Skarphedin, for whom music was precious and wonderful. These songs of loss and longing would have touched him when all the screams and flowing blood could not. It was as if one part of him had been left gentle and one part only. It was a strange thing for Odin to overlook.

His head swam a little, both with thinking and the drink.
What was he to say to Maelsechnaill? Should he leave this
warm hall and escape? But the night beyond the hall was cold
and comfortless, if it cost him his life he would rather stay
here. Again the harps throbbed, a tumbling river of sound that
went from the bottom of his heart to the top in the space of
time it took those long fingers to pass across the strings. His
eyes filled with tears, for nothing and everything. Through
the mist he saw the girl.

She was walking down the hall, small, upright, her green
skirt swinging against her legs. As she passed him her head
turned and he met her eyes, those cat's eyes, and at once he
rose and followed her. The night air hit him from beyond the
door, he knew himself to be on fire, and he knew also that
she had bewitched him. If it was a trap he did not care.

It was very dark outside. A torch blazed somewhere in the
gloom and on the edge of the light was the girl. She stood as
if waiting, but she did not look at him, so was she waiting,
and was it for him? Her hair moved in the blackness, a gleam
amongst the shadows and he went to her.

"I saw you," he said. "In there."

"Yes. I watched you."

"I wanted—" He stroked a finger on the pale, bare flesh
of her arm. "What is your name?" he asked.

"I am Rafarta. The daughter of Maelsechnaill."

He breathed a long "oh" and took each of her narrow
wrists in his hands, because she was beautiful and she looked
at him with green eyes out of a cat's face. She laughed at him
with a wide mouth and he bent his head and kissed her.

She dug sharp nails into his neck, but her tongue joined
his, hot, twisting inside his mouth. He could not bear it to
stop, but as he wound his arms around her she pulled free and
stood apart from him. "I will tell my father," she whispered.
"You will die for this."

"Why tell anyone? You are so beautiful, I want you so
much."

He reached for her again, his hand finding an apple of a
breast beneath her tunic. She gasped and writhed, her fingers
clawing. He had never felt such exquisite pain. They began to
fight, but even as she scratched and struck at his crotch with
her knee she kissed him and pressed her belly against his hip.
He began to laugh for she was wild and he was going to

mount her, she was asking for it. He dragged up her skirt and found hot thighs with between them curls of tight damp hair. She growled deep in her throat when he touched her there and her body arched backwards.

"You'll have a mating, my little hel-cat," he whispered. "Where can we go?" She said nothing but only growled again and he thought of the wagon with its bales of cloth and good thick cover. A better bed than some he had tried and he was in no mood for dawdling. He had never wanted a woman more, if she was a woman, this girl-cat. He caught her arm and dragged her down the dark paths. When they reached the wagon he flung back the cover and pushed her under, catching only a glimpse of wide young eyes. Then he was in after her and there was only the dark and soft, writhing flesh. He loosed himself from his breeks and hung over her, savoring the moment.

"Rafarta," he breathed and on the word plunged. As he broke into her body the girl shrieked.

When it was over Bjarni lay on her gasping. "I was the first. Why didn't you tell me I was the first?"

She put sharp white teeth against his shoulder. "Now my father will kill you."

"Only if you tell him. Don't tell him, my sweet, I'll make you love me. In a little while we'll do it again and it won't hurt at all. Darling. Beautiful one." He kissed her but she moved her mouth aside.

"Suppose you've got me with child."

"It never happens the first time. Do you like this? Tell me if you like it." He licked at her nipple and she clutched at his hair and groaned.

This time he was gentle and eased himself into her torn flesh, though she was as hot for it as he. Towards dawn, when she wanted him again, he thought she was truly a cat that will howl for a mate as well as claw it. He had never had such a woman, but he was spent. The air in the wagon was foetid with passion.

"You'd better go," he said. "It's getting light."

Her eyes gleamed in the dark but she said nothing and Bjarni thought, she is the daughter of Maelsechnaill. A thrill went through him and he lifted her hand and kissed it. The strings in it were like the veins of a leaf, quite visible.

"Don't tell anyone" he whispered, but she was gone, running lightfooted through a grey dawn.

There was a groaning and rumbling from underneath the wagon. Bjarni sat with the cover round his head, all his limbs weak from the night, and watched Colman crawl blearily out.

"So there you are," said Bjarni.

"Who was that?" His fringe of hair was on end and his eyes half closed. Dew had soaked his clothing and he was shaking with cold, it made Bjarni laugh to look at him.

"You've been drinking," he said, giving Colman a hand up. "Did I not tell you the stuff was strong?"

"It is a brew of the devil, and truly so. At first I thought I could hear angels singing. It is an evil temptation."

"Brewed by Christian men, Colman, don't forget that. Come up, man, and get warm. What a night, eh? What a night." The Viking gathered the cover round the pair of them and exhausted, they both slept.

They woke to sunlight and a circle of spears.

"What is this?" Bjarni blinked at them, forgetful for the moment of where he was. Beside him Colman smiled awkwardly, like a man who has entered the wrong house.

"Maelsechnaill wants you," said one.

Remembrance was filtering back. Bjarni gulped. "He can at least wait until a man has had a piss, can't he?" He climbed from the wagon and went against the wall. He had an ache in his groin, may the gods protect him, what had he been thinking of? His knife was lost somewhere in the wagon and the only things under his shirt now were nail marks, clear and unmistakable. Oh, but she had been good. Tight as a man could wish for.

Colman came and stood beside him. "You have done something," he said worriedly. "Is it stealing again? I should never have taken up with you, it is the worst thing I ever did."

"I can't say you've brought me much luck," snapped Bjarni, fastening himself up again. "I needed you last night when you were swilling your head off, the chief nearly killed me."

"Perhaps better for us all if he had," said Colman, hitching up his habit and sending a thin stream of urine to splash the Viking's feet. Bjarni muttered a routine curse and moved away to comb his hair. He felt panic very near the surface. Oh Thorkil, he thought to himself, why did I ever leave your side?

They were hustled to the hall like guilty men and when they entered it was to a hard silence. All four of Maelsechnaill's sons were gathered about his chair and they seemed to Bjarni like trees in a forest, every one huge.

Colman hissed to him, "Is that the king? The old one?"

Bjarni muttered to himself. The monk was a child and if he needed Thorkil the monk needed him. "Just be quiet," he said patiently. "I'll get you out."

Maelsechnaill glowered down at them. "Good morning, lord," said Bjarni politely, his guts churning themselves liquid.

"Shut him up," growled Maelsechnaill and a man dealt a blow to the Viking's back. His hand flashed to where his sword should have been and then fell slowly to his side. He straightened up. If he was to die it might as well be bravely.

"The monk has done nothing," he said. All at once he felt calm, as before a battle with Skarphedin, and he knew it to be because a course was decided upon. It is the deciding that is hard he thought, and smiled to himself. How strange to find such a thing out just before the end.

"You smile," said Maelsechnaill, with iron. "Does it amuse you to deflower my daughter?"

"Your daughter is very beautiful," prevaricated Bjarni.

Maelsechnaill lifted a finger and one of the sons reached behind the screen. Rafarta half fell on to the dais, supported only by her brother's hand. Her flame hair was tangled about her pointed face, which was disfigured by a hugely swollen jaw rapidly turning purple. Her eyes were fixed on Bjarni.

"They have beaten you," said Bjarni and turned angrily to the chief. "It is not right to hurt her so. The fault is mine."

Beside him Colman gulped, squeaked, and began to pray. Maelsechnaill half rose in his seat, shouting, "You come to my house. You eat my bread. I honor you with my welcome. And in return you take my daughter, sending her to her bed stained with her own virgin blood, filled with your heathen seed. You think to give Maelsechnaill Viking bastards? Is that your thanks? If I had my strength I would tear your heart out myself."

Bjarni lifted a soothing hand, looking from the chief's grey lips to Rafarta's green eyes. She was so lovely. He could desire her even now.

"Perhaps you could pay—" It was Colman, piping up. All heads turned furiously towards him.

"Pay? Pay?" shrieked Maelsechnaill, spitting foam. "He will wed the girl, that's what he'll do. And then he will die. You have my word on it, the word of Maelsechnaill who is still great. Let no man think he is done. No man." But his voice was trailing weakly into silence. He fell back in his chair and slumped there, panting. The sons seemed not to know what to do and Bjarni saw that the chief had cause to be afraid, because there was none coming after that could rule.

Maelsechnaill's strength had not passed on to this generation, though it might come again in the next. Or perhaps not at all, great kings were rare but great lines rarer still. The eldest son bent his head to his father and then straightened.

"Take them away," he instructed. "The girl will be made ready and then you will wed. The monk can see to the words."

"Me? Me? I cannot." Shocked, Colman began to bluster noisily. He had never done more than hold a vessel cover, he could not now marry someone.

"Be quiet, man," growled Bjarni as they were hustled away. Once again he had the feeling that fate had him in its grasp. To die on the day of his wedding, that was a thing indeed. No wonder Thorkil had always steered him clear of matrimony.

They were locked in a shed with some half-cured sheephides. "I could get a good price for these," said Bjarni mournfully.

"I cannot marry you," whimpered Colman. "You're not even Christian!"

"As to that, it hardly matters. Do you think she might ask him to spare me? After we are wed, I mean? He doesn't seem over fond but it might be so."

"He'll kill you when he finds he's married her to a heathen," said Colman. "I must baptize you, it is the only thing to do. I have thought from the first it would be best for there is badness in you that must be driven out."

He began to fiddle about with the flask of water that was all they had been given. Bjarni took no notice but flung himself down on the smelly hides and locked his hands behind his head. He could not believe Maelsechnaill would really kill him, not when the insult was made good by marriage. But perhaps they took these things more seriously in Ireland, though when he thought about it they took them quite seriously everywhere. She had smelled of the earth, of grass after rain, and when he took her he felt that he burrowed into the womb of the land itself. It was the land that bewitched him, it was that he had wanted to possess.

"You must listen," said Colman settling himself down on the hides beside him. "I am to tell you of Christ Jesus who was born of a virgin."

"Oh yes," said Bjarni scornfully. "So were we all no doubt."

"Most truly he was, it was a great miracle. And by God's grace we shall be saved, even after death, so you should listen most carefully."

"I do not think I shall die," said Bjarni and realized that indeed he did not think it. This adventure could not end here, when he had traveled so far and had yet so far to go. He was still looking for his place.

Colman told the tale as a simple man tells it, bluntly and with truth. Bjarni thought, is this what they hold so dear, just this? He had always thought there was more. But he knelt at Colman's bidding while the monk marked his head with a wet thumb.

"Now you can die a Christian," said Colman with satisfaction. Bjarni lay back again on his hides and thought of a hayfield in the sun, where he had lain and slept until Thorkil woke him, peering out of the radiance like a golden-haired giant. Where would Thorkil go when he died? To Asgard, it had to be, for he was a warrior and a mighty one. Bjarni would not see him for now he would be in heaven, which was quite a different place and perhaps more suited to him. He was not born a fighting man.

A little while later the door opened. "It's time," said the guard, grinning. Bjarni wondered at it for it was not a laughing matter, but he rose and straightened his clothing. He would smell of the hides which was a pity since the girl at least deserved better. Colman was white with nerves.

They were taken to a little wooden church, bare and draughty, but the king was not there and they stood waiting. After a time the girl came in, surrounded by her tall brothers. She seemed tiny and frail in the midst of them.

"Rafarta." He took her hand. The bruise on her face was darkening to black but when he looked in her eyes there was something that repelled him. There seemed no softness there but only calculation. She did not seem the guileless virgin of the night before.

"Is it true that they will kill me?" he asked her softly and she looked up at him and said, "If my father wills it. He is Maelsechnaill."

When the chief entered he was swaying, his gaunt giant's frame wrapped in a grey fur cloak, wolf's fur. He looked at the girl and she at him, and a slight nod passed between them. "Get on with it," he muttered and Colman cleared his throat.

Bjarni understood none of his mutterings, which to his ears seemed to repeat themselves endlessly, as Colman stood wide-eyed and panic-stricken, his mouth talking by itself. But in a while it was over, and they were wed.

"We are to feast this night with my father," said Rafarta composedly. He bent his head to kiss her and tasted again the greenness of her tongue.

"Will we have a bedding, my sweet?" he asked. "At least we must have that."

There was something in her look, he sensed it was almost contempt. "It is what you want, my father knows it."

The smoke hung thick in the hall and to Bjarni it seemed that it moved amongst his thoughts. There was something strange here, he could feel it, he could see it in the false smiles of the people around him. Rafarta, his wife, leaned her firm young body against him, urged him to drink from her cup. Why? He did not feel that she was young and innocent, instead she seemed a deceiver. But in what way? What was it that he did not know?

He looked for Colman, who of them all was the only one that he trusted, because he was too simple for guile.

"Drink," whispered Rafarta, "then you shall bed me." She held his beard and turned his face to hers, sinking her tongue deep in his throat, her free hand stroking his thigh. He pulled away and got to his feet, walking unsteadily amongst the tables looking for Colman. His new wife watched him, still and catlike.

"I must speak with you!" Colman had found him and was hanging on his sleeve, his raw finger-ends with their bitten nails digging into his arm.

"What is happening here, Colman? I don't understand."

"It is a trap! They are saying—I heard—she is not his daughter. Or at least, she is his but by a concubine. They sent her to your bed."

Bjarni gaped. "But—why?"

"They have heard a tale about you, that you are truly a chief with a fierce band, traveling this land to spy out the rich places. They say you are great in battle."

"It isn't true."

"Isn't it? They want you to fight for them." Colman looked at him so faithfully that Bjarni felt a surge of love for him, for the one honest face amidst so much treachery. Curse that Viking need to make up a tale, curse the nights in the taverns that had spread it. These Irish did not know that you took a Norseman's wordfame, cut it in four and swallowed one piece only; they had devoured it whole and trusted it. They would certainly kill him now, for he could not buy back his life with a warrior band. At best he could scratch together a few journeyman fighters, hardly more.

He looked back at Rafarta and she was watching him, her fingers stroking the hair that lay across her shoulder above those small, hard breasts. Oh but she had trapped him sure enough, with her slut's writhings.

"Keep close to me," he said to Colman and crossed to her, catching her narrow wrist and jerking her to her feet. "We shall have our bedding," he whispered to her, "and such a bedding it shall be, you schemer." He pushed his hand into her dress and cupped her breast, before them all. She gasped and the people roared.

"I do not understand this," muttered Colman. "I wish I was back with Father Abbot."

"Never you fear, Colman," said Bjarni. "Stay close to me and you'll be safe from such as this." He placed a sucking kiss on Rafarta's neck and all but dragged her to the door. She had a smile fixed tightly to her lips as he pushed her past tables and benches, the air filled with lewd shouts and singing. At the door Bjarni turned as if to say something to the shouting wildmen within the hall.

"Friends," he declaimed, and paused. They watched him like drunken hawks. "Friends—you can keep her!"

On the word he flung Rafarta back into the hall, sending her sprawling amongst the tables. He heard the girl scream and thought, that's the cat howling, but he seized Colman's stunned arm and ran. The monk clutched his skirts around his waist, thick legs flashing in the gloom.

"We must climb the fence," hissed Bjarni, but it was so dark they could not see and the fence was very high. He remembered the wagon, drawn up close to the rath, and he headed for it, once almost losing his way. Torches flamed in the night behind them, he felt wildly, drunkenly excited.

There was the wagon, they flung themselves against it, cracking muscles as they pushed it close to the wall. He could not have done it without Colman's brawny arms, he was a good friend, a true friend. They scrambled up on the wagon and from there to the top of the fence. Only then did they wonder if the ground below was staked as they hung in wind above the blackness. But there was no going back.

"In the name of the Father," wailed Colman and they dropped together. When the men came soon after they were away in the dark bog and lost to them.

They looked out across a tossing sea to where the island loomed, black and rocklike. No tree could be seen, nor any grass, but only spray, and seabirds swirling about. Drawn up on the shingled beach was a tiny currach, old and weather-battered. Not even the shorefolk came here to build their seaweed fires, it was desolate and entirely lonely.

"I am not at all happy about this, Colman," said Bjarni, today as for many days past. "It is surely no part of your duty to die of hunger."

"It is my duty to be obedient," said Colman miserably. "If I do not go then there is no life for me, I shall be an outcast. But if I do this and survive I can go home."

"But what shall you eat? We have lost everything, we are half starved now and there is nothing there but birds and rock. I doubt that God will send down dinners." During the past days they had begged a meal or two from a poor house, picked berries and eaten dismally of a fox's leavings.

Colman's plump cheeks were being smoothed into flatness. "If I were holy enough, my God would feed me," he said, but without conviction. Both he and Bjarni knew that he was not the stuff of which martyrs and saints are made.

The Norseman sighed. "I must take care of it, that's plain. I shall come across with you, Colman, and see you settled, then I shall row back myself and find some work hereabouts. Some supplies would see you safe enough out there.''

''What if Maelsechnaill hears of you?'' They both had a healthy fear of the king's wrath.

''We are far from him here. And I think the king troubled enough in his rath not to spare men to hunt me down. I am a Christian man now, friend, and in the care of a Christian God. We shall both trust Him and see what comes of it.''

He was cheerful in the face of Colman's despair. The monk was no more suited to loneliness than a dog, that will turn its face to a kennel wall and die for lack of company. As they trudged down the beach together slow tears trickled down Colman's glum face and he wiped his nose on his sleeve.

Together they pushed the little boat out into the waves, soaking themselves to the knees. The wind was bitter, whipping spume from the water and sending it against their faces in harsh slaps. Bjarni took the oar, rowing in the way he had learned from the fisherlad, sweeping it to and fro across the round end of the boat, and Colman baled, scooping green water out of the tub with his hands. The wind was with them and soon they were bumping a rocky shore.

The island knew no shelter and it was very cold. They were sodden with spray. The seaweed-covered rocks sent them slipping and sliding as if the whole island conspired to reject them, crying, ''This is no place for men.'' But men had left their mark here, in the little curved cell made of stone that crouched within a fold of ground above the beach. This was to be Colman's home, a little beehive with a hole for a door.

Inside there was a bench, a stone bed, two thin blankets and some bowls and cooking pots.

''It's more than I expected,'' said Colman bravely. Bjarni felt a little pride in him that he was taking this so well. Perhaps this Father Abbot was right, that even for such as Colman this trial would prove worthwhile. He wondered how he himself would sustain it, and flinched at the thought. A man's thoughts were best avoided, it took a great simplicity to look in upon oneself.

''I'll go now, then,'' he said, wishing to hurry and have it over.

Colman sensed his need but still tried to keep him. ''I shall light a fire,'' he wheedled, ''won't you stay and get warm? Seaweed burns quite hot, so they say.''

"The sea's getting up," said Bjarni. "Never fear, Colman, I'll be back in a day or so with some good bread and a fur or two, and in a better boat than that leaky old tub. Keep your courage, friend."

Colman tried to smile. Bjarni gripped his shoulder and then bent to go out into the air.

The wind clutched at him even before he had straightened, flinging his beard into his mouth and his hair into his eyes. A gale was blowing, and even before he turned his streaming eyes to the sea he knew that he should not cross it. The green waves stood like mountains topped with snow, and flung themselves about as if in rage. But the distance was small, and besides he could not bear to spend a night in this place, being cheerful in the face of Colman's misery. What was a Viking if not a seaman? He launched the currach into the waves with a firm purpose.

Without Colman's weight the vessel skittered on the sea, but with the wind blowing off the land he had a hard task to row it. He found his feet were splashing in water, not as he had thought from splashes over the sides but from leaks where the hides had split. The first cold whisper of fear brushed his cheek and he rowed harder. But the land seemed no nearer, and for all his sweeps with the oar the little craft sank lower and lower still into the sea. Was he to die after all? So foolishly when he need only have waited till tomorrow? Suddenly it came to him, the truth of it. He had angered the gods of his youth, and in forsaking them had offered himself up to their revenge. They did not loose their hold so easily, he had been foolish to think it. But what had Colman said? That Christ had walked upon the water, that he had calmed the wind and the waves.

"Save me! I am your creature now, save me!" His shrieking joined with the storm and in the howling his little boat was spun like a leaf, round and round, until at last it sank into a green and swirling sea.

Chapter
Ten

IF YOU DO not know fear, look behind you sometime when your ship is running before a sea; see the grey hills chasing you, bigger than trees, with their tops flecked white and the wind in them roaring. Watch one come for you like a hunting dog, closer, closer, until the teeth are snapping at your life— and at last feel the good ship lifting herself. Then you will rest a hand on the strong oak and give thanks to the man that made her; and perhaps if you are the nervous type, you will give up voyaging and vow to stay at home—until the next time the sun sets on a gentle sea.

When we left the mouth of the river I was faced with a problem, and it was the first of many. Were we to creep south, hugging the coastline, before risking a crossing? That way we were seldom in open water and in our present state, unpracticed and tender, it could be said to be the wise course. If we made a straight crossing we were risking a lot, for it might be days to a landfall, and in foul weather Thor alone knew where we might end up. But it grieved me to be dithering. In a time not so long past I should have scorned to be cautious and would have launched into the ocean without a waver. I was spurred to pretend to be the man of my youth, that careless fellow who was a lifetime braver than me.

"Are you fit, men?" I asked them. "You're coming together nicely so we'll make our crossing now. Drink your fill

and eat hearty for we sail on the morning tide and it may be
our last hot meal for a day or so.''

"If ever," muttered Olaf. "What are you about, Thorkil,
we're no more fit to face a storm than a boatload of babies.''

"We'll do," I said confidently.

Then, with thinking, I added, "Do you sense a storm then,
Olaf? I thought it seemed settled enough, though the blow's
somewhat eastward.''

He sniffed. "I don't know. There are some seabirds here
that I would not expect, and sometimes that means bad
weather. This coast is strange to me.''

"The sun's a good color," I said. "And there's not over
much weed on the tide.''

"Is the water cold?''

We each put our hands in and thought about it. How should
we tell, who had spent years on dry land? All water felt cold.

"I'll not creep about like a rat in a barn," I said. "We will
put our trust in Thor, who holds the waves in the palm of his
hand. If he chooses to end it, then so be it.''

Olaf glowered at me, saying, "If I'd known you were
running this mad I'd never have come," but he settled happily enough to his food. It pleased him to see me heedless
once again, as if the marks of my youth made his age more
distant. If he had known what a bad stomach I had—but then
who can ever know? We are always hidden, even from those
closest to us.

So it was that we found ourselves, no more than a day out
from shore, being tossed on the waves like a feather. There
was no-one who was not sick except me and Olaf, and the
men lay on the deck lashed to their benches for safety, and
careless whether they lived or died.

We kept the sail up as long as we could, but as I told you,
we had not the right resin and it stretched most alarmingly
when the gale filled it. In my ignorance I backed it twice,
trying to sail an unhandy boat too close to the wind, and each
time Olaf swore through clenched teeth with his eyes glitter-
ing. "I'll give you the stitching of it, you offspring of a
snake," he cursed, watching the sail bang like a slammed
door. I'll never know why it didn't split and when the storm
worsened we furled it rather than lose the only sail we had. I
had pinched at a second, but foolishly, for in that sea the
money saved seemed very small when set against our lives.

I sat with the tiller in my hand, my beard thick with salt spray and every now and then drenched by a big sea, and I thought of Emma. The boat was getting sluggish as water filled her, it hung under waves too long. What if it was the end of me? Would she sense it somehow, taking the knowledge from the wind to cloud her sea-grey eyes? We were too strong for each other, she and I, we were like iron and flint, striking sparks but with no true mating. In that sinking boat I saw it clearly, the best matches are when strength meets softness, when one takes and the other yields. Yet Emma and I had each found it in us to be gentle once. Only our anguish had put an end to it.

A thought came to me. I lashed the tiller with stiff hands and crawled to where Olaf lay, shouting in his ear, "We can put a drag on her. Then we can bale." He nodded, as calm as ever, and we set to making a drag out of waterskins, lacing them together with thin ropes. The wind's howl was never-ending, it filled your head with all the sound that there is in the world, from the deepest roar to the highest screeching that you thought never to hear outside your dreams. The man nearest to me lay like the dead, but his lips moved in prayer. All at once my fear left me. It fell away like the shell of a nut. I was not scared of dying, nor even of life; the wind held no terrors for me on the sea. I reached out a hand and took the man's arm in a strong clasp. "You'll tell tales of this in Birka," I bellowed above the gale. His eyes opened a crack and he tried to smile and he watched as Olaf and I heaved the drag over the stern.

At once the movement of the ship changed, she was held at the stern by a giant hand, no longer were we buffeted this way and that, swamped by whichever wave desired it, we took the seas evenly, bow first. Our lives were our own once again, bought back with only a little thought from the demons that waited to clasp us in cold green arms.

But now we must work. I went round the men, urging some and kicking others. "Bale," I told them. "Bale, you whoreson lepers, or it's over the side with you and you'll never see your mothers again."

"My mother's been dead these ten years," complained one, and I grinned. I had forgotten that the boys I used to take to sea had become thick-muscled, canny grown men.

"Think of your wives and children, then," I bellowed.

"I'll jump now," shouted Thorsteinn, who had been given the fur cloak. We all laughed a little to ourselves, and felt a touch of pity for Thorsteinn's wife that he should mock her so. Why, the woman would be heartbroke if he died. The thought made me laugh a little more.

The boat began to come up soon after we began work. After a time I was able to let some rest while others labored and we passed round some biscuits to chew. Even a sick man does better with something in his belly.

When you pass a night in a storm there comes a time when you forget that daylight exists. It seems that the world is black forever, that part of your suffering is to be forever in the dark. It is a cruelty to a man to shut him in a whirling night with his head full of roaring and keep him so till his courage is a shivering mouse, and seasick at that. When the sky above the waves turns from black to grey it seems the greatest blessing, and when I looked at the drawn faces of my crew I knew that I was not alone in my thoughts.

"We must give thanks," I said and there was a general searching for a bottle of unspoiled wine. We spilled it into the waves that even now raged about us.

"The wind's easing," said Olaf.

I had not noticed it. Yet perhaps the howling was less.

A seagull sat on a wave beside us, riding it with impertinent ease, his little black eye seeming to say "You should have stayed home, sailor!" as if we did not know it.

"He thinks it's past," I said, "and I'll wager he didn't expect to see us this morning."

"He's not alone in that," said Olaf and we exchanged looks. We had been lucky.

There is no rising of the sun on such a day, only a lightening of greys until the faces of comrades show their weariness clearly. We were in poor case, with everything soaked, the rudder smashed and two of the planks spread and taking in water. I set all the men on to baling, each taking a turn regardless of how ill he might be, for every one of them had been keen enough to come. Bent, whose hair was grey and his face now greyer, groaned like a walrus as he worked and was plainly very sick.

"It would not hurt to let him stop," said Olaf out of the

side of his mouth and indeed the men were looking at him and muttering.

"Bent," I said, "if another will take your place he may do so. But it will be the end of it, I will put you ashore as soon as I can. It is the same for all of us."

His dark eyes watched from holes of wrinkled flesh, all sunk in now with misery but with a spark burning that I knew to be hate.

"I will take the turn," said Thorsteinn, and I thought to myself, that is a good man, he is cheerful and strong. His wife was right to weep for him.

I could feel salt sores forming where my clothes rubbed, in the folds of elbows and in the groin, at every moment reminding of how soft we were. Yet the wind was now no more than a strong breeze though the sea was short and angry. Towards noon we saw the sun, all wreathed about in cloud as if it were a woman's veiling, one of those eastern women that they keep all parceled up in cloth. They keep them like cattle there but they seem not to mind it. I amused myself wondering what Emma would say if I told her to go about like that, though I knew that what she said would be the least of it; she would box my ears for me I dare say.

"Thorkil. There's a sail."

Olaf pointed and I looked along his arm. Truly, there it was, a Viking sail, red, and as we rose on a wave I could see the dragonpicture.

"Thank the gods! We are saved!" cried Bent, pulling himself up to his knees.

I glared at him. "We weren't drowning," I snapped. "Would you have them see us like this? Pull yourselves together and let us face them proudly. They may tell us our bearing, it is all we need."

The ship had seen us as we had seen them and was skimming the waves towards us. "She sails most smartly," I said to Olaf, and he grunted. I knew he would rather be with such seamen, they had mastered the sea as a bird on the wind. I could see the foam creaming the prow, and the heads of men ranged along the sides, the pale sun glinting on their helms.

"Olaf," I said uneasily. "What would such a ship be doing here? They look as if they put to sea only this morning."

"Perhaps they did," he replied, seeing nothing beyond

what was there. I swallowed. Was this a real fear or again the caution of age? If I was wrong I should look a fool, but if I was right—was I to let my pride send us all to our deaths? But they could be just a boatload of warriors, taking news from a ship such as ours and giving casual succor. They were Viking after all—and I'd taken Viking crews in my time and killed a few, though I never sold them for slaves. They would be on us in a moment, I had to decide.

I spun round to face my men. "Listen to me, all of you," I said urgently. "Your lives depend on it. That ship looks to me like a pirate vessel, preying on storm and shipwreck. We seem helpless, and that must be our strength. Take your arms and keep them hidden, and if it should come to a fight remember this only—in the afterlife there is room at the table for few men, and those the warriors who gave up their hearts bravely. We will stand to each other comrades, it is the only glory."

Their faces looked at me, like so many anxious children. Then without speaking they took swords and laid them at their feet, and daggers were placed close to hand on the benches. The old one, Bent, had a bow.

"You'll be one of us yet," I said to him, and dropped my hand to his shoulder. He said nothing and I thought is an enemy made so easily? I took my hand away and ordered, "Make your first shot their leader, you see him? The one with the gold locks, standing all godlike at the prow."

"If I take him now it might settle it," said Bent.

I glanced at him quickly. "Not yet. They have more bows than we, they could stand off and take us at their leisure."

"If we let them in close they will slaughter us!"

I shrugged. "That is the way of it. But it's not over yet, put your faith in World Tree, who has never failed the man that holds him." Then, seeing that he was not comforted by such stuff I added, "Besides, we shall surprise them. Fit as they are, a dagger in the gut will see to it."

"But they may not be pirates at all."

"Oh, go fuck your mother," I snapped, and abandoned him. I found myself hoping that he met his end a deal sooner than the rest of us.

I made some of the men lie down, as if desperate sick, but myself I placed square on the deck, letting them see that I carried no sword, letting my hair and beard stream in the breeze. I watched in wonder as they slipped the wind from the sail as they approached us, taking the way from the boat with four oars at the stern.

"If you're right, we're dead," whispered Olaf. "They're good."

Their leader hailed us. When I looked at his tall and slender body, with his golden hair curling from his helmet, I thought at once of Bjarni. But there was a slyness in him that came to me like a stench across the oarslength between us, his words were touched not with honey but the rankest oil.

"You seem distressed," he purred. "We are come to give you aid."

"We need no aid," I said, and even to my own ears I sounded harsh.

"But your men are sick. Come, let us take you in tow, we shall see you safe to land."

"They aren't pirates after all," hissed Bent and began to rise, but someone kneed him.

"How far is it to land?" I asked and the young man smiled at me, sensing a softening. "Barely half a morning. Look, here is our rope all ready, you can be safe in harbor and enjoying a good meal in the time it would take you to put up the sail."

"And what would you want for this service?"

He waved an airy hand. "A trifling payment only. We can discuss it later, when your men are safe ashore."

I pretended to think. If I let them take us to shore we were finished, for they would be certain to have others of like mind waiting for them. No, it must be here and now if we were to fight at all. I felt a griping in my guts and that dryness of mouth that tells a man he will never outlive fear. I lifted my head and sucked the air through my nose, smelling the sea and the wind, feeling the lift and drop of the waves as Skimmer labored beneath me.

"We are taking in water," I said. "Let us put some men in your good ship, it will make the tow easier."

"They seem very sick," he said doubtfully. Thorsteinn set up a groaning that would have done credit to a cow.

"It is the sea only and also some bad water," I offered. "If you want us to take your tow you must lighten us."

"That man sounds as if he is dying," said the pirate.

"Would that he were. Stuff it, Thorsteinn, and get on your

feet! I've a solid ship for you now, you've been praying for one long enough.''

"Little wonder, I'd give anything for a change from this tub," complained Thorsteinn. "Bad food, bad water, the boat leaking and the chief sleeping all day, it's the last time I take ship with you, I promise." He levered himself up to his knees as the pirate ship began to draw alongside. "Where are the riches you promised us? Coming, always coming. You're lucky the trade goods didn't sink us, I said we were too low when we set out. What use all these hides at the bottom of the sea I said, do you hear me comrades, I told him—"

The pirate crew were laughing at him as he clung to the side like a wild man, ranting for all he was worth. I put my hand to my sword where it lay beneath the sail. Olaf fingered within his shirt to where his dagger lay snug. Another stroke and they must ship their oars or break them against our hull, and in that moment we should have them.

A movement caught my eye. I watched amazed as Bent lifted his bow from the bench, drew it back and fired. Even before the arrow landed, thudding useless into the other's deck, the young chief was yelling for them to pull away. But they could not make the change so swiftly, one oar struck us and splintered as I leaped forward yelling, "Take them lads! We have them!"

There was a distance between the boats. I stood on the gunwale, swayed to take my balance and leaped, landing sprawling on a man unsheathing his sword. The space was tight, I could not wield World Tree, but I was roaring like a bull and I trampled him like one also. His shipped oar was before me, I rammed it one handed out again, hoping that it would reach Skimmer and the men could seize it and board also.

"Pull! Pull!" Olaf's voice, but I was too busy to look. Four of them were at me, two with spears, but I had found my feet and swirled my sword to keep them back.

"You think to trick Thorkil Sigurdsson?" I bellowed. "You think he is fool enough to fall for your schemes, you young snake?" There was a shriek as my blade caught the hand that held a spear. Cut at the wrist, it flew in the air and landed twitching on the deck, the fingers wriggling by themselves. After a moment the blood spurted down on to the deck and the pirate leader turned and called out "Sven!"

It was the last thing that he said. I felt no sorrow for him then, nor any later, though I grieved to learn that his mother lost two sons on that ship. She should have taught them better habits, I think.

But these thoughts were not for a battle. In a moment Olaf and Thorsteinn were beside me and I saw with pleasure that others of my crew had put a hook in the pirate deck to hold the two vessels close. They might not be seamen yet but they were warriors. One whose name I had forgotten took a dagger in the throat, and his friends drowned his cries with their battleroar. There was no fear in any of us but only strength and courage and a comradeship that is unknown to men who have never faced death together. We began that day a rabble and ended it a warrior band.

It was soon over, as such shipboard fights must always be. One or two men jumped into the sea clutching a jar or whatever else they could take that might help them float, but for the rest we took prisoners, some ten in all. One was so bad hurt that we let his friends finish it for him, though strangely I could not watch. I was grown squeamish as a girl.

For ourselves we had four men gone and we were in difficulties. Our own ship was in sore need of beaching for she was very battered, but we did not know where we were. Our captives would of course send us straight to a hostile shore, and if we went somewhere that they did not advise it might be that they had thought of that and misinformed us deliberately. So we could not trust them at all, except lashed to their oars to row. All the same I questioned them, and it seemed to me that they were Danes, hunting out of a foreign port, perhaps on the south coast of Frankia. Perhaps we were blown southward, in which case that was a troubled part of the world. I sniffed the wind and thought a little. It would be best to trust to luck and go north a little to strike Denmark or even Norway if the gods permitted. We could take ship in the pirate vessel and draw poor old Skimmer behind us.

Olaf caught my arm. "We must see to the burials."

"What?" I looked at him without understanding. Then it came to me, of course when warriors are slain their chief must see to the burial, it was only that in all our adventuring with our little band no-one had ever died. The Danes saw to their own and we took small part in it, I had never before had to deal with such a thing. I did not know what to do.

"We cannot make land and do it," I whispered. "I had just this minute decided we had better sail north. This coast is a viper's nest."

"We should put them in the ship."

I goggled at him. "A good ship? For common seamen? Why, my own father only had a currach and he was—my father. Can't we give them the things in a sack and tip them over the side?"

He picked his teeth and scratched at his nose. "If we had a whore or two to send with them perhaps, that always makes everyone happy."

I nodded, remembering when I too had shared in that. The girl is sent to the grave for a man to use, for he will need her just as much as the weapons and food that he takes with him. But to honor him, and to remember themselves to a comrade, his friends each serve the woman before she dies, and strangely there is little lewdness in it. She is going to her death and she will be as if awake in sleep, because of herbs and wine usually. She passes from man to man and when each has planted something of himself in her there is a calmness and a remembering. Her death comes quickly, in the midst of a great shout, and she and her master go on their journey together. But we had no women, which was a troublesome point.

I cleared my throat. "Men," I said firmly. "We have a difficulty. Our own good comrades have fallen in battle and in our grief we must honor them. For myself I am sure that they are now nearing Asgard, leaving only their bodies for us to weep over. But it is our duty to send their goods after them and I am happy to give my own dagger to the grave." I laid it down somberly, though in truth I had only taken it that day. Still, it was a good dagger.

"Do we put them in the ship?" asked one.

"If there were no other way then indeed I would," I said grandly. "But instead we shall build them a raft, for we have spars and goatskins. They will sail away in honor."

There was a little murmuring, but soon silenced when I poured out some ale for the graveship. It was running low and they all knew it. One by one they each gave something, be it a pin, a belt or a comb. I knew that every one of them was thinking that they themselves would be ashamed to receive so little to take to a new life, but none was prepared to give more. They were comrades only, there were no ties of kinship.

Meantime Olaf was building something to float, even if only until we were out of sight. It was a makeshift affair and each body was lashed to it with his grave goods stowed about him. When we lowered it into the sea it sank very low, and water lapped about the dead faces, splashing into their blind eyes, moving like air into their lungs. For a time it stayed close to the ship, but gradually the waves took it away, at first hiding the color of their skin, then the look of each face, and at last taking our friends from us and leaving only some raft or other bobbing at a distance.

"That is finished," I said then. "Let us set sail and go before someone else comes to seize us."

One of our captives looked up to me from where he was bound to an oar. "You have not buried our man. He is my brother." It was at once a demand and a plea. All the others had been tipped over the side, it was only this last one, who had been so bad hurt that remained. So I took a pinch of bread and I soaked it in ale, I found an old knife and a couple of beads and I put all in a bag and slipped it inside the man's jerkin. Then I blew up a goatskin and tied it to his head, and he too went forth on his travels.

"That is a debt you owe me," I said to my prisoner as he bent his back at the oar.

In the next days the full extent of our troubles became clear to us all, in the creaking of Skimmer's mast whenever sail was set and in the constant need to bale water out of the hull. She was sore wounded by the storm and Olf began muttering. "She was never meant for a long voyage, we should keep to the coast only. Look at her, it makes your heart bleed to see her so distressed, for she's a fine ship and deserves better than a fool to steer her. If she sinks it will be only what she deserves."

I ignored him for as long as I might, for the pirate ship was very fine. But when it began to blow and we were forced to drop Skimmer's sail a long while before the other was even filled, well I saw that we either saved her or sank her.

I told Olaf to make course for the coast, the raider towing Skimmer in its wake. I feared that a storm was approaching and I sat in the bows of the raider, sipping wine and looking

out to the horizon. Before the battle I should not have be-
haved so, but now I had the men's trust and respect. Only
Olaf still snapped at me, but from such a friend one takes
anything. Besides, he was good for me.

So I sat there and watched for the first faint smudges of
land, hoping that by some chance I should know where we
were. Soon I saw what I looked for, a thin, flat coast that
could have been anywhere, but smelled to me like Denmark.
Men who have not traveled will say to you, how can you
know which place you are come to after days tossing about on
a faceless sea, and to them I say the sea is never faceless; in
its deeps and shallows it speaks to us, in the color of the
weed and the movement of the waves against the hull. A man
can tell how far a wave has traveled only by looking at it.
And when he sees a coast before him he will say to himself it
cannot be here or here, or even there, but must surely be this
one place only. Most times he will be right.

I looked down my ship to where the prisoners sat,
hunchshouldered and miserable. There was the one whose
brother I had buried and he sat with his young face turned
brightly to the land. I knew that he looked towards home and
I pondered if this could be useful to me. We needed succor
for ourselves and our ship, and that was not easy come by in
Denmark, where all the towns have walls and the people are
as sure and fierce as wolves in the forest. I called for the lad
to come to me, and he moved stiffly, for we untied them as
rarely as possible.

"Where is your home, lad?" I asked, fatherly, you know
what I mean?

He swallowed and you could see his mind working behind
his face, with the longing and the doubt, the fear and the
sureness that is youth of a good ending to it all. "It is a
village . . . near Ribe."

"We are near there now, I think." In truth I knew only
that it was Denmark, no more and no less.

"With this wind we could be there in half a day."

I began to smile and then remembered Emma saying that I
looked like a thief when I smiled, so I nodded like a wise
man instead. "Your mother will be glad to have you home,
lad."

"You mean—you are setting us free?"

I sniffed and rubbed at my nose. I was going to seek

payment, but not in money. "Do they build ships at your home?"

He nodded, hot and hopeful. "Some. There is a man who makes fishing boats, we bring some of the wood from Norway."

"I knew it. Come, lad, drink with me and seal our bargain. You and your friends to go free in return for good old Skimmer to be put to rights. Can I trust you to it, boy? You have seen my honor, I think."

"My father will pledge his word on mine. It is agreed." The lad drew himself up and clasped my hand before taking a sup of wine. He was a fair enough boy if a trifle dull in the head, but that is Danes for you. Mind you, if they set their minds to a thing it is as good as done, and I speak as one who knows them better than most. All I can say is, don't tell them jokes.

Olfa's snoring was never sweet, but that night he was louder than a pig. He did not wake when I threw a shoe at him and by then I was itching all over and quite sleepless. I put on my clothes, which was not easy for Olaf was lying on my shoe, and I went out.

It was a clear sky with half a moon showing. The light sparkled silver on the water, like a shoal of herring in the net, and against it rose up the raider's mast and that of Skimmer, a new pine pole on a new mast fish. The old ship was as good as she'd ever be and we were as fat as cows, thanks to a mother's gratitude. But it seemed to me time to move on, before they fell to thinking that it would be useful to have the raider back in Danish hands, whatever words had passed from a young boy's foolish lips.

That night I felt sad and heavy, yet there was no reason for it. I had won a prize and now had two fine ships and even some of the Danes were asking to sail with us. If it is wealth a man looks for then I had it, and if it is glory then I had that also. Why then did I feel as if at any moment I could sit on the shore with my head on my knees and sob? I moved into the shadow cast by Skimmer as she lay angled on the beach and I snuffled into my beard a little, part of me a grieving child while another part stood aside and wondered how it should be that a grown man wept, and for nothing. The planks of the boat were cool and hard against my cheek, uncomforting, being themselves far from the quiet forests of their begetting, more lonely even than I, though I was miserable enough. How long had the oak trees stood before they died to build a ship? How long would the ship go on living, taking into itself the years in the wood even on the day of its birth.

Suddenly I longed for Skarphedin, who felt a certainty and faith that was not mine. My strength was only in my arm and my happiness a fragile plant that flowered in the snow and withered in warm breezes, or so it seemed to me.

When I had done crying I went back to the house. Olaf lifted up on his elbow as I entered.

"You've been a long time. I was going to come and look for you."

"Can't a man take a walk by himself any more?"

"If it is only a walk. I thought the Danes might have done for you, they're beginning to think."

"I suppose even Danes must do that now and then. We sail in the morning, for if we don't get rid of those hides soon they'll rot. Some of them are barely cured. We'll sell them at Hedeby and then move on to Birka to see what we can pick up." Now that we had two ships we could trade in earnest and I had a fancy to see what was come out of the east in those times. When last I was at Birka market there was a cup so thin you could see the light through it and the man that owned it said it had come across Lake Ladoga on the ice, and before that on a sledge from the mountains. That is a very far place. Hearing of such things makes a man know his own littleness.

Olaf said, a little gruffly, "I thought we were going home. We're near enough, Thorkil, surely."

If he had something to go home for I had not. I said, "There's time enough for that. I will sleep now, don't bother me."

When we took ship next morning we left Bent standing forlorn on the beach, watching us. I had warned him but he had not believed me, or at least he had looked for some payment or other.

"I owe you nothing," I said to him, and he stared at me white-faced, for he was without goods of any sort, or money. So we left him, in part for his own fault and in part to show the others how it might be.

*   *   *

I know what you are thinking; how did we fare in the Skagerrack? It is no better now than it was I may say, with pirates like flies on a dungheap, biting each other half the time. We were lucky that we were two ships together, they thought we were stronger than we were. I set every shield that we had along the sides, each man held his spear so it could be seen and we kept a fire burning in a pot on deck, for arrows if need be. I was wondering all the while if we should fetch up on a lee shore, for the wind is as treacherous as the ships thereabouts. But I was raised in that fjord.

I was in Raider while Olaf captained old Skimmer, to squeeze all speed out of her because even with the new mast she was not quick. It was misty when we began, but by some curse the sun got up and it was as clear as polished silver. We saw a ship at a distance, and though first we thought the worst of them when we saw how she labored we thought perhaps they were honest men, like ourselves. I shouted to Olaf and together we began to beat towards her, for if they were in such trouble I thought we might offer aid. Or take them if it looked worth it, there's no point in making a habit out of virtue.

As we got close I saw that the sail was patched, showing grey streaks where it had once been as red as our own. It seemed to me that they were taking water, for the ship was down by the head and wallowed in the troughs of waves. I looked back to see how close Skimmer came and she was near enough, the two of us making a fine sight no doubt with our high painted prows and the shields catching the sun. I remember that I shivered, partly from cold, for the snow was dusting the high ground and in the morning the decks were bristled with ice.

A voice from the boat ahead hailed us. "If you value your lives you'll come no closer. We are poor men going about our business."

"I thought you might be in trouble," I shouted back. "You are down by the head."

"If we are it is our problem only."

By now we were only a spear's shot distant and on every ship men were fingering their weapons. But I was wary. If we took them it had to be worth our while.

"Where are you from?" I asked, trying to come close

enough to see how many of them there were behind the shieldwall.

The reply was cautious. "Skringsall, near Kaupang, in Vestfold. We are on our way home."

Olaf's voice rose in a great shout. "Knut Gunnarson, you old whoremonger! I thought it was a wonder the boat was afloat, she's sailing like a washtub!"

Olaf began to roar and Knut to roar back and soon Olaf was leaping the gap between Skimmer and Knut's ship, to clasp his cousin and punch him harder than an enemy.

I swore beneath my breath and spat into the water. For what else could we do but lay down our swords and see our friend safely home, to the village that was ours, to the friends of our boyhood, to the women who had kissed us long ago?

They gathered on the beach to welcome us, they stretched out fond arms to bring our ships to safety. Here and there I saw a face I knew and I would call out a name and then there was amazement and glad cries. I leaped from my ship and splashed forward, reaching out to embrace my friends, and to a man they seemed surprised and less glad than I had thought. I felt apart from them.

Olaf and his cousin were calling and shouting to family, and the lack of my own people was like a knife. Where was my mother, my sister with her new husband, that would be an old husband by now? Why, it was years since I trod the gentle paths of Skringsall, and smelt fish and pine forest. I should have left it years longer perhaps. Never gone back in this lifetime.

Olaf caught at my sleeve saying, "Come, Thorkil, we are going to Knut's house. You see how they are looking at you? It's wordfame you have here it seems, they're all overcome.,

I tossed in a belly laugh that was all wind, and turned to summon Thorsteinn. He would see to the men this night, find them a barn as lodging and a pretty girl or two.

"I want no trouble," I said to him quietly. "No torn dresses, you understand me?" He nodded and grinned. I don't know how it should be but you take staid men, with wives, give them a few weeks at sea, and they're as randy and wayward as boys fresh from their mother's skirts.

I took up World Tree and a pack with some few gifts inside it, the sort of thing it is good to bring home though I had no thought of who would receive them. This place had stayed set in my mind since the day that I left it, only now did I think that while I was changing this was changing also. I had a feeling of guilt, like a child out playing too long and worrying his mother—there was a question on my tongue, and I looked around to ask it. I could not. Instead I smiled and strode long-legged after my friend.

If I drank one horn of ale I drank twenty. The fire had a deep red throat and the faces round it swam in the smoke like creatures in a sea-mist. They called me hero. They fed me herring baked with herbs and they asked in dread of the great Skarphedin, that only I could tame, who held such magic in his hand that kings were afraid.

"How many have you killed?" the young boys asked and I shook my head at them and said, "A man doesn't count."

Girls looked at me with their great round eyes, looking out of faces too young and plump, seeing in me something that was not there, or if it was I did not know it. I heard Olaf tell that in Northumbria we were rich, that we had a great farm and that there I had left a noble wife. The girls all dropped their eyes and one whispered "Is she beautiful?" to which Olaf replied "She has skin like silk. And her courage is the equal of any man's." The they all looked at me again and I held my horn out for more ale.

In the morning my skull was splitting, but at least it kept me from thought. Olaf's mother's sister, that had Knut to answer for, gave me a cup of hot wine and some bread with a look that said "They're all boys, however long their beards." I knew that in a day she would be sewing my clothes and trimming my hair, and making me tasty things to eat as if she mothered me as well as her own. I sat down gratefully in the warm place by the fire and watched her make bread on a floury table. The memories flooded thick and fast, I had sat so often in a house like this and watched a woman cooking.

"I will travel to my uncle's later," I said. "For news of my mother."

Her hands stopped working. "I did not know if you had heard," she said slowly. " She went last winter, quite quietly. We lost a lot of old people in the cold."

I sat for a moment. How could I feel grief now for something that had happened months since, that made no change in my life but only put a final ending to a tale long forgotten? Besides, I had known it from the moment we put in at Skringsall, I had only waited for the telling.

I took a sip of wine but could not swallow it. My tears dripped into the cup. I was glad there was only an old woman to see me.

In a little time I asked "My sister? I've heard nothing—surely she's not—"

Knut's mother sighed. "You've been away too long, Thorkil Sigurdsson. The brave and hearty ones have gone, and your sister and her man amongst them. I think in the spring that Knut will go too, he's only come back to court young Ingrid. And she's no better than she ought to be, there've been a few hands up that skirt." She banged at the bread as if she wished it were Ingrid's head. I wondered which one she was, I had thought Knut fancied the shy, plump one.

"These girls are all the same," I said sagely. "Tell me, mother, where are people going? Is it England?"

"We leave that to the Danes. Our people are taking ship for Iceland now. It is empty, there are no battles to fight. But there's little else good about it if you ask me."

Any place that took her son would be hard thought of, I could see. "Iceland—do you mean Thule?" I had heard of this place, days from Norway's coast, where the mountains spout fire and the ice falls like rivers into the sea. I had not thought it a place to settle.

"They're all flocking there like so many hens, and it's Finehair's fault. He has trodden too many necks."

I lifted my brows and thought for a little. My sister had always been wilful, we'd never been close, and there was no reason for she and her husband to keep to the home country. Still, I had thought myself to be the wanderer, I was surprised to learn she'd gone to a place I had only heard spoken of in legend.

I went thoughtfully outside and the wind was like a slap from a cold hand, it smelled of snow and hard frost, coming early. In England the summer's end is a gentle thing, as the summer is gentle, but in Norway it is a dog with teeth.

Olaf sheltered in the barn, yarning with his cousins. "I am telling of that night in Jorvik, when we found Emma," he said happily.

"You talk too much," I said, sour as new wine.

"She sounds fierce," said Knut, presuming on a short friendship.

I waggled my head at him. "If she sounds anything I am sure it is no concern of yours old fellow. What is this I hear of a girl called Ingrid? Your mother says she's light."

Knut's face flushed dark red. "It is not for you to repeat a lie. She is good and sweet, I know it."

"They are all sweet apples, the better for keeping, crisp to the bite and oh, so juicy—" Olaf was very drunk. "Give me a woman!" he cried. "Fat or thin, short or tall, all that I ask is a good tight fit between her thighs. Isn't there a girl in Skringsall would like a sticking?"

There came a giggle from around the door and we looked out to see one of the girls that served in the house passing with a jug. She blushed to her hair and ran off, with her skirt rising up past her knees.

"Try that one," I told Olaf. "You like them soft."

He pulled at his breeks and stood straight, staggering a little. "I need something to give her."

We laughed lewdly and Knut said, "I've got something if you haven't!"

"There are some brooches and things in my pack," I said. "You can take them."

"You're a good friend to me, Thorkil. I tell you, when I was alone in Jorvik I didn't know myself. We're brothers, you and me—" he stretched out his hand to me but I caught his shoulders and pushed him to the door.

"Go and make the girl happy, you old waster. And make sure the old lady doesn't know or she'll chop off something you hold most dear, mark my words."

When he was gone Knut and I were quiet together.

"He's a good friend," I said at last.

"He speaks most highly of you."

I shrugged. "That's Olaf for you. A good friend."

Knut chewed at his nails a little and I saw that it was habit of his, for there was nothing left to chew. "I was familiar about your wife," he said. "I'm sorry."

"I was unkind about your girl also. What is she like?"

"Ingrid? Very small and sweet, with the biggest eyes you ever saw, and so shy—"

"I think I saw her. She was in the red dress, near you, and blushing when you spoke?"

"That's her. We hope to be wed."

I nodded and dropped a hand on his shoulder. "She'll make you a fine wife. Your mother says you are leaving here though, to settle in Iceland."

"If I go it will have to be soon, or all the land will be gone. It's a fine place so they tell me, with the sea boiling with fish and the fields so green the cattle get fat just looking at them."

"What of the fiery mountains? What of the ice?"

He looked me straight in the eyes. "It will be hard, Thorkil, I know that. But there comes a time when a man needs his freedom, he needs to breathe his own air. You've been away a long time. It was bad here when you went and it's worse now. A man can't call his shit his own."

"But Thule—I tell you, Knut, there are better places. In England now, you need a strong arm but I have won myself some land. Grant that most of it goes to the Danes, but—"

"That is not what I want," he burst out. "I want a place with laws and peace, that is owned honestly, where Ingrid can sleep sound and know that no-one will come and kill her in the night. I have had enough of terror."

"There is no such place," I said sadly. "Believe me, I've seen it all."

"No, you haven't."

I glanced up at him. "Now see here, lad, I've been trailing about since I was a boy—"

"There is a place you haven't seen, that is all I am saying. Look, I don't want you to spread this about—it's not something I want people to know. But on the last voyage—I found a place."

He was staring at me very hard, as if to see into my mind. He had a tale to tell, that much was clear. "Come, lad," I said, drawing him further into the barn. "Let's go back among the cows, it's warmer there and more private. Tell me the tale."

It was hard in those days to live in Vestfold, as it is often hard to live under a great king. For Harald Halfdanarson was great, even his enemies acknowledged it, and he came of a great line, for his grandmother was Queen Asa. She it was who was taken in marriage by force and when she had borne her first child, Halfdan the Black had her husband murdered.

Then she took her son home to Agdir and ruled for him until he was grown, and could demand Agdir and his father's lands of Vestfold as of right. Harald was Halfdan's son and by the strength of his arm he took and held Norway's kingdoms. But he fed on the people, taking from them so that he could prosper, and always reaching out for more and more conquest.

Skringsall was small, but nearby was the market of Kaupang, where beads and cloth and bronze were worked and traded. When Knut decided to marry Ingrid he thought he would try a trading venture, and he gathered his funds and loaded a ship with goods to sell elsewhere. He thought he would beat up Norway's coast to Trondelag, to sell his wares and see if life was any easier there than under King Harald's thumb in Vestfold, but it seemed much the same to him, except colder and more out of things.

It was on the return voyage that difficulty arose. One of their number had made a crossing before to the islands north of Britain, where he thought some of their goods might fetch better prices than in Trondelag, where the people haggled so. They decided to try their luck in the Faroes before setting off for home. The wind was getting up when they started, and before a day was out it was clear that they were in for a great blow. They lashed everything that moved, themselves huddled in the stern, and waited for the storm to exhaust itself. It blew for four days, always westward, and when at last the wind dropped it was only enough for them to eat a hot meal. There was a howling in the air like the cries of the dead, screaming at the end of the world, and the seas tossed the boat like a twig. The days and nights were inseparable, filled with wind and rain and the screeches of a ship near to breaking. Knut lost count of the time, which seemed only a ghastly passage to death, when their own spirits would howl in the wind.

They were so cold and wet that their feet lost all feeling, and when at last the storm eased and they took off their leggings and shoes there was more than one man found a toe came off with them. But what use are toes on the edge of the world, where they must surely be after so long?

They were despairing, quite without hope of ever seeing home and hearthside again.

Knut was as hopeless as his men, but as the leader he tried to rally them. "There may be land here," he said. "If we can only find a little water and some food, we can try to get home again.''

"The boat's near smashed to pieces," said Bjorn, his voice hoarse from the days past when they had screamed to each other over the storm.

"We may be able to mend it," said Knut, though in truth he did not think it was possible. Yet they were not dead, the gods had brought them here alive. Were they then to reach the place where the seas meet the sky, to be the first to fall into the underworld, without death's dusty cloak? It seemed a terrible thing. Knut and his men sat silent and grim-faced, watching their stained sail push them onward.

In a few more days they were thin and drawn from lack of food, and still they saw no land. The water was deep and they caught few fish and at night the stars shone so bright that they could see each other's faces, a man could pare his nails by the glow. Knut hated the nights, he could not bear to look at the great vastness of the sky and know that they in their torment were so tiny a thing. In such a world one man's anguish makes as little sound as a raindrop.

The day came when there was nothing to eat at all but some moldered biscuit. "Let us offer it," said Knut, and since none could think of a better plan they did so. The crumbs floated away on a green sea and that night they slept well, as starving men do. Death creeps upon the hungry and always takes a man in sleep. Those who have left their friends dead on the ice floes will tell you the same.

Next day they saw land, looming black in the morning mist. As they came closer, believing at first that it was some foul place, they saw that it was green and seemed to those men to be lusher by far than anywhere they knew. There were no houses, no fires, no people. The beach sloped gently and they grounded some way out and had to splash their way shorewards, with the wavering steps of men who have been very long at sea.

There was grass near to the shore, and stiff bushes with berries on. They ate them though they were bitter. When they had gathered their wits they walked further on, amazed to find themselves in such a place, and alive. Towards evening Bjorn caught a salmon in a river, and they gathered round a brushwood fire to cook it.

"I tell you, Thorkil," said Knut, "I shall never feel such

happiness again. We were saved from death, and after so long. We had not looked for it.''

I nodded wisely and urged him to go on, but it was as you might expect. They mended the ship, gathered what stores they could and came home, this time making a landfall on the coast of Britain, from which they were chased by the Picts after one night. They crept back to Skringsall as poor as when they left, with two men dead and the rest missing teeth as well as toes. Our meeting them in the Skagerrack was the least of their luck by all accounts.

"But why don't you tell this tale?" I asked. "You'll be famous for it!"

Knut looked unhappy. "You know how men are. If I tell it then half will believe me and half won't, and of the half that do someone will want to go there. And I'm never making that trip again, not in this life. I'm taking Ingrid to Iceland and that is the last journey we shall make, whatever we find there. If I was an adventurer like you it would be different, but I have not your courage, Thorkil.''

So I thanked him for telling me and we went into the house to drink a cup or two by the fire. And I do not mind saying that whatever Knut's faith in me I was a deal happier in that warm house than crossing the seas to the world's end.

In a couple of days I thought we would never leave the place. It was so good to be among friends and if they all complained about taxes and so on it had little to do with me. Olaf was keeping himself warm at night with the serving girl, and there would be a swollen belly there before long. He was deceiving her and promising to take her with us, which I did not like. A girl hasn't so much as a man, you shouldn't trick her into giving it. When I spoke to him about it he was amazed, and ranted on about girls past, but as I said to him, "Olaf, that was different. We were young then."

We learn little enough in this life as it is without turning our noses up at something because we did not know it sooner.

I took a day or two myself and went inland, to my uncle's farm, to learn what I could of my mother. The weather was cold, of course. I set off late on the first day and the pony went lame before I had done half the journey and I had to walk, so when it came on dark I thought I had better find a house to take me in. No man in his senses spends a night in a field when the wind is blowing little flakes of snow into his beard. A light burned in the gathering dusk, I could just make out a cluster of buildings at a steading. I could hear the cows in the barn mooing to be fed, so it was close on milking. It was a comforting sound and made me think of times past. There would be no winter on my own farm yet awhile.

A man was crossing the yard as I approached. He stood staring, and said in a voice rough with fear, "Who goes there? This is a peaceful house."

"And I am a peaceful man," I replied. "Have you a bed for a night for a traveler? I am going to my uncle's farm after years away, and would you believe that this nag has gone lame? I am sorry to be a trouble to you."

I was close to him now and saw that he was small and round, coming barely to my shoulder. He looked askance at World Tree and said, "I'd be obliged if you'd leave your sword outside, stranger."

"No, I'll not do that. You may put us both in the barn if you wish but where he goes I go also. We love each other, you see, and between us we manage to stay healthy. But I'm honest, I promise you that. My name's Thorkil Sigurdsson."

"Thorkil Sigurdsson! Well! I don't know what to say!"

I have never seen a man so stunned by just a name, and it puffed me up a little. As Olaf said, I was famous. I chuckled modestly and gestured to the house, and the little man led the way like a lamb.

There was a woman tending a pot on the fire, taller than the man and it was as well for she carried more flesh than you'd look for on a heifer. A couple of brats were playing in a corner but I wanted to make my peace with her before I took notice. After all, she was cooking dinner.

"Well met, mistress," I said. "Your husband has been so kind as to offer me a bed—"

I got no further. She turned with the ladle in her hand and her mouth a round hole in her face, and underneath it three chins at least, every one of them wobbling. She looked as if she might be mad, and I felt my own smile sliding back into my beard. Thank the gods for World Tree I thought to myself, I had no wish to end my days at the ladle of a lunatic.

"Thorkil!" she cried. "Thorkil! Don't you know me? Your own Bergthora!"

Well! I've had shocks and frights aplenty in my life but

that stopped my heart beating, I can tell you. There was the
husband, looking all to pieces, and there Bergthora that I
remembered as plump enough to please, as fat as a pig off to
market. All of a sudden I remembered fondling her breasts in
the dark of the barn, which was as much as she would let me.
If one of those dugs was let loose now it would take both my
hands to hold it, and if both swung free a man could be
smothered! She flung her arms out towards me, so naturally I
embraced her, feeling those great breasts like pillows against
my chest and her thighs all trembling.

"I didn't know you were wed," I said gently in her ear,
and I saw that she was crying a little. The husband and the
children were standing looking at us, their faces miserable. I
put Bergthora away from me and she began to cry in earnest.
Her skin was pink and still as smooth as in her girlhood. I had
forgotten that about her.

I patted her shoulder and her cheek, and then the great
mound of her bottom, and after a time she cheered up and
went back to cooking the dinner. And I told her of what had
happened to me, and the grievous wound that had prevented
me coming home—I could not decide where to have it, but
fortunately no-one asked—and how happy I was to see her so
well settled after the anxious years I had worried about her.
She was a marvelous cook. She did hare with herbs better
than I have ever tasted it, and I said as much to her husband.
"You're a lucky man," I said, and he agreed with me. I saw
Bergthora blush and look at me a little sideways.

After supper I played a game with the two little boys. They
were fine lads, but soft in their ways, crying at the least thing
and bringing their mother to cuddle them. I could not help
thinking that my own son would not have been so, for he had
strong blood in him. Perhaps these boys would be different if
I had been the sire. I said to Bergthora, "My own son died."

She put her hand out to me, with her face troubled. "What
of your wife?"

I did not know what to say. I wanted her to think well of
me and if I told her the truth I thought that she would not. But
again, there was no point in lying, I would only tangle myself
further. In confusion I stood up, saying "I must see to the
pony," but Bergthora's husband, who had sat quiet in the
corner watching us, said, "Stay you, sir, as the host it is my
task. Anyway you want to talk."

When he was gone Bergthora and I sat watching the fire and the children.

"You left her," she said, and there was no denying it.

Still, I tried to put a gloss on it. "When the child died it all went bad between us. She did not want me. But she has the farm and a lad to help her, she'll not starve."

She looked at me sorrowfully, her girlish eyes that I remembered looking from a face I did not know. She had been so pretty once.

"I knew how it would be," she said. "You always leave women, you don't know how to stay. If we'd wed you'd have left me and said it was because I was fat. At least now I've got a husband that loves me in spite of it." She sniffed into a handkerchief and I patted the great round bolster of her shoulder, that was so soft it seemed boneless.

"She wasn't as pretty as you," I said.

"I'm not so pretty any more. But I have a good man and good children and that is more than your wife has. So you see, it's turned out for the best. Olaf said as much."

"Olaf? When did you see him?"

"As if a brother wouldn't come to see his only kin! He was careful not to tell you, that's all. The way he ate you'd think he hadn't seen food in a month."

I thought of the tale I'd told them, putting myself in a good light all along.

My face began to redden and I bent down to where the boys were playing at Vikings, with a wooden boat and wooden figures. "That's it lads, whack 'em! You going to go adventuring when you grow up eh? That's the spirit!"

"I knew Skarphedin was no good for you," said Bergthora and it was as if I heard my mother speaking.

"We can't all stay home and grow corn," I snapped.

"The world would be a deal less troubled if we did," she retorted, and I looked up at her, to where she sat like a puffball on her chair, round and white and swollen. Women grow strong-willed when they get older, they're sweet enough when you wed them but give them a few years and they're tougher than leather. Emma was the exception to that of course, for marriage had softened her. If it hadn't been for the baby it would all have been different I told myself again, and chewed on a sweetmeat Bergthora had made with a whole cherry inside the honey coat. Those children would grow up to be puffballs too, they'd take up half a boatslength between them.

"Olaf says you're going to winter in Birka."

I shrugged. "I don't know. Kaupang's got so big I reckon we could get as good a price for our stuff there. Besides, I've been to Birka and when you've seen one ant's nest you've seen them all." I said this to impress her, for I well knew she hadn't been more than twenty miles from Skringsall in her life.

"I wonder why Olaf doesn't have an idea of his own, I swear you could lead him over a cliff. Where then, if not Birka?"

Where indeed? It seemed very nice and warm where I was, thank you very much.

Just then Bergthora's husband came back in, with his hair white with frost. I moved aside to let him in to the fire, and Bergthora took his hand and rubbed it warm.

I said, "Ah, what a lucky pair you are to be sure," and that pleased them both.

"I was asking Thorkil what he means to do next," said Bergthora. "He can never be still for a minute."

"That's a true Viking for you," said her husband. "Where's it to be then, I wonder?"

I felt like screaming, "Can't a man rest for a minute? By Frey's prick, I've been on the go for months and here I am planning to pass a bit of time in Skringsall, yarning and keeping warm, and all anyone can do is pack me off again."

And the little boys were saying, "Where are you going, Uncle Thorkil? Tell us, please?"

So I put back my head and laughed like the great adventurer I was and said, "I've a fancy to do some fur trading. It's the land of the Rus for me.'

So we sold our goods in Kaupang and bought knives and bowls and the pretty beads they made there and we waited for the seas to freeze hard so we could travel by sledge. It was clearly time to be off, for the authorities were asking questions about us and although we had been away a long time it might be that someone had a long memory. When Olaf, Skarphedin and I fled Skringsall all those years ago we left some dead men behind.

I had a problem though, in the waiting, but after all those

fine words to Olaf I could not solve it in Skringsall. For that
reason I found myself one night in Kaupang, looking for a
clean whore if there were any to be found. When you don't
want one they all look fine, but when you do they have spots,
or they smell, or they're old or look as if they've had five
men before you that night. Sometimes you find a man trying
to sell a slavegirl so young you feel like killing him, except
you know that then the child would starve. The Arabs are the
worst for that, it's very shocking.

I found a girl at last, leaning against one of the stalls. She
had long bronze earrings and they gleamed against her skin in
the torchlight. She was of the east I think, but she was brazen
and knowing, with a hard beauty.

"Buy me a drink, stranger?" she asked and I got her a cup
from the stall; mulled ale I think.

"Do you have a place?" I asked, watching her hands move
her cloak aside so I could see what she was selling. She wore
only a shift, in that cold, and the tips of her breasts stuck out
at me.

"Come for the night," she said. "I'll make it good for
you. I squeeze a man like no-one else, all the men say it."

"Not all night," I said and she tried to change my mind,
slipping an arm round my neck and saying, "Come on! A big
boy like you?" But it's one thing sleeping beside a whore
when your friends are nearby and quite another when you're
as like to wake dead as anything else.

She took me to a stable, and the noise of the stalls and the
light from the torches came in through the planks. It was
cold, even there, and our breath formed clouds. Right next to
us a pony stood champing and every now and then looked at
us. The things a man is driven to sometimes. The girl still
thought she'd get a lot from me so she did some fussing
about, kissing me and rubbing her body on me like a cat. But
I wasn't sure that her keeper wasn't going to put a blade in
me so I unfastened my breeks and told her to lie down. That's
what I hate about whores, they always do what you tell them.
I put my knife by her head and got into her, and when a man
has been without it for a while it is certainly good.

"You can have a bit extra for that," I said when my head
had stopped spinning. "It was good."

"Like I told you, all the men think so," she said proudly.
"You haven't seen my tricks yet, you want to come home

with me and see my tricks? I like a man who can get it up, I can see you're a real sailorboy—"

But I was dressed and leaving her, slipping out of the door with a careful glance to make sure there was no-one waiting for me. The girl stood in the lane and called after me, "Come again tomorrow, sailor. I'll give you it cheap." I looked back and her earrings were catching the light. "You're worth twice as much," I shouted and saw the men looking at her. She'd have a few more that night.

When I got back to Skringsall it was very late. I went softly to bed and lay there thinking about what had happened. It was the first since Emma you see, and I could not help remembering my marriage bed, with the talk and the closeness and the laughter and the fights, and in the end the cold. I wondered what my wife was doing, if she lay down when a man told her and said, "You're big enough, sailorboy." It was possible. That's what happens when you leave women alone.

Chapter
Eleven

MARJOLEIN CAME SLOWLY up the hill, her basket pulling her thin body down, her skirt blowing in the cold wind. Emma watched her come, her face set and still. She stood like a pillar set to guard her lands.

"Why, Emma! You look so oddly there I thought you must be turned to stone. Here, I've brought you some bread and some eggs, I came with the carter. Jorvik is so smelly at this time of year, I felt I just had to escape." She flashed a girlish, ingratiating smile but Emma did not reach for the proffered basket.

In the silence Marjolein's grinning became at first fixed and then drooped miserably, her pale skin and fluffy hair seeming more akin to age than the summer's end of youth. "I thought you might at least pretend to be pleased," she murmured.

Emma sighed. "It is scarce a week since you were here," she said crossly. "What is the point of it? You have a home and a husband in Jorvik, Marjolein, what use is all this trailing about?"

Marjolein stood with her head bent, sniffing back tears. Emma clasped her hands together in helpless exasperation. "You'd better come in then," she muttered and marched to the house, her friend trailing feebly in her wake, the basket impeding her every step. Even the geese flapped at her, hissing with outstretched necks and by the time she stumbled into the house she was sobbing openly.

"I don't know why you have to be so unkind," she gasped, her eyes like a rabbit's, seemingly lashless in her white face.

"I'm not unkind!" snapped Emma and then as Marjolein sobbed she turned away. She pulled off her green cap and let her hair tumble down, taking up her comb that had been a gift from Thorkil and pulling it sharply through her bronze mane. It eased her mind a little and soon she parted the strands and peered out at Marjolein. "It is something new that has happened, I can see. Tell me."

"Oh, it isn't new, it's the same. Except that now he's begging in the alehouses. The young men get him drunk and he sits like a log while they laugh at him. I ask you, Emma, is that any way for a man? They make him do tricks, silly drunken tricks—I want no more of it and that is the truth."

"I think you imagine much of this, you know. It is not so bad surely."

"It is so bad and worse! Only two days since Attar came with a message for him to take and when I went to find him—but I shall not tell you. You won't believe me anyway."

Emma eyed her thoughtfully. There was more here than was yet told, that was plain. She began to unpack the basket Marjolein had brought, merely for something to do, and it seemed to her that always she was asked for help when there was no-one anywhere that could give her aid. Marjolein thought they were friends, but Emma herself felt friendless. It was very hard.

The basket yielded stale bread, a few dirty eggs and a bundle of cloth. When she shook it out she saw that it was Marjolein's other dress. She looked up sharply and Marjolein blushed. "If you'll let me stay for a little—I can't go back. I'll work, I promise you that, I'll be no trouble to you." Emma's face contorted in a grimace of pain and she put up her hand to hide it. It might well be that no-one asked for much, but when all was added together the burden weighed her down. How was she to feed yet another mouth? The cow was going dry, they had eaten most of the corn and harvest was a long time away, the wheat was still green. Would she manage? How would she manage?

But Marjolein was watching her, eyes full of hope and fear.

"Let us have some wine." Emma took up a small pan,

filled it from a wicker-wrapped carafe and set it to heat. She added a sprinkle of herbs and when it was ready poured it carefully into two bowls. The two women bent their heads to sip, their hair in contrast, the one so rich and brown, the other worn gold.

Marjolein sighed a deep and weary sigh. There was a patched hole in her skirt and she picked at the threads as she spoke. "I know if I tell you this it will be secret, Emma. You've been such a friend to me. When I went to find Gunnar he was too drunk to stand, which is not unusual these days. The men began laughing at me and pointing, calling me a hag, you know how they can be. Once they would never have dared. Gunnar just grinned like an idiot, but I got him to his feet and dragged him outside. It was useless, I could get him no further. You know what he's like, Emma, there's no reasoning with him."

"Did you leave him?"

Marjolein shrugged. "I had no choice. Was I to pass the night on a dunghill just because he was too stupid and stinking—so I left him. I went back to Attar. I don't know what it is with Attar, he is never as kind as you expect. It wouldn't hurt him to give a little, he has so much. I told him Gunnar was ill, he knew what I meant. I asked for a little money, not a lot, just to buy some food. He—he laughed at me Emma. What is there that's so funny about a destitute woman, that's what I'd like to know? All I have is that bread and the eggs, and half of them are addled, what's so funny about that? We lived on Attar's messages, he knew the state I was in. You should know that about him, Emma, he has a mean heart."

Emma gave a thin smile. "I know that, I have known it a long time. Was it then you decided to come here?"

"No—not then. I thought I would get some money. There's no-one to care what I do any more, what is there for a woman on her own? I washed myself and let down my hair, then I put on my beads, the green ones, you've often seen them. Gunnar gave them me when we were wed. I went into the town, there's a street there, the women wait in the shadows for the men. I've watched them a long time. When you're hungry it's like a waking dream and that helped. The others frightened me, the real ones, they seemed so fierce and they watched me all the time to see if I got anyone. But there weren't many men about, I stood there until I thought I would die standing. I was so tired and so miserable, Emma, I would rather be dead than know that again. When a man came by I caught his arm. "Would you like something, stranger?" I said. I wasn't sure if I could do it, he smelt of horse piss. But he asked how much and I tried to think because I don't know how much it should be. Then I saw the others coming, the women. I tried to run but they caught me, I thought they would cut me, anything. They kicked me a bit, that's all. And they took—my green beads. My own—green beads." She dropped her head into her hands and shook with misery.

Emma went to sit by her, encircling the thin shoulders with her arm. "You should not have gone there, Marjolein, did you not think to come to me first? I would have helped then as I will help now."

"What is the use? I'm what they called me, I'm a hag, not even a drunk will buy me."

"You are tired and sad, a good night's sleep will improve things," soothed Emma. She stood up and began to move chests and benches around. "We'll put up a curtain to make a place for you. I'm—I'm sorry if I was harsh, Marjolein. I have not been kind to you."

The other woman looked up, her face puffy and blotched. "I don't deserve kindness. Only please don't let Attar throw me out, I don't know what I should do, only let me work for my keep, Emma, please."

Emma's face stiffened a little. "It is still my own house, whatever Attar thinks of the matter. Watch what you say in front of the men, Marjolein, they are Attar's creatures and not mine. If I could get rid of anyone it would be them, they'd kill me at a word from him."

"But he loves you still, doesn't he?"

"He loves himself best of all. And I have borne him no children, there is that to remember. I think the time will come when he would like this farm without its barren wife, and we must watch for that, both of us. He is sweet enough yet but for how long? I tread carefully, I tell you."

When the household was gathered to eat that evening, Emma put it that Marjolein had come to keep her company and was thus a welcome guest. The men-at-arms, that were Attar's men and lodged in the barn doing nothing, ran their eyes up and down Marjolein's thin charms. Once Emma would have challenged them but they sensed the wind changing and she did not dare. These days she held to her authority as if it were a twig, saving her as she tumbled over a cliff. Too strong a pull and it would come away in her hand, but if she once let go she was lost. Leif and her own people were loyal, that at least she was sure of, but they could not be asked to give up their own lives for hers. She expected little of them.

On the next day Attar came to the farm. He rode a neat bay pony with bronze stirrups and the leather of his reins was expensively frilled. There was a smugness about him that repelled.

"That is new," said Emma, nodding at the horse. Attar bent to kiss her and she turned her head aside so that his lips touched her cheek.

"I picked him up in trade. He came from Francia, I think, or at least his dam did."

"You'll believe anything," said Emma and went into the house. "Are you hungry?" she asked as Attar flung himself down, dropping sword and jerkin and pouch with all the familiarity of a man in his own home.

"Only for you, my lovely one," he said and reached up under her wool skirt as she passed.

Emma slapped at him, well knowing that Attar never savored easy meat. "We have a guest," she said.

Attar jumped and looked nervously about, causing Emma to hide a smile. He had been more than anxious since Bjarni made a hole in him, it was then he had sent his men.

"It is only Marjolein," she soothed. "She has come to live with me."

Marjolein herself peeped out from behind her hanging, nervous and apologetic. In her youth she had been as soft and gay as a primrose but now, in her ragged dress, she had the faded worth of washed linen.

Clearly she was not to Attar's taste. "I do not like this, Emma," he said stiffly. "I cannot have such people taking advantage of you. My apologies, Marjolein, but Emma must consult me before making these arrangements,"

"It is my farm," said Emma, and put a playful finger against Attar's chest.

"You think so?"

"Yes." She twined an arm around his neck and slid her leg against him. He chuckled and took the weight of her breast in his hand, kneading it to make her gasp. He smelled of some scent that caught in her throat and she knew that she must pleasure him, though it choked her. How had she once been hot for this? He was groping between her thighs, in front of Marjolein, and when she pulled away he held her with surprising strength. "I think you must be kind to me" he said softly.

Emma looked full into his hard brown eyes. "I will be— very kind," she said.

At once Attar spun her round and pushed her before him to her room. "I see this is not so bad after all, Marjolein," he said over his shoulder. "Emma grows tender.'

At the evening meal Attar was a satisfied man. Marjolein fluttered round him paying the little attentions that Emma would never stoop to and his plate was piled high with delicacies. Meanwhile Emma sat with her lips bruised for all to see, and her neck marked where he had sucked her. He leaned across to her, almost striking Marjolein who was again fussing about him. He glared at her and she drew back with a frightened squeak.

"Some news came today, sweet. From Guthorm."

Emma's fingers, that had been breaking bread to pellets, froze. "It is not—is it Skarphedin?"

"By the gods I hope not, except that he was with the army. There has been a battle. Guthorm has been defeated."

The men-at-arms, the serving girls and the farm lads all gasped. But Emma said only, "You have the news wrong."

"Indeed I have not! The Saxons stood at Edington and they won the day. It was a great slaughter, I am told."

"And who was it told you? Why, they've been chasing poor King Alfred in and out of the marshes all winter. He had not an army."

"He gathered them up after the spring sowing. Guthorm was not expecting it."

A finger tapped at her red lips. Attar thought how well her cap suited her, drawing her hair back from the firm lines of her face, with her only softness the droop of dark lashes on a white skin. Never pretty, she was grown to handsomeness.

"Is Guthorm dead then?"

"No. There's been a settlement."

"A Viking settlement! Much good will that do Alfred, when has Guthorm ever kept his word?"

"This will surprise you, Emma. He's taken baptism. Alfred stood sponsor to him at the font."

They were all dumbfounded. Emma stood up and wandered around the room, her mouth set in a hard line. "It has to be treachery," she whispered. She believed nothing of Attar, nothing of anyone, it was all false.

Attar shrugged. "I think not. The men are tired of fighting, they want to settle the flat lands in the east. For myself I am glad, for it is hard enough to trade with a marching army. Now we shall have farms and towns to supply."

A tremor touched Emma's swollen lips. "I am so tired of the fighting. When I was a girl honest folk went about their days in peace. Nowadays when a man gets back to his house of a night he's like to find his wife raped, his children dead and the cattle gone. This is a godless time."

"That's what happens when women are left unprotected," soothed Attar pointedly. He was surprised, for he had rarely seen her upset. "There are things for which you should be grateful, Emma."

She gave his turned shoulder a weary look. "You think so?"

In a day or so Attar was gone, leaving Emma more restless than her people were used to seeing her. She wandered from her spinning to the cow byre, from pig stye to shed, setting them all tasks that she stopped an hour later. At last she said to Marjolein, "I want to talk. Let's go into the fields."

They went up to the high grove. The summer was cold that year and damp, the ground beneath their feet was thick with early falling leaves and no birds sang high in the windswept trees. It would be a poor harvest.

"Thorkil believed that his god was here," said Emma absently, looking up to where the sky showed.

"You should be afraid," whispered Marjolein.

"I was once. It is not gods that I fear. Marjolein, what has happened to Skarphedin?"

"By all the saints! Don't say he's coming here, Emma, is he?"

"I don't know." Now it was Emma that whispered, in case

the trees should hear her. Skarphedin had been lord here once, he it was that made the trees bow down. "I don't pray any more," she whispered. "And I don't go to church, not since Attar."

"There's hardly a church left to go to round here. They gather at the cross in Shipton, I believe," said Marjolein absently.

"I thought, if he was dead, that I would feel it here. But there is nothing, I came yesterday and it was the same. Do you feel anything?" She turned piercing eyes on the pale woman before her and Marjolein quailed.

"It is heathen talk and not for a Christian woman. I am going back. If that creature comes near me I shall lose my mind, I know it!"

Marjolein ran from the wood, leaving Emma alone beneath the tall trees. When the sound of footsteps died she went to sit on a log, closing her eyes the better to think.

It had been so long since Thorkil left and in that time she had heard only once, from Norway. But he was much on her mind these days and in this wood, that was his as much as Skarphedin's, she looked for some sign of him. That she had a skill and a craft that reached back into the old, dark times she well knew, but somehow when it touched the things of her own heart she was as helpless as anyone. What use now were her leaves and feathers, her herbs and waking dreams? If Thorkil was dead she did not know it, if he loved her still the warmth was far away. When she looked at Attar's neatness it was Thorkil's lack of such that came to mind; when Attar loved her, his body white and soft, she thought of a man's great weight and his hands gentle on her skin. Now, when all was ended, she thought of Thorkil's kindnesses, when she labored and before, when she was sad. The baby had been all their longing, shared between them in equal portions. It was she that had taken all the grief, and left him nothing. When she thought of the comb he brought her, as a comfort and a gift of love, slow tears dropped onto her hands.

Where was he now, when she needed him? Here, in the grove, she knew that Skarphedin threatened, he hung in her mind like a dark cloud, coming ever nearer. He had wished her dead when he had no cause to do so, and now with Attar in her bed he had every cause. Skarphedin would never understand her need, that Erik over the hill stole fields by

inches and waited only for a sign of weakness to take everything. At least Attar was not so obvious a thief. Skarphedin
would see only that she had sent her husband away and taken
a stranger to her bed, and for that she would die. She pondered what to do. He was close now, she was sure of it, and
to sit and wait was beyond her patience. The fear was eating
into her soul, at night it came out of the dark and engulfed her
until it seemed that he was in her head and out of it, breathing
curses into her ears and putting bloody fingers on her tongue.
She had made charms against evil and placed them everywhere, though since he still came it might be that the evil was
in herself. She, who brought women safe through childbed
and cured fever with but a potion, was faced with something
greater than she could know. But at the very least she could
discover what was to come.

She stood up, shivering in the chill wind that rustled the
branches about her. Word would have traveled to Jorvik by
now and it was there that she would go to hear it. Lame Leif
would go with her, for he had a house of his own now, set
apart, in which he lived with his serving girl and her baby.
Emma had given a rich cloth at the birth, embroidered by her
own hand with flower patterns, and she had asked for nothing
except loyalty. Now was the time to seek her payment.

Emma looked dubiously at the inn, which seemed full to burst-
ing and smelled of bad meat. "You are sure they can take us?"
"Why yes, mistress. The lady said to come right in."
She grimaced but stepped down from the wagon. She was
stiff, it was late and it had drizzled for most of the day. Now
they were come to Jorvik she would give anything to be home
again, with a warm fire and her own things about her. The
strangeness of the place leached away her courage; she was
not a traveler, she had always known it.

Jorvik grew each time she came and now was bigger and
noisier than any place she knew. Thorkil had spoken of towns
with streets as wide as rivers, but she took that as traveler's
tales, growing with the miles. Jorvik was as big as she could
think of with tall buildings crowding so tight together that
sometimes only one man could walk between them and whichever way you turned a different smell choked you, whether of
hides or dung or burning horn, which was of them all the
most sickening.

Emma turned her back on it all and went into the inn, hoping for some comfort. Men sat drinking around a fire, though the day was not chill. They roared as she entered, for she was tall and bright and stared at them disdainfully.

But the innkeeper's wife bustled towards her. "We have room, we have room. Come this way sweetheart, we'll soon have you tucked up."

Emma followed through damp passages to a lean-to fixed draughtily at the higgledy-piggledy rear of the house. It smelled of wet and rotten things, which was a breeding ground of lung sickness as Emma knew well. But there was a bed and a pitcher of water, and she was too tired to go on. She sighed, accepted it and told Leif he could sleep by the door.

"What has happened to the world?" she said miserably. "When I was a girl travelers lodged in comfort with the monks but all that is gone now. Everything is in pieces nowadays. We are a people cursed."

"Cheer up, mistress," said Leif and Emma saw that she embarrassed him.

She forced a smile on her face and said, "It is only the journey, it has tired me. Please, Leif, find me some food, I am very hungry."

A meal lifted her misery a little and she unstoppered a flask of wine. She trickled it slowly between her lips, wishing so many things different that for a moment it seemed there was nothing at all in her life that was good. She was as lost as a child in a wood, who could think of nothing but to sit down and wail. Her throat closed on tears that she dared not let fall.

The farm swam into her mind. Without it she would be truly lost, for it gave her everything, from her warm wool dress to the money in her pouch, to the flesh on her bones. She closed her mind on the thought, forgetting the damp and discomfort around her. The farm was a good thing, and it was hers. She would fight to the last to keep it, for it was all that she had and Attar would not drive her from it, nor even Skarphedin. A small, tight shudder went through her. Why did everyone think only of taking, Thorkil alone had opened his hand to give her things. She had not valued them as she should. But then, she had been very foolish in the past and she had done many foolish things. Must we always suffer for them she wondered, each to the full extent? It seemed now that it must be so.

At last her thoughts drifted back to her task. She stood up, smoothing the folds of her dress which was taken from wool to dye by her own hand, and with nothing to guide her but her own good sense. She admired it for a moment. Whatever clouds threatened she had achieved much.

"Come, Leif," she said purposefully. "We must go out."

He looked anxious. "But mistress—not you. This is no place for a lady, the town's full of soldiers, it's very wild. Go in the day, mistress, if you want something now I will fetch it for you."

"But you do not know Gunnar, Leif, and he it is I am looking for. And like an owl he comes out at night, to roost in alehouses, I believe. It is not so bad a place, it is only that we are not used to towns, you and I. We will be brave together."

"Only put your money safe. They are still robbers, I swear it, even when they sell you things. I should be ashamed to ask these prices, I tell you, mistress, they are all thieves."

Emma agreed and tied her purse under her skirt.

Even town air smelled fresh after the close little room. Emma felt braver out in the torchlight, with all around her bustling and alive. Still, at this time, the shops were open and the people buzzed like the flies on Butcher Row, jostling her this way and that in the narrow places. Leif was white with nerves but Emma opened her eyes to see the leatherhard sailors with rings in their ears, the soldiers with their easy confidence. This was the world, and at the farm she had forgotten it. A man was selling beads from a tray, red ones that would look so well against her dress. She watched from a distance and he called to her saying, "Come along, sweet, don't be shy. Buy yourself something pretty for once." Breathless, she picked out red beads for herself and some blue ones for Marjolein, who was sitting dull at home and had no money. Leif was watching her scornfully.

"We'll look in the alehouses," she said, remembering that she had told him that they were to do things of importance in Jorvik, yet here she was buying beads. She blushed a little at herself and scurried after Leif who was hobbling on his lame leg. She must be sensible or he would cease to respect her.

It was still early and the alehouses were thin of people. They trailed from one to the other asking for Gunnar and they found several men of that name but none the one they sought.

Leif's leg was hurting and Emma began to worry that they would never find him and the journey would be for nothing. She pushed ahead into still another low door, with the thatch dripping greasily down her neck. The torches were smoking and she could barely see, but she crossed to a group of young men. In their midst and already drunk was Gunnar.

Emma barely recognized him for his hair was black with grease and his good looks vanished beneath dirt and bleary skin. There were traces of dried vomit on his jerkin.

"Gunnar," she said but he did not hear her. There was a cup of ale before him and he was grinning at the lads and trying to lift it with the stump of his arm. Emma saw that this was a trick of his that he kept to amuse those with money to spend and when the cup went flying the lads roared and Gunnar giggled hopefully. Emma could not bear to see. "Gunnar," she said again, and pushed through to him. He looked up at her owlishly. "How can you let them do this?" she asked.

"Let him alone, mistress, he's having fun," said one of the lads, almost as drunk himself.

Emma caught Gunnar's arm and tried to pull him upright, but he hung like a log and mumbled.

"Come and cuddle me instead," said the lad and made a face at her, clowning. She saw that they were only boys.

"You do not know what you are doing," she said stiffly. "This man once fought beside the great Skarphedin and I will swear that you have not such courage. Why do you tease him now when he is crippled? It is very wrong."

"He likes it," said one. "If we buy him the drink he doesn't mind."

Gunnar's legs were like cloth, they would not hold him. Leif limped across to help.

"D'you like them crippled, then?" teased a boy. "Come on, give me a kiss." He pursed up his lips and smacked them at her and she pushed him. Suddenly they were crowding about, shouting and touching her, she felt a hand grab at her breast. She struck out with her fist and between them she and Leif dragged Gunnar into the street. She was shaking and her hair was coming down.

"I told you what this place is," said Leif, as white as she was.

"They were only boys. It is all fun to them. Will you try to stand, Gunnar, don't you know me? It is Emma. Emma!"

He reeled against a wattle wall and slid into the water channel, wetting his legs to the knees. When Emma caught his arm to hold him upright he was noisily sick down her skirt. She shuddered and let him go. The man was a wreck, only touching him made her want to scream.

"I'll take him, mistress," said Leif.

"He's too heavy. We'll both do it. I know your leg's paining. Come along." Between them they hauled Gunnar to his feet and back to the inn.

They dumped him on the floor of the room while Emma washed her skirt. When it was clean she washed Gunnar's face, at the same time picking lice from his hair.

"I need a drink," he belched and Emma held a bowl to catch the vomit. He revolted her and yet she pitied him, for she had known him when he was young and golden. It was like watching a corpse decay. She wondered if they would all come to this, and Gunnar's only difference was that he did it too soon.

"Could you fetch some hot water Leif?" she asked. "If I made him a posset it might help."

"You'll get nothing from him till morning," said Leif but nonetheless went.

Emma shook Gunnar's shoulder. "Gunnar! I must ask you something."

He rolled a pus-filled eye at her. "I've got nothing. Even my wife's gone and left me."

"And what do you expect? If you could see yourself—"

Gunnar began to mumble, pulling on her sleeve and whispering confidingly. "You know—after they took my arm she never once let me touch her. Did you know that? A man's still got a cock, whether he's got one arm or two, and I kept the end part covered with a cloth so it didn't upset her. That's a bad wife, isn't it? That's not what a wife should be?"

"I don't know what a wife should be. I have something to ask you—"

"What's your name, sweetheart?" he said and grinned at her. Two of his teeth were missing. Emma got up and sat on the bed, wondering where in this sodden lump was the sharp, crisp man that had once been Gunnar. As Leif said she would get nothing before morning.

She wakened him at dawn, shaking him to consciousness

and bad air. He slurped greedily at the now cold posset that he had cursed at the night before. "What are you doing to me, Emma?" he croaked, and she blessed the saints that he knew her.

"Keep your voice down," she whispered, for Leif was still sleeping. "I need some news of Skarphedin."

"Who knows anything of him? Who would want to know anything?"

"I do. You know how it is with me and Attar, how it has to be. I think if Skarphedin comes to the farm he will kill me."

Gunnar nodded. "I think that is very likely. Have you a drink here, Emma? There is nothing to do about Skarphedin, he does as he wills."

"But where is he? I feel—I know that he is near. Attar tells me that the battle was lost and the armies stood down, I have heard that here also. But nothing about Skarphedin. I came to ask you."

Gunnar pulled at his beard with his one hand, clearly turning over thoughts in his mind. His fingers were long and slender as a girl's, but each nail was broken and black-rimmed. "I heard something a week or two ago, but I don't remember it. It is the drink, you know, it feeds on a man's memories and that is no misfortune. There was a falling out, but who was it that told me? I can't think."

"But you must remember. It is more important than you know." Emma's voice trembled, try as she would to steady it. She knew Skarphedin was coming for her.

"Was it Snorri, I wonder? Yes, I think it was Snorri, we shared a cup or two and he was with Guthorm. He will tell you about Skarphedin.'

The soldier sat thoughtful, holding his cup with a hand callused by the battle-axe. He had drunk a little and eaten a lot, watched all the while by Emma, her nerves jangling. Sometimes he fingered a brown, wizened thing hung on a leather rope about his neck. When at last he began to speak it was gently and without heat, as a man will who knows his tale is strong. Sometimes he put his mouth close to her ear and whispered, as if even the walls might hear him.

"If I hadn't a charm in my hand I wouldn't be telling you any of this, my girl, that I can promise. If a man had no belief in magic before he would have plenty now. For I ask you, how can it be that a king, a slight boy-king, could summon an army from nowhere? An army that fought like a tribe of demons, whose swords flashed as though each was twenty? I tell you, that battlefield was cursed. There is a man I can bring you to that saw the black spirits coming, flying through the sky to choose the slain, and for every Saxon there were ten Norse dead. Guthorm it was that paid, and though I hold this charm tight I still whisper it. Guthorm was cursed.

"We fell upon Alfred in midwinter, in his stronghold in the fens. The ground was hard and white and they were all celebrating. We should have had him like a rat in a shoe, but perhaps the magic was working even then, for he slipped away into the wilderness. Long months we chased him, in a hostile land, but he struck us more often than we him. There were tales sprang up, of his courage, his victories, his care for his people. It was said he spent a night in a cottage, deep in that damp country, and a wife there made bread and set it to bake. And Alfred, king though he was, himself turned the loaves rather than see them burn, and his people told each other this and said 'This is a wise king. He will care for us nobly.'

"I think then we could still have had the victory. Guthorm had not entirely turned the gods against him. It concerns the berserk, Skarphedin, and I see from your face that you know him. Who has not heard of his greatness? Who shall not tremble even at the sound of his name? So dear is he to his god that he is saved from all harm, so great is his honor that men die from the light in his eyes, should it chance to fall upon them. I will tell you of the great wrong that was done him, and by Odin's one eye, I hold this charm tight.

"There was a coldness between him and Guthorm, it came about when Guthorm sought to bind Skarphedin's honor. Is such a man a servant that must be held by this or that payment, by some debt? As if honor were not enough. As if a name could hold more glory. If there was any reason to it I think it was that Skarphedin was Halfdan's man and there was a doubting there, though Guthorm was equal in friendship with Halfdan. Perhaps he wanted to be greater, I don't know. But the men honored Skarphedin, even if Guthorm did not. They knew the strength of his magic and had seen it proved time and again, when he stood at the center and roared his battle-cry. He held the luck. We all knew it, except Guthorm.

"Well, Guthorm was bad-tempered because he had not caught Alfred and it was wet and cold and his guts troubled him. I think also his wife was nagging at him to make some kind of peace and it was said she had turned him from her bed because of it, though I don't know the truth of that. If she had he was sure to be bad-tempered, because he liked to use himself, he thought it strengthened him. Anyway he had enough reason, or so he thought. He decided to play a trick on Skarphedin when he came to his hall, for Skarphedin had a way of chilling the place just by entering it. There was this woman that had been in a fire. Half her face was smooth and pretty, but the other half was all charred, like a piece of wood. One hand was burned too, but the rest of her was all right. Guthorm set it so he was on his high seat, his guard all around in case Skarphedin turned nasty, and this woman cloaked before him. Her good side was turned to the door if you understand me, and she had her hood up. Not one of us knew what he was about, except Guthorm and one or two others. We would not have believed if we had been told because Guthorm's a finer man than many, he's not coarse cloth. It might be that he disliked in Skarphedin, the wildness. He sent for Skarphedin. He said he had a gift for him.

"In he came. It was very quiet. His hair was black with wolfgrease, it hung in braids on his shoulders. He wore studded leather with his jerkin made from the skin of a sheep, belted round with a thong that held Claw of the Raven. Has any sword known such greatness? It is lightning trapped in metal form. 'I have a gift for you,' said Guthorm, and waved his hand to the girl. Skarphedin's head came up, like a pony at a bridge, he sniffed the air. He smelt dishonor. 'There is nothing that I hold,' he said, and Guthorm was confused because of course berserks take nothing. 'It is for your use. I thought you might like her,' he said and waited for Skarphedin to step forward. He did not. He stood in that hall, with the great roof filled with smoke from the torches and all around men watching and he went apart from it. His face was empty. It seemed he was gone.

"After a time, which seemed like forever to Guthorm and his men and still Skarphedin had not stirred, he leaned down from his seat and said to someone, 'Take the girl to him. Let him see her.' And a man caught the girl, who was stiff with terror, and took her by the arm down the hall, to where

Skarphedin could see her and the wreck of her charred face.
They stood, the three of them, and it was as if Skarphedin
saw nothing. At Guthorm's signal a harp began to play. And
then with a roar that was like the howl of Hel itself we saw
Claw of the Raven rise up and strike in one blow the heads of
the girl and her captor, so that they flew to the floor, and
afterwards their bodies stood, headless, before they fell. I
remember that in the stillness afterwards with the roar echo-
ing in our ears, there was still a hum of harp strings in the air.

"Skarphedin lifted his blade and wiped it with his fingers,
as gently as a mother with her child. 'A web of man's own
weaving,' he said softly, but it was heard by all. 'A curse
from a man's chosen god.' He looped his sword across his
shoulder and went out into the night.

"That was the last we saw of him. No-one knows where he
went but the word spread in the army of what had happened
as you might imagine. When the day of the battle dawned and
he was not there, we had no spirit for the fight. One or two
others tried to ape him, by eating mushrooms and suchlike,
but no-one was fooled. Only Skarphedin held the luck, and he
was not with us.

"So, when the battle was lost and the dead thicker than
flies on bad meat, Guthorm did the only thing he could. He
made peace and became a Christian, to turn aside the curse,
you see. It was Odin's curse alone, not another god. And I
think I might do likewise, for I haven't done so well since
that day in the hall. There's worse things than being a Christian I can tell you."

Emma gave the soldier coin and she was careful not to
touch him, for a curse can be passed on even in the breath, so
who knew what the sweat of a frightened man might do? As
she turned from him she crossed herself, and when she went
out Gunnar was waiting for her.

"Emma. Give me money now. I need it." He threatened
her, though it shamed him. He would not meet her eye but his
one hand bunched into a fist.

It was useless to argue, but she said helplessly, "Could
you not try and find a trade? You have still one good hand,
and two strong legs—" but he lifted his head to glare as if
she were an enemy, and his lip wrinkled up like a dog's. She
reached for her purse, saying, "If you wish you could be my
packman, to deal honestly for me. I don't trust Attar and—

Gunnar!'' He kicked at her and reached to grab the purse from her hand. She felt his spittle on her face and in a short stab of terror she thought he might kill her, he was desperate enough.

''You're a prattling bitch, Emma. My life is my own and I need no pink-faced charity. If I choose to drink then I choose it, as you choose to whore for your bread. Save your speech for Attar, though I doubt that's what he pays for, and I'll take the payment with thanks. You can spread your legs for more I dare say.''

She shrank away into the mud as Gunnar came at her, his breath making her flinch. Then he turned and shambled away to the alehouse, leaving Emma alone in the street.

Her hands were shaking and she was very cold. She pulled her cloak about her, wishing for somewhere private that she could go and cry. If even a drunk despised her how much must everyone else? Attar told that she took him to her bed, and it was this as much as anything kept her at home. If they did not call her whore it would be witch, though as to that she had little enough power. Truly she could know things, but it brought no peace. Sometimes she needed all her courage just to go forward to another day.

A cur-dog was sniffing in the black slime oozing from a dung-heap. It was very thin and scabrous, every rib could be clearly seen and there was an oozing sore on its back. She clicked her fingers at it and it lifted its lip in a silent snarl, as nasty a thing as she had ever seen, unloved and unloving. When she stepped closer it cringed down warily, turning its head up ready to bite. She bent down towards it.

''I'd be careful if I was you, missus.'' A man had come to sling rubbish on to the heap. ''He's a mean one. If he wasn't such a good ratter he'd have been knocked on the head long ago.''

''Does he belong to anyone?'' Emma reached her hand cautiously forward and the dog quivered on a snarl.

''Not him. Watch it, he'll bite. D'you need a sharp dog then? You'll catch him easy enough with meat, I dare say.'' He slung his basket at the rubbish heap and the dog, startled, leaped and snapped at it. The man recoiled with a nervous laugh. ''Don't blame me if he kills you,'' he said. ''Funny things, dog bites.''

''Yes.'' Emma studied the brute, that was surely vicious

enough. If there was anyone needed a dog it was she, but would it love her? Perhaps love was dead in it and could never be revived. She had thought that of herself once, as in a white winter when you cannot believe in spring. Yet it comes, it comes, and one day there are buds on dry twigs. She resolved to take the dog.

They came back to the farm late the next day, with their saddles laden and the cur-dog swinging in a wicker basket next to Leif's pony. The paths were scattered with leaves and the sound of their passing drowned whatever else might be heard. Emma found herself looking nervously at the dark places in the trees and at each bend she held her breath until they were safely round it. She did not know what frightened her, for it was not Skarphedin, he would never hide round corners. And since he was not yet come what could there be to fear? All else was mere anxiety. But rabbits made her gasp and a swooping owl, out early, brought a stifled shriek to her lips.

"Steady, mistress," said Leif, who had been sorely tried on this venture. She knew he had lost faith in her, because away from the farm she was not strong or brave or sure."

"If only we could be home," she said jerkily.

"Nearly there now. Look, you can see the light across the fields."

It was a torch, set on the barn as a guide to them, in case they should return that night. When they plodded into the yard and the household spilled out to welcome them, Emma said querulously, "You should not have shown a light. The hills are full of robbers, do you want to lead them straight to our door?"

Attar's men-at-arms, lounging in the door of the barn, picked at their teeth and laughed at her. "Don't you worry, mistress, we'll look after you. All this gallivanting's making you nervous." It was the fat one, that Emma hated because he did not work, and smelled.

She turned her back to him in a swirl of cloak, saying stiffly, "I have brought a dog, in that basket. Someone bring him into the house."

While she ate she dropped pieces of meat down into the basket. The dog gobbled them, all the time looking at her with a yellow eye.

Marjolein, who seemed to Emma to have gained flesh in the few days she had been away, said, "I don't know what you want with him Emma, he's horrible."

"I want him to guard me." This time when she fed him she held the meat so that his nose brushed her fingers.

"Against—him?" Marjolein almost whispered.

"No man will stand against him. I thought perhaps a dog—I shall feel safer with a dog."

Marjolein drew her knees up and hugged them, a gesture that seemed too young for her. "We oughtn't to stay here, it's foolish. We should leave."

"There's nowhere to go." Emma snapped like the dog and felt unkind. "Don't think I haven't thought of it," she said more gently. "I should not have told you, it could all be my imagining. No-one's seen him in months, he could have gone after Thorkil, anything."

"But you know he hasn't! When have you ever had a feeling that wasn't true? I remember in Jorvik, you spoke to that smith and afterwards said to me 'He won't live long' and he drowned the very next week. And when we heard it Skarphedin looked at you and said 'We stand too close, you and I.' I've never forgotten it."

Emma shivered. "Neither have I. And I do feel it, Marjolein, still! What are we to do?"

"Can't you put a spell on him?" said Marjolein shrilly.

"Shhhh! None of my charms work when I want them to, I can never do anything for me." She pressed a hand to her lips, choking back fear and a terrible sense of loneliness. It was the waiting made it worse, if it went on much longer she would be out of her senses. Her mind searched for something to dwell on, and suddenly she remembered the beads.

"I brought you a present, Marjolein. Look here."

Marjolein's pale cheeks flushed pink. "For me? Oh Emma!" She unfolded the cloth with childish haste and gasped at the treasure within. Then her face crumpled into tears. "You are so kind to me! I don't deserve it when there's nothing I can give back. I know you don't really want me here."

Emma put a hand on Marjolein's shoulder. "Not at first perhaps. But our lives go together somehow, I don't know why. I have not Thorkil any more and I need a friend. You're good for me."

Marjolein sniffed. "He would have stayed if you had asked him. He had a great tenderness for you."

Emma sighed hugely and her hands closed in the folds of her skirt. She could not remember now why she had let him go, it seemed a great foolishness. Had she not seen what would come of it? How had she thought to live? "I was never cold in his shadow," she said miserably, feeling as cold as she had ever done.

The cur-dog was whimpering in his basket and she bent to peer in at him. "Will you bite me?" she asked him. "I think that you will. But tomorrow you will not, because like me you must learn to bend. It is a hard lesson for us both but we will come to it. Here, eat." She dangled meat into the cage.

Emma spent long days with her dog. At first she dared not touch it unless its teeth were occupied with meat, and twice she was too bold and he grazed her fingers. She could have asked one of the men to hold him while she washed his thin body and cleaned out his sores, but she would not. Instead she waited until the creature trusted enough to let her do him hurt and then she was as gentle as a dove. In the evenings it lay at Emma's side, seeming never to sleep for no-one ever saw it do so. Its yellow eyes watched fiercely, windows to his bitter heart that had yet one spot of warmth left in it. He was a cur but he comforted her.

But as Marjolein warned, Attar did not like it. "I am very tired of Attar," whispered Emma to herself and knew that it was true. She was tired of his smooth charm that he gave everyone in equal measure, and his cowardice that you had to know him well to see. She knew he had other women and she knew also that he was bored with her. Sometimes when they coupled and he pumped in and out, using her body that could have been anyone's, she would have liked to close her hand on a knife and stab him, deep into his smooth flat back. But of course she dared not. Without Attar she would lose the farm, though it might be that Erik would keep her a while if his wife did not ask questions. So what was there to do but lie there and pretend love, letting this man bite her and biting in return, hearing her cur-dog snarling outside the door and wishing that she too could snarl. In those nights she almost longed for Skarphedin to come and end her servitude, to put a clean blade in her flesh and make it pure.

When Attar snored in sleep, his mouth slack and open, she crept from the bed and went to soothe her dog. His bare tail wagged at her anxiously. "Do you care for me so much?" she asked. And she knew that she was his god and he would give his life for her.

In the morning Attar was fractious and sat bad-tempered by the fire. He was paring his nails with the point of his knife and when Marjolein strayed too near he pricked her with it. She shrieked. "You have cut me! Emma, look, I'm stabbed!"

Emma went white. Was it today he meant to end it then? Whatever came, she would not beg. She crossed to Attar and stood tall above him, her flat face quite still. Marjolein was mopping blood from her thigh, trying not to show herself.

"Is this some new game?" asked Emma quietly. "Marjolein is my guest and my friend."

"Be careful, Emma. I may turn to you next."

"It is you who should be careful. I am told that Skarphedin travels this way, and I think it would surprise him to find you here. He is my husband's friend."

It was Attar's turn to pale. "This is not true. He'd cut you first, girl, remember that."

"First or second, it makes little difference. As to the truth of it, wait and find out."

She went to tend Marjolein, and her leg was not cut badly though her dress was slashed.

"What will he do?" whispered Marjolein. "He'll set the men on us."

"I don't think he'll dare. Oh Marjolein, you thought I was good to take you in but you see what I've come to. There's no help for us anywhere."

Marjolein hobbled to the door and peeped out to where Attar talked hastily to his men. "I just wish he would go away. He's a weasel of a man, no more than that."

Emma pressed cold fingers to her cheeks, trying to make herself think. Attar would do nothing at present for he never acted without due thought and would ponder and discuss until he had decided. But, as Marjolein said, they would be a deal happier if he did that thinking elsewhere.

She clasped her hands and turned to her friend. "I think it is time we had a pigsticking," she said firmly. "The weather's cool enough and the pig won't get much fatter. I will speak to Leif today."

*   *   *

That afternoon the house was filled with pigmeat and scalded pigskin; it was a demon's dwelling littered with bones and boiling blood.

Emma looked at Attar across a pile of offal. "You see how I work to feed you and your leeches," she said.

"Not for much longer, my sweet. None of us can know what is about to happen in so lonely a place as this. But I see you are busy and I shall be on my way. Be sure to use enough salt, I like my house well stocked with curing."

She gave him a bitter look and he smiled back at her. For she was trapped on her farm while he could go where he pleased and if Skarphedin came she alone would be there to meet him. Her head throbbed horribly and when Attar's horse had trotted away she went to lie down on her bed. Her belly ached where he'd pummeled her in the night and she was still wet from him.

He would have loved her still if she'd borne him a child, of that she was sure. It was the only thing that held men to you, everything else passed away. If she had swelled for Aelthyn she might now be in Mercia, conquered but a wife still. If Thorkil's seed had prospered she would have suckled a tribe for him and lived in strength and riches. And if Attar had bred her he might have stood by her now instead of scheming to see her damned.

But she was barren and had only a sharp yellow dog to love, that himself could find no other. She put her hand to the cur and he licked the tears from it.

The next day she left the women of her household all chopping meat and vegetables and herbs and took herself and her dog to the hillside. Her sense of doom was very strong today, it weighed on her like the grey clouds resting on the far slopes of the moor. Her dog, that was raised amidst buildings, clung close beside her and she gentled him. Below stretched the track to the farm, winding within trees and then snaking out onto uplands where in summer sheep grazed with lads set to watch them. Now the sheep were within walls, or folded on to fields to dung and add goodness to the soil, but Emma had few sheep because there was no-one to tend them.

A pony stepped out of the forest and the man riding it was as shaggy as his mount. They seemed to be one animal, bound together in some way, for the rider's legs were so short they barely stretched to the pony's belly. Emma's hand closed on her dog and he shuddered.

"You do right," she said. "It is Skarphedin."

She rose and dusted the grass from her skirt, then pulled her cap more closely over the coils of her hair. This day had been coming a very long time and she had twisted this way and that to escape it. Now there was no escape and it must be faced, and there was peace in an end to the waiting. She felt almost calm because there was nothing now to do but go down to the farm and meet Skarphedin.

But as she went down the hill, leaning back against the slope and feeling the good earth firm beneath her feet, thoughts blew into her head. Aldwulf dead, with blood swelling his head, filling a night with black horror. The pain of her child's birth, that was like knives ripping and was Skarphedin's blame. Her heart began to thump within her and the dog pressed close against her legs. The warmth touched her and her eyes swam with tears that she blinked away. She did not run but when she came to the house she was breathless. Skarphedin was within and Marjolein and the girls all looked at him, their eyes more round and scared than a hare's. A pot on the fire was boiling, sending gobbets of water splashing into the flames, but no-one tended it. A fat maggot-fly buzzed over the piles of meat.

"Kill the fly, someone," said Emma from the doorway. "It will spoil the meat."

Skarphedin turned quickly, with that speed that was so frightening because it was least expected. The dog cringed against her legs and Emma stared, once again taking in the livid scar that twisted his face into a mask, the dead-black eyes that were always cold. There was a blankness about him. She wondered if he knew her.

"Well met, Skarphedin." She whispered, though she had intended to speak out.

He nodded. "I am come."

"And I welcome you. We have killed a pig, I am sorry we are in such turmoil. Will you sit by here, I will bring you warm ale."

But he twisted round and stared again at the table, saying, "I did not know it was a pig. Only a pig. Well then."

"Just a pig," said Emma. "Sit down and I will cook you some of it, the inside parts are very good."

Obediently he went to sit down but all the time his eyes moved round the faces in the room. Emma worked at the fire, tossing small pieces of chitterling in butter and clumsy in her nervousness so that the fat spat and burned her hand more than once. When it was done she took it to Skarphedin.

"Where is he?" he asked.

"Thorkil is gone. We've had no word in months."

"And the other one?" He put his hand to his head. "Was there another one? I remember—another."

"If it is Bjarni you mean, then he is gone too, I don't know where. There's only me. But you must eat, Skarphedin, eat and rest."

He dipped his hand into the food she offered and did not flinch at the heat. He ate very slowly and everyone watched him.

"Get on with your work, girls," said Emma shrilly and herself paced the room while her dog lay and watched Skarphedin, his nose lifted to catch the warrior taint. It is death, thought Emma, and mine to be added to it. Ah well.

When he had eaten Skarphedin drank a cup of ale, spread his cloak on a bench and slept. The women looked at each other.

"What shall we do?" whispered Marjolein.

"Nothing. We'd best leave him."

"We could kill him while he slept, mistress," said Leif's woman, lifting up the long bright knife she was using on the pig.

"I don't think he can be killed," said Emma. "He has made a bargain with his black god. The knife would turn aside, I am sure of it."

The woman sighed. "Leif said as much. It is a dreadful thing when we needs must bow down to heathens in our midst."

"Lie down in your case, I think," said Emma with a grin, and they all laughed a little and felt better.

She was bemused, because this was not as she had imagined. Skarphedin seemed strange and weary, almost like a warrior coming home to rest. But he would soon see how it was with her, he would soon realize how she had lived. She wondered a little, thinking of the soldiers lodged in her barn.

Towards evening Skarphedin woke. The weary women, that had worked all day, were preparing a meal, moving and talking quietly. The berserk's mouth was slack and his eyes unfocused and without thinking Emma crossed and touched his hand, a thing she had never done before. The skin was cold and dry.

"You are here," she said. "At the farm. With Emma."

His eyes blinked and looked at her. He clasped her hand. "Emma."

"Yes. We are going to eat now. Come."

He ate little and that very slowly. His presence hushed the talk and though the silence made others uncomfortable Skarphedin seemed unmoved, only eating and looking about him.

At last, when it seemed that there was a weight of unuttered speech sitting on Emma's head she said, "Skarphedin!"

They all jumped except Skarphedin who turned his head slowly.

"You—you have not told us your news," she went on breathlessly. "What has been happening."

His lips moved once or twice as if he was attempting speech but nothing was heard. Then, with a strangled effort he gasped, "News! What is not known to the gods? It is all nothing. I can only see the blood, it is in the rain, I have seen it."

Emma gestured to the girl to fill the cups. Now she was sure he was mad, he had been halfway to it before but without this twitching lack of sense. It made him no less dangerous.

They all left the house as soon as may be, even Marjolein going cravenly to sit with Leif's wife. Emma found herself at the head of the table, with only her cur-dog for company and Skarphedin like a brooding dwarf close by. She watched his twisted face, that had once been like stone and now quivered and moved with the thoughts that came and went behind it. He might once have been handsome she realized suddenly.

"What was it happened to your face?"

He put up his fingers and touched the scar, that seemed to have grown out of his skin. He followed its course, from within his black hair to the corner of his eye and down to where it pulled at his mouth.

"In my home country," he said in his high voice, "they move the longships sometimes. They put them on trees to take them across the land. My nurse was careless with me. A great ship fell and I was crushed beneath it. When they pulled

me free I was not dead but my lower parts were broken in
many pieces and my face—was torn. Small as I was the
anguish is with me still, the sense of crushing. Many said I
should have died. But in those months of my torment my
spirit was forged, as a smith forges iron into a sword. It was
then that Odin claimed me, gave me healing and took my
service in return. This mark—this scar—is his sign.''

"He is all wickedness," said Emma.

"He is all knowledge.''

The fire cracked a little and the dog sat up to scratch a flea.
It seemed strangely companionable, as if two old friends sat
together. Perhaps friendship is made by years, thought Emma.
At the hour of death even an enemy's hand, if known, is
better than loneliness.

"Lately," said Skarphedin, "I am much troubled. In my
mind.''

"How are you troubled?" she asked curiously. Such talk
from him was unknown.

He turned his black eyes on her. "I see things. They are
not real. I see blood where there is only ale, I see rank flesh
where all is still wholesome. It is a sign. I ask you, as a
witch, to tell it to me.''

She put her hand to the dog and he licked the meal's grease
from her fingers. Suddenly she burned. "You cursed my
child," she whispered harshly.

"The god's work only. You asked for his gift, if it is not to
your liking do not ask it. Ah woman, you know so little. You
do not know your own littleness.''

"Then why do you ask me things?" snapped Emma.

"Because you have the power. I feel it." The cold light
burned again in his face and she fought a shudder. The dog
rose at her side and snarled silently, his thin hair bristling
along his spine and Emma knew herself to be a mouse in the
claws of an owl. She must squeak to make him drop her.

She cleared her throat. "I too am troubled," she said
stiffly. "There is a man that threatens me, his name is Attar.
I think you know him.''

He said vaguely "I knew a man once—he was weak and
threatened no-one.''

"He threatens me, because I am alone and have no-one to
help me. In my barn lodge two of his men, they were at table
this night, you saw them.''

"I saw two men. But they did not speak and I was not sure if they were flesh. Only yesterday Odin sent a stag to me, it followed me all the day."

"They are real enough," said Emma. "Attar puts them here to watch me and soon he will drive me from this farm that is Thorkil's and take it for himself. Will you save me from that, Skarphedin? Will you help me?"

He sat for a long time before he spoke. "What a spider you are, woman, catching such flies in your jeweled web. You think to deceive me, I see your heart. I warn you only, do not trick the gods, you do not know their power."

Emma felt chilled, as if the door had swung wide in winter. "I offer my own small magic. Do this for me and I will cast my spells for you. My husband is far away and I need a man's strength." She gazed at him beseechingly, her breasts swelling against her dress, but Skarphedin's face was cold.

"What a witch this is," he said softly. Then he rose and took up Claw of the Raven, binding it about him.

"Now?" said Emma shrilly. "Won't the morning be soon enough?"

"You ask for death, and it does not wait for the dawn," said Skarphedin. He pulled his cloak loosely around him. "Come you."

When the door opened the wind rushed in and flared the fire. Emma left it swinging wide and went after Skarphedin, feeling a horror that had something in it of excitement. Was this how men went to battle, she thought? With a fever that put flames in their blood?

Within the barn the soldiers lay on their beds, one with his fat belly spilling out like the bulge of a cow's udder. The tallow dips were poor and the air was dark and greasy, and in it Skarphedin's shadow loomed up onto the walls. "What is this? We have done nothing." The man sat up and his belly became sausage resting across his thighs. The other rolled off the bed and scrabbled for his sword, Emma heard herself laugh at his foolishness. A little noise began that was Skarphedin humming, and it grew from a thread into a cloth that hung above them all and the men that were to die screamed like rats when the club begins to fall.

Skarphedin stepped once into the room and his hand held Claw of the Raven, that had come there because he willed it. One more step and it might be that the sword struck, though no-one saw it except perhaps a god, and a man lay dead upon the floor. His blood was water from a spring, the spring of death. And his friend, that still lived cried, "Save me, lady! I never harmed you," and Emma put up her hands not to hear him. When he fell the blood came up into his mouth and splashed her skirt.

Skarphedin turned and there was madness in his face, there was nothing in him that was human. Emma stepped back, knowing stark terror, knowing that for him the curtain of reason was gone and that she too would die. Slowly, more slowly than was possible he lifted Claw of the Raven and his face became exulted but even as he smiled and struck, her cur-dog leaped at him. His teeth closed on Skarphedin's wrist and as the blade fell it twisted. Emma felt a breath, like the brush of a butterfly's wing and when she looked one lock of her hair fluttered down. The cur-dog hit the wall with a solid thud.

All was still. The dog whimpered softly and Emma went to him, one leg was broken. She gathered the creature into her skirt to take him back to the house, feeling on her fingers the slime that was blood but closing her mind to it. That way was madness, that was the path of Skarphedin. He stood in the door, he was a husk, there was nothing in him, the folds of his face hung slack.

Emma looked for her voice. "It is finished. Come now and rest."

He followed behind her, his step shambling. Outside were Leif and the girls, huddling together like cattle. Emma lifted her finger and brought Leif to her side. "Go you and look," she said. "Then ride to Wicstun and tell what has happened, that Skarphedin has taken the farm once again for his friend. If you tell it right we shall not see Attar again."

Leif nodded jerkily and Emma went on to the house. In the short time she had been away the fire had burned down and she put wood on it, moving slowly and purposefully. She dared not cease movement for that would permit thought. The dog seemed very ill. She strapped his leg to a stick and laid him down by her bed, whispering to him and promising to love him for ever. When she went out Skarphedin was slumped on a bench.

She brought a cup of spiced wine and held it to his lips and he drank like a greedy baby. "Lie down now," she whis-

pered and obediently he did so. She began to cover him with
his cloak and then thought of the wrist the dog had bitten,
which should by rights have been leather strapped but tonight
he wore no armor. But when she looked at the flesh there
was no mark at all.

Emma stood and went to fetch a blanket. She swept it over
Skarphedin and bunched it up to pillow his sleeping head,
watching her hands quiver and feeling the sobs rising hot in
her throat. When all was done she found the quivering had
spread until even her hair shook and before her eyes came the
piece with its crisp, cut end. She stuffed her hands into her
mouth and ran to her bed, casting herself down in agony.

On the next day Skarphedin was quiet, only eating and dozing. In the afternoon as she worked she turned and found him
watching her.

"Do you want something?"

"I do not. I have been dreaming of my good friend Thorkil."

Emma stepped closer to him. "Was it a good dream? Tell
me."

"It was a dream of days past, when we marched together.
Green days with a high, bright sun. We would still march
now but for you."

"Nothing stays the same," said Emma. "The days pass for
all of us, and even you must grow old."

Yet when he looked at her she wondered if there was age in
him, or if even that had passed him by.

They stood in the grove together, he and Emma. The trees
were without leaves and it was a sunless day. Far away was
the crying of gulls, feeding inland, which was sure sign of a
storm at sea. She held a bowl for him to drink and she sipped
also. There was a spice in it for she knew magic herbs.
Nearby was a wide bronze dish that she had brought with her
and filled, as he watched, with water. Now she peered into it,
looking for a sign.

"What do you see?"

She shook her head at him, for she was unsure that she had
cast the spell right. It was hard to remember exactly, it had
been so long since her mother told it her. The water gave
back her own face, so flat and harsh that she hated it, and
behind she could see the high clouds passing. She sipped

again at the potion, for she had to see something, he expected it. It was his payment. The water was stirring in the wind, forming wrinkles and waves, it moved like a lake, like a river, like the sea. She looked into it and saw Bjarni.

"May God forgive me! Sweet Jesu save me!"

"You have the power. Tell me what you see."

Her hands were flung over her face. "I cannot do this! I don't wish to, you don't understand. Skarphedin, let me go."

"Woman! Tell me!"

She could not hide from him. She shivered and wished for her cloak, her house, for anything. But he was waiting. "It was Bjarni. He was drowning, I saw the waves, I watched him call to me."

"You screamed. There was more."

"That was all. I know he's dead."

"Then look again, spider, or I will prick you a little." He menaced her with his legs spread wide and his body springing between. She felt terror again, for fear is of the body, it asks no permission of the mind to turn bowels to water and coat the palms with sweat. But he needed her. She had the power.

"I'll look no more today," she said sullenly, and turned away from him. She gathered up her things, her bowl, her herb pouch, and she bent to pour the water from the dish. It fell in a clear stream and she thought, I saw nothing. It was a dream and there is no truth in such. It is water, clear and good and only a witch could see more. I am only Emma, and she is not a witch.

Suddenly Skarphedin shrieked, like a tortured hare, and fell to his knees crying, "What does it mean? Tell me what does it mean?" He looked up at her and said wonderingly, "It is blood again. The water is all blood."

Chapter
Twelve

THE DAY WAS clear and fresh, with seabirds hanging on the wind and swooping about the island's rocky shores. Colman was scrambling to look for eggs, his habit, now ragged and dirty, hitched up around his waist. Bjarni sat at the top watching and occasionally calling to point Colman to a nest he had missed, but the wind snatched at his words and mostly left Colman bewildered. Sometimes a gull dived at the monk and clawed at his matted head, and he lifted his arms and beat at it, in fear for his life if he should fall.

Bjarni gave a hand to him as he struggled back up, the precious eggs tied in a cloth. They were neither of them strong now and such forays down the cliff exhausted them. But as Bjarni said, hunger gave a man a view of things, it cleared his mind quite wonderfully, cleansing it of all passion. And Colman pretended to agree, although in his case his mind was cleansed of everything but the thought of food, endless delectable food.

They went slowly back to the cell, two threadbare sticks of men who had lived so long together that there was nothing left to talk of. There was only one thing that roused Colman to speech these days, now that Bjarni refused to talk of his women, and it was escape. He prayed daily for rescue, and each night when he went to bed hungry he felt that he most certainly deserved it, a pure and empty vessel waiting to be filled with God's grace. He could hardly be else, trapped here, yet still they waited and still no-one came.

They took three eggs each and one to be shared between them. From past experience they knew it was best to make a tiny hole in the shell and suck out the contents and each man drilled gently with his knife. Colman's egg was brittle and cracked right across, giving out a stench.

"It is addled," said Colman in disbelief. "All that for an addled egg."

"We have more," said Bjarni.

"Aye, and every one of them bad I dare say. What is God thinking of to leave us here? Why doesn't anyone come? We've been obedient and we've sought forgiveness, so why are we still here? We're forgotten, Bjarni, and we'll die and our bones will go all white like those beyond." He put his raw, chilblained hands to his face and sobbed.

Bjarni put out his own hand and gripped them. "You should not lose faith, Colman. Your God saved me from the sea and he will save us both again, it is only a matter of waiting. And I have told you before, those are not a man's bones, only some creature. This is a holy place."

"They look like a man's to me," sniffed Colman. He picked up another egg and hacked at it, this time with success. The rich yolk dribbled down his chin.

"You see, we are not forgotten," said Bjarni, giving him a cheering shake. "He gives us good and wholesome food, we should be thankful."

"I am, I am! It is only—Bjarni, an egg is not so filling for a man as a good stew. I would give anything for a stew."

The Viking gave him a rueful grin. "I know, I know."

He felt a great pity for Colman, caught up in another man's trial. He had no thought but this was meant only for him, and that Colman, a mere instrument, was a fish trapped in the same net. These days had been set aside for thinking and now he saw his life as a journey, twisting here and there through difficult ways. He had been set here, on this island, to find his path and each day he felt he came a little closer to it. He had lived wrongly in the past, that was clear, he had worshipped black gods and been sinful. Yet this was not enough of the answer for still they stayed on the island. Like Colman, he was beginning to be a little desperate.

In the cold, dank evening he went out onto the hill and

lashed himself with a rope made of seaweed. He knew that in
the grey skies something watched and he thrashed at his loins
to show that he was lustful no longer and was coming close to
grace.

Colman, who had once joined him in penance, sat glumly
watching. "I will cast myself into the sea and drown," he
said crossly.

Bjarni stopped, panting, and coiled up his rope. "Go down
to the shore, man, and see what you can find. There may be
some wood washed up, we have not looked this day. Go
along, Colman, do." He felt like a mother with a fretful child
that will not work and will not play but only keeps others
from their tasks. This time was too hard for Colman, much
longer would unstitch his mind.

He stood on the cliff, feeling the blows from the rope
stinging pleasurably as Colman pottered about down below.
He did not feel like sleep which was strange, because hungry
men sleep easily. Perhaps he had caught Colman's restless-
ness. The monk was stopped now, and stood peering out
across the water to where the land loomed up darkly, and
Bjarni knew he could stand so until pitch dark and then come
to bed miserable. "Come away, Colman" he called.

"But—I see something. Look, Bjarni, on the shore."

Truly the man was near madness. "There is nothing. Come
Colman, we'll look at your picture together."

"My picture be damned. Look, look, I see men!"

"There is nothing. All I can see is waves and shingle
and—by my mother's honor. I see men!" He felt faint and
his head swam. Still he stumbled down the cliff to stand
beside Colman, only to find he could see better from on high.
The two of them scrambled back and peered out into the
gathering gloom.

"They were there, two of them. Tell me you saw them
truly, Bjarni."

"I did, I did. We are saved, we are come to grace!"

"Only if they come here and fetch us. We must light a fire."
Suddenly purposeful Colman rushed to gather their dried
seaweed to burn it on the cliff. Bjarni had difficulty in
preventing him from burning their wooden bowls too, for
Colman could see no further than rescue. Suppose it was only
shorefolk? Or someone else, now gone? His own heart sank
at the thought and it depressed him further that he should so

long to escape. He had learned nothing during this time, he was as weak as ever.

The fire blazed in the darkness, smelling of salt and long-dead fish. The sparks flew up into the night sky, making it darker still in contrast to the flame. So it is with God, thought Bjarni, the nearer we come to him the blacker the night. We must trust in him to bring the morning. Colman muttered to himself, piling their whole stock of fuel on to the fire, crying sometimes amidst snatches of prayers. Bjarni gripped him, saying, "Calm yourself. Be at peace with what is to come, it will be well."

Colman sniffed and said jerkily, "It is only that I long so much to be back at the monastery. I cannot do with all this thinking, I cannot." But Bjarni thought, here is a man who has something to go back to. I am changed and I cannot go back, and the way ahead looks very hard. What is there for me? Oh God, if you are God and I think you are, take my hand.

At last the fire died and in the east came the pinkness of dawn. The two men stood on the cliff and looked out into the wind until their eyes streamed, two wildmen mad with hope and loneliness. The sea was wrinkled like an old woman's neck and at last, where the land chinned it, they saw two figures. They were black monks and they carried a boat. Slowly they crossed the water and the little craft dipped and bobbed, bringing to mind Bjarni's near drowning. He trusted that this time he was saved, but they rode above a sea-god these monks. When at last the currach came within the island's shelter he let out his breath in a long gasp, surprised to find that he had given up taking in air for some minutes past. Now he and Colman found that they were shy of meeting them. They looked at each other and saw that they were ragged, filthy, uncombed. They brushed at themselves and at each other, then went slowly down to the beach.

"Brother Donald! Brother Liam!" The sight of friends brought tears to Colman's eyes, he fell on their necks, weeping openly.

"It has been too long, Colman. Father Abbot looked to have you home months since, what has kept you?" This monk was greyhaired and somber, he greeted Colman like a father himself.

"The boat was wrecked, my friend here was near drowned.

I am sorry—this is too much for me—'' Colman turned away, unmanned entirely.

Bjarni made polite greeting on his own behalf. "Bjarni Sigurdsson, saved by Brother Colman's good offices. You are most welcome.''

The younger monk, Liam, looked confused. The two men whispered to one another. "You are—Viking,'' said Liam cautiously.

"But a Christian, sir. Colman brought me to faith.''

"Colman?'' They looked incredulous and Bjarni saw that here was his chance to make Colman's reputation. "He baptized me, and so by a miracle I was saved from drowning. It was all Colman's doing.''

"Yes. Yes, it was.'' Colman brightened at the truth of it.

Brother Donald, plainly feeling that they were wasting time in such chitchat, rubbed his hands together. "I think we had best make a start, if you would gather your goods together—? By the by, did you lose any teeth, Colman, I hear it often happens.''

"Only two at the back. We have nothing to bring, nothing at all.''

They went down to the boat, but as Colman stretched a leg to step into it, one foot already deep in the surf, he remembered his picture, lodged in a crevice in the rock wall of the cell. For a moment he paused, he must go back for it. But the path up the cliff seemed a mountain to him and here was freedom, so close. His foot acted for him, stepping firmly into the currach. The picture must stay where it was, for he had at last learned obedience and it was a bitter medicine. Perhaps one day some other would come to the cell and find his work, and would see in it the radiance of creation. As for Colman, he would paint what they told him, and be glad of it.

The currach, though small, was sound. Bjarni sat close to the waves and looked down into them, remembering. He had seen death and it had an ugly face. He had much for which to be thankful. Brother Donald rowed with a strength the younger men could not match, they were weakened even by this excitement. Bjarni knew that he must eat and rest if he were to go on, but he could see no way to it, the monks would not feed him. The days to come seemed perilous.

At last they came to shore. From here the island looked soft and unforbidding, as gentle as a breast to lay one's head.

Colman said, "Will you travel with us some way, Bjarni?"

Bjarni looked at him and saw it was only politeness, and that the others were unwilling. Suddenly he felt quite alone.

"We have been raided again since you left, Colman," said Liam stiffly. "They burned all that was not in the tower."

"But Bjarni is a Christian," said Colman uncertainly, "and he has nothing." He was fearful that too strong a plea might see him back on the island and he dared not ask too much.

Bjarni said, "I would rather go my own way, Colman, I'll find some work hereabouts, it was what I intended before. I shall keep you always in my heart, friend, let us meet in eternity."

They parted with smiles and tears, Colman to the road, Bjarni along the beach to where Liam said there was a village, some few miles down. Bjarni turned again and again to wave, but at the last time Colman was not looking and after that there was nothing to see but sky, and grey-blue hills. He felt weak and very hungry, soon he left the beach for the easier walking behind it and there he found bushes with a few bitter berries for the picking. The monks could have given him bread at least, he thought. It should have angered him but he was past that now, the island had driven all that out of him. He found himself staggering a little, as if he was drunk, and the world seemed far distant.

He thought of the eggs they had eaten, he thought he was in an egg, out of which his leg protruded like a hatching chick, and he walked on those legs and carried his shell around with him. He was in a shell and it was made of green glass, everything outside of it was green, even the faces that loomed up to him. He would speak to them but for this green glass shell, that walled him in and out. He would shout to them if his voice would come.

And the shorefolk peered at the tall, thin man, his hair and beard saltwhite and his eyes more blue than flowers, and caught him as he fell.

They fed him bread and fish and drink strong enough to take a man's breath away. They lived in huts of twig and bracken that they left and came back to, moving to a rhythm that was unseen by others and perhaps unnoticed by themselves. Bjarni could talk to them a little and he found that they were shy and nervous people, preyed on by the people in

the bothies, who were themselves devoured by the kings and
their stewards, that in turn were meat to a Viking sword.
Though they had so little they did not grudge it, and in a day
or two Bjarni felt well enough to go on.

As he took his leave he saw that the people were leaving
also, gathering their things and setting out into the sun. He
turned another way, heading always for the village that might
give him work.

In the evening he saw it stretched before him, peaceful
smoke rising from the fires. He thought to himself, I have
come upon places before like this. It is the same every time,
we must fulfill a task until at last we have it right, going over
and over again to a thing until we have learned what there is
to learn and done what we must do. I am no conqueror now,
no warrior, I am a beggar, looking to be allowed into the
houses for no payment but myself. This is what I am come to.

He went purposefully forward, ragged, wild, and when the
men stepped out to him with fear in their faces he stretched
out his hand and said "In the name of Jesus Christ. I come in
peace."

Bjarni lay on his bracken bed, feeling the creatures captured
in it making their tiny movements beneath him and gazing up
at a roof so low that if he sat up he would crack his head on
it. Once he would have lain here wondering what treasures
they hid within that thatch, but that time seemed very far
away. Now he worked, moving from place to place mending
chairs and making bowls, lending his muscle to cut corn or
holding down a beast while they lanced an abscess.

They were beginning to know him, these people: when he
came to a steading they smiled and cried, "Bjarni! We have
been looking for you, take your old place and join us at table
this night." He knew their songs and their ancient tales, of
giants, dark magic and gold. And when the priest came by
with his bread and flask of wine Bjarni knelt amongst friends
to take his portion. Never in his life had he known such
peace.

It was early still, but the sunshine filtered through the
boarding and made him restless. He got up, sluiced his head
in the trough outside and combed his hair and beard. These
days and since his breeks had fallen in pieces he wore the kilt
of orange cloth that the men here favored with his legs

strapped in leather. It was practical because the land was so boggy and the weather so wet, for a man could be soaked a dozen times in a day and the fields were so full of thistle that a test of good pasture was to turn a horse into it and count the burrs on its legs when you caught it again.

The cow was restless in its stall, he could hear her mooing gently. He fetched a bucket and went in to milk her, settling himself on the stool he himself had made two months since. The cow bitched at him, flicking a back leg up and switching her tail into his face, so she was bulling again and that was another task, to take her two miles to the next farm. They had suffered there of late when the steading was burned and all stolen, but the bull was left to them since it was fierce and would not go quietly.

Being sour of temper the cow held her milk back and Bjarni struggled to squeeze it out of her. He cajoled her in Norse, which somehow came more easily to him when he wished to be sweet. Little by little the cow relaxed until the milk was swishing into the bucket, and he leaned his head on her flank and gave himself up to the pleasure of it, turning the clean, creamy streams into seafoam.

There was a sound in the doorway.

"You need not fret, Dougal, I am doing your work for you," said Bjarni cheerfully. When no reply came he cast a glance over his shoulder, never pausing in his milking of the cow.

A woman stood there, black against the brightness of the day, and she held a child in her arms. Unease came into him, like a grub in an apple. He put his hand to shield his eyes against the glare.

"Who is this?" he said harshly. "Do I know you?"

The woman stepped fully into the byre, and as she did so her hood slipped from her head. It was the face of a cat, small, pointed, with eyes like moss and hair like a sheet of flame. It was Rafarta.

"I have brought you your son," she said.

Bjarni sat by his cow. There were no thoughts in him. "I am milking," he said.

"I have heard of the work you do. Are you sick in your mind perhaps? You are a warrior, are your men hereabouts? I saw no-one." She went to sit on a barrel and Bjarni saw that her child was thin, but with yellow hair and blue, blue eyes. That was a Viking babe.

"Is he—truly mine?" he asked.

"As you are truly my husband. I know we were wrong to deceive you, I deserved what you did. Of course you would have a warrior's pride. But I need you now. We were wed and you bred me, it is for you to provide."

Bjarni turned back to the cow, but she had tired of waiting and there was no more milk. He stood up and took a wooden cup from the rafter, filling it with a scoop of milk and handing it to the woman. "Give this to the child. He looks starved."

She looked at him despairingly. "Is it any wonder? My father is dead and all lost, it is for you to take it back! His hall is charred ruin and my brothers are all dead. If I had not run I should be a slave now. You are my husband, Bjarni Sigurdsson, we were wed. You must help me."

"Give the child the milk, he needs it."

But she pushed the baby into a pile of straw and reached out her hand to Bjarni and clutched his arm. "And I need a man. To be a husband to me, and a father to my boy, you can't deny me! You were the first, you took my honor from me. Don't you remember how it was? I don't forget."

She breathed on him and her breasts swelled beneath her dress. They were heavy now from childbirth and of a sudden he found himself wondering what it would be like to lie again with his head on a milkwhite pillow, to drink again from a perfumed cup. Her tongue was pale pink within her mouth, as he watched it licked lightly at her lips. He felt himself swelling to stiffness, she was so close to him he could not think. He stretched out a hand and touched her hair.

"I have nothing for you," he whispered. "I am what you see, no more than that."

"I shan't ask what you plan, I promise. Don't turn me away, husband, if you do we shall starve. I am the daughter of Maelsechnaill, when my father was alive men begged him for my hand. He chose you! Am I not worthy? Aren't my kisses sweet?" She pressed herself to him, her mouth with its sharp white teeth begging for his own. Bjarni shuddered. With an effort of will that was like a pain he pushed her aside.

"You don't understand," he said. "I'm no-one. I have

nothing except my two hands, I work for my food. If I've wronged you I'm sorry for it, but there is nothing I can do. You must find someone else.''

"You don't desire me," she said heavily.

"It is not that! You are lovely, more than any woman."

"I have borne you a son." She was close behind him now, if he turned he could hold her without taking a step. He longed to turn.

"Is it mine?" He felt bemused, there was a roaring like the sea in his head.

"You know it." She dug pointed fingers into his shoulders, her breasts pressed his back, they burned him like hot coals. The girl writhed sensuously, sucking air on a moan, pressing her narrow thighs against his. Bjarni sank to his knees, turned to put his face up to her. He saw that her dress was open, her nipples were dark plums against milky, blue-veined skin. His hands reached up of their own accord, to clutch and caress. Rafarta gasped at his touch, he remembered how it had been before, the need, the tightness that would not let him through and then the explosion into her that was like a thrust into heaven. How had he thought never to taste that again?

Somehow she was under him, their clothes a flimsy barrier to lust. Oh, how she smelled, oh how she tasted, she was all desire, all woman. When he sank into her flesh it was of all things what he wanted the most and his pounding release left him drained.

He rolled away. He could not think how this had happened. "I—I did not mean—I'm sorry. I can't look after you."

She gave a little laugh, drawing her skirt down over fleshless legs. "I am not a whore that you can have as you please. I am a king's daughter and your wife. You must take me to your house."

"I tell you I have no house!"

She lifted her narrow brows, colored as red as her hair. Clearly she did not believe him. Bjarni began to feel desperate. "What do you think I am?" he asked.

She considered. "Rich. A warrior. You came out of the Viking stronghold to look into the country and see what was there, but I hear you have a brother who is mighty and that you yourself are great. So you must care for me, and for your son." She got up smoothly and went to lift the baby from its straw bed. A sense of doom weighed like stones in the pit of Bjarni's stomach.

Outside he could hear the household stirring, voices sounded and children wailed. He was hungry, and looking at Rafarta he saw that she was large-eyed from many days without food. No wonder the child was thin.

He put a hand to his head. "Go down the road a little. I can't tell these people—it would be hard to explain. I'll come to you soon."

She nodded. "They do not know what you are, I see that. It seemed to me that you planned something. I can help you. I know the rath of my father's neighbor, I will tell you how to take it. You need not waste your time with these little places, with me as your wife you can be a great king!" Her green eyes flashed with a hunter's zeal and again Bjarni felt helpless. She did not know him at all.

He watched as she walked off down the lane, small and straight-backed with an air of scorn even for the mud beneath her feet. He wished that the ground would open up and swallow her, or him, to part them totally. If it were not for the child—what? Would he run away? He was more afraid of his future than of death.

The farmer and his family looked surprised when he took his leave; the daughter, that had been hopeful even though he gave her no encouragement became silent and her face went red. When they asked where he was going he lied and said he went to see his family. When he thought he realized that it was no lie at all, he had a family whether he liked it or not. Why did he not like it when she thrilled him so? His one sure feeling was that he did not.

She stood beneath a crabapple tree, the child asleep in her arms. She smiled when she saw him, as if all was as she expected. He thought, she does as she wants with me. He knew even then that he must fail her, that all she wished for was not his to provide. He told her that they must travel to Dubhlinn and she said, "Is that your stronghold?" He did not know how to answer her.

They lodged at night in poor houses and Rafarta sat like a queen while the women of the place waited on her. She would be royal in a cess-pit, thought Bjarni, haltingly trying to explain to her what he was. Little by little he saw that what he said to her made no difference, that in her mind she had decided and that was that. At night she loved him wildly and even while he reveled in her softness he thought, what will she think when at last she finds out? He began to feel that he was truly a deceiver.

When they came to Dubhlinn at first she looked about her with eager interest, at the ships, at the jewels, at the people. This was as she had expected, a great stronghold. Grim-faced, Bjarni asked around for lodgings and Rafarta, not understanding, waited to be taken to her home. He had little money and could afford only the smallest place, a lean-to hard by the river. He knew that when it rained the floor would run with mud.

She looked at him in amazement. "I cannot stay here. Where is your house?"

"I told you. I have no house."

He had it in him to be sorry for her. She, who had dined all her life in a king's hall, with her wrists hung with silver and the harp music playing, had somehow become shackled to a poor laborer. For the first few days, as he went around asking for work, her face wore a look of shocked surprise. She did not know how to cook, her only sewing had been fine linen, yet now she must struggle with a smoking fire and patch breeks worn by toil. And the town was less prosperous than formerly, money was hard to come by. The Irish kings were grown stronger and rich pickings from the country were not so easily had.

In the evenings Bjarni would come home to his cold, damp house, to his stone-faced wife and wailing baby, and he would wonder what was to happen to them all. One night when he reached for her under the thin covers she turned away and from then on she denied him, though the damage was done and she was breeding again. It was all wrong and he did not know what to do.

The child began to cough, as did his mother. One day she said dully to him, "I shall die here. You have killed me."

Despairingly, knowing he could not make her understand, Bjarni said, "I never meant to take a wife. I'm not suited to it, my brother now, he's different. He has a good farm in Northumbria, though he's gone traveling I hear—he always knows how to manage things, does Thorkil."

Her eyes were clear no longer, they were tinged with mud. "We should go there." She spoke without hope, because nothing she wanted ever seemed to be within her grasp any more. She, who had graced her father's hall, whose suitors had begged to be allowed to touch her hand and offer gifts was now without friends, or lovers or even a warm bed. It had all come from Bjarni, this misfortune, luck had left her the day she saw his face. He had tricked her, that was all there was to know, he had done it with his smile and his blue, blue eyes. He spoke of a brother and riches but probably he lied. Rafarta looked at him with icy hatred.

Bjarni looked around the poor room, and outside it was raining once again. He thought of Emma's warm dry house, and the flowers called monk's hood on the floor. Here there was only mud. A great longing for his own kind came to him, for Thorkil who would take away his load. He would be home now, surely, for who could stay from such a place for long? Rafarta was coughing again, her thin shoulders shaking. Surely her words had been guided.

"We will go there," said Bjarni, his voice catching on excitement. "We will go to the farm."

Chapter
Thirteen

SNOW TELLS A man something about things, don't you think? It is lovelier than a jewel, sparkling in the sunshine, and it'll see you dead quicker than a blade. Man has no use for it, except to look. Give me ugliness any day, for it means life. Beauty has no kindness in it.

The snow nearly had Olaf, Thorsteinn and me that winter. The others dropped out along the way but we three went on together with horses pulling the sledge across the ice and down the trails. You can hear another sledge coming a long way off, for the sound carries in the air, even down to the men shouting and the jingling of the harness. In that cold you all go muffled to the eyes, you could pass your brother and not know him. But I will tell you what happened, it was like this.

We'd been going for a long time, stopping at the houses along the way, they'll always find a place for a stranger by the stove. The food was terrible, they cook in bad butter, that has stood without salt too long, you know? A man can get used to anything, I suppose. We had a fair number of goods which we were going to trade for furs further east, and we had silver though we were careful to hide it. All the same we looked prosperous, with our good clothes and two shaggy ponies. One night we lay in a house with some Slavs, who were traveling the other way to us. We had no common language but we played a game or two with them and drank some disgusting stuff the people brew round there. I'll swear that has butter in it too.

They're a strange lot, the Slavs, with wide flat faces and slanted eyes, set back in so you can't see their eyelids. It makes it hard to know what they're thinking, except that a man can guess. We went our two ways in the morning and thought nothing of it, and for a day or so all was well. We should have known they'd have a short cut or two, in their own country. Towards evening on the third day we passed through black forest, with the snow heavy on the branches of the trees. It was a dead place in winter, with only sometimes a hare to be seen, or the tracks of bear and wolf. We were anxious to find shelter for the night, the forest being no place to rest with ponies. Wolves won't often come for a man, but they'll take a pony all right.

By the hammer, it was cold, Thorsteinn's spittle had dried to ice on his beard. I was wondering if we should stop before it was quite dark and build two fires, putting the ponies in between. Every now and then we would look into the trees and see shadows that moved and wove about like spirits. My feet had lost all feeling and I knew if I was not careful it would be the end of some toes.

The trail swung round a bend and the ponies snorted, which I thought meant they scented a house. Our swords were close to hand, but we were not expecting trouble and as it turned out they were not close enough. The Slavs fell upon us as we rounded the bend, six of them, and their own sledge standing by. They shrieked like the Valkyrie and I remember my brain stood still for a moment, frozen stupid. A man rushed towards me, a spear balanced for throwing and I did not duck until it was flying through the air, and even so I moved slowly. Then I found myself and closed my hand on a friend whose teeth would bite for me, I embraced World Tree and brandished him, roaring. I ran at a man who could not throw his spear for fright. At the last he cast it, but I struck it aside and killed him.

An axe dealt a blow to my shoulder, but my clothes were thick and I only felt the weight. I drove him off with my sword and felt for my dagger, to have it in my free hand since I did not have a shield. I saw Thorsteinn gripping a club as a Slav tried to smash his head with it and I leaped to his aid and let World Tree do what he might. Olaf was fighting well, but

then he went down and the axe was there to finish him.
Thorsteinn saved him that time, but when Olaf rose up on his
knees I saw there was blood on his head. It enraged me to see
my friend hurt, and the rage drove me to end it. In a moment
there were six men dead in the snow, one slain as he ran
which was no more than he deserved. No-one should run
from a battlefield when friends stand beleaguered.

Olaf was groaning and his eyes rolled, so we picked him
up and laid him on the sledge. When I looked at his wound
my heart went tight within me, for his skull was pressed in
above his eye. I thought to myself, not Olaf, not my good,
dear friend, and I felt the tears freezing on my cheeks.

"He's not gone yet," said Thorsteinn, who as I said, was a
good man. "I've seen men come back from worse than this."

It is good to hear a lie sometimes. By now it was quite dark
and as our blood cooled so did our flesh. It would be killing
Olaf more quickly than any wound as he lay there with his
wits gone.

"We'd best camp here," I said. "At least we've got their
sledge, we can draw it up as shelter."

"We'll need a fire," said Thorsteinn and we both looked
out into the dark woods. Fetching wood in there was not a
task to savor, with wolves, bears and no doubt Slavs to deal
with. In the end we wrapped Olaf in a cover and went
together, to watch each other's backs, and we brought back
what we might, though much of it was wet with snow. It took
a very long time to get a blaze going, and in that space I felt
the slow weariness that takes a man in such cold, the sleep
from which there is no waking. When we had a good fire
at last we drew Olaf up to it and also set a pot of snow to melt
to give us all a drink. I could not bear to look at my friend,
and then when I looked I could not bear to look away. The
blood had stopped flowing and was matted red ice on his hair
and beard, and though his eyes were open they were rolled up
in his head. From time to time he would twitch and stroke a
hand to his cheek, though soon we had him wrapped so he
kept still.

It was then we found the one good thing of that day, in the
sledge belonging to the Slavs. When we searched it, looking
for more covers, we found it was heavy with furs that they
had been taking to trade at Birka no doubt. There was snow

fox and bear and wolf, and a thick lustrous pelt from some sort of cat I think.

"What did they want to rob us for?" asked Thorsteinn. "They were rich!"

"And fancied being richer," I said. For once I could not rejoice in our wealth, with Olaf lying by the fire with his head bashed in.

I swear I have never been so cold. The part of me that was nearest to the fire kept warm enough, but any part that was not so near shuddered. My back felt as it did when someone put a snowball down it when I was a lad, but instead of shouting and wriggling and being free of the chill, I sat there and felt it spread. I knew I should have wrapped myself in the fur and walked about from time to time as Thorsteinn did, but I could think of no purpose to it. If a man should live without the love of his fellows, what is there for him? Is there anything more awful than to be friendless in the dark?

I felt my head nodding dangerously, and I remember that I could not think of a reason to fight it, this death that was taking me so quietly. Then Olaf groaned and rolled his head, and I creaked up to see to him. I saw that if I washed the blood away a little it did not seem so bad, or perhaps I had simply become used to it. That was the end of acceptance that night, the rest was all cold and hunger. Towards dawn when the fire was low and the wood gone, the wolves gathered in the trees, looking at us out of green eyes, and the ponies stamped and screamed in terror. So we screamed at the wolves and threw lumps of snow, so that they backed off for a while and then came creeping back, slipping between the trees. But at last when it was light there was no sign of them.

Then of course we had to decide what to do. There was no point taking the furs we had won back to where they had come from, no point at all, and with Olaf like this we needed to rest up until he recovered. I looked at Thorsteinn and wondered.

"What are your chances taking that lot back by yourself?" I asked.

He made a face at me. "Bad. Except that I'd be going the way we've just come. I could put it about that we were robbed and the both of you killed. With the sledge covered like that no-one need know what's on it, I could say it was the bodies." He rolled his eyes and laughed and I tried to laugh with him. A good man but somewhat wooden was Thorsteinn. He had less feeling in him than a tree.

"Go you then," I said, and he helped me make Olaf comfortable in a bearskin first. Then we hugged each other and he said, "I'll keep your portion safe friend," which he no doubt meant but I did not believe, men being as they are, and we parted.

I lodged that night in a warm house, and the people were kind. They took Olaf in and the wife poured honey milk between his lips, for all her flat face, and she bathed him and poulticed his head. She had no children, and that was probably the cause of it. We stayed there three days and on the third day Olaf seemed almost awake, though he kept slipping from us again. So I took a knife and I heated it in the fire until it was red, and I put it on his leg. Such a shriek as you have never heard, and there was Olaf again, cursing me and shaking his head. The wife struck at me with a poker and her husband was laughing and holding her, but all the same I had to hide behind a chair to stop her beating me. When we left in a day or so more I gave her some silver and a good big kiss.

Naturally Olaf had headaches. We made slow progress to give him time to rest, for sometimes the pain was so bad he sat groaning on the sledge with his head in his hands. Othertimes he seemed well and I said to myself, "He is mending. Soon all will be as before."

One day I said to him, "Do you remember the cakes Emma made for us? I'd give anything for one of them now," for the food was the usual bad meat and sour bread.

And Olaf answered "Emma? Who would that be?"

I felt my stomach dropping away, I almost sicked up what we had eaten. I said, "You remember Emma. My wife."

And he looked vague and said, "Oh yes. Of course."

That seemed strange to me, so in a while I said, "How about that time you went fishing from Jorvik? You remember that, don't you?"

"Yes—yes," said Olaf.

"Who was it went with you? I can't recall."

"It's a long time since." He put his hand up at his head.

"Was it my brother Sven? Was it him? Sven?"

He nodded. "That would be it. Sven."

I felt tears pricking at my eyes. Did he even know me, that

was his friend from years past? I began to watch him closely
and saw that he was altogether changed. As each day passed
so it was lost to him. He could remember what had happened
an hour since, but more than that and there was nothing.
Sometimes he forgot my name, sometimes even his own. We
journeyed on because there was nothing else to do, and my
only comfort was that he did not know what had happened to
him.

We began to trade our wares here and there in the forested
wastes. Nothing wonderful you understand, only furs and
bear claws, for the best stuff we had to go still east. Olaf
could pack a sledge for me but nothing more, even the money
was beyond him. I was like a father with a simple-minded
son.

But the day came when we reached the great frozen lake,
and to my amazement it was thronged. There were traders
there from all over, sheltering within tents and wood huts,
gathering as such men will, to drink and tell tales of where
they have been. There was an Arab who had set a rich red
carpet on the snow in his tent, it was amazing to see, and
there were short, hard men that swallowed their gold go keep
it safe when they came to wild places. Some of them had
slaves, mostly young, and they waited for the rivers to thaw,
so that they could trade them further south. It was judged to
be safer to brave the torrent together. That river claimed lives
every year.

I made a friend of a man that had a Saxon girl in his tent,
he had bought her last year in Francia. I found it pleasant to
talk to her in her own tongue, it brought back times past, it
shortened the miles between me and my home. For with each
day that passed and I went further from Emma I found myself
thinking of her more. You see, it's a strange thing, but with
Olaf almost witless all I could hold to was Emma. My brother
was set on his own path, and as for Skarphedin, you did not
build a life round such a man.

But Emma—in all these days of travel I had never once
met a woman to compare, and I don't mean looks, by the
gods, a fist in the face makes any girl ugly. It was her. She
was not sweet and she was not kind, but she was strong and
brave as any man, and when she was soft—it was like a
blessing. She could take what a man gave her and win in the
end, and she had almost loved me. It was my own foolishness

stood between us, nothing more. And here I was risking my neck in this cold place, with Olaf lost to me and no friend but a slant-eyed trader that scented his crotch, all because I had not the courage to stand by my wife.

The thaw was beginning, each morning when I woke there was the sound of water, running into the tent as like as not. Olaf slept more and more, I dreaded the day that I could not wake him. All around us men were preparing to go down the river, the Arab picked up his carpet and my trader friend took it in exchange for his woman. She was none too pleased, I can tell you, for these Arabs have filthy habits, they don't know what a woman's for. Also he made her wear stuff so thin you could see through it, which besides being disgusting was very cold. Still, it was good to watch her breasts bounce when she coughed, a sight like that can take years off a man.

The trader asked me if I'd go with him down the river, for he wasn't a seaman and his boat was a mite clumsy. I agreed if he'd give me the carpet, but he was loth. In the end when everyone was going and it looked as if he'd be left behind, he gave in, so I loaded Olaf and a couple of bales of goods into the boat, topped it with the carpet and set off.

The first part was easy, a broad river filled with icy water and only some tree branches to avoid. A couple of days of that and I thought I had a good bargain, as I sat in the stern and steered and drank wine. I was drinking too much wine, I know that. It was because of Olaf, sitting slumped at my feet, too sick to row and too far gone to speak. Sometimes he would dribble. Each day I had to tell him to eat.

Then we caught up with some boats that had gone before us, moored to the bank and anxious. "It is Gulper," they said. "We have never seen it so full." They were speaking of a rocky stretch with a little fall in the middle, which by all accounts did not sound so bad. I told the trader to strip off his clothes and I put a man in the bow and myself at the stern, each with a long pole. The danger was that the bottom would be torn out on a rock, or that we would be grounded and battered to pieces by the water pouring down, because it was thawing in earnest and the river was very full. And this I must tell you. I would have waited with the others if I had not been drunk, I was too drunk to know sensible caution.

We started on our way, with everyone watching to see how

we fared. Every now and again I would hold on to a rock and
send the trader over the side to feel for the bottom with his
feet, telling him all the while that this was the best way and
would do wonders for his manhood. Soon his teeth were
rattling together and he began to be difficult, so I cursed him
and threw him over whether he wanted to go or not. He had
thick hair on his shoulders I remember, and even so I could
see the goosebumps.

"May you drown, you whoremonger," I shouted, swig-
ging my wine, and he crouched naked on a rock, hugging
himself and shrieking. The man at the bow was getting
nervous for we were racing along now and sometimes a rock
would deal us a blow that sent us swirling away. I ceased
punting with my pole, I had no care at all if we died, though
everyone else was wailing and crying to their gods. The
bowman leaped over the side and struck out for safety, but in
that white water he had not a chance, and sank from view. As
for me, I was flying, I was high above them all and the luck
held me. When we struck I was laughing with my beard in
my mouth and the wine tasting sweet on my tongue.

I never thought to look on Olaf dead and not weep for him.
We had lost six. He lay amongst them with his skin puffed
out with water and his hair straight that had always been
curly. I touched his hand and said, "Olaf my friend." I could
not believe that he would not now open his eyes and smile in
his old, slow way. A man's years can be measured in the
passing of friends, his life is a pot filled with memories.

Everything was lost. The trader had been rescued and
would have killed me if he'd had any guts, which he hadn't.
All that grieved me now was that I could not send Olaf on his
journey with a proper respect, so I wandered around the slow
pools below Gulper and fished out some silver and a sodden
fur or two, and I traded them for the things that I wanted; an
old boat; some bread and wine, a knife and some shoes, for
his own were lost and who knows if a man might need them
in Asgard? I settled him down so tenderly, in an old wool
cloak that I wished he'd had in life, when he could feel it. I
rested his head on a pillow. It should have been the sea of
course, for he was a child of the waves, but this river would
flow to it, as all must. So do we all travel to the homeland.

At the last, when I torched the boat and pushed it off, I let out a great shout of anguish. The echo of it came back from the rocks, the smoke of my friend's burning filled my eyes and I was lonely, lonely, lonely. This was no place for me.

"Go home," my voice called to me, and again the rocks cried out "Go home."

Chapter
Fourteen

As THE LONGSHIP swung up the river it was plain to see that the men were veterans. Their shoulders were thick from rowing, the leather and wool of their clothing stained with long use. But their spears gleamed bright in the sun. In their eyes too you could see hard confidence, that they knew themselves and feared nothing.

Marjolein put her hand to her throat, for whatever one thought of these men, in their longships they were mighty. Perhaps she knew one of them. But as they shipped oars smartly she saw no face that was familiar.

She had come to buy fish and see if there were any whelks to be had, for rich ladies liked their colors gaudy. Today there were none and Emma would bite her lip in that way she had, as if she was tried too far and too long. No wonder, thought Marjolein, and looked at the sailors. He's not like them. He never was.

The place was thick with people and they made her nervous, jostling her this way and that. She held tight to her purse for she could not afford to lose coin, not since Attar went. Perhaps she might see Attar. Her heart shuddered at the thought and when a hand caught her elbow she choked on a shriek. But when she looked it was Gunnar, slack-jawed, dirty-haired, but her husband.

"I knew it was you. Done well for yourself, haven't you?"

He stank, he made the town smells sweet. Marjolein pressed

a hand to her nose and tried to pull away, but he held her. "Let me go. I want nothing to do with you, there's nothing to say." But he held on to her, his one-armed grip surprisingly strong and she could not shake him off.

A man said, "Here you! Let this lady alone!"

Gunnar glared at him out of a mass of lousy beard and spluttered, "This is my wife!"

The man looked at the couple, shrugged and went on.

"Let me go, Gunnar," hissed Marjolein, squirming against iron fingers.

"You must talk to me. I have something to say."

Only to be rid of him and the stares of the crowd she said, "All right, all right! Only let it be somewhere quiet."

He led her down an alley she had not known existed, a dank, dark place warmed at night by the backs of pottery kilns. Gunnar reeled against the wall and she winced as his stump met stone. It revolted her, but less now than the rest of him. If she looked into her heart she thought she might wish him dead.

"This is where I sleep," he said, pathetic and defiant at one and the same time.

"You disgust me," said Marjolein. Her skirt trailed in filth and she pulled it up out of the way. There were rats here, she had seen one running.

"Very high and mighty you've become, I see. You weren't so proud before, I remember when we've both begged for bread. Do you remember that, huh?"

"Is it money you want? It is all Emma's, I can't give you it."

He leaned back and eyed her speculatively. "Grown ugly now, haven't you? Who'd have thought your looks would wear away, like paint on wood. You're paler than water, you know that?"

She knew it. Her youth was gone and the knots of ribbon tied girlishly above her ears were a foolish pretense. But what was she to do, be old and lonely and not even try? She was suddenly desperate to be rid of this creature, she would give anything to be gone. "Here, take some coin, it isn't mine, but I can lie a little. Emma's a good friend, it's all I can spare."

But Gunnar's hand grabbed at her purse and took it. "She's

a good sort, is Emma, she won't grudge me. You can always tell a real lady.''

"You can't take it all, it isn't mine!'' Short, dry sobs made the ribbons shake but Gunnar only grunted.

"You can tell her you bought something from me. Listen, girl, and I'll tell you a tale.''

"I don't want to listen to you, you filthy, drunken beast—''

He shouldered her hard against the wall and his mouth breathed at her ear. "Tell her this. Attar's getting some men together, they aim to take the farm. He's fierce against Emma, reckons but for her he'd have taken a wife long since and be a father by now. Terrible thing a barren woman, eh Marjolein?''

"Get away from me. If you'd left the fighting when I asked you'd have two good arms now.''

"I took my chance with the rest of them. Is it my fault you won't lie with a one-armed man? I've still got what it takes, I had it then, look, it's just the same. Like a rub then? Come on, have a feel.'' He thrust at her, a drunken, leering monster of a man and as she backed away he laughed and chased her, shouting, "Coy now, aren't we? Come on girl, you always liked a good screw.''

Marjolein fled, back down the alley, back through the square, her basket and all her money gone. She would not stay in town that night, she would ride home and brave the dangers. But how would she pay the man who kept the pony? Gunnar always did this to her, she hadn't known misery till she met him. In all her careless girlhood she had never foreseen this.

The Dane who stabled her gelding was dour-faced, and though solid was not unkind. "I was robbed,'' she said tearfully and he nodded and believed her. But he took one of the panniers to hold against payment next time, if he saw her next time since she was making that ride in the dark. The roads were dangerous nowadays. Marjolein knew it but she had to be gone, to Emma and her certainty. She passed through the bar only an hour before dusk, the pony shuffling through the mud.

The forest was black and threatening, rustlings came from the trees and the path behind and ahead. Marjolein was so tired that she thought she would fall from her mount and be lost, eaten by one of the forest creatures, one of the wood-spirits that still haunted these places for all no-one believed in them any more. The inside of her knee was rubbed raw against the saddle, she was not made for life's harshnesses but for pillows and prettiness. Where Emma was strong iron and neither bent nor broke, Marjolein was bronze, pretty enough at the start but no good for anything. She saw nothing good in herself, she almost wished to be devoured.

At last the dark mass of the steading loomed before her, quiet and brooding. The dog in the house began growling and the gander and his tribe of wives rose hissing from their bed.

"It's me, Marjolein," she called, and the pony shied away from these geese. What a welcome, what a homecoming. Marjolein was dull with misery.

But Emma was at the door, with a torch in her hand. "Is it really you? Why do you come so late?" Her voice was high with nerves, no good ever came in the night.

"I had to. I'll tell you all, only get these geese away do!"

Emma came out with the torch and drove it at the geese, her hair catching sparks it seemed and blowing in the wind. The pony whinnied, the geese hissed and in the midst of it was suddenly Skarphedin, his sword upraised and ready.

"No! No! shrieked Emma and flung herself back, but the blade swirled and took the gander's head. His body strutted for some steps, spurting blood horribly and Marjolein screamed, "He's mad, he'll kill us all!"

Leif hobbled up from his house, a dagger in his hand but when he saw Skarphedin he made off, dragging his bad leg and yelling, "Hide, mistress! Get away from him!" In the torchlight Skarphedin looked mad and ghastly, his head sunk between his shoulders and searching for a foe.

Emma, crouched beneath the neck of the pony, gathered her wits. She stood, very slowly, and went to where the torch had fallen and still blazed amidst the blood. She lifted it and said softly, "Skarphedin. It's over now. Come and sleep." Her voice seemed to pierce through his confusion. His head turned and he seemed to know her.

"We are attacked?" he asked uncertainly.

"Not this night, it is to come. We will know when it is time." She looped her free hand through his shieldarm and it was as if the touch drew spirit out of him and drained the madness from his face.

"I dreamed again. I saw them come."

"Then it is a sign of what must be. Come now, my friend, come and sleep. We are safe and you can rest with honor."

He allowed himself to be led away. In the yard the geese called for their lost master, Leif's wife sobbed by her house and Marjolein sat her pony like a statue.

The next day, when they had gathered their wits a little, Marjolein went to Emma. "I have to tell you what happened. I'm no use to you, Emma, I lost the money, the stableman has one pannier and I lamed the pony. You should send me away."

Emma smiled wearily. "And what would that make better? The luck has gone, that is all there is to it. I can't get it back. It is as Thorkil said, we are trapped in a web and try as we might we can't get free. I am so tired of it."

Marjolein said, "It was Gunnar stole the money."

"That man is a leech! If ever a man ought to die it is he, preying on women, robbing his wife!"

"He told me—Emma, he says Attar is plotting to take the farm, that he is quite turned against you and will kill us all. He is gathering men."

Emma's face became very still. She has not lost beauty, thought Marjolein, she has gained it, she is all bones and smooth white skin. She rubbed at her own cheeks, whose fragile surface was long since roughened by the wind.

"What is to come?" said Emma suddenly. "I see us all in the light, in a circle of light. Outside it is all dark. Soon we must go out into that dark, and what will become of us? In the light everything's known, even the pain is understood. But in the dark—it is all mystery."

Marjolein sat frozen. "Are we to die then?" she whispered.

Emma looked at her, bemused. "That is nothing of it," she said. Sometimes she felt that only Skarphedin understood, that he was as close to her as he was distant.

"But what of Attar?"

Shrugging, Emma said, "It is as I expected. Perhaps he won't come and if he does, we have Skarphedin. I know his sense has gone, but perhaps Attar does not. Or if he does he must still fear him, we all must. We shall see. But tell me of Gunnar, was he drunk?"

Marjolein flushed, to the roots of her faded hair. "He—he

was very drunk. Emma, he waved himself at me. He undid himself and—waved it.''

Emma put her hand to her mouth, went pink and began to giggle. "He didn't! What did you do? Did anyone see?''

Just as pink and looking somewhat coy, Marjolein began to tell the tale. They drank a little wine. In a while, seated in their circle of light, they forgot their fears.

The rhythm of days formed a shell around Emma, keeping her from thought and anxiety, making a rigid frame on which to hang her life. She did not hope any more, for it seemed to her that each time a traveler came to the farm and it was not Thorkil, who alone could save her, she was weakened by disappointment. She no longer thought, "If he came he need not know about Attar, I could tell this lie or that,'' for she did not think he would come. Her life was a string of partings and once parted she seemed never to meet again. There was a pattern to it, and it could not be changed. So she stayed on her farm and cared for Skarphedin, that she alone could manage, and all around people moved at her direction. In fear of Attar, and even of Gunnar now, they did not travel to Jorvik, but traded with Wicstun, the little town at the foot of the hills that held a market twice a week. Emma sent Leif to it, she had no wish to go herself. To leave her farm was to see herself as weak, defenseless and poor, while at home she was Emma, and mistress.

One day Leif returned from market to say that there was a man there asking for Sigurdsson's wife. He had not known what to say and had come away before anyone pointed him out.

"Who was it?'' asked Emma.

He shrugged. "Laughed a lot. Seafaring man, I should say.''

"And you did not ask what he wanted?'' Emma gaped at him. For a sensible man Leif was often half-witted it seemed to her. Here was news, and from Thorkil, and he ran away rather than hear it. She fetched her cloak, and spared a thought for the pony that must travel again this day.

"You'll not go yourself?'' said Leif.

"Since you won't speak to him, it seems I must,'' said Emma waspishly, and knew herself unkind.

"How will we manage—him?" said Marjolein. It was what everyone was thinking, they looked at her, big-eyed and nervous. Her excitement paused a little.

She went to where Skarphedin sat watching the road, his fingers tracing the intricate patterns on the hilt of his sword. "I am going to market," she said. "Will you come?"

"Am I a dog to cling to my mistress's skirts?"

She grimaced. Her own dog was not fit for much more, hobbling about at her heels on three legs and a bent and twisted fourth. But Emma treasured him, and would leave him tied to a post, otherwise he would follow her till he dropped.

She went back to the others. "Skarphedin is well today. Leave him alone, don't bother him."

"You must take care," said Marjolein nervously and Emma, impatient, nodded.

The afternoon was warm, the air scented with wild thyme. But the pony moved sluggishly, for he was cross at being asked to leave home again. Emma thought, the man will be gone and I shall never know. The noise of chopping came from within the forest, and that was Erik most like. These were her woods, or so she liked to think, but she could not drive him from them. That was a thing to clear the head, that she might meet Erik on a lonely trail. It would not be a happy meeting.

It was not far to Wicstun and soon she stood by her pony at the edge of the market. It looked like a poor day, with few stalls and fewer customers, so she haggled a good rate to have her pony stabled. The man looked at her curiously, for she was not known and besides, she was handsome. Most women of her years were slackbellied from childbearing, or wizened and wearied from work, so when men saw Emma, deep-breasted, strong, with a neat waist and shining hair they nudged each other and said "Look at that. Who's she?" Emma swirled her green cloak and looked back at them.

In the alehouse, when she asked for the man that asked after her, there were knowing looks and grins. Her heart shrank in her, for if everyone knew of Attar how could Thorkil fail to know? She had been foolish. But she said for all to hear, "I thought my husband dead. Does the man bring news?"

"Hanged if I know, lady," said the innkeeper. "Try at the blacksmith's, his horse was wanting a shoe."

"My thanks," said Emma, and when she turned everyone was staring at her. She felt herself flushing and became haughty in consequence, sweeping from the place with the manner of a queen. The men sniffed and rubbed their noses.

At the blacksmith's a man sat on a plough while his pony was shod. Emma knew him for the one, he had a gold ring in his ear and a dagger tucked into his shoe, and the backs of his hands were drawn all over with birds in dark blue and red, as sailors often did. There was one man she had seen wore always a sleeveless jerkin so that men might look at the snake that coiled around his arm, its mouth hissing open on the back of his hand. She disliked it very much.

"You have news of my husband," she said breathlessly, and the man turned and looked at her. He stood up.

"I was looking for the wife of Thorkil Sigurdsson. If you are she I don't know why he went to sea."

"I am his wife. Is there news, tell me please. He isn't— he's not—is he well?"

Thorsteinn sighed and sat down again. "Lady I can't tell. We went east to trade in the snow, and after one thing and another I brought back some furs to sell. I heard no more of him, I thought perhaps he'd come home before me. Now don't! Now there's no need for that!"

To have hoped so much for so little. Emma sat slumped beside him on the plough, her face in her hands. What was to become of her, with Attar against her, and Erik too, and Skarphedin half-mad and Leif only good for breeding from his fat wife, that he did every year without fail—why did Thorkil stay away?

"Has he quite forgotten me?" she asked tearfully.

"Why never. He spoke of you the day long, I swear it."

"How is he?"

"How can I say? He's a man like no other, his name goes before him. A dragon in the fight and at sea he's more cunning than a snake. I swear he calls the wind to come to him."

Emma put out her hand to Thorsteinn and lifted drowned eyes. "Thank you for this news, it was kind to bring it."

Thorsteinn, who was very susceptible, blinked. He gripped

her hand a little tighter. "Er—I've something for you. From the furs. Come where we can be private."

They sidled behind the forge. Like sun after rain, Emma gasped, "Is it money?"

Thorsteinn lowered his voice. "It is gold. That's why I came, to give him his half. Look." He opened a heavy pouch and Emma said, "Is that all for Thorkil?"

"Yes, it is his share." Emma thought, less a gold piece or two. Still, it was good of him to bring any of it.

"You are an honest man," she said, and moved closer to him. He was very large and hairy, he made her ache a little.

"In the east," said Thorsteinn, "they cut off a man's balls and leave him to guard the women. I'm surprised Thorkil didn't leave you such. Very surprised." He was eyeing her breasts, that were as full as ever and thrust out against her dress.

Would he be good, she thought, or all sailor, shoving an oar through a wooden boat? It was hard to live without a man at all, it made her cross.

She lifted up her hand to pat at her hair. "Do you have a wife?" she asked softly.

"We live at Kexby."

At once Emma took a pace backwards, she did not like him well enough to have him on her doorstep after. He would have his reward some other way.

"I will buy you a drink," she said. "I have the money now."

He cautioned her. "Don't show that around here, sweetheart, someone'll slice you for it."

"I have some lesser coin. Come, tell me everything."

When she rode back to the farm it was dusk, but she was made brave by excitement. Money! And from Thorkil, who would surely come back to her soon; he spoke of her constantly, Thorsteinn said. She would tell him Attar forced her, and then he would kill Attar and all would be well. Where was he now? What was he thinking? She gazed up at a young moon and dreamed.

The door of the house stood wide. Suddenly Emma thought, is it Attar, now? She thought of turning and riding away, but then there was Marjolein running to her, as full of news as a baby with wind.

"You'll never guess—Emma, what a day! It is Bjarni, and he has brought with him a wife and a babe, and he's turned Christian, I never thought I'd see the day! Just think Emma, Bjarni has returned to help us!"

"Bjarni? I'll swear him drowned, dead—Bjarni?" Emma slipped from the pony and ran to the house. Her heart thudded, she was sure she had seen him die. She looked for a ghost and did not at once see that the man beside the fire was truly Bjarni. Still, she hardly knew him. His eyes were as blue and his hair as golden, but he was thin and strained, all the laughter was gone. What had happened to weary him so? Her heart went out to him on a wave of warm memories.

"Brother!" Emma went to embrace him, unsure whether to laugh or cry. "You have been through trials," she said softly.

"More than you know." She saw that his hand trembled and she took it to give him strength, but at once he pulled away, saying, "This is my wife, Emma. Rafarta."

Emma turned her mind to the girl, sitting straight-backed on the bench. She was small and as fragile as thin ice, and she rose to greet the mistress of the house a little too slowly for Emma's liking. When they stood together Emma felt like a giant.

"You are welcome," she said stiffly.

"My thanks to you."

It was enough and no more. Perhaps she was still unhappy with the language, thought Emma, but she looked at the small, proud head of her guest and thought not. The girl seated herself again. For all the world like a princess, thought Emma, bustling about with food and drink for them all. As she worked she saw Bjarni tip his head to speak to her, and to him too she seemed formal. Leif and the farmboy gaped at her flame hair and narrow hands and all the girls looked round-eyed.

Marjolein whispered "She is certainly noble," and Emma snapped, "No more noble than I. She should offer to help."

"But she is with child, Emma, can you not see?"

Emma sent a piercing glance across and saw that Rafarta, who had combed her hair with languorous content, swelled. She had remarked only the green-eyed cat's face, that made her own hair rise on her neck as it did for her cur-dog, who even now crouched at Emma's feet.

What did Skarphedin make of this she wondered, and looked for him. "Where is Skarphedin? Marjolein?"

She made a face. "Brooding in the sewing shed."

Emma dried her hands and said, "See to this." She took up a flagon and cup and went out.

Skarphedin sat silent by a dead fire. Emma went to him and put her hand on his shoulder. "Are you well?"

His eyes slowly opened, he spoke on a shallow breath. "I need—herbs." He was in pain, she had seen it at once. Quickly she poured a measure from her flask, it was her most precious medicine bringing sleep and an easing of pain, though too much caused vomiting. Skarphedin took the cup, blind-eyed.

"Bjarni has come," she said. "He has a cat of a wife, she thinks very well of herself."

"One sniff and you know this?" He almost mocked her.

"We shall see if I'm right. She makes Bjarni sad, that is plain enough. She's borne him one babe and swells with another."

Skarphedin looked at her out of hooded eyes. "Odin is jealous but a barren woman is his mirror."

"It is not that! Do you come to the house, Skarphedin, I have work to do."

She swept out and he followed her slowly. When he entered the house there was a silence, all faces turned to him. The child, that crawled around Emma's busy feet, whimpered a little. Rafarta watched green-eyed as Bjarni rose in greeting.

"My friend." He moved to clasp the berserk, but Skarphedin threw back his head and stared. Bjarni dropped his hands.

"Are you known to me?" said Skarphedin.

"For all that we had—" said Bjarni anxiously, and his forehead wrinkled.

"It is for those who honor it. You have chosen your path, walk it, do not look to others on a different way. Put your slobber on your wife."

He went to his seat, that was kept for him, where Emma spread his blanket and set his cup. Bjarni turned slowly back to his wife.

"What is this man?" hissed Rafarta, pink with excitement.

"He is a warrior," said Bjarni hesitantly, "he worships another god—"

"As did you once," said Emma in ringing tones. "He is

Skarphedin and you do well to remember it, Bjarni. Don't try
to make him small.''

"You're playing a different tune," said Bjarni in amazement.

Emma met Skarphedin's eye, briefly. "We know one another, he and I."

At table Emma and her girls fetched and carried, served and
poured, while all the time Rafarta sat unmoved. Even her
child was left to Emma to feed, slicing up meat into small
pieces and mashing bread to a wet paste.

"What is his name?" she asked, and Bjarni said "Liam"
which Emma thought dreadful but it was the child's and must
be used. He looked less well to her than one of her cattle and
she said sharply, "Has no-one fed this boy? A sheep hurdle
hasn't so many ribs," to which Bjarni replied "It was hard in
Dubhlinn, there wasn't so much work."

"The northmen spoiled everything," said Rafarta contemp-
tuously and Emma surged and said, "You tell that to me? I
am Mercian nobility, I'll have you know."

But Rafarta only smiled and Bjarni said apologetically,
"She's the daughter of a king, Emma."

"Oh aye," said Emma scornfully.

She gave the couple the room in the barn where the soldiers
had lodged. Bjarni was mysterious and would not say if he
planned to stay, or was perhaps traveling somewhere. Time
and again she resolved to ask, and then looked into his tired
blue eyes and could not. She began to feel uncomfortable,
and to wonder if in fact he meant to take the farm from her.
She remembered how they had parted, and that he at least
might remember Attar. She began to find it hard to sleep at
night.

At last she said, "Things are difficult with us nowadays,
brother. We are poor." It was barely a lie, for the money was
Thorkil's and she had buried it beneath her loom. She looked
innocently at Bjarni. "Everyone has to work," she hinted.
"There is no place here for people that will not bend their
backs to a task." They both knew that she spoke of Rafarta,
who sat all day like a queen to be waited on, but Bjarni said
nothing. "I trust she's lusty, it's all she's good for," said
Emma sharply.

Bjarni said "I have the right to bring my wife here, Emma. It is my brother's farm."

"That he left to me, not you. I've held it, I've worked it, don't think you can come now and take what is mine. I won't let you, and I won't let Attar, or Erik, or anyone else. It is my farm, Bjarni, and we all have to work to keep it. You are welcome as Thorkil's brother, and also because of your sword. I'll not keep idlers, that's all I say." She felt tearful, and angry that he should dare to think of displacing her. But in that moment he had looked like Bjarni again, bright and living, though as she watched the vigor drained away and he seemed only tired, dispirited and hopeless. She touched his hand. "You are welcome," she said softly. "It is only—I don't like her."

"She—she finds it hard in a strange land, amongst strangers. I want you to be kind, Emma."

"It is very hard to be kind when you must work every moment while others sit with their hands folded! At the least you should speak to her. Why don't you?"

He looked harassed, and suddenly Emma thought, he is afraid of her. He cannot stand up to women, that was always his trouble. He could charm them and love them, but in the end he could not master them.

Bjarni said, "I'll talk to her. She feels ill, with the baby coming—" and she knew he would say nothing.

"You should think about building a house," she told him, and he looked vague, as if he could not bring his mind to it. He had become very dreamy, she thought.

But life on the farm opened up a space for the newcomers and the pattern of it changed, uncomfortably to Emma's way of thinking. Twice a day Rafarta came into the house and took food for herself, exactly as though she wandered into the palace kitchen to see what was provided there. It enraged Emma, especially since Liam was left entirely to her care, as if she was the appointed nurse perhaps, she said furiously to Marjolein.

"But Emma, you like it."

"What has that to do with the case? I warn you, if she once comes and says again 'Is this meat salted?' and then turns up her nose at it I shall fetch her a clout with the barrel so I shall. Except that then she would say 'How useful to be so

strong, Emma, when you are as small as me it is so tiresome.
One has to ask a man's help all the time.' If there were more
a man than Liam round here we'd have trouble.''

''She'll be different when the babe comes,'' said Marjolein.

''I do not think so,'' said Emma, and hissed with bad
temper.

It began to be all she could do to hold her tongue when
Rafarta was there, and always the girl seemed to strive to
annoy. When Emma wore her amber beads Rafarta admired
them, saying, ''I suppose this is all you can get here. What a
pity you have not a silversmith, then you could have something really fine.'' And Marjolein, Emma's friend, gazed
wonderingly at the slut and heated water for her and brought
her wine, as if she were as royal as she pretended.

Not for one moment did Emma believe it, and if she had it
would have made no difference. When Bjarni came in from
the fields with a cut hand it was Emma that must tend it,
Rafarta only watched. When the child fell on a stone it was
Emma quieted his sobs, though she knew Rafarta heard.

She began to feel she could not escape the woman, that she
was the cause of the bad luck that dogged them. Skarphedin
was ill; in Jorvik the chiefs were squabbling which would
mean a loss for someone, and if Attar was without a place
where would he look to but here? Once in the forest she saw
Erik, looking down on the steading, marking it. Bjarni went
to look but found no-one, and said she was mistaken. So
perhaps it was Rafarta bewitching her sight, for if witch there
was she was Irish, thought Emma.

Rafarta swelled like a plum on the bough, and Marjolein
was her wasp, darting round and tending her. One day Emma
found them together, Rafarta seated while Marjolein combed
the long, red hair. She was using Emma's comb, that was
Thorkil's gift. For the space of half a breath Emma could not
believe it. Her house, her friend and her comb! She sprang
towards them, a growl in her throat, and Rafarta's pink mouth
made a hole in her face.

''Give me my comb!'' shrieked Emma, and swung her arm
to slap. At the last Rafarta ducked away, and the blow struck
the side of her head. Emma had wanted to leave the mark of a
red hand on her flesh, perhaps even to draw blood. She stood

turning the comb in her fingers, knowing it to be spoiled while Rafarta crouched looking up at her.

Marjolein sobbed, saying, "Please Emma! We've done nothing! The baby's crying."

And when she looked Liam was in the doorway, grizzling unhappily. Emma picked him up, hating him for being Rafarta's and loving him for himself. "It was my comb," she said defensively.

"You are a witch," said Rafarta. "My husband told me and I see it is true."

"You're no sort of mother. If it wasn't for me you'd all have starved. You've no right to come here and live off me, you're nothing but a slut."

A slight smile touched Rafarta's lips. With Marjolein's help she lifted her swollen body back on to the bench. "I at least have never played my husband false," she said sweetly. "Marjolein has told me all about it." She tossed a strand of hair back over her narrow shoulder.

Emma flashed Marjolein a look of congealed fury. What else had she betrayed? What other secrets were known to the world? The words that would send Marjolein away rose to her lips, trembled there and were swallowed again. She could not do it, not when Marjolein wrung her hands and wept. All at once Emma too felt like crying.

"Here. Take the child, if I can trust you to it." And when Marjolein tried to take her hand she thrust her aside saying, "Don't speak to me!"

Outside, in the cold damp air, she could breathe again. Her chest hurt. She put the comb in her pocket and went to look for her bronze bowl, to take it up to the grove. It would be peaceful there in the quiet of the woods, she would not feel that she lived amongst enemies. Sullen birds sat in the bushes, they watched her passing. Today she longed for Thorkil, he was real in her mind but he was far from her. She was most terribly lonely.

The water was clear, as it should be. She crouched over it, feeling the damp grass on her knees through her skirt. A tiny leaf blew on to the surface and whirled about, she put in a long finger and rescued it. The water shivered. She saw a mist, and in it was Skarphedin.

She sat back on her heels, her mind filled with horror and success. Why could she not see what she wanted? Why did she see anything at all? "I am a witch," she whispered and wondered why she did not prosper. She did not wish to look again, for it was Thorkil she longed for and she knew he would be denied her. She gathered up her things and went slowly back to the house.

Skarphedin sat outside, watching her, and she could not look at him. She felt his will straining at hers, and at last she gave in, and met his eye.

"It is my death," he said.

"Is that what it means?"

"I have felt it. I think sometimes I am dead already, all this seems—far away." He looked down to the road in the trees as if from a very great height.

"Are you in pain?" asked Emma, but he had left her, passing into that other world which now he left so rarely. There is no fear in him at all, she thought. He has trust in his god.

She went into the house and found Marjolein working, red-eyed and silent. Bjarni was at the forge, she could hear the hammering, which meant Leif and the farmboy alone in the field, bringing in a poor harvest. There was weed in the corn and it did not ripen in these sunless days, so it would give them all gripes even when made into bread. She felt desperate. The baby's nose was running and she wiped it, resting her cheek a moment on the soft hair. What was to be done, how should she care for them all, that cared not at all for her?

She stood up and said to Marjolein, "I will go out to the fields and help the men, Bjarni must come also. Why did you not take them the basket, Marjolein, instead of tending that cat? She won't feed you."

"I'm sorry," whispered Marjolein and handed the food that should have gone to the men long since. Emma was surprised they had not come back for it.

Bjarni was mending a ploughshare, though they had no need of it now and it was a task wasted. She held tight to her temper and said, "Will you come into the field, please, Bjarni? We have a harvest to gather and not enough men to do it. I shall help myself."

He looked at her coldly. "Rafarta tells me you struck her."

"I told you, people here have to work. She does nothing—

except take my things. My special things. You'll have to speak to her about it."

Bjarni said nothing, but plunged his hot metal in the water barrel. They stood in billowing steam, and when it was cold Bjarni left it and pulled on his jerkin.

They walked together into the fields, Emma's dog limping at her heels.

"This is no life for me," said Bjarni. "I need peace."

Emma sighed. "You should not have brought her here."

"You're a jealous woman. I never knew that about you."

"I am not! It is just—I'll never like her. What is it you want, man, it seems to me you have tried everything and none of it suits. Why are you here if you don't want to be?"

He shook his head a little and swiped at a grass, dragging the seeds through his fingers in a bunch and then letting them flutter away in the breeze. "I know what I want," he said sadly. "I cannot have it, but at last I know." Emma said nothing, only watching as he walked, slightly stooped now where once he had been tall and straight. If she had not made Thorkil happy, at least she had not brought him down. That was something better than the cat.

"I would go for a monk," said Bjarni suddenly.

Emma stopped in her tracks. "That's rubbish."

"I tell you I would. It's what I need, I don't need women, or fighting, or drink, I've seen enough of adventure. If I was a monk there'd be—peace." He caught her hand, and he was alive again, saying "If I could leave here, Emma, I know Thorkil would do this for me, he wouldn't grudge her a place in his home. I could go into Wessex and seek Guthorm's sponsoring, he is Christian now—please Emma. I'll ask nothing of you ever again."

"You want—me—to care for your wife? Your children? You ask me that?" She could not believe it.

"I tell you, Emma, I have to go."

There seemed to be no words in her head. Dumbly she began to walk again, feeling in turn furious and triumphant. For all her noble blood, for all her beauty and fecundity, Rafarta still could not keep her man. And Thorkil would have stayed if she had asked him, he spoke about her daily, Thorsteinn said. But the thought of Rafarta night and day, watching with her green cat's eyes that told a silent tale of riches and unknown splendor, she could not bear it. She did not know what to say.

When they came to the field she wondered why they had come. No-one could be seen, Leif and the boy were asleep somewhere no doubt. Did no-one round here ever work if they were not watched? "Leif! Leif!" she called and went up and down the stooked rows, the basket heavy on her hip. She'd take the food back so she would if she waited much longer.

A pair of feet stuck out from the standing corn and she kicked at them, saying "Get up man, do!" One foot lolled heavily on its ankle and Emma felt her irritation drain quite away. In a moment she knew she'd be afraid.

"Bjarni," she said quietly. "There's a dead man here."

He came to her side and went into the corn without a word. The place seemed to threaten her, with its silence and grey skies.

"It is Leif," said Bjarni. "The boy is further on."

It was a small field. She put her hand to her eyes and spun round, searching the trees that surrounded them. Anyone could be there and she would not see them. Was it Erik? Attar? Some other that she did not know? Leif's scythe was lying on the ground and she lifted it. Her dog was licking the blood from the ground and where Bjarni had trodden down the corn she could see a hand, the fingers half-severed where they had caught at a blade. These men had been defenseless and it was her fault. She had been warned and she had done nothing.

They ran back to the house and Emma thought breathlessly, at least I have Bjarni, he will take a sword. Skarphedin will hold it for us, he must. But the steading was peaceful still, the only smoke came curling from the chimney. They all looked up when she rushed in, their faces full of mild surprise.

"They've killed the men," gasped Emma. "We must fight!"

Leif's woman gave a shriek and fainted dead away, and her child began to squeal and the girls set up a wailing until Emma shouted, "Be quiet all of you! We must—be strong. I've been expecting this. We must make a stand in the house."

"They will fire the thatch," sobbed Marjolein, and it was true, it would happen. Without men to fight they were lost.

Emma turned to Bjarni saying, "Have you your sword to hand? If not there is one in the barn, not good but all I could afford. It was for Leif. I never gave it him." She blinked back desperate tears. He had been a good lad, he had done his best for her. But this was not the time for weeping and she forced her mind to think of what must be done.

"Go fetch your wife," she said sharply to Bjarni, who still had not moved, though it was her thoughts that raced and not the moments.

She looked for Skarphedin and could not see him. Where was he now when she needed him, where was Thorkil, now, in her distress? She ran to the door and looked wildly about, half expecting to see Attar and his men riding down on her. When would they come? Suppose it was days, should they all run away and have done with it? A low mumbling came from her sewing shed and with fear sobbing in her throat she ran to it. She stopped at the door, shocked into stillness.

Skarphedin sat naked to the waist, rocking his head from side to side and whispering. The scar on his face was the least of it, the mark ran down his neck to his shoulder and spread like the gnarl of a tree across his chest. She had never seen him like this. Now you could see that his swordarm was all there was of him long and straight and true, the rest was all crushed and twisted.

"Skarphedin," she said. "They are coming for us. We need you."

But he mumbled and she thought, his wits are gone and just before the fight. If there is a god he has deserted us. She went to him and touched as she had never done before, stroking him, pleading and begging. Sweat stood on his brow and she knew that his pain was come again. At last he seemed to know her. She begged him to come to the house.

Bjarni had fetched Rafarta in, and she sat composed, with her hands folded above her vast belly and her pointed face almost smiling. "This is very foolish, Emma," she said. "In my country we build caverns for when the raids come, where the women and children can hide. You should have spoken to me of this danger, I would have advised you."

And Emma, with her thoughts darting like minnows in reeds believed that she was right, because she alone had brought them to this. But they had not the men to build such a cavern, there was no-one to cut wood for the fence that should surround them, behind which the men should now be sheltering. In her mind she saw them all dead, Liam with his throat slit, the girls ravished before they were knifed. Her own death seemed without meaning when set against this, she felt more fear for them than ever for herself. Before this that night in Jorvik, when first she met Thorkil, had been for her the pinnacle of terror. If she had known it would come to this would she have done different? Would anyone if they knew what was to come?

A horse was coming, galloping up the track. The girls shrieked and Bjarni yelled at her to bar the door, but she would not. Instead she stepped out into the yard, her hands clasped before her, without a weapon, without anything. It was for her to ask for their lives, it was her task to face Attar and plead with him. He was not a brutal man and he might still have a kindness for her. She looked back into the house and saw that Skarphedin sat slumped on the bench and some-one had draped a jerkin over him so he did not frighten the children. He was old and ill and he had failed her. She felt quite calm.

The horse skittered into the yard, foam and sweat flying. Its rider, a big man, leaped from the saddle and ran at her. It was not Attar. Emma shrieked and ran, swinging the house door closed on him, but the man was too quick and put his shoulder to the wood. She could not hold it. The door swung wide and cracked against the wall. He stood and looked at her and he was tall and blond haired, his eyes wreathed in wrinkles.

Emma found that she was crying and she put up her fingers to wipe away the tears. "I cast spells to bring you home," she said.

"And you force the door against me. Come, wife, kiss me. I've waited a long time."

She put up her face to him and when he held her she twined her arms around his neck and tangled her fingers in his salty hair. He pulled off her cap and wiped his eyes on it.

"Ah, such a homecoming. I have dreamed of this day, I have lived for it. And you are so lovely, I wish I was half as grand, you are like a pretty green bird. There there, sweeting, don't cry. I am come back to you."

She clung to him, saying, "They are coming for us. I think it is Attar, he means to take the farm."

Thorkil nodded and went further into the room, pushing the door behind him. "This is not news to me, I was told it as soon as I stepped from the boat, it is why I came so quick. And a man tried to stop me on the road, so I thought as his body went cold, there is a plot stirring here. I fear I have done for the pony. Send the boy to see to it."

"The boy is dead," said Emma dully and Thorkil made a face to hear something so tiresome. He looked round the room.

"Well met, brother." Bjarni stood blushing, like a boy again, turning his sword in his hands.

Thorkil went to him, crying, "Bjarni! I had not looked for you, this is a fine day indeed. What have you done with yourself then, have you stolen my farm, eh?"

"I have a wife now, and a son."

Now Thorkil noticed Rafarta, watching with her green cat's eyes, and he grinned a bit and sniffed. "Such stuff as you found on your travels, lad, and you've been busy again, I see. Tell her not to drop it yet, we've a battle to fight." He swung round and looked at everyone. "So many people! So many women!"

He put his arm round Emma's waist and squeezed her. Then his eye lighted on the slumped figure of Skarphedin.

"He is ill," Emma whispered. "His wits wander."

"And for that I should not greet him? My friend. My long good friend, it is I, Thorkil. Stretch out your hand to me, I have waited for this day."

Skarphedin slowly raised his head, as if it pained him to do so. He took the hand offered to him. "My good friend," he whispered. "Here at the last."

"As at the first. We will fight together, I think, there is no better ending."

Skarphedin breathed weakly. "This is a kindness—of the gods."

Thorkil held his friend's hand to his lips and kissed it, the tears running freely down his face. He took up Skarphedin's sheepskin and his belt of black leather and eased his twisted frame into them. Then he lifted Claw of the Raven and put it in his hand.

"It is lighter than before," said Skarphedin.

"The gods hold it with you."

Unseen, Emma went out to the pony. She was sobbing to herself, and if her body was shaking so was her mind, she had no will left to her. She was helpless in a gale. The simple task she had set herself took a long time, because she could not think of it. Yet the pony was past everything, it stood with sweat dripping from its nose and the point of its belly. He's near burst its heart, she thought, and it was for me. She led the animal to the barn, though she could not see for tears.

She took off its pack and washed its mouth with water. Strapped to one side of the saddle was a cloth-wrapped bundle and at one end, where the cover was unfolded, she could see tufts of red and golden-brown. It was a present but it did not interest her. She could not believe they were saved.

In the house the men were talking of the farm's defense. She put her hand on Thorkil's arm, to see if he were real. She had thought of him often and now, when there was no time left to them, he was come home. They went out into the yard and Emma held her husband, but he said, "Go in the house, Emma. We hear them coming."

"Where is Olaf? Does he come later?"

Thorkil bent to her. "He is dead, sweeting, and went on his journey in a far place. But I'll be surprised if he does not look at us now and laugh to see us so. Ah my friend, if we join you this day you must keep a place at table and a stoop of good ale."

"Do they let women come there?" asked Emma, sobbing. She could hear the sound of many horses.

"You will sit beside me as a queen." He kissed her forehead and they clung together. "How should I have left you?" murmured Thorkil.

Emma threw back her head and looked at him, her own man. "Stay with me for ever," she whispered.

"Go to the house. They are come."

Skarphedin took the center, at his shield was Bjarni, to his right the elder brother. The berserk swayed on his short, bowed legs, the sweat already standing on his brow. He was keening to himself, the high, thin sound of death walking abroad. When the enemy band rode up they stopped. At the front was Attar, in a new and shiny helm.

"We have waited for you," called Thorkil. "Did you need to gather courage to fight a woman all alone?"

Attar stared at him. "The berserk is ill, Sigurdsson, and there are fifteen of us. Take the women and go, we won't stop you."

"But I like this piece of ground, Attar, my friend. I've a fancy to stay on it. Get back to your sewing, you're more suited to the task."

Attar began to spur his horse forward, but one of his men caught the rein and whispered fiercely to him.

Bjarni called out, "An honorable man would step down from his horse. You were ever a coward."

Attar's band looked unhappy, they had not expected to face this. Everyone knew of Sigurdsson's wordfame, he and the mighty Skarphedin. Attar had said he was old and sick, but there he stood, swaying and singing to himself.

"We'll take them now," called out Attar in a rush. "Come on!" His pony raced forward, before the others, and Skarphedin stepped out and swiped at it as smoothly as if cutting corn. The pony screamed and fell to its knees and there was Attar on the ground and behind him the mass of his men, riding on.

"He is mine," yelled Thorkil and cut Attar between shoulder and neck. The blood spurted and the man howled as the sword was pulled free and there was bone and the ends of sinews. Thorkil left him and the three moved forward as so often before, calm, assured in their task. The horses would not face the blood and backed off, milling. If the men had been cowards they would have turned and gone, but they were not. They were desperate men, seeking to grab a life for themselves and one by one they dismounted and came forward. Attar was calling for his mother. Between the two bands rested the dead pony, it's blood greasing the earth and making it treacherous.

"This is the time. It has come," sang Skarphedin and touched bloody fingers to his lips as if he held a flower. Beside him Bjarni was laughing to himself, watching the men come slowly on.

"Let them come round the pony," said Thorkil and they fell back a little, so the others were split in two round the corpse. Before they could join together again a howl broke out, Skarphedin's howl, and the three were on them, cutting and slicing as if it were truly a harvest and they were winnowing bones. Men fell, groaning. At the back a man cried, "Fire it quick. That'll finish them."

The two bands stood back, breathing hard. They could see a man striking flame to light a torch, he went around the house looking for a good place to fire the thatch.

"Emma," called out Thorkil. "Come out now, girl. I want you with me."

She came out, slowly. The others followed, Marjolein with the children, the serving girls and the swollen figure of Rafarta, looking haughtily at them all.

"They are firing the barn too," said Emma, and thought of the horse. Poor brute, they would all be dead soon. Smoke began to fill the hollow that sheltered the buildings and they all began to cough. The thatch was damp and burned slowly, a smoldering flame that dropped lumps of smoking straw into the buildings, to light what was there. Emma thought of her cloth, so carefully put to one side, that had taken so long to prepare and was now burning. She saw Attar watching her, crouched in a pool of his own blood.

"You have done this to me," she said bitterly. "I hate you."

Thorkil turned and held something out to her. It was a knife. "Here, my lovely. It is for you to decide on an ending."

She smiled at him and took it, letting their fingers touch. They had dragged the pony aside and were coming again, out of a grey fog of smoke. She held her knife and watched the thick plaits of Skarphedin's hair, swinging as he fought. She thought, he is true to himself, it is that makes him mighty. Looking down she saw Attar's trembling gaze; although so near death he still feared it.

"Don't do it," he pleaded. "Emma! Remember what we had."

"I remember," she said, and stooped to him. With one thrust she plunged the dagger into his throat.

She turned away until he was gone, carefully cleaning her knife in the midst of the smoke and blood and turmoil. Men were shouting and crying out to each other, she would not look to see if Thorkil had fallen. Her dog pressed close to her. When she put down her hand to him he licked away the blood.

The others were all clinging together, except Rafarta, who was watching. She had picked up the scythe that Emma had brought from the fields and was plainly considering how to use it. The child will be born in blood, thought Emma, and hated her bitterly. As she watched Rafarta shouted. Bjarni had fallen, struck by a spear in his swordarm. At once Skarphedin stepped over him, and where he stood no-one would come. At his side Thorkil was roaring, like a bull held at bay by dogs and his sword was very red. Attar's men fell back, weary. They stood and stared at each other across a carpet of corpses, six alive now where there had been fifteen.

Calling for help, Emma went to fetch Bjarni, but no-one came, not even his wife. She struggled with the weight and dragged him to one side. He was losing blood fast and was near senseless, so Emma chopped at her skirt to find a piece to bind him. The white end of a tendon gleamed deep in the slash and Emma thought, that is the end of his fighting days. He'll only be fit for praying.

Skarphedin was leaning on his sword, something never seen before. Thorkil rested a hand on his shoulder. "Not far now, my friend," he panted. "It is the last hill."

Skarphedin ducked his head for a moment. When he raised it there was blood running from his lips. "At last he calls me," he whispered. "I am to come home." Again he swung his sword and again they came at him, flinging themselves at the blades as men will who have nothing to lose by death. Yet Skarphedin was passing from them, journeying across the slain and they could not hold him. Soon only one man stood alive.

"Go you," said Thorkil to him, and he had barely the breath to speak. "Tell of this day. That Skarphedin, sick and ailing, stood to his friends in the service of his god. Where Claw of the Raven strikes no man shall live. At the last he served only the master."

When the man was gone, shambling and exhausted, Thorkil turned to his friend. "Are you ready?"

"As these many years. I cannot see you, it is all dark. Touch me a little."

Thorkil put his fingers to the one smooth cheek. "You do me great honor," he whispered.

Then he took up Claw of the Raven in both hands, holding

it above his head like a mighty dagger. On a cry he plunged,
and drove Skarphedin through the heart.

His place was in the grove, in a shipsetting, that is, where
the stones are set into the earth like a ship. He took with him
nothing but Claw of the Raven, held in his dead hands as it
had been in life. Emma watched but Bjarni, still weak and ill,
would not.

"There is truth in this," said Thorkil to him. "You know
it."

"I have left that god," said Bjarni. "This time I shall hold
to my path."

In the trees above the rooks clapped their wings, rising up
into a wintry sky. Below the worms began their feast and the
earth took man's flesh back into itself in the dark, quiet
places. Those that were left held each other in gladness that
they still breathed the air.

So it was that Thorkil and Emma wandered in the woods,
listening to the wind.

"What now?" she asked fearfully. "We have nothing, not
even a bed. Even the cow must be killed, we can't feed her.
What's to happen?" She held tight to his strong arm, letting
her thigh rest against his.

He laid her on the ground. He took her cloak and wrapped
it around them both and in the warmth of its folds he rejoiced
in her. Her breasts were heavy in his hands, they were
billows of the sea made flesh. When he put his lips to them
they tasted only of Emma, there was no other woman in the
world that he had loved like this. She spread herself for him
and he entered her, huge and tender, gently plunging. She put
her fingers in his long yellow hair and they smiled at each
other. It was all new. Out of an end was come a beginning.

When they went back to the farmstead, now blackened timber
standing against the sky, scattered about with the wreckage of
things rescued, they found Rafarta lying on straw, laboring.
Marjolein fussed about her but Bjarni sat apart, thinking his
own thoughts. Emma looked at the girl's drawn face that did
not now smile at some secret inner joke, and wished her
anywhere but here. She was digging her nails into herself,
fighting the pains and Emma knew she must help. She brought

water to bathe her face and held her hand until the nails drew blood. There was a potion that could help, but that was lost now. She and the girl struggled together, neither liking it.

Thorkil came and stood over them. "Is it stuck, do you think?"

Emma shook her head. "She is small, that makes it harder. She'll open soon."

"It will be a boy. The grandson of a king," groaned Rafarta and Thorkil lifted his brows in surprise. "If it's a boy it'll be a Viking first," he said. "The male line's strongest."

Emma pulled the girl up, a little too roughly for kindness. Rafarta started straining, the veins on her forehead bulging under the thin skin as if they would burst. She uttered foreign curses and sometimes a deep, short scream. Thorkil shook his head. "Poor creature. To begin life out of such pain, it is a strange thing."

He moved to touch Emma's hand and she looked up at him, remembering. Her time had been far worse than this. But it was long past and they were different people then, looking with different eyes. If their hearts were the same the pain was gone, it was distant, there was no sharpness. If I had known it would come to this, thought Emma, if I had known the agony would pass. It would not have been so bad.

At last, on a groan, the child's head burst out and in a moment it slithered long and grey on to the straw. "It is a boy," said Rafarta and sank back, her task completed. Blank-faced, Emma cut the cord and put the child to suckle from its mother. It was cold, the wind cut deep. She took off her own warm cloak and wrapped them in it.

"You have a son," said Thorkil to his brother.

Bjarni stayed where he was, saying, "I heard." After a time he got up, looked perfunctorily at the child and went away.

Thorkil sighed and shook his head. "It is the truth to say that I do not understand him."

Emma was shivering and Thorkil put his arm around her and drew her into the shelter of the sewing shed wall, the only structure left half standing.

"I have been thinking," he said. "We could build again, but this country's very lawless. Good enough, but there's never a moment's peace it seems to me."

"And whose fault is that?" said Emma, cuddling into his warmth. In this desolation he seemed all that was good. He lifted her chin and kissed her, and so sweet was it that he almost forgot himself again.

"You were a people grown soft. Rich pickings got too easy, there is no blame for us. We only took what was offered."

"No-one offered it. You stole from another man's table, that is all there is to say."

She turned restlessly, but he held her and said, "Don't let's fight, sweeting. I brought you a present but I think it's burned, it was a lovely carpet. All gone now. I have lost a fortune since I saw you, won it and lost it, see how badly I do without you?"

"I had troubles left alone," she said, picking at his jerkin. Did he know about Attar, she wondered? Had he guessed?

"Hmmm." He looked down at her. "We thresh our own corn, I think, and live with our own poor harvest. This is a new beginning for us, we must go somewhere lucky."

"I'll not go to Ireland, it's barbarous. Look at that girl, look at Bjarni."

"I've heard it's strange, they have giants still. And it's very wild. No, no, the place I have in mind is far away. Empty. Rich. A home for us, Emma."

She pulled away from him and went distractedly to the wreck of the house, looking for something to wrap around herself. The fire had been casual in its destruction, leaving here some ale, there a wooden bowl, and in the corner nothing but charred ruin. Thorkil stood watching her.

"We have Marjolein to think of," she said. "And that creature of Bjarni's, he'll not care for her. I don't know what it is with him but he'll settle to nothing, how long will he be content as a monk, do you think? I doubt they'll even have him. Then there's Leif's woman, and she's expecting again, they look to me to look after them, Thorkil. I can't go."

"If they will work, they can come. I've a fancy to be master of something, with a gaggle of women working in the house. They can weave me new clothes, I'm dressed in rags, wife. It is not fitting."

She sniffed at him. "If it's weaving you want, they are none as good as me. My cloth was asked for in the markets, you know."

"So, I made a farmwife of you after all! I always could choose a good heifer."

Emma ducked her head. "What use is a cow if she's barren?" she said harshly. Thorkil made to take her hand but she pulled away. He looked at her bronze hair and long white neck. "I'll have Bjarni's brats to father it looks like. And who knows, there's a tree in the east can live half a man's span without bearing fruit, and then one year they can pick it by the handful."

She looked at him under her lashes. "Did you see it?"

He grinned. "I was told of it only. And you're right, they lie a lot. But who knows what the gods plan for us, we could die tomorrow. Over all the world, Emma, I have only found you. If you are a friend to me, and a true friend, you will be more than all the others and they I loved above all else. I am lonely without you."

She had found some green cloth, blanketed with charred straw. She took it out and wrapped it around herself, her white face smudged and weary. "If that is how it is," she said, "then I have something for you." She led him to the sewing shed and scrabbled in the earth beneath her wrecked loom.

"Not a good place, Emma," chided Thorkil. "Women always bury things there."

"As you would know, you robber. Here. Thorsteinn brought it, he sold some furs."

Thorkil weighed the gold in his hand. He chuckled. "A good man, Thorsteinn, more honest than he should be. If he were not so cheerful, I'd ask him to come with us. I might ask him, though his wife loves him more than is good for her. See here, Emma, we can buy a ship."

"Surely not? There isn't enough."

"You think not? I dare say you're right, I'll get Thorsteinn to pay half. We shall go to Iceland and be happy."

She drew back. "What is it called? Iceland? What good is a frozen place? I tell you, Thorkil, I'd rather stay here."

He tweaked her nose and she blushed a little. He treated her like that when the others could see, but she liked it. "It is only a name," he chided. "They have great ice cliffs in parts, but the farms are rich as can be. The fish jump out of the sea into a man's nets and the good land is there for the taking. It is ours, Emma. Nothing stolen, nothing robbed, a man able to walk abroad without even a dagger in his sleeve.''

She moved away and began to walk about, looking at the wreck of what she had built and loved. It was spoiled now but it would rise again. Did she want to leave it? Thorkil had won it but she had made it her own. The brook murmured to her and high in the sky the wild geese called, a wailing sound. Yet over the hill was Erik that sooner or later would gather some men and make a fight of it, and as for the rest the hills were swarming with landless, lawless men.

Marjolein came towards her saying, ''The barrel of salt meat's spoiled. What shall we do, Emma?''

Behind her was Leif's wife, red-eyed with her children at her skirts. ''Mistress, they want food and I've nothing to give them. What shall we do?''

Even Rafarta looked at her, lying helpless with a newborn babe that needed food, warmth, safety. And she had nothing now to give them. Thorkil was breaking her shattered loom into sticks for a fire and she watched him working, bending his broad, strong back. He was right. They would leave this wild place.

Chapter
Fifteen

WE FOUND A good big *knorr* that would take the cattle bedded
deep in the center, and we took grain and flax and wool as
well to see us over the first difficult time and of course water
for the days at sea. Emma took her pouches of herbs, but she
was very nervous. It is hard for a woman to leave her home,
they put such value on things. I let her take her cur-dog,
though it bit me, you see how much love I had for her. She
was more dear to me than anything, I would have parted with
my life before her. At such an age to be in love like that, it is
to be a fool and not care. I would take her behind a house and
kiss her and she would push me off, all pink and laughing,
with her hair coming down. Such sweetness.

My brother Bjarni left us. It should have grieved me more
perhaps, but then, how well do we know our brothers? He
had always been soft as well as wild, and at last he seemed to
have found a way to draw his life together, like a woman
plaiting her hair. It was not my way but I was past judging
and I took his sons as my own. Their mother was a different
problem and that is another story, I shall tell it one day, and
of Marjolein and her disgrace. Not even death is an ending,
the words are not forgotten.

All at once the day was on us, with the ship loaded deep
and the children crying and Emma white-faced and short-
tempered. I said to her, ''Don't be afraid,'' and she turned on
me.

"I'm not afraid. It is Thorsteinn, your block of a friend, that keeps laughing. He's a fool."

"And I am a bigger fool, to give my head for a bitch to chew on," I said, and left her. I stowed some last goods in the stern and checked that the rudder was fitted properly.

All the time she sat on a bench and watched me. Suddenly she was catching my arm. "Thorkil."

I grunted but kept on with my work.

Again she said, "Thorkil," Just like a little girl that wants a ribbon.

"What do you want?" I asked, trying to keep my voice distant.

"What is it like—the sea? It—frightens me." She was as pale as sea-foam and I could not be angry with her.

I took her and kissed her and said "Sweet, there is nothing to fear, I am here with you in a good strong ship. Trust me."

"I don't want to drown," she said and I laughed at her.

"We cannot choose our ending. To sleep in strong arms, it is all we can hope for, and I am with you to the last. As I have trusted World Tree so shall you trust me, to be your strength in danger. Come, wife, settle yourself. We are going to Thule, to a new beginning."

And because she was brave and as true as my sword, she smiled and kissed me and went to her place.

I called to the men and they unshipped their oars. The cattle in the hold began lowing, sensing their adventure, and I gathered up the ropes that bound us to the quay. In my distraction I almost called for Olaf to see to the sail, for there was never a man that understood ships more than he. Our friends live on in the love we bear for them, and it was Thorsteinn stood to the sail.

Voices called from the bank, saying goodbye and wishing us well, and I know the women were crying. The river took us swiftly away and I leaned to it to offer bread and wine to my god. May Thor always hold me in his palm.

And so we went away, to a new, far country.

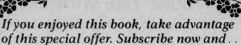